CRUSADER

JOEL GALLOWAY

This is a fictional narrative. The storyline of this novel and the characters are for entertainment purposes only. It is not intended to imply any real person actually made statements nor acted in any manner consistent with the storyline of this novel.

Published by Joel Galloway
Printed in the USA

For information about special discounts for bulk purchases or this author's availability for speaking engagements, please contact:
jrgcrusader@gmail.com.

Paperback ISBN# 978-1-7320652-3-9
Hardback ISBN# 978-0-692-06496-2
eBook ISBN# 978-1-7320652-0-8

Cover Art by Jake Hounshell
Interior by Debbi Stocco

Distributed by Ingram Spark

Visit www.crusaderbook.com

Dedicated to the innocent victims
of the so-called Mexican drug wars.

Part I—1997

It is 1997. The United States' crackdown on cocaine trafficking in Florida has forced the Colombian drug cartels to search for new smuggling routes. The Colombians have found success in Mexico. Institutionalized corruption, widespread poverty, the recent passage of NAFTA, and its northern neighbor's insatiable drug appetite have combined to create a perfect environment for organized crime.

The original, monolithic Mexican drug cartel has splintered into several warring factions, battling for the most lucrative turfs. The next-generation drug lords exhibit a type of ruthlessness and barbarism that has not been seen before. Military and law enforcement personnel are actively recruited by the new deadly Mexican cartels, as well as all manner of criminals and U.S. gangsters. Thousands flock to their ranks and waves of violence sweep across the land. Multitudes lose their faith and an ancient evil religion has risen from the ashes to become an insidious inspiration for gangsters and criminals everywhere. As it fights its descent into darkness, the country desperately searches for heroes...

Chapter 1

Chihuahua Desert, Mexico

Light from the October moon revealed blood-soaked ground near a saguaro cactus. The huge plant stood over the man like a gravestone. It took a few surreal minutes for the man to assemble the events of the last few days. His mutilated body had been buried up to the neck in some barren wilderness. He forcibly raised his left eyelid and stared at the gory remains of his right eye ball. They had purposely allowed him to keep his left eye, in anticipation of this moment. All he could think of was pain. The man's lungs exploded in a hellish roar. The demonic noise sent a bearded lizard scurrying towards the mountains and a fountain of white heat erupted into the man's brain, releasing him back into unconsciousness.

It was quiet again in the Mexican desert. A few hours later, four glowing eyes emerged from the darkness as two coyotes, searching for food, picked up the blood trail. As the animals closed in on the burial site, the man woke once again to his new, brutal existence. Pain devoured him. Agonizing minutes passed as his mind regained its focus. His first thoughts were of his family; how they found them, he would never know. But he had seen both his wife and daughter, in person, right before the bastards broke his jaw with a pipe wrench.

He hoped they died fast. He choked up and wept for a few minutes before succumbing to rage. He stared at the coyotes and lashed out in fury. But his limbs were trapped deep inside the desert soil—completely immobile.

Violent obscenities erupted from his throat. He screamed with some desperate hope against all hopes that he would be allowed to have his vengeance. The coyotes fled as if they had crossed into cursed territory. On and on he screamed until, eventually, his lungs surrendered, and the excruciating pain replaced the anger. He blacked out. Hours marched on. The fiery Mexican sun creeping over the eastern mountains unveiled more of the sinister handiwork. A buzzard swooped down near the saguaro, scooping up the jelly ball-like substance once belonging to the man's right eye socket. It crowed wickedly in delight at the taste of human flesh, waking the man once more.

Slivers of sunlight danced across his blood-crusted face, attempting to vitalize his mind. But the mental abilities that had once served him so well had been butchered as badly as his physical body—the hate-fueled energy was now gone. His thoughts went to his wife and young daughter and he sobbed. A fanatical desire to join his family overwhelmed him and he now craved death.

Stinging memories of his betrayal and subsequent torture resonated in his mind. He had finally been defeated. There would be no winning this time. His family was dead. He himself would die an agonizing death in this godforsaken land and it would not come quickly. The thought was chilling. *How long can I possibly survive? Surely I must soon succumb to the pain?* He struggled again to move his arms and legs. They would not budge. He had suffered before, immensely so, yet never anything like this.

Any glimmers of hope or peace had drained out of his soul, much like the blood that flowed from his body. He could not fathom how any living creature could go on in such a state. Yet the seconds turned into minutes, and ultimately, the minutes turned into hours. And every single instant was a torture beyond anything he ever imagined a human being could withstand. Bizarre memories of crunching bone and burning flesh ravaged his thoughts. He wondered if he was losing his mind. Eventually, he concluded it did not matter; a plunge into insanity might alleviate the pain. *How long can I go on like this? A day? Two days? Three days? More?* He felt the panic coming on. The death for which he so desperately sought would be prolonged, just as his torturers had planned. *Can I endure?* Disturbing images of their workmanship continued to dominate his thoughts. With exhaustive effort, he shut his eye and calmed himself into some level of tranquility.

Memories of salient life events seeped into his mind. He pictured his wife's long, jet-black hair laying gently against her skin. He had loved her. God knows he loved her. Tears welled up once again as he thought of his daughter. She was six years old and absolutely adorable, his pride and joy. He had wanted to give her the world. The train of thought was too unbearable and he forced the images out of his head. He reminisced about his time in the Middle East and North Africa, old friends long forgotten, early childhood years, successes and failures, joy and agony.

His bloody lips twisted into a gruesome formation. He had only been with the DEA for eight months and, like Camarena, he was going down. Kiki Camarena had been a DEA undercover agent. In 1985 he had been abducted in broad daylight by corrupt police officers on the payroll of narco kingpin Miguel Ángel Félix Gallardo—the reigning drug lord in Mexico at the time. Camarena had been brutally tortured and, when his body was discovered a month later, the DEA launched the biggest homicide investigation ever undertaken.

But there won't be any investigation on my behalf. He knew beforehand that the agency would deny any connection should he fail. Their informant was in trouble and he went after him, despite explicit instructions to the contrary. Tejada, the only one who might have looked for him, was gone. They would never find his body. *Not that it mattered; there was no one alive who would care if it was found. Not anymore.* They would come up with some story to account for the disappearance of his wife and daughter. He and his family would go down as casualties of the ever-expanding drug war.

Physical pain returned savagely to wipe away the images of his family. *I'd almost gotten away,* he realized. *Almost.* He could recollect the moments leading up to his capture in painstaking detail. Adrenaline pulsed through his veins and he worked himself up into another fury before the brutal truth of his predicament tempered its flames. There would be no vengeance. He would suffer out here in this wasteland interminably. The knowledge was so unnerving it caused him to fall out of consciousness once again.

As the sun moved towards the center of the sandy sky, his eyelid slowly opened. Every muscle in his body was fatigued. The pain came back fiercer than ever and with it, the dark understanding of his situation. He would die. He knew that and relished it. Time was the enemy now, and that terrified him. The returning realization that his death would be delayed launched new waves of panic. He forced his breathing to remain steady. Agonizing sensations in his knees and elbows caused his mind to focus in on detailed images of his torture. They had first used pliers to pull out his toe nails. When he kept silent, they smashed his toes with a hammer. After the fourth toe he blacked out and did so again before they went onto his fingers. And then other body parts. Drugs had been injected to maximize sensations as well as keep him conscious. He infuriated his captors with his silence; they became more barbaric. He screamed when they burned off patches of skin. When the man called Vásquez removed his eye ball, he spit in the bastard's face before blacking out.

Emotionally, he shut out the disturbing thoughts. He looked up at the sky. *God, make it stop. Please let it end.* Though his mother had taken him to church every Sunday, he had never been particularly religious. Yet he now drew upon the primitive instinct embedded in all human beings when faced with their greatest trials and challenges. Throwing aside anger and logic, he pleaded to his Creator for death. He prayed and prayed for hours and hours. More time passed and, eventually, even this final optimism began to fade with the passing sandstorm. His eye scanned the sky as he held on to his last hope of a merciful ending to his life. And as the red sun disappeared under the western flatlands, he learned the painful law of mankind so many desperate souls had understood before him: He was on his own.

CHAPTER 2

OAXACA JUNGLES, MEXICO

MAJOR HÉCTOR VÁSQUEZ JUMPED OUT of the helicopter with the agility of a jaguar, swearing as his feet touched the ground.

"¡Chingatelo!"

The major was clad in the standard olive-green uniform of the Mexican military. Medals decorated both breasts and gold epaulettes draped from his shoulders. His upper body muscles were so large that the uniform had to be tailor-made. Even then, he was cautious of ripping the fabric.

"¡Pinche gringo culero!"

Blood dripped from his nose. The *gringo* bastard had broken it.

Wiping away the blood with a handkerchief, he raised up his giant arm to block out the sun. Ramón was off in the distance to his left. Major Vásquez nodded his head sharply and walked over to his commander. He was a bit on edge and aching for more heroin. He had used up the last of his stash a few days ago and he knew that Ramón always had an ample supply on hand.

Colonel Ramón Acosta checked his mobile phone for new messages as he watched the big man move athletically across the clearing. *The American was finally finished.* There was something about the *gringo* that unnerved him. He disliked the feeling; it was unfamiliar.

Ramón's upper lip curled. The fury rose within him once again. His jet-black eyes darkened even deeper. The American had discovered one of his stash houses and the colonel had been forced to destroy over fifty million U.S. dollars' worth of heroin. The knowledge had been needling him for more than a week. But more critical was that somehow the bastard had found about General Huerta and the American agent was hell-bent on taking him down. *If Huerta were to be exposed by the DEA, I would go down with him.*

Unlike Major Vásquez, Colonel Acosta was wearing sandals and dressed in a simple red loincloth and blue cape that hung loosely over his powerful shoulders. A headdress lined with vibrant green quetzal feathers covered his full head of thick hair and accentuated his sharp, pointed nose and high cheekbones. At the base of his neck was a jade skull. The eyes in the skull slightly bulged out and were plated, along with the teeth, in gold.

"*Joder,*" Ramón said. "*Puto cabrón.* You're late, you big, ugly son of a bitch."

"*Me vale madre. Vete a la chingada,*" replied Héctor.

Colonel Acosta broke into a grin. The two men embraced and Vásquez quickly recounted the details of the last few days. The colonel's grin grew wider. He presented Major Vásquez with a needle, syringe, and large quantity of heroin which he knew the big man so desperately craved. Colonel Acosta had once again sent the right man to do the job. The hulking Vásquez stood nearly six-feet-five inches tall, possessed inhuman-like strength, and was a ruthless killer. Time and time again Vásquez had proven himself and he had been faithfully rewarded with money, women, and this corrosive substance which had destroyed his soul. Several years ago, he had looked forward to a promising boxing career before he was arrested for the rape and murder of a fifteen-year-old girl. Colonel Ramón Acosta had intervened on his behalf in exchange for unconditional loyalty. Vásquez had not disappointed him.

Ramón possessed an uncanny ability to recognize the most vicious of killers. It bordered on the supernatural. He pondered the strange phenomenon as he strolled down the ancient limestone pathway lining the jungle floor. Excitement was bubbling within him. He needed it now, he realized. He had become an addict, just like Vásquez. Not a chemical dependency on any sort of drug—he never touched the poison. It was the indescribable power that he craved, the godlike omnipotence of destroying a human soul. The adrenaline rush exceeded the effects of any artificial stimulant.

Ramón's demeanor loosened at the train of thought: to feel the flow of energy into his being as another human pleaded for mercy, offering up to him all that he or she held most dear in the world. He smiled at this thought. Colonel Acosta lusted for control, and he was on track to become the most powerful figure Mexico had ever known.

Wildlife noises blared from the jungle. The cacophony echoed throughout the stone edifices as Ramón walked to the center of the ancient ruins. Fresh lime whitewash coated the rough exteriors of various buildings to present a silvery, dazzling appearance. The outer walls were covered in murals and carved images of serpents, eagles, jaguars, suns, stars, moons, and various other entities. Many of the stone architectures possessed towers and roof crests, somewhat resembling fortresses, recently painted in brilliant reds, blues, and greens.

The site had been discovered three years ago. It would have made world headlines had not Ramón used his influence and wealth to silence the publicity. People asking too many questions disappeared. Ultimately, the site was declared a strategic military location. Colonel Acosta had rocketed through the ranks of the Mexican Armed Forces and reported to no one save General Huerta. Huerta was aware of the site but granted Colonel Acosta full control, for a hefty monthly payment. Ramón bristled at the thought. He despised Huerta and hated having a formal superior. *But that would soon change.*

Colonel Acosta gazed upon the nearing temple. It stood atop a bright red step pyramid that rose some 250 feet in the air. The entire structure was decorated with colorful frescoes of animals in human form and cleared of the heavy vegetation that still clung to some of the other buildings.

Standing at the base of the temple, robed in a jaguar skin, was an ancient hunchback. White fangs, projecting from the mouth of the dead beast, were situated over the old man's forehead and reflected the last remnants of the red sun's rays. Two pieces of forest-green jade hung down from the hunchback's earlobes to help mask his facial deformities. The old man was called Tlaloc. No one present knew the old man's real name, and the hunchback had gone by the name of the wrathful Aztec god for as long as Ramón had known him, almost twenty years now. Tlaloc was the only man whom Colonel Ramón Acosta respected.

He is a genius, thought Ramón, *the key to restoring power to Mexico.* Ramón looked at the newly restored statues of Aztec deities standing everywhere amidst the temple grounds. Tlaloc was obsessed with the ancient Aztec civilization; he knew far more about the enigmatic culture than anyone else on the planet. His personal collection of artifacts surpassed that of any museum, and he possessed every paper and book ever published on the ancient people. Tlaloc had painstakingly undertaken the task of restoring every representation of the gods he could find. His favorites, standing a short distance south of the temple, were an alignment of nine magnificent sculptures, carved out of obsidian and onyx.

Each figure was authentic and the absolute best of its kind among the world's remaining Aztec artifacts. They represented the Lords of the Night—a set of nine gods that ruled over the underworld. In the middle stood the largest of the collection, a ten-foot statue of a hideous creature that Ramón had known for many years. Large staring eyeballs protruded out of its deathly skull along with several prominent, bared teeth. On top of the skull sat a headdress composed of owl feathers. A chain of human eyeballs lined the base. Two gigantic skeletal arms gestured aggressively towards the pyramid as if to welcome new arrivals. It was Mictlantecuhtli, the Aztec god of the underworld, the deity which Tlaloc considered the most powerful.

Modern ornamentation also embellished the ancient site. Human skulls, housing glowing red candles, lined the foundation of the pyramid. Vibrant portraits of another skeletal figure, clothed in the robes of the Virgin Guadalupe and armed with a scythe, hung upon every limestone wall. This was Santa Muerte, the angel of death, and its popularity was soaring among criminals across the country. Tlaloc embraced the morbid entity. He had been among the first to make the association between Santa Muerte and the second coming of Mictecacihuatl, the wife of Mictlantecuhtli and queen of the underworld. The hunchback believed this royal couple was the key that both he and Colonel Acosta would turn to restore power and glory to Mexico. Ramón knew that the old man was never wrong.

From atop the pyramid, at the temple base, Tlaloc looked down at Ramón and nodded. The cripple lifted his left arm—a primal drum unleashed a chilling beat, a wicked tone reeking of death. Hundreds of men stood at the base of the pyramid, naked save for loincloths, skins covered with colorful tattoos of Santa Muerte, Mictlantecuhtli, and gang insignia. The elite wore headdresses like Colonel Acosta's. Major Vásquez, now dressed appropriately for the event, stood among them.

Most of the men were military, serving under Colonel Acosta's command, and had participated in the sacred ordinance before. Through acts of terror and treachery they had proved themselves loyal and devout. Many came from abject poverty, seduced by Ramón in their teens with the lure of money, drugs, and women. And, perhaps even more important, Ramon offered them a semblance of self-respect. They were soldiers in a revolution for the soul of Mexico. They believed they were doing something truly monumental and were intent on achieving victory by any means possible. Most were heroin addicts, and all understood that Colonel Acosta would satisfy their needs in exchange for unconditional loyalty. They also understood that the slightest hint of insubordination would not be tolerated. Several new initiates were scattered among the crowd and Ramón knew the ritual would solidify their allegiance.

The drum rhythm reached a feverish pitch—then abruptly went silent. It was replaced by maniacal screams from a young woman being marched up the eastern side of the pyramid. The victim was scantily clad in tattered robes and her slender, dark-skinned body was painted blue. Two large, muscular men forcibly escorted the young woman up the top pyramid steps. They were, like the others, clothed solely in loincloths. Both wore bright blue and red headdresses assembled from tropical bird feathers. The young woman was hysterical and she had recently descended the slippery slope of insanity. Upon discovering she was not a virgin, Tlaloc let an entire division of Ramón's men rape her. Bruised, bloody, and violated, she now stood at the top of the temple in absolute, unfathomable horror, desperately trying to decide if this was reality or the demonic scenes within some unimaginable nightmare.

She had been kidnapped several days earlier in the outskirts of Juárez. The young woman had worked at one of the newly constructed *maquiladoras,* factories built by foreigners designed to optimize the use of cheap labor. When her family died in Guatemala she had traveled to the fabled northern dreamland and ended up getting stuck in the border slums where she slaved away for pennies. There would not be an investigation into her disappearance. There never was.

Tlaloc stared into the girl's eyes, grinning fiendishly. Shrieking, she struggled violently to free herself from the grip of the two priests and failed. Tlaloc turned to face the statue of Mictlantecuhtli and spoke in a clear booming voice, strangely unnatural given his frail appearance.

Yet he spoke slowly, taking deep, ragged breaths. He spoke in perfect Nahuatl, the ancient language of the Aztecs. No person present, save Colonel Acosta, could understand his words.

"To the one ... most powerful ... we present ... this offering ... of life. May your glory ... be restored ... upon this land." He sucked in the jungle air. "As devoted ... servants ... we praise ... your name ... and ask for ... your help ... and blessing ... to defeat ... the enemy." Then, suddenly and adroitly, Tlaloc picked up an obsidian knife and plunged it deep into the young woman's abdomen. He ripped the blade upwards, expertly removing her heart from her rib cage. Her body went limp and the two priests harshly tossed the corpse down the ancient steps. Tlaloc cried out with bestial jubilation and raised the bloody heart upwards, in the direction of Mictlantecuhtli. The assembly of men cheered violently. Ramón's eyes homed in on the crimson heart held high in Tlaloc's right hand. It was still beating.

The two priests entered a chamber and returned carrying a gold platter, encrusted with precious gem stones. All eyes were upon Tlaloc as he lowered the beating heart to his open lips, indicating that each of the new initiates was required to partake of the offering. He placed the mutilated organ onto the platter. The two priests carried the platter down the steps and marched through the center aisle of men. One young man had turned a sickly shade of white and was sweating profusely. He attempted to perform the appalling act and failed. Colonel Acosta strode deliberately over to the man and killed him with his bare hands.

A few days later, Colonel Acosta returned to his palatial home in the suburbs of Culiacán. All traces of hatred and anger had disappeared from his handsome face, replaced by the charm and charisma that his family knew so well. He greeted his lovely wife Mónica with a warm embrace and presented her with an exquisite necklace of perfectly formed pearls. Mónica squealed with delight, wrapped her arms around his neck, and kissed him passionately. She loved her husband. And despite all his infidelities, he loved her also. She was his oldest friend.

The reunion was interrupted by their son Rene. The youngster came bounding down the stairs and latched onto his father's leg.

"*¡Papi!* You're home!"

Ramón picked up his child and twirled him around in the air. "*¿Cómo estas Mijo?* How's my little tiger doing? Hey, I heard some funny noises out by the truck. I think you better come with me to check them out."

Rene grinned and eagerly followed his father outside to the lavish driveway. In the back of Ramón's armored Chevy Tahoe was an ornate bird cage housing a beautiful scarlet macaw with rainbow wings and neon red and blue plumage.

"*¡Hola!*" the bird squawked.

Rene howled with delight. The young boy had become fascinated with pirates and he had been begging his mother for a parrot. Rene loved the bird.

"*Gracias Papi, gracias,*" he said joyfully. "Can I take him up to my room?"

"*¿Por qué no?*" replied Ramón. "Think you can help me carry him?"

Rene howled again and helped his father hold the birdcage while making the long journey up to his room. A few hours later, the boy fell asleep with a smile across his face. When Mónica was ready to go to bed, sometime after midnight, she also had a smile upon her face. And as she drifted off to sleep, she was still thinking of how lucky she was to have such a husband.

Chapter 3

Outskirts of Ceballos, Durango, Mexico

An eerie silence crept through the air as the aged priest walked through the *barrio.* Fog seemed to enshroud every object in his path, making the journey more difficult than anticipated. His spiritual instincts were on high alert. *It is too quiet.* Gently kicking aside a tumbleweed, the priest pondered the meaning of the strange tranquility. His much younger companion, Father Gómez, did not appear to share his uneasiness.

"Hey, Father Navarro," he said in English, "What do you call a sleepwalking nun?"

The aging priest turned to look at Father Gómez with a bemused smile but remained silent.

"A roamin' Catholic! Get it?" Father Gómez laughed at his own joke. The young priest had volunteered to accompany the old man. He did not really believe the stories surrounding the veteran priest. He did not really believe in his own faith, for that matter. But he was not unhappy with his decision to join the clergy. It was a fairly easy life. He did not have to work at Father Navarro's monastery, thank God; he would have to do something over there. And there were many, many benefits for an ambitious young man of the cloth. Certainly having a good relationship with the legendary Father Navarro could not hurt his career.

They had been the only ones who would come. Narrowing his dark, deep-set eyes, Father Navarro ever so slightly ground his back molars together. He tilted his biretta to the left. He perceived that most of them did not believe in these strange happenings sweeping across the land, that they did not yet quite grasp the power of the Adversary. But he knew better. He had witnessed the evil firsthand. *They are good men, for the most part,* he reflected on his brethren in Christ. *Yet they are lacking in faith for the tribulations that are now upon them.* A frown formed upon his lips and his brow furrowed. He rubbed the white stubble on his jaw. Disturbing thoughts had plagued him for some time now. *Focus,* he warned himself. *Concentrate now on the job at hand.*

The pair of priests had difficulty seeing the house numbers as they strode deeper into the arcane neighborhood. The old man walked with a slight limp, a remnant of the polio he had contracted as a teenager. He'd been a great athlete until the disease crippled him; now his legs grew unevenly. He was eventually forced to quit playing soccer and baseball. Even after all these years and all the surgeries, his right leg was an inch shorter than his left.

The priests continued their course for several more blocks before the old man focused on the silhouette of one particular dwelling faintly illuminated by a rustic oil lamp. It stood out elusively next to a rundown auto garage; as if it did not want to be discovered. *Or,* Father Navarro pondered, his gaze hardening, *as if it invites us.* He felt uneasy. Cold. *This is it.* The evil presence was so pervasive it made his stomach churn. Decades of battling the Enemy had finely tuned his spiritual senses. He could internally recognize the forces of darkness when no one else could.

Father Navarro's fingers fumbled around the left breast pocket of his cloak to search for his trusted Bible—the one his grandfather had given him a half century ago. Feeling the leather binding had always given him comfort. He turned to face his companion.

"We are here."

The old man gazed upwards for a few moments as if trying to pierce through the fog. "We must be cautious and we must have faith. The Adversary is ruthless and will not hesitate to destroy the weak. Do not trust in memorized rites, rituals, or physical objects of superstition. Trust in the Lord with all your heart and let His strength and energy flow within you."

Father Gómez nodded his head and feigned understanding, slightly amused at the gravity in Father Navarro's tone. *Finally,* Father Gómez thought. He was incredibly bored and beginning to regret his decision to accompany the old man. *Let's get on with it so we can go home.* He patted his canvas *mochila.* His colleagues had semi-jokingly equipped him with an assortment of holy relics to prepare for the ordeal.

Father Navarro made the sign of the cross. He walked towards the gated door of the humble house, trailed by Father Gómez. The adobe walls were dusty pink and had not been painted in decades. Rusty iron bars covered two outside windows and the front door. The familiar face of the Virgin Guadalupe, robed in turquoise and surrounded in dirty-yellow light, greeted the old man as he went up the final doorstep. Known as the "Queen of Mexico," the virgin's image was plastered across every house, store, and cathedral in the entire country. In 1531, an Indian peasant named Juan Diego experienced a vision in which the Virgin Mary appeared as a beautiful Aztec princess. Presenting herself as Santa María de Guadalupe, Mary proclaimed her love for Diego and his people. News of the vision struck a chord in the disillusioned Native Mexicans and the event is believed to be responsible for the conversion of millions.

Father Navarro reflected for a few seconds on the vision of Juan

Diego before retrieving a key chain belonging to his own place of worship. He gave three sharp knocks on the metallic door gate. Two minutes passed before the door creaked open, revealing the mahogany face of a small woman. She appeared almost as old as the weathered priest himself. Tears flowed from her beady eyes. "Padre, Padre—I knew you would come. *¡Ayúdenos!* Oh! Please help us!"

The priest bent down to kiss the old woman's wrinkled cheek. He gently cupped his own wrinkled hands under her chin and looked into her eyes. "It shall be well, Hermana Queiroz. Have faith and courage. Your family deeply needs your support at this time."

Father Navarro introduced the young priest behind him, who smiled politely and extended his own right hand. Behind the old woman stood a sniffling, ten-year-old girl with curly brown hair, thin limbs, and abnormally large brown eyes. She was wrapped in a wool blanket and cradled a stuffed animal somewhat resembling a dog. Hermana Queiroz reached back and took hold of the young girl's hand. "This is my *nieta,* Gladys."

"What a lovely name," the old priest said, smiling warmly. "Hello Gladys. You are a beautiful young girl." His eyes went to the stuffed animal. *"¿Te gustan los perritos?* Do you like puppies?"

The girl, tears dripping from her big brown eyes, glanced at her grandmother and then nodded feebly. Father Navarro extended his hand towards the back of her right ear and magically pulled out a silver coin. Minted on its face was the portrait of a Chihuahua puppy. "Take it Gladys. If your grandmother consents, I can exchange it for a real one."

For the first time in weeks, a flicker of light sparkled in the young girl's countenance. She looked up longingly at her *abuelita*. Hermana Queiroz gave her approval. The old priest looked deep into the girl's eyes. "Be strong, little one. Your brother needs all of your faith and *oraciones.*" Gladys nodded her head enthusiastically with a hope she had not felt in sometime. There was something different about this dark stranger. Something strong. Something good. The dark stranger turned his eyes back to her grandmother. "Take us to your grandson."

Hermana Queiroz collected a soft glowing lamp and led the two men through the back door to the outside yard. Gladys, in accordance with Father Navarro's request, remained behind, praying near the fireplace in the living room. Twenty-five yards away from the house stood a shack, constructed from crumbling concrete blocks and rotten plywood. A thick, ugly, oversized door was attached to the entryway of the shack with an iron chain and steel padlock. Hermana Queiroz walked over to the dismal abode, pulled out a key, and heaved to unlock the crude barrier. The door slowly swung open and, with a slight hesitation, she walked forward.

As the two priests followed the old woman they were struck by the sudden drop in temperature. For the first time on the journey Father Gómez showed signs of apprehension. There were no air conditioners in this region and the neighborhood was much too impoverished for swamp coolers, especially in this makeshift dump. Father Gómez was also surprised to see a primitive staircase that seemed to lead into some sort of a basement. Hermana Queiroz gathered her courage and cautiously took the first step downward.

A foul stench permeated the lower-level air. Halfway down the staircase, the young priest started to gag and his legs wobbled, forcing him to cling to Father Navarro for support. It was silent. Dark. The lamp's light diminished with each step downward. When the old woman reached the bottom, an infernal howl pierced through the air—followed by riotous clashing. Father Gómez froze. The noise was chilling, unlike anything he had ever heard. Hermana Queiroz also stopped walking; her frail body trembled and she almost dropped the lamp. The howling grew louder. Father Navarro gingerly put his hand on the old woman's shoulders, collected the lamp, and brushed past her.

He turned around momentarily. "Be strong and have faith."

Father Navarro picked up his pace and headed down the narrow corridor which led to a bedroom. He entered it. Hermana Queiroz gathered herself, as did Father Gómez, and they both followed the old man. A fourteen-year-old boy was bound to a ragged bed, shaking so violently the bed was coming up off the floor. The boy's face was a strange shade of yellow. *"¡No me jodas—hijo de tu puta madre—hijo de la chingada!"* Vile profanities spewed from his bloodied, cracked lips. The heinous scene caused Father Gómez to recoil in shock. He felt his limbs go numb and his muscles go weak. He tried to turn around. His feet would not move.

With a quick alertness, Father Navarro took notice of the surroundings. To his left was a small closet and a worn-out clothes dresser. On top of the dresser was a mess of empty bags of chips, cigarette butts and roach clips, and a cocaine free-base kit. The priest's eyes examined the dresser for a couple of seconds, then he rotated his head in the opposite direction.

There it is—again. Hanging on the right wall was a medium-sized portrait of the angel of death—Santa Muerte. The picture was an imitation of the Virgin Guadalupe decorating the front door, except the face was replaced by a deathly-white skull. Ignoring the boy's blasphemous screams, the old man walked over to the portrait. He quietly removed it from the wall and handed it to Hermana Queiroz. "Take this outside and burn it. Then go inside your home and wait with Gladys. Do you understand?"

Quivering, the old woman nodded.

"Good. Do it quickly."

Hermana Queiroz hastened to obey the priest's command. As the old woman exited the room, her grandson shook even more savagely. Putrid green vomit erupted from his mouth. Blood gushed from his nostrils. The old man set the lamp on the dresser, moved closer to the boy, and pulled out a vial of holy water. As Hermana Queiroz scurried up the stairs, he removed the soft plastic plug.

Father Gómez remained frozen, bulging eyes fixated on the boy. He mentally commanded his fingers to open his *mochila*. His fingers would not obey. The boy stopped vomiting and sick laughter burst from his lips. His bloodshot eyes stared at the terrified young priest. "You think you can defeat me, you hypocritical son of a bitch? A man of the cloth who does not believe in his own religion? A false priest who impregnates nuns and visits prostitutes? Sister Nuñez had an abortion. Did you know that? *¡Chinga tu madre, pinche puto!*"

Father Gómez turned ashen. His fingers went limp and the canvas *mochila* fell to the floor. Urine trickled down his pants and formed a pool around his shoes. Somehow his bladder failure triggered a mental wire; the priest recovered mastery of his legs. He quickly turned around and sprang out of the room like a jack rabbit. He sprinted down the hallway, climbed up the stairs, and fled into the safety of the dark fog. Father Navarro never saw him again.

The laughter spewing from the boy's mouth turned into a throaty, threatening voice. The bloodshot eyes turned towards the more formidable opponent. "We are coming for you, Navarro. We will destroy you, your friends, your church, and your country."

Ignoring the demonic words, the priest walked over to the bed and sprinkled holy water across the boy's twisted body. The voice roared and the boy's right arm shot forward, snapping the cord that bound him. Immediately, and surprisingly quick, the priest's left hand grabbed the boy's wrist before the fingers could reach his own throat. Growling with a force that shattered the glass vial, the voice raged on in Spanish. "You cannot win, priest. For every soul you save we will destroy ten more. Everything you hold dear will be annihilated. *¡Vete a la chingada!*"

Holding the boy's wrist, the old man stared directly into the malevolent red eyes. He stared for a long time. He stared with an intensity that rocked the very core of hell itself. Finally, the ancient priest spoke. He spoke in a voice that was calm and clear. And he spoke in flawless Nahuatl. "Your loyalties are misplaced, Itzpapalotl. Your fate has been determined and, in the end, you shall be crushed."

The boy's eyes bulged out as the demon inside heard his ancient Aztec name. His face contorted into a supernatural expression of fury. Father Navarro slightly adjusted the golden cross around his neck and lowered his right hand onto the boy's head. An unseen power surged within his being. "In the name of Jesus Christ of Nazareth, the Holy One of Israel, I command you to leave this body at once."

Gladys and her grandmother huddled together next to the fireplace. Both were shaking. They had witnessed Father Gómez scamper out of the shack and run into the night. The commotion coming from outside sounded like an ancient battle of titans of which they wanted no part. Minutes slowly turned into hours and then, silence. Serenity. The contrast was surreal. More time passed and then, finally, they heard the back door open. It was their beloved brother and grandson Raúl, followed by the old priest.

"Raúl!" screamed Gladys. Her tears morphed into sobs of joy. She rushed over to hug her brother, acutely noticing his skin color and complexion were normal. Raúl's grandmother walked closely behind Gladys to join in the family reunion. After embracing her *nieto,* Hermana Queiroz, weeping, faced the old man.

"Thank you Padre, oh thank you. How can we possibly ever repay you?"

The priest, both physically and mentally exhausted, made every effort to generate the warmest smile he could. "You are very welcome

Hermana Queiroz. Raúl has promised to come to mass every Sunday and I expect you and Gladys to join him. Remember the Messiah and seek to do his will and pass on his word. And Gladys, I shall return with your puppy."

The old woman hastily nodded in acceptance. "Of course Padre, of course."

Then, with a slight tip of his hat, the priest made his way out the front door and started on his journey home.

Chapter 4

Chihuahua Desert, Mexico

Young Ignacio Jarabo was after a buck. A giant buck. He had spent too many dinners listening to his family's good-natured ribbing about the last hunting trip, during which he had fired seventeen bullets at a six-point mule deer from 300 yards and missed every last shot. His older brothers Gabriel and Fernando had been especially tough on him, continually joking that their little sister, Adela, could shoot twice as straight blindfolded. Grinding down on his back teeth, he dejectedly concluded that maybe he was not the hunter a Jarabo should be. Having lived all his fifteen years on his family's secluded cattle ranch, he was a skilled horseman, cowboy, and outdoorsman. He knew the wilderness land surrounding the outskirts of the ranch like the crescent-shaped scar on his left thumb. He could stalk a deer. He could field dress a deer. He could trail a wounded deer for miles. But for the love of everything holy in Mexico, he could not shoot straight. He had been on the hunt for two days now and he had fired his Winchester .270 rifle multiple times at three different deer. He missed every shot.

Ignacio stared at the dying fire and carefully stirred the coals with his right foot, clad in one of his favorite cowboy boots. The boot was made from armadillo skin; the shafts were green, white, and red. Embroidered into the white portion of the shaft was a brown *aguila* grasping a serpent in its talons, perched on top of a prickly pear cactus, the national emblem of Mexico. As he heated up coffee and ate the last of his *tortillas,* Ignacio looked up despairingly at his best friend, his trusty mare Blanca.

"*¡Ay, Chihuahua!* I don't know if we're going to do it this time, girl."

The pale-white animal gazed lovingly into the boy's eyes, gently scuffing her front right hoof into the dirt as if in agreement. Ignacio had promised his mother he'd be home by now but he didn't want to return empty-handed. Disgusted, he downed the coffee and cleaned up his campsite. Fifteen minutes later, he loaded the last of his supplies into Blanca's saddle bags and mounted up. He had not traveled more than 100 yards when he saw it—he shook his head and blinked several times. *Was that actually real?*

Looking at him, no more than fifty yards to the north, was the biggest buck he had ever seen. Huge antlers protruded from the beast's head in every direction, glimmering radiantly in the early morning sun. It was the trophy of a lifetime. Ignacio became so excited a brief period of confusion set in. Pinching himself, he slowly dismounted and placed the .270 across the back of Blanca. He nervously pointed the rifle scope in the general vicinity of the deer and experienced a twinge of anxiety trying to get the deer in his crosshairs. Adrenaline replaced the anxiety as he confirmed he had not spooked the buck. Ignacio centered the crosshairs in the middle of the deer's chest. And fired. The animal jumped sharply to its left and then jolted away towards the mountains.

"*¡Maldita sea!*"

He had missed yet again. For a few minutes he stood in disappointment. Blanca impatiently snorted.

"*Cálmate*—we're going." Blanca knew that every time Ignacio shot the rifle he would take her to new territory. Just as his father had taught him, Ignacio would painstakingly search the area for blood, in case he had wounded his prey and needed to track the animal. Counting off the yards, he mentally calculated the vicinity where the buck had originally stood and led Blanca to the site.

One hour later, after patiently scouring the scrubland for any signs of a wounded animal, Ignacio was confident he had completely missed the shot. Blanca was feasting on desert grass. Ignacio faced her, calling out her name, and in the process noticed something strange in the distant landscape.

What was that?

He had discovered a new enemy, one on whom he could focus his rage. And he had chosen to go to war. For what now seemed like an eternity, he had taken to cursing God—even if He was imaginary—every moment of his being. He would count the number of blasphemies to pass time. Eventually he would get confused, lose count, and start over. *If indeed, God exists, I'm gonna go after that bastard before he sends me to hell. And hell will be a relief.*

He felt as if it had gone on forever and he had learned it was simply not possible to will himself to die. But his primal instincts now informed him it was almost over. His vision was so blurred he could scarcely distinguish between day and night. Grotesque, swollen lips attempted the formation of a deviant smile. *I did it without you God,* he reflected, victoriously. *How long had it been?*

He had lost count a few days ago and had given up on any form of divine intervention long before that. *But the pain will soon end. Death will be sweet and it's almost here. Will I see my family again?* Images of his wife and daughter caused him to mentally wince. *Probably not,* he concluded. *God does not exist. Or maybe I just really pissed him off. It doesn't matter anymore. Just let it be over. Just let the pain stop.* He was fading fast. His dreams were becoming more and more bizarre and he realized his mental capacities were dwindling. He heard a voice and peacefully realized he had just left this earth. *Is it God or the Devil? It doesn't matter now.*

"*¡Dios Mío!*" exclaimed Ignacio. Horrified, he realized the strange object protruding from the ground was a human head. He quickly made the sign of the cross and said a silent prayer to the Virgin Guadalupe. Dismounting Blanca, Ignacio surveyed the landscape and cautiously walked over to the seemingly lifeless head. It lay at the base of a giant saguaro cactus. He knelt to the ground for a closer examination and recoiled: the face was brutally disfigured. The gaping hole in its right eye socket turned Ignacio's stomach. Vomit rose to his throat. He popped up and ran a few paces before puking out coffee and *tortillas*. Upon gathering himself, Ignacio realized that this person had been tortured and left here to die—out in the middle of nowhere.

A sudden sense of dread swept over him. He raced back to Blanca and quickly mounted her. He dug his spurs into her flesh but for some unearthly reason the animal disobeyed him. She turned around and trotted straight towards the burial site. And that's when he saw it. *The lips moved! Or did I imagine it?* He cleared his vision, blinked several times, and took another long, hard look at the face. Ever so slightly, he saw the grotesque purple lips make a strange formation. He stared intensely at the lips. It was almost as if they were talking—communicating with some invisible entity. *This human being is alive!* The revelation jolted Ignacio. *What should I do?* His first thought was to ride back home to tell his father. *But he is miles away—this person could die any moment!*

Ignacio started to panic. *What would my father do?* From an early age, his father had taught him how to work, hunt, and fish. He had also taught him wilderness survival skills, including first aid. His mind reflected on the lessons and knowledge instilled within him since childhood. *During a crisis, never panic. Relax and think clearly. Base your decisions on logic and common sense.* Ignacio could hear his father's resounding voice. He took a deep breath.

¡Agua! Of course! This person needs water!

Ignacio quickly untied the canteen from Blanca, walked back to the head, and poured a few drops of water onto the purple lips. And then a few more into his mouth. Careful not to overdo it, he dumped the rest of the water on top of the head. The results of the actions were immediate. Ignacio heard a gargling sound dislodge from the person's throat and it gave the boy a boost of confidence.

Forty minutes later, with the help of his camp shovel, Ignacio had dug out a hole about two feet in diameter around the wretched survivor. He could now definitively make out that the individual was male. The man's large arms had been tied together behind his back. Ignacio spent three minutes cutting the man's limbs free with his hunting knife, slicing his own left index finger in the process.

Using the spare rope in the saddle bag, Ignacio made a honda knot and lassoed the man's torso. He made sure the rope was placed underneath the arms, up to the armpits, and then tied the other end to Blanca's saddle. He urged the horse forward. With little effort on behalf of the mare, the man was ejected from his desert prison. *Now comes the hard part,* Ignacio thought. He pulled out the remaining apples from the supply bag and began expertly soothing the animal. Five minutes and three apples later he had the mare lying down. Twenty minutes later, physically drained, he had the man on the back of the horse.

Chapter 5

Catholic Monastery—Durango, Mexico

Rain pounded the cathedral. Father Navarro, in bed, stretched his aching legs and tried to relax. He had not slept in three days. *Things are getting worse,* he reflected. *Poverty is on the rise and charity is on the decline. Kidnappings, murders, torture—the barbaric acts are becoming more and more commonplace. Not since the revolution has there been so much turmoil. People across the country are losing hope.*

The old man sighed and shook his head in disgust. He had just returned from the Vargas family funeral. It had been pure anguish. Fernando Vargas, his wife Verónica, and their four beautiful young daughters had been killed Saturday night as they were traveling to Mass. Their Dodge Minivan had been gunned down by assassins from the Sinaloa Cartel, a major player on the Mexican drug-trafficking scene. Fernando was an attorney who had helped convict Héctor Luis Palma Salazar, one of the top leaders in the criminal organization.

Father Navarro closed his eyes and attempted to block out the thoughts, desperately trying to sleep. He was unsuccessful. He didn't sleep much anymore. Right now, however, he could not remember ever being more tired. The old man lay still for several minutes before he finally gave up and walked over to the library. The collection of books at the monastery was impressive, yet it composed only a fraction of the literary material he had read throughout his lifetime.

It was well known in the clergy and in certain academic circles that he possessed one of the sharpest intellects in Mexico. However, for those who knew him best, it seemed the more he learned, the humbler he appeared. Throughout his life of piety, he had developed a very deep belief in the existence of a supreme creator and in the divinity of Jesus Christ. Yet, he subscribed to a philosophy in which he was not afraid to revise aspects of his faith upon encountering new historical information. He read and studied relentlessly to further understand the complex nature of mankind. Such a methodology allowed him to empathize with human weaknesses and deficiencies as well as sharpen his own spirituality.

He possessed a rich Mexican heritage and could trace his Spanish lineage back to the Crusades. He could also trace his Indian ancestry back several generations to before the conquest. The Navarros were very wealthy and one of the most respected families in the region. They had been staunch Catholics for generations. The priest was nine years old when his father and several older siblings fought in the Cristero War in the late 1920s. Two of his brothers had died and, despite being very young, Father Navarro remembered the period well.

Those were dark days, the priest recalled. The bloody revolution inspired secularization, instituted within the 1917 constitution. The revolutionaries had finally had enough of both the real and perceived abuses committed by the church over the centuries. It was an oppressive overreaction. Priests were fined for wearing clerical garments in public. Clergy could be imprisoned up to five years for criticizing the government. In the state of Chihuahua, the measures were incredibly tyrannical. The government seized church property, deported foreign priests, and closed convents, monasteries, and religious schools. Peaceful resistance by church members eventually escalated to bloodshed. Catholic peasants were hung from trees, telephone poles, and lamp-posts alongside railroad tracks. It was estimated that 70,000 Mexicans perished in the Cristero War. Father Navarro shivered at the memories. And then he shivered at the comparisons with the present times. His country was a ticking bomb. It always had been. It was one brutal, cy-clic power struggle against a search for justice.

The current narco violence caused his soul to quiver and his spirit to quake. He could almost feel the pending implosion of his land. The level of fear and pessimism prevailing among all classes of Mexican citizens was becoming unprecedented. Centuries of dismal political and economic policies had decayed the country to its core. Poverty had bred a widespread acceptance of corruption, injustice, and orga-nized crime. The cartels were growing exponentially and with them the reemergence of an ancient evil: Santa Muerte. The dark religion was increasing its traction. The hearts of many had become cold, and the disease was contagious. Father Navarro wept for his country and his people. In these last few years he had spent more and more of his days on his knees, pleading with the Lord for guidance, answers, and the salvation of Mexico.

The old priest pushed the genealogy book back on the shelf and walked on. His eyes continued to scan the shelves; Aristotle, Socrates, Locke, Hume, Confucius, Nietzsche, Shakespeare, Miguel de Cer-vantes; the authors went on and on.

Eventually Father Navarro's eyes fixated on a large antiquated book with a worn-out black leather cover—*La Santa Biblia*. He retrieved the book, carried it to his bed, and opened it. Throughout the years of his long life he had practically memorized the text, yet he continued to discover new lessons and insights. He was reading the book of Jeremiah when his exhaustion finally overtook him; he fell into a deep sleep.

It was a sleep unlike any he had ever experienced. Comfort enveloped his being as bright light ushered out the darkness of his innermost fears. Familiar faces and old friends long gone seemed to welcome him into some imperceptible, yet familiar domain. He recognized the younger face of his long-deceased father, holding the hand of a smiling young woman wearing a dress of such whiteness that it seemed to transcend the spectrum of human visibility. It was his mother. *Am I dead?* the priest wondered. *Did I die in my sleep of exhaustion and sorrow?*

As if in answer to his own question, the brightness faded, replaced by earthly images of the land he loved. Diverse peoples and tribes appeared before him, and he saw wars and battles. He saw the emergence of a victorious tribe that became all-powerful; he recognized them as the Aztecs. A giant statue of gray limestone and basalt materialized. It was Mictlantecuhtli, the Aztec god of the dead, one of the principle gods of human sacrifice.

Aghast, the priest watched as thick scarlet blood oozed from the mouth of the statue. More sculptures of various macabre deities appeared and Father Navarro saw neighboring tribes being hunted down and systematically slaughtered in ritualistic fashion—all to appease the blood thirst of the gods. A poignant reminder that the Adversary had grown strong in the ancient land.

The texture of the dream changed. Father Navarro saw serpents rise across the land, poisoning the soil and destroying the people. The priest's eyes focused on a gang of serpents, fangs bared and dripping with venom, chasing down a brown hare. Above, in the cobalt sky, soared seven majestic eagles. One of the eagles spotted the ambush and swooped down to rescue the hare. With one swipe of his talon, the eagle decapitated the lead serpent and fought the others. But other gangs of serpents joined the battle and, despite his most valiant efforts, the eagle was subdued. The retaliation was merciless. The serpents struck the eagle again and again, shredding its flesh. Flames shot out from a serpent's nostrils; the eagle caught on fire. The serpents slithered off, leaving the site of the massacre to march on in their path of destruction. The earth moaned and the stars shuddered. And then the priest saw a gentle movement at the scene of carnage. A pale-colored horse emerged and nudged the bird. Out of the ashes, the eagle rose and transformed into a hideous beast. The serpents returned to fight against this new grisly opponent. The beast drew a silver sword and mounted the horse. It then turned its head to look directly at Father Navarro. The beast had one eye and was shedding a lucid tear

The priest woke abruptly as thunder boomed in harrowing fashion. It took a few sobering moments for Father Navarro to realize where he was. Shivering, he reached for a towel to wipe his forehead, beaded with sweat. The reality of the dream stabbed his consciousness. As the rain continued to pummel the monastery, the priest attempted to process the meaning of the strange dream and he reflected again upon the strange, one-eyed beast. Lightning streaked across the dark sky, illuminating an ancient grandfather clock. It was 1:20 a.m. Thunder again rocked the monastery. He went to the bathroom to clean up and regain his composure. In the process he heard another sound between the intervals of the storm. The telephone was ringing.

Who could it possibly be at this hour? Instinctively, he recognized something was wrong. He geared himself up to prepare for the next tragedy and stepped to pick up the phone. It was Aracely Jarabo, the wife of a dear friend whom he had known for thirty years. The priest listened for a few moments before cutting Aracely off. He said he would come immediately.

It was 3:30 a.m. in the main house at the Jarabo ranch. Father Navarro sat next to Aracely and her nine-year-old daughter Adela, both extremely worried about the male members of their family. Ignacio had not returned from his hunting trip and Alfonso Jarabo, along with sons Gabriel and Fernando, went looking for him. They had been gone for thirty-six hours. The old priest was sipping tea when Aracely suggested reading from the Bible. Father Navarro forced himself to smile.

"Una muy buena idea," he said gently. "Adela, would you be so kind as to read a few verses to your mother and I?"

Adela picked up *La Santa Biblia*, randomly opened the book, and began to read. Half-heartedly, the priest stood up and walked over to the living room window while he drank from his cup of tea and listened to the sweet voice of the small girl. He immediately recognized the verses as coming from the book of Revelation.

"...and power was given to him that sat thereon to take peace from the earth...and there was given unto him a great sword...And when he had opened the fourth seal, I heard the voice of the fourth beast say, Come and see. And I looked, and behold a pale horse: and his name that sat on him was Death, and Hell followed with him..."

Thunder cracked so loud that Aracely Jarabo jumped from her chair. Adela dropped the Bible onto the floor. White lighting flashed across the sky and, for just a split second, Father Navarro could see Alfonso Jarabo and all three of his sons walking outside. They were guiding Blanca up to the house. Lying across the horse, the ancient priest could clearly see a bloody human body. The dream returned to his mind vividly and forcefully; he dropped the porcelain cup of tea and while it shattered against the ceramic tile floor the priest made the sign of the cross. The bloody head of the man on the horse had only one eye.

Chapter 6

Catholic Monastery—Durango, Mexico

He had not believed the afterlife would be quite like this. He didn't know if the personages interacting with him were angels, demons, or some other immortal beings whose nature he did not comprehend. In truth, a large part of him had believed he would have simply faded away, his essence wiped out of existence. The most surprising aspect of the experience so far was that he still had physical sensations. It was as if his body had been transformed into spiritual matter in conjunction with his soul. *Perhaps,* he thought, *I will come to understand the process as time goes by.* The physical pain had diminished, but still tormented him. *Maybe God exists and the perception of physical pain is punishment.*

For what seemed like earthly weeks, or perhaps even months, he had teetered back and forth between semi-consciousness and nightmares of his wife and daughter dying. He couldn't decide which was worse. But time continued to pass. Eventually he recognized his thoughts were becoming more and more cogent. Recently, in his most lucid moments, he could almost make out the conversations between the strange beings associating with him. It struck him as extremely bizarre that Spanish was the language spoken in the afterlife. And then one morning it happened. His left eye opened and he stared at an old man dressed in black vestments, gold cross hanging from his neck. The old man smiled and spoke in perfect English.

"Greetings, young man. Welcome back to the world of the living."

It took him several minutes to process what was occurring. *What in the hell happened, and why am I still alive?* He painfully forced his lips to move. "My family?"

The old man, looking deeply pained, slowly shook his head.

Fuck. So that was it. The news was not unexpected. He already knew his family was dead—just as he should be. *Through the justice of every God that mankind has ever worshipped I should be dead. I should be with my family in heaven, hell, or some version of the afterlife. Or, perhaps even better, I should have vanished.*

Rage swelled within his brain and brought with it a rush of adrenaline. He tried to clinch his fingers together. They would not move. The old man, whom he now understood to be a Catholic priest, gave him a look of sympathy. There was something very strange in the priest's expression, something he couldn't quite recognize. And he hated it. He hated this priest who was now standing before him. He hated Mexico. And, if there was a God, he hated him too.

"My name is Father Navarro. You were rescued by a young man named Ignacio Jarabo and now reside at my monastery in Northwestern Durango. One more day out in the desert and you surely would not be with us anymore." The priest did not miss the patient's acidic glare. The old man pretended not to notice. "We have been looking after you for some time, anticipating your return. I feared to take you to a hospital or alert the authorities in fear of retribution from your enemies. They are powerful and their network is vast. However, I do have medical skills which I believe are adequate for your recovery. How would you like me to address you during your stay here?"

The patient's single eye narrowed. It bore venomously into the eyes of the priest for some time before surveying the surroundings. The man discovered he lay in a plain, yet comfortable bed. Next to him was a nightstand, the Holy Bible on top. A painting of Jesus Christ calming the storm on the Sea of Galilee hung on the wall to his left. A window with green velvet drapes decorated the wall to his right. Directly in front of him was a large bookcase. His eye scanned a few of the books' titles, and with effort he made out some of the wording. Something about wealth and nations and Roman empires and conquests of New Spain. He recognized none of them. He looked back into the eyes of the priest and said nothing. The priest softly smiled.

"Very well. I suspect you are hungry. We are having *huevos rancheros* for breakfast. I shall have Sister Arámbula bring you up a plate immediately." Father Navarro turned to the door and took a few steps before looking back at his reluctant patient. "The pain shall subside and your strength shall return in time."

Minutes slowly passed as the man with no name lay in bed and pondered his predicament. He was completely incapacitated. He could control certain facial muscles. That was about it. Images of his wife and daughter once again crept into his mind; tears started to flow. *Will I ever see them again?* He quickly extinguished the troublesome thoughts and attempted to shake his head. He was racked by pain. *How long had it been?* He concluded that his life as he knew it was over. There would be no going back. *If I could, I would make it all end right here.*

He recollected a movie he watched in high school about some kid going off to serve in World War I who was hit by an artillery shell. The kid soldier lost his limbs, ears, mouth, and eyes but retained all his mental faculties. *Johnny Got His Gun* was the name of it. The military had kept him alive as part of some medical experiment and the wounded soldier went through an unimaginable hell of being trapped in his own body. He finally communicated to the military that he wanted to die by tapping his head on a pillow in Morse code. He would have remained in that hellish state forever had not some sympathetic nurse assisted the soldier in suicide.

The mental imagery made the man shudder. He tried once again to make his arms or legs move. The effort resulted in failure. *My God, I'm just like the soldier in the movie.* Waves of cold fear swept through his brain, heart, and gut. *What if I'm not as lucky as the soldier? What if I remain in this condition forever?* The thought terrified him. Frantic, his eye scanned his body in desperation. In doing so, he abruptly realized he possessed vision. *I can at least see. I am somewhat better off than the soldier in the film.* His eye went to his arms, encapsulated in orthopedic casts. His fingers and thumbs had been placed in splints. He could still make out the swelling. *Holy hell, are those things really attached to my body?*

His fingers had been brutally smashed, he recalled, as another wave of dark despair swept over him, his toes also. He was pretty sure his knees and elbows had been treated likewise. For a brief instant he vividly pictured the faces of the bastards and that evil son-of-a-bitch Vásquez, and he remembered their cruel, sadistic laughter. It enraged him. Adrenaline rushed through his veins. He thirsted for vengeance, dreaming of finding those responsible for his betrayal and killing them. All of them. He forcibly expunged the emotions from his mind. Neither vengeance nor justice would be attained.

The old man had told him that his strength would return but he knew it was untrue. *The best doctors in the world's best medical clinics could not repair the damage.* He made his eye work in tandem with his facial muscles to more thoroughly evaluate his condition. The priest seemed to have reset every bone in his body. Casts and splits made it impossible to tell if he had lost total control of all his major muscles. *Just let me die. For the love of God...just let me die.*

The opening of the door disrupted the harrowing train of thought and a heavyset nun came into the room carrying a platter of food. The expression on her face said volumes as she saw the man fully awake for the first time. She quickly regained her composure and feigned her best smile.

"Buenos días, Señor. My name *es* Sister Arámbula. *Espero* you are feeling good. I have a plate of *desayuno."* She walked over to the night stand, removed the Bible, and slid the platter on top. She looked at him hesitantly. "El Padre Navarro *me dijo—¿cómo se dice?*—to help you eat—to give you something to eat."

He shut his eye in defiance but the aroma won out. He was absolutely famished. He found himself nodding slightly and made a mental note that he possessed some control over his neck muscles. When the nun put a spoon between his lips he also realized he could use his mouth and throat. Every bite was a combination of agony and dull satisfaction as his belly slowly filled with enchiladas, eggs, beans, and rice. Between mouthfuls Sister Arámbula gave him sips of freshly squeezed orange juice.

"You want *más, Señor?* Something else?"

He looked at the nun intently and pieced together the first word of his new life.

"Cerveza."

The nun gently smiled at the reply. "I sorry, *Señor*. Padre says no to this. *Pero* he gave you some *medicina* in your*—¿cómo se dice?—jugo de naranja*—oh *sí*—orange juice."

With those words she collected the plate, glass, and silverware and departed. His eye followed her footsteps out the room. *Bastard*, he thought, as he envisioned smashing the priest across the mouth, right before taking his own life with a bullet to the brain. With that, he collapsed into another deep, dark sleep.

Against the cacophony of electronic warnings and human screaming, a grinding mass of molten steel and titanium crashed into the concrete structure on the outskirts of Baghdad. Shards of metal fragments from two of the Black Hawk's rotors pierced through glass, flesh, and bone. His body was flung from one side of the cabin to the other and in a moment of insanity he saw Jimmy's body crumple near the GAU-19 Gatling gun. Half of Jimmy's face was blown off. When the motion of the demolished chopper finally halted, he could hear outside voices screaming in Arabic amidst the chaos and carnage. Through the semi-blinding smoke he stared at the bloody and disfigured remains of the Army Rangers and Delta Operators. He attempted to move his limbs and discovered, to his amazement, that he could do so.

It appeared he was the only survivor. He looked again at the remains of his brothers in arms and his heart wept for a few moments before the jubilant cheering of the enemy awoke within him a new, darker emotion. His eyes, burning from the rancid smoke and toxic fumes, quickly focused in on a loaded M-60 machine gun lying near one of his dead companions. It was splotched with red but appeared functional. Outside he could hear the mob thirsting for more blood. Instinctively, his fingers fondled the Beretta M9 on his left hip and he picked up the M-60. He peeled a grenade off his harness and prepared for battle. To survive, he would have to fight his way out...

He awoke from the nightmares of the war to the hellish reality that now defined his existence. The days drifted into a similar routine. The priest came by every morning, noon, and evening, presenting the same smile and encouraging words. The man with no name, whom Father Navarro had named "G," short for *"Güero,"* a common term of endearment for a white person, ignored him. Sister Arámbula would follow the priest with a platter of food and a few pills and fill him to his satisfaction. G did have to admit that the food was good. Perhaps the best he had ever eaten. And whatever medicine they were giving him did seem to take the edge off the pain. Every evening after supper the priest would lay his hands upon G's head and bless him in Latin. During such religious sessions, though not understanding anything, G made every effort to stay mentally alert in order to silently curse both Father Navarro and God.

Flashbacks of his torture wreaked havoc upon his mind. He would regularly wake up to nightmares of his family being tortured. The thoughts and images terrified him and shredded his brain.

G could talk and be understood, though all his communication efforts consisted of one-word commands directed strictly to Sister Arámbula. He now had control over his head. His neck muscles had healed. To pass time, and to clear his mind, he performed thousands of repetitions of 'Yes/No's,' an exercise consisting of simply moving his head, something he had learned a long time ago as a kid in wrestling practice.

One day he discovered, despite all his body casts, he could sit up a few inches and with that action he created an exercise regimen—an outlet to escape his mental anguish. When physically exhausted from his primitive training routines he would then turn back to the task of silently blaspheming God, cursing him with the vilest words and phrases he could come up with in both English and Spanish. He even tried to commit suicide. For five days he stopped eating before Father Navarro inserted an IV tube into him. The next day he ate the bowl of *menudo* brought to him by Sister Arámbula. He tried to stop breathing on hundreds of occasions. He only succeeded in dramatically increasing his lung capacity.

G did notice that his pain, true to the word of the priest, was indeed subsiding. Physically, the discomfort he now felt was trivial to what he had experienced alone in the desert. Still most excruciating was the knowledge that his family was dead, that he was physically incapacitated, and that he could do nothing about it. He could not obtain the vengeance he believed might save his soul. It was difficult to think about anything else and it was slowly destroying him like a cancer.

Still, he reminisced about his previous life. He thought of the brief time spent as a DEA agent; the plethora of Mexican people whom he had met across the spectrum of society. He thought of his own father and imagined what he would be like. *The bastard.* His father had come from German descent, or so his mother had told him, and his mother's family was Scotch-Irish. G had never known his father. He had died of a heroin overdose when G was two years old. But his mother had somehow been able to endure the tragedy and worked endless hours to pay the mortgage on their small house and buy groceries. His mother also allowed him to pursue his love of sports. He discovered at an early age that he was physically gifted and sports came easy to him—especially wrestling. He received a wrestling scholarship in high school. During his junior year in college he had been the top-ranked wrestler in the nation before abruptly quitting everything to be with his mother when she was diagnosed with terminal cancer. After her death, he enlisted in the U.S. Army and a few years later became an Operator in Delta Force.

Time slowly turned into an unexpected ally. His neck and stomach muscles had regained some of their former strength and Sister Arámbula had witnessed the transformation. Although G did not speak much, the nun enjoyed practicing her English. She had also started reading the Bible to him, beginning with Genesis. He spaced out during most of the reading but occasionally would concentrate to help focus on anything but his own miserable existence. His Spanish comprehension was becoming better. With effort, he could understand about 30-40 percent of what the nun was reading. He had managed to get assigned to Mexico with the help of Tejada, one of his former military buddies. As a DEA agent, G's Spanish was poor, but he had picked up enough of the language to get by.

The daily routines went on unchanged for months. One afternoon

Sister Arámbula was reading the Book of Mark when the priest came in with a pair of scissors and a leather bag containing an assortment of medical tools. "Good afternoon, G," the old man said in his usual, friendly voice, "today we shall observe your recovery." G remained silent, giving the old man his normal look of disdain. *Why the hell does he keep calling me G? Maybe I should have told him to call me by my own damn name.*

Father Navarro started with the toes and, with the precision of a heart surgeon, delicately removed the splints and casts. "Try to wiggle your toes," the old man commanded.

Out of pure curiosity, G obeyed, and to his amazement, discovered he had regained control over all the muscles in his feet and ankles. He looked down at perfectly healed scars on each toe and on various locations over his feet. Each crimson red line stood out with mathematical precision. The priest proceeded to cut open the casts that bound G's legs. Both knees had the appearance of overweight, ripe plums. But again, to his surprise, and with some prodding by Father Navarro, G discovered that he could bend, ever so slightly, both his gruesome knees. As with his toes and feet, G's legs displayed an assortment of surgical scars flawlessly etched into his skin. G reluctantly conceded the workmanship could only have been performed by a master.

In silence, the priest went on to remove the upper body and arm casts confining his patient. Newly revealed skin exhibited an almost evil appearance of bone white and violet. Patches of fleshy peach and dull red covered his chest, a reminder of the burning he had been subjected to. The ghastly sight reminded G that he had not seen his face since his abduction. He had no desire to do so now.

G's elbows did not bend as easily as his knees but he could clinch his fingers together. The priest quietly watched G experiment with his new body. After almost five minutes, the priest spoke to break the uncomfortable silence. "*Descanse*. Get some rest now, G. Tomorrow Sister

López shall provide your first session of physical therapy and I suspect it shall not be pleasant. However, I do believe that you shall be walking by the end of the week."

Chapter 7

Military Headquarters—Culiacán, Sinaloa, Mexico

In the armed forces, and in high-level government circles, Colonel Ramón Acosta was a rising star. It was widely accepted that he was the most charismatic military figure to come around in a long time. His handsome appearance and charming personality made him a lady's dream. He displayed a keen intellect and it was said he possessed a photographic memory. Friends and guests were astounded at his ability to converse in minute details on various worldwide contemporary and historical political events. His manners and social skills were impeccable. Among the feminine elite, a common topic of conversation was the comparison of his finely groomed mustache to that of the late Emiliano Zapata, the magnetic Mexican revolutionary. Ramón had been intimate with almost all the important women—wives and girlfriends of high-ranking military leaders and upper-level government officials; the secrets he discovered were priceless.

Despite his many talents and successes, Colonel Acosta was bitter, angry, and constantly on edge. Today, he was livid. He walked into his office red-faced and slammed his fist on the desk.

"¡Hijo de la chingada!" Huerta is holding me back.

Ramón's breathing quickened; blood rushed into his hardened muscles; his pupils danced wickedly. He envisioned wrapping his arms around Huerta's fleshy neck and squeezing; crushing his windpipe with the heel of his boot; stomping his skull until brains poured out; ripping his gut open with an obsidian blade. Acosta had just been denied the promotion to General. Huerta had intervened again; he was sure of it. Ramón sensed Huerta might be on to him but simply didn't care; his own lust for power had become too great. He was smarter, stronger, and more ambitious than Huerta. It was becoming too galling for him to take orders. He had been in Huerta's shadow for far too long and it was his turn to rise—just like Tlaloc had predicted. He was defying the fabled military commander openly now and flirting with disaster in the process.

Completely out of spite, he had slept with Huerta's young wife, as well as his favorite mistress. Colonel Acosta sat down and cursed General Huerta one more time. Tensions were running high; the situation was unsustainable. *Something would have to change and it would have to change fast.* Ramón acknowledged Huerta's talents and power. At one point, he had been the best. Acosta gazed up at the picture of President Ernesto Zedillo. After a few moments Ramón's eyes went to the left of Zedillo to the portrait of President Carlos Salinas, then to President Miguel de la Madrid, and then to President José Portillo. Each president conjured up images of crucial time periods within his mind.

Huerta had been entrenched from the beginning. He joined the army at age eighteen, and his cunning and ruthlessness propelled him through the ranks of the service. Huerta had a cousin of the same age with whom he was close and remained so for decades to come. His name was Miguel Ángel Félix Gallardo. Félix Gallardo joined the Federal Judicial Police at age seventeen, enabling his advancement in *el narco*—"drug-trafficking." After a successful stint as a police agent, he became a bodyguard for the governor of the state of Sinaloa. The position allowed Félix Gallardo to create a strategic network of political connections with important members of the ruling Institutional Revolutionary Party (PRI).

In the late 1960s, Pedro Avilés Pérez (a.k.a. "Don Pedro") established an organization that would serve as the foundation for the more modern cartels. Don Pedro built large-scale marijuana and opium plantations, the likes of which had never been seen in Mexico. He established new smuggling routes, implemented strategic communication channels, and pioneered the use of aircraft to get drugs into the United States. Don Pedro also put together a group of people who were visionary, inventive, and utterly ruthless. One of these individuals was Félix Gallardo. The criminal organization became known as the Guadalajara Cartel.

Huerta became a three-star general and took command of the Third Military Region covering the states of Sinaloa, Sonora, Durango, and Chihuahua. He shielded the cartel from over-zealous *fedérale* intervention and provided its members with military-grade weaponry, armored vehicles, communication systems, and other valuable equipment. Huerta also recruited his own group of men and scoured the army and police forces for talented individuals who would help make him more powerful. In 1978, Félix Gallardo conspired with Huerta to take over. They orchestrated a police crackdown with surgical precision in which Don Pedro was killed in a shootout with the *federales*. The treachery exemplified the fractures that would splinter the cartels for years to come. Félix Gallardo emerged as the new leader of the Guadalajara Cartel and became known as "El Padrino"—"The Godfather."

Under the leadership of El Padrino, and with the military protection offered by Huerta, the cartel thrived and acted with complete impunity. Political leaders in all levels of government got in on the action. Officials who refused cartel bribes or fought to expose corruption suffered tragic accidents or mysteriously disappeared. *Plata o plomo*—

"silver or lead"—became a popular idiom.

El Padrino ran the narco empire brilliantly and adopted strategies used by Colombian cartels and Italian mafia. He established well-ordered hierarchies and franchised valuable pieces of drug-smuggling real estate known as *plazas*.

General Huerta ruled with a ruthless iron fist, setting the mold for the brutality to occur in later years. He became known as "El Pozolero"—"The Stewmaker." If *plaza* payments were missed, Huerta would submerge offending individuals in vats of hydrofluoric acid. He became one of the most feared men in Mexico, as well as one of the richest.

The policies and actions of the United States changed the landscape of Mexican drug-trafficking. In the early 1980s, the Reagan administration declared war on the Colombian cartels and specifically targeted their pervasive influence in South Florida. Reagan was a tough president; his campaign was so successful the Colombians became desperate for different drug routes into the United States. Inevitably, Félix Gallardo was introduced to Pablo Escobar, head of the Medellín Cartel in Colombia; a partnership formed that shifted the balance of power in the international drug trade.

As Colombian cocaine began to flood into the United States through Mexico, the profits of El Padrino's cartel skyrocketed; the organization blossomed into one of the most powerful criminal entities on the planet. Reagan turned his attention away from Florida to confront the new growing threat on the southern border. In 1984, undercover DEA agent Enrique "Kiki" Camarena infiltrated the Guadalajara Cartel and provided information that led to the destruction of a mammoth marijuana plantation known as "Rancho Bufalo" with an estimated worth of eight billion U.S. dollars. Unfortunately, Camarena was discovered as the informant and in 1985, El Padrino ordered his kidnapping and murder. Camarena was brutally tortured over the course of a 30-hour period. He finally died when a screwdriver was stabbed through his skull.

The DEA was outraged. In response to the murder, the Reagan administration launched "Operation Leyenda," the largest DEA homicide investigation ever undertaken. Special agents were dispatched to Mexico and identified El Padrino as a primary suspect. El Padrino retained political protection but was on the run. In 1987, two years before his arrest, El Padrino decided it was time to change course. The response from the U.S. DEA to the Camarena murder had poked holes in the cartel and revealed vulnerabilities. El Padrino divided his empire into five distinct territories to be ruled by the narco elite.

The Tijuana *plaza* was given to the Arellano-Félix brothers. Control of the lucrative Juárez *plaza* was placed in the hands of narco kingpin Amado Carrillo Fuentes. Miguel Caro Quintero was given control of the Sonora Corridor. Drug lord Juan García Abrego retained control of the Gulf Region. Finally, Joaquín Archivaldo Guzmán Loera (a.k.a. 'El Chapo') and Mayo Zambada inherited the Pacific Coast operations, later known as the Sinaloa Cartel.

General Huerta had close relationships with all the newly crowned drug lords; he continued his role as an enforcer and received a percentage of profits from each of the cartels. In 1988, the general discovered Ramón Acosta. Huerta quickly recognized his brilliance and within a few months, Acosta became his right-hand man.

Like El Padrino, Ramón had served time in the police force before joining the military. With help from Tlaloc, he made important connections within an impressive number of federal, state, and municipal entities. Tlaloc spent a fortune on bribes, and soon Ramón controlled a significant number of police officers and began cashing in on the action. He was generous with his money and possessed a rare ability to connect with men, as well as leverage their strengths and exploit their vulnerabilities. Unbeknownst to Huerta, Ramón made a deal with the

Medellín Cartel and García Abrego to broker shipments of cocaine to the Gulf Region with a much lower commission rate than the general.

Colonel Ramón Acosta looked at the ceiling and contemplated the ramifications of the shakeup of El Padrino's empire. *Chaos ... creates ... opportunities.* Tlaloc's wise words echoed in his mind. *The old man had been correct once again.* The Arellano-Félix brothers were proving to be psychotic; their actions were creating havoc in Tijuana and, more interesting, among the other cartels. They became known as the AFO (Arellano-Félix Organization). They struck fear in civilian populations. And they had created a lethal blood feud with El Chapo Guzmán.

As General Huerta continued to rise and became the top commander of all military regions in Mexico, he flexed his muscle. When he discovered three top-level Sonora Cartel officers were withholding *plaza* payments he had them dissolved in acid, alive, in front of Miguel Caro Quintero and all members of the Sonora Cartel. He invited each head of the other cartels to witness the event.

But in the new atmosphere of fear and unpredictability, Colonel Ramón Acosta had also risen in power, though unofficially. Through his brokerage of cocaine shipments between the Colombians and Gulf Cartel, he amassed more than 300 million U.S. dollars. He created key allies and informants within all cartels and, perhaps more important, built up his own army with his vast social network. Through bribes, drugs, and promises of power, he won over large numbers of men in all levels of the police, military, and government. He suspected Huerta knew about at least some of his activities and was digging for more information. Colonel Acosta also now knew that the two men could not coexist together. One of them would have to go, and it would have to be soon.

Chapter 8

Catholic Monastery—
Durango, Mexico

G looked at the Virgin Guadalupe on the grandfather clock. It was 2:21 a.m. He had faked taking medicine from the nun to maximize mental alertness. Now his mind was racing. *This is not going to be easy.*

As quietly as possible, G rotated his legs off the bed and planted his bulbous feet onto the carpet. Adrenaline drowned out the pain that jolted through his bones and muscles. Carefully, he moved one foot in front of the other. His balance was misaligned but he managed to adapt. His left arm seemed to be functioning better than his right. He reached for the doorknob with his left hand and, ever so gently, twisted it counter-clockwise. The door opened more quietly than he anticipated and, as he suspected, there was someone outside his room—a man sitting on a wooden stool wearing a black poncho, face covered by a wide-brimmed *sombrero,* snoring heavily. G turned to his right and found himself staring directly into a colorful portrait of Jesus Christ engraved into a stained-glass window. Inside the face of Jesus, he saw his own reflection. *Damn, I am one ugly son of a bitch.*

He turned to the left and discovered he stood at one end of a long, narrow corridor, dimly lit by candles housed in iron sconces. He started to limp to the opposite end. As his feet became more and more steady, his single eye searched feverishly for anything that might help accomplish his mission. He failed to notice the man behind him lift his *sombrero* and rise to his feet.

G lumbered past paintings and tapestries of Christ, the Virgin Guadalupe, and a slew of various saints before discovering a spiral staircase. After a grueling twenty-minute struggle, fueled by sheer will power, G managed to somehow stagger to the bottom step. The stairs led to a large room that functioned as some type of intersection. Fifteen yards to his right were two large wooden doors, ornately crafted, encrusted with bronze crosses, and partially open. G slowly hobbled through the doors and into the church.

Massive stained-glass windows adorned large areas of both the ceiling and upper walls to capture the moonlight and provide a primitive level of visibility. The worship area was plain compared to other churches in Mexico, but G found it impressive nonetheless. Pews covered most of the floor, with one large aisle dividing two main sections. G stumbled down the aisle to examine some sort of altar. A lifelike statue of the Virgin Mary stood to his left, cradling the baby Jesus. An adult Jesus, blood trickling from his thorn-covered head, hung on a wooden cross in front of him. This was his first time in a Catholic church. *And it will be my last*. Feeling very uncomfortable, he considered backtracking when he noticed an exit door positioned in the back-left corner. He limped towards the exit door, pulled it open, and gazed out into the dark.

G breathed deeply as a gust of eastern wind cooled his sweating forehead. And then he saw it. A deteriorating limestone sculpture of a man, resembling a priest, rose in the middle of the courtyard. He had a stone Bible in his left hand and a sword in his right. *Was the sword real?* Turbulent emotions swelling within him, G hobbled towards the sculpture and examined the blade in the priest's hand. It was old, rusty, and dull. But it was real enough. He pressed his left thumb down on the edge hard enough to draw blood and then broke the weapon free from the statue's crumbling grip. The moment was surreal.

Has it come to this? He'd fantasized about death for months and now, finally, the opportunity presented itself. He envisioned piercing the sword through his gut and slicing it up through his lungs, just like a defeated Samurai warrior. *It would be so easy,* G thought, gripping the hilt with both hands.

Unexpectedly, he thought of his father. *The bastardly heroin addict.* It wasn't until he himself served a few years in the army did G learn of the extent of the heroin epidemic among Vietnam vets. A whole slew of the U.S. Military had gotten hooked on the drug while in Southeast Asia and it had destroyed most of them. G also discovered, according to some of the old-timers, his father had been a war hero in Vietnam. A real badass. Before the heroin had decimated him.

The more G thought about his father and heroin, the more it had pissed him off. He'd developed a fanatical hatred for drugs and especially for those who trafficked them. When he completed his tour of duty, he promptly joined the DEA.

He figured service in the DEA would be a nice change. Perhaps allow him to settle down a bit. His wife had just completed her service and he had wanted to spend more time with both her and his daughter. Former Delta Operator Sergeant Tejada had been with the DEA for a few years and climbed its ranks. Tejada had given him an open invitation to come on board—said he could pull some strings and get him into Mexico, despite him not speaking Spanish. The DEA liked ex-military. And perhaps, just perhaps, it might bring some family closure. It might help bring peace.

What would he think now? Does it matter? He tightened his grip on the sword. *Will I see my wife and daughter again? If so, is this what they would want me to do?*

His wife encouraged him to join the DEA. He was deeply in love with his wife. Always had been. They met during his first few months in the Middle East, shortly after his first injury—a bullet wound to the abdomen, just above his left hip. The wound was superficial, his wife had told him, the first day they met. The bullet had missed bone and intestines. His wife had recently graduated from the Baylor College of Medicine, paid for by the U.S. Army, and arrived in Saudi Arabia about the same time that he did, for her first residency program. Their daughter was born one year later.

What about my mother? Would she understand or would she be ashamed? Is this how I want to be remembered in the afterlife, if it exists, by all who have known me?

Life memories flashed through his mind: childhood, high school, college, military—the brutal, yet sweet time spent in the Middle East, victories and defeats, emotions of joy and pain, love of his family, innermost secrets; everything that composed his very existence and defined his human essence. He looked down again at the blade and the trail of blood trickling from his thumb.

Is this who I am?

In despair, he pondered his choices. *What is there to live for?* As the anger and frustration mounted within him, he sliced the sword through the midnight blackness. The thrust was weak and he winced at the pain; more self-pity swelled within him. He turned to face the sculpture. The look on the man's face annoyed him.

Who is this guy?

His eye bore into the limestone face and he wondered why the expression was so irritating. He recognized the answer immediately. The face displayed the confident look of a warrior; the expression of a man not afraid of anyone or anything. It was the look that he himself once possessed, and the knowledge that he had been transformed into a miserable cripple obsessed with death enraged him. In a crazed fury,

G brought the sword to his shoulder and prepared to do battle with the inanimate object. Snarling, he swung the blade so hard it sunk into the limestone. Torment rippled through his muscles. He almost blacked out.

"No one knows exactly from whence the sword came."

The hell?

The voice pulled G back into the realm of reality. He spun around fast, too fast. His legs gave out and he fell.

Damn Father Navarro!

The old man grabbed G's arms and pulled him up with surprising strength. He then dislodged the sword from the statue and put it back into G's hands. He continued talking as if nothing had happened.

"But I thought it a fitting addition for Miguel Hidalgo, though some of my brethren would turn me over to the Vatican for keeping such a relic in the monastery. Hidalgo is one of Mexico's greatest heroes."

G said nothing and simply stared at the old man. He had no idea how long the priest had been following him or who the hell this Miguel Hidalgo was. And he found it bizarre that the priest would attempt to lecture him under the circumstances. Undeterred, Father Navarro looked up into the night sky and went on.

"The history of our land is often referred to as 'Fire and Blood.' Unfortunately, such a description is apt. After the Spanish conquest some 500 years ago, a brutal caste system was implemented in which every human being in Mexico was classified according to their ancestry, skin color, and place of birth. The caste system was complex and detailed. An individual's social status and life opportunities were defined by the caste to which he or she belonged. Denigrating terms such as 'Miserable Zambo' were codified into Mexican law and helped create an environment nothing short of a ticking time bomb."

G stared at the priest, stoic. His eye rotated to look at Miguel Hidalgo and then back to Father Navarro. *The hell was this old man on about?*

"Miguel Hidalgo was a Criollo priest who, in the early 1800s, served in the small town of Dolores in the state of Guanajuato. He was shocked at the misery and poverty he discovered there and decided to do something about it. Hidalgo went on a one-man crusade to provide a better life for the people whom he served. He taught them various skills such as grape farming, leather making, silk production, and even beekeeping."

The old man slowly directed his gaze to the statue and cleared his throat.

"Even more shocking to Hidalgo than the widespread poverty were the outrageous injustices committed by the top caste of people known as 'Peninsulares.' In 1808, a devastating drought plagued Mexico and caused widespread famine across most of the northern regions, especially in Durango. The 'Peninsulares' deliberately withheld grain from the starving people to boost crop prices. Countless numbers of people died. Hidalgo reached his breaking point in 1810 when a large group of dissenters were imprisoned unjustly. On September 15, he rode with armed men to free the prisoners. A day later he gave, perhaps, the most famous speech ever recorded in Mexico. The essence of it is printed on the plaque below the statue."

G, astonished at the strange turn of events, looked down at the metallic plaque as if in a dream. Father Navarro slowly translated the wording: "My children: A new dispensation comes to us today. Will you receive it? Will you free yourselves? Will you recover the lands stolen 300 years ago from your forefathers by the hated Spaniards? We must act as one...Will you defend your religion and your rights as true patriots? Long live our Lady of Guadalupe! Death to bad government! Death to the *gachupines!*"

G looked back up at the priest blankly.

"Even with your U.S. schooling you must have heard of '16 de Septiembre'?"

Without waiting for an answer, the old man shook his head and continued: "Hidalgo put together a ragtag army that swelled to a size of more than 80,000 men. They adopted the Virgin of Guadalupe as their symbol and declared war on the 'Peninsulares' and their injustices. Bloody battles were fought throughout the land with heavy casualties on both sides. Eventually, however, Hidalgo was betrayed and captured by Spanish authorities without achieving his stated goal. He was excommunicated from the Church and sentenced to death. In his final days, Hidalgo wrote a letter to his jailers, thanking them for his humane treatment. In front of his firing squad, he refused to wear a blindfold and placed his right hand over his heart so the marksmen would know where to shoot. After his death, he was decapitated and the 'Peninsulares' hung his head at the granary of Guanajuato as a warning to all those who would follow in his footsteps."

After months of the silent treatment, G finally spoke to the priest. "Why do you tell me this?"

The priest directed his gaze once again towards the night sky.

"Hidalgo's enemies hoped the display of his death would serve as a powerful deterrent. They were, of course, 100 percent wrong. His movement ignited a fire which led to sweeping reformations across the country. Today, Miguel Hidalgo is known as the father of Mexico and his legacy is cemented within Mexican nationalism. This land has seen some of the most abhorrent acts of injustice and bloodshed ever known to mankind."

The priest slowly lowered his gaze to stare directly into G's single eye. The old man's countenance transformed to portray an almost mystical appearance.

"But in its darkest hours, heroes have risen to combat the evil and protect the innocent."

The old man's eyes flickered to the sword in G's hand and then to the deep cut in the statue. "The level of strength needed to inflict such damage, especially by a man in your condition, is impressive. But the blade you hold, though effective in its time, will be of no use against your adversaries. To defeat those who have done you wrong, you must have a clear understanding of their origins. You must understand their culture, you must possess knowledge of what they want to achieve, and you must know what they will do to achieve it."

Without another word, Father Navarro slowly walked back to the church and went inside. G stared at the door in which the mysterious man of God disappeared through for some time before looking back at the deep scar he had inflicted upon the statue. And then he realized it. *This morning I was completely incapacitated, doomed to remain in a bodily hell forever. And now...* The realization jarred him, bringing back some of his mental toughness.

His body had been horribly damaged and mutilated, but he was capable of physical movement. *The old priest had been correct,* G admitted to himself. *My strength will return.* He could feel it now in his muscles, in his blood, and in his soul. *I will find Vásquez and I will kill him. And I will kill the others.* His lips quivered in rage. *And I will kill whoever sent him. Every single person involved.* His fingers tightened around the hilt of the sword; he swung the blade with a ferocity that made the night air sing. *I will find vengeance.*

Chapter 9

Military Headquarters—Culiacán, Sinaloa, Mexico

General Jorge Huerta puffed on his Montecristo Cuban cigar and then took a swig of Pere Magloire Fine Calvados brandy. He stroked his impressive mustache, now streaked with gray, with shaking fingers. He had gained weight in recent years; a monstrous pot belly hindered his agility, yet his wide shoulders and barrel chest were still powerful.

The chair on which the general sat had been built with 100 pounds of solid gold. On his fleshy right hand he wore a platinum ring, studded with a 10-carat orange-pink padparadscha sapphire. A diamond bracelet worth two million U.S. dollars snaked around his left wrist. Tahitian black pearls and Colombian emeralds adorned the edges of his Carpathian elm desk. Paintings from some of the most sought-after artists in the world decorated his office walls. At home he even possessed originals of Van Gogh, Picasso, and Cézanne. General Huerta was one of the wealthiest men on the planet but his appetite for extravagant possessions was insatiable.

His favorite piece of artwork was housed in a glass exhibit podium standing just a few feet away. It was a human skull with gold teeth and a pair of 50-carat Burmese star rubies embedded within its eye sockets. The skull belonged to Don Pedro, the founding drug lord whom Huerta had betrayed and murdered. The general had prized the skull for more than a decade.

Right now, however, Huerta's quest for the latest treasure had been abandoned; any thoughts of the precious skull were gone. The general's flabby face was scarlet. His lips quivered. His nostrils flared. *¡Hijo de puta! He really thinks he can pinche get away with this, the insolent pinche puto bastard. After everything I've chingado done for him.* He took another drink of brandy and, trying to calm his shaking hands, picked up his phone and called for the girl.

As Huerta hung up, he looked up at Benjamín Arellano-Félix. Benjamín had just informed him of Colonel Ramón Acosta's business with Juan García Abrego and the Gulf Cartel. The AFO recently tortured three high-ranking Colombian Cartel members and one of them had talked. It wasn't the information they were looking for, but nonetheless valuable. Benjamín smoked a cigarette while casually leaning against the wall, right hand toying with an ivory-plated pistol garnished with Santa Muerte insignia. He wore a white hat, black silk shirt, designer blue jeans ornamented with a wide, gold-buckled belt, and beige snakeskin cowboy boots.

"*Gracias,* Benjamín, I'll see you in a few *chingado* days *cabrón*. You will be well rewarded for your *chingado* loyalty." Benjamín saluted the general and left. Fuming, Huerta took another drink and waited for the girl. She arrived fifteen minutes later dressed in a black miniskirt, pink tank top, and white leather boots running up to her knees. Splashes of velvet enhanced the hue of her dark eyes. She smiled seductively, revealing white teeth.

"*Hola,* the usual General?"

Huerta nodded.

Twenty minutes later, the general was lying down on the floor.

Blood dripped from his naked body. The freshly healed scars on his abdomen, chest, and buttocks had been reopened. His genitalia were stinging. His anger had subsided. He was in ecstasy. And he knew exactly how to handle Colonel Ramón Acosta.

One week later, Huerta arrived unannounced at Ramón's office, laughing heartily. "Ramón! *¿Qué onda, cabrón?* How are Mónica and Rene?" General Huerta had a wife also, many, in fact, and so many children he had lost count years ago. He didn't give a damn about any of them, though they would help cement his legacy. But he knew that Colonel Acosta genuinely loved his family.

Ramón remained stoic and simply nodded at his commanding officer. *Joder. What do you want, you fat bastard?* He envisioned crushing the general's jaw with the broad side of an axe. General Huerta went on undeterred. "I thought I'd come by and see if we can talk things over, bury the hatchet in all the *chingado* goat shit. Here—I've brought a little something for you and your wife." Huerta stretched forth his hand and presented Ramón with two small gifts. "Go ahead, open them. You can re-wrap the one for your wife however you want."

Colonel Acosta opened the gifts. The first was a gold Rolex watch, the second an exquisite diamond necklace. Ramón stared for a few moments at the fine pieces and then slowly looked up at General Huerta, mind racing to analyze the strange turn of events. "*Muchísimas gracias,* Jorge. You are extremely generous." Ramón spoke slowly and deliberately, his facial features void of emotion. "To what do I owe this unexpected pleasure?"

"We *chingado* need you. A *puto* large shipment of merchandise arrived a few days ago from Medellín. It's perhaps the biggest *chingado* stash ever delivered on Mexican soil and our friends want help getting it across the border. It's going to be *pinche* lucrative, all the way around. Let's go take a look and see what you think. How about it, *cabrón?*"

Ramón shrugged and stared at the gifts. He sensed trouble. But he also recognized the inklings of an opportunity. "Come on *cabrón,*" the general urged. "You will not regret this opportunity. I *chingando* guarantee it."

Colonel Acosta remained silent for twenty seconds before cracking a smile. "Alright, you *gordo* bastard, I'm in. Let me go grab Héctor and let's see what they got."

Huerta held back the makings of a frown and forced himself to grin. He hated the *chingado* giant thug Vásquez almost as much as he hated Ramón. "*¿Por qué no?* We could use *el cabrón. ¡Vámonos!*"

Ramón felt a twinge of uneasiness upon entering the black VCR-TT 6x6 but acted cordial, confident, and charismatic. The VCR-TT was an armored personnel carrier Huerta was fond of. He had a flying phobia, worsened in recent years, and now refused to travel in airplanes or helicopters. Major Chalino Lugo, one of Huerta's bodyguards, drove. Major Vásquez sat up front. All four men were dressed in military attire. Two more VCT-TTs, one sporting desert camouflage and the other painted in a traditional three-color camouflage pattern, served as escorts.

Huerta drank from a fifty-year-old bottle of Chivas Regal Royal Salute. He offered the bottle to Ramón knowing the young colonel never touched the stuff. Ramón smiled, politely declined, and asked more about the shipment. He finessed out pertinent information and praised Huerta's skill and leadership. As the VCR-TT cruised through the downtown streets of Culiacán, they came across a group of Afro-Mexicans crossing the street. Major Lugo hit the gas pedal and the vehicle narrowly missed a teenager by a few inches.

"*¡Que vivan los Negros!*" yelled General Huerta. "Long live black people!"

"Pero que vivan muy lejos de mi casa," replied Colonel Acosta. "But let them live a long ways from my home."

General Huerta roared in laughter. Everyone joined him. Soon they were reminiscing about past women, adventures, and the fortunes they had accumulated.

Eventually, the vehicle emerged onto a remote highway leading towards the Pacific Ocean. Sometime later, as the Mexican sun descended into the distant horizon, they entered a secluded port area, lined with rundown cargo ships, ancient fishing vessels, and deteriorating warehouses. General Huerta disengaged from the jovial conversation and looked outside the window. "Ah, we are *chingado* here already. You are going to be amazed at this, Ramón." Huerta put his plump hand on Ramón's shoulder. "I want you to know that I could not have become this *puto* powerful without you. I mean that *cabrón*. You have a bright future ahead of you, Colonel."

The VCT-TT parked outside a particularly ugly-looking warehouse showing few signs of maintenance or human activity. All four men exited the vehicle and the escorts drove off. It was dark outside, blankets of clouds blocked out the moonlight. Ocean waves crashed against the docks. Major Lugo led them to a partially hidden door on the opposite side of the main loading gate. Lugo entered through the door first, followed by Vásquez, Ramón, and then Huerta.

The inside of the warehouse was dark and dank with few windows. Any chances of visibility were dashed when Huerta closed the door behind him. The general was unperturbed by the darkness, however, and spoke loudly as he continued to walk into the deteriorating building. "The *cabrones* who designed the place put the main light switch near the center office just up ahead. Give me a few *chingados* seconds."

Five seconds later waves of light abruptly flooded the entire inside of the warehouse. The contrast resulted in a few moments of confusion for Ramón. He tried to get his bearings. Twenty yards directly in front of him were his wife and son. They were gagged, tied up, held at gunpoint, and standing next to two large vats containing a liquid-like substance that Ramón knew was Huerta's favorite acidic concoction. Colonel Acosta heard the familiar cock of an AK-47 and felt the cold steel barrel gently touch the back of his head. It was Lugo.

Fifteen men, dressed in military uniform and armed with AR-15s, swarmed onto the scene. Two large muscular brutes with hard jaw lines and scarred faces surrounded Vásquez and pointed an AK-47 and Heckler & Koch P7 pistol directly at his head. They were brothers from the slums of Tijuana, Roberto and Pancho, two of Huerta's most ruthless enforcers. Huerta cracked an iron rebar across Vásquez's knees. The large man went down hard. Pancho fired his pistol to the left of Vásquez's face, annihilating his ear.

General Huerta, holding the iron rod firmly in his right hand, slowly and deliberately walked up to Ramón. His face was swollen and purple. Droplets of saliva streamed from his lips to his chin. His whole body shook and his now ominous voice hissed into Ramón's ear. "You dare take *chingado* money from me *hijo de puta?* You really thought you could get away with this? After all I've done for you? I am the one who *chingado* made you!" The crazed general looked at the terrified woman and boy and then back at Colonel Acosta. Huerta raised the iron bar high in the air.

"You will give me the locations of your stash houses. If we recuperate enough money your family will be set free and you will die a quick death. Otherwise, you will watch your family's flesh slowly dissolve from their bones and you will suffer beyond your wildest imagination!"

Instantly after Huerta spewed out the last words, Ramón ducked hard and fast. A Ka-Bar combat knife appeared in his right hand. He sprung up with incredible force and plunged the knife brutally into Lugo's throat as three rounds from the assault rifle missed his head by several inches. Before Huerta could comprehend what was happening,

Ramón seized control of the AK-47 from the lifeless Lugo and put a bullet through the general's kneecap. Roberto and Pancho stared at their commander for a split second in disbelief before Pancho's facial bones shattered from a thunderous left hook from a maniacal Vásquez.

Roberto went down a microsecond later as two expertly placed bullets from Vásquez's Beretta 92FS pistol penetrated deep into his heart. Ramón's left arm shot out like a rattlesnake and wrapped itself around Huerta's neck. He yanked the wounded general up to his feet and pointed the machine gun at Huerta's stunned men. Vásquez had retrieved the AK-47 from the bloody pool on the concrete floor and was standing next to Colonel Acosta with the weapon aimed at his enemies.

"Tell your men to drop the weapons," Ramón whispered into Huerta's ear. The tone of his voice was strangely calm. General Huerta hastened to obey his command and the soldiers slowly relinquished their arms. Colonel Acosta gave an ever-so-slight nod and then proceeded, in unison with Major Vásquez, to open fire.

It was a massacre. Most of Huerta's men had been too slow to realize what was happening—only a handful managed to pick up their guns and retaliate. All the soldiers were ripped to shreds by the 169 rounds spraying from the assault rifles of Ramón and Héctor.

Colonel Acosta took a bullet to his right shoulder early on. He had kept on firing. Another bullet slightly grazed the left side of his head, just above the ear, and left a deep scarlet gash about two inches long cutting to his skull. Vásquez had a gory hole in the flesh of his upper right thigh. The floor was thick with blood and littered with bodies. One of the large vats of acid had been pierced with bullets and was leaking its contents onto the bloody mess.

Colonel Acosta violently shoved the horrified Huerta over to Major Vásquez and walked towards his family. He gently removed the cord that bound his son's mouth.

"¡Papi!"

Tears streamed down Rene's face as Ramón freed him with the Ka-Bar combat knife. Acosta was moving onto his wife when the gunfire blasted into his ears. His response was immediate. The knife rocketed from the colonel's hand, sinking into the ribcage of one of Huerta's gunmen—a lieutenant named Chávez. Despite being riddled with seven bullets, the wounded lieutenant had somehow managed to come to his knees and fire his weapon. Lieutenant Chávez had missed his target—Colonel Acosta was unscathed. But Mónica had taken three shots to the chest and a single bullet had struck the forehead of Rene. Both their corpses fell to the concrete near Ramón's feet.

Colonel Acosta rushed over to the dead lieutenant and stabbed him over 100 times before running back to his family. Collapsing onto his knees, he unleashed a primal scream—the likes of which neither Vásquez nor Huerta had ever heard. The colonel screamed for what seemed like an eternity before finally kissing his dead wife and son on the cheek. He carefully collected both bodies and carried them out to the VCT-TT.

Vásquez dragged General Huerta to the south wall of the warehouse. Héctor's massive arms twisted the iron rebar tightly around Huerta's neck and he shoved the general against a thick glass window. Though Huerta weighed close to 300 pounds, Vásquez lifted him several inches off the floor. Colonel Acosta re-entered the building and strode towards Huerta in silence.

Ramón's eyes bore into Huerta for a full minute. It was then that Huerta realized he had underestimated Colonel Acosta for the last time. The general desperately struggled for air and looked back into Ramón's eyes. And he felt true fear upon recognizing the underlying essence behind those eyes. It was power and it was evil. It was a dark evil that far surpassed anything he could have conceived. The tone of Ramón's voice was chilling. He spoke slowly and methodically.

"Your time has passed, Jorge, and you are going down, just like Don Pedro. But your death won't be as easy as a simple bullet to the head. You will suffer for this."

Vásquez dropped the general to the floor and Huerta gasped for air for a long time before squirming up to his hands and knees like a wounded wharf rat. He ignored the crushed bone in his knee cap. When he finally looked up at the two men, his body was wobbling as he urinated in his olive-green pants.

In a tomb within a secret cavern, Colonel Acosta kissed his wife and son for the last time. Just a few minutes later, he exited the pyramid. Shielding his eyes from the Mexican sun, he nodded at Tlaloc. The drums began to beat at the hunchback's command.

General Huerta finally came to his senses. The first thing he sensed was the pain. But it was not from his shattered knee cap. It was a cruel, nefarious throbbing in his feet that he never fathomed a living creature could experience. Despite the agony he absorbed the rancid odor ripping up through his nostrils and into his brain. He recognized the smell immediately. It was his own special concoction of hydrofluoric acid.

He looked down and screamed. Both his legs had been implanted in two large buckets; the skin on his feet and lower legs had disappeared. His body was dissolving before his very eyes. There was a man next to him with a syringe who General Huerta knew was a doctor assigned the difficult task of keeping him conscious and alive.

The drums were beating to a wicked rhythm, a macabre music he had never heard. Yet, somehow, it was vaguely recognizable. It only took a few seconds for the general to make the connection. The music was death. He looked up to his left and saw nine haunting statues, mystically calling out to him. The pupils in Huerta's eyes dilated; he unwittingly focused on the giant statue in the middle: it wore a necklace of gory human heads. The statue's own eyeballs bulged out of their sockets and pierced into Huerta's soul. Huerta stared at the human heads and horror flooded into his very essence. He recognized the faces. They belonged to his bodyguards and most loyal henchmen.

The general now knew where he was—at the ancient Aztec site he rented out to Acosta. But he had been completely unaware of its use. Huerta's body went limp. His skin turned ashen. He shook his head in disbelief. He looked to the right and discovered a scene even more sinister. The ancient pyramid had been resurrected and though somewhat distant, Huerta could visualize a hideous human being at the top of the structure. He was clothed in a jaguar skin robe and held a blood-stained obsidian knife. The beastly human stared down at him, grinning wickedly. Huerta screamed again. To the right of the jaguar man stood a line of sobbing humans, painted in blue, to honor the Aztec rain god. They were Huerta's wives, children, and mistresses—all of them. Huerta watched in diabolical fear as the shrieking members of his family and concubines were steadily sacrificed by the jaguar priest, one by one.

After the last sacrifice, two men descended the steps of the pyramid and walked over to the now-unconscious Huerta. One man was draped in a crimson robe held together by jade at the base of his neck. He was otherwise naked save for a green loincloth and an elaborate headdress composed of brightly colored feathers. The other man wore a loincloth striped in resplendent colors of blue, green, red, and yellow. Polished gold bracelets snaked around his huge wrists and biceps. A gold necklace, studded with turquoise and engraved with images of jaguars and eagles, wrapped around his massive chest. The man in the crimson robe looked at the lifeless Huerta and turned to the doctor at his side.

"Wake him up."

The doctor injected another dose of drugs into Huerta's arm; a few minutes later the general's eyes popped open, he found himself staring into the face that haunted every moment of his existence. In his right hand, Colonel Ramón Acosta gripped the blood-soaked obsidian knife Tlaloc used to worship the Aztec god of death. He held it up to Huerta's nose.

"Over the course of the next few days you will experience a suffering known only to a few people who have ever lived on this planet. Just before you die, I will use this knife to cut out your heart. Then I will devour it. I want you to know that I will have power over you in the afterlife."

Ramón turned to face Major Vásquez before walking away.

"He's all yours."

Chapter 10

Catholic Monastery—Durango, Mexico

"Daddy, I love you!" cried the five-year-old girl. She wrapped her arms around his muscular neck. He grinned and softly rubbed her button nose with his own. She was the most beautiful little girl in the world, and he absolutely adored her.

"I love you too, Princess. Now it's time to go to bed."

The little girl's lips formed a pouting expression until a stunning brunette in a red dress gave the girl a mocking frown and clapped her hands.

"Now—it's time for you to get some sleep. You can play with Daddy in the morning."

The little girl looked at her daddy one more time and then grudgingly followed her mother upstairs. A few minutes later her mother came back down, now dressed in a black silk nightgown...

At 8:00 a.m., the alarm clock emitted an irritating buzz that yanked G back into reality from a rare good dream. Most of his dreams still centered on his torture and his ultimate horror, the suffering of his family. His eyelid opened. His right arm slowly emerged from the cotton blanket to fumble around the nightstand. For a few brief moments, he considered smashing the damned clock. Yesterday he had shattered its predecessor and slept in past noon. Instead, he softly hit the off switch. He pulled his hand back under the blanket and closed his eyelid. He pondered what it would be like to go back to sleep in the comfortable bed and never again wake up, fade into the numbing darkness and disappear forever. The only outlet he had for serenity was sleep—when he was not having nightmares. And the only thing that kept him going was his thirst for vengeance. He lay in bed for five full minutes contemplating whether to go back to sleep.

"Shit!" He rolled off the mattress and onto the floor. Ignoring the pain, he forced himself into position and performed as many push-ups as possible. As expected, the number was not high—twelve. But it was a new record in the start of his brand new, miserable life.

G stood six-feet-one-inch tall and in his prime had weighed a very lean 219 pounds. He doubted now whether he weighed 180. Heavy amounts of scar tissue threaded around his muscles, joints, and bones, which caused agony in most of his bodily movements. His eye glanced down at his aching arms, reminding him once again that his singular purpose in life was to remodel body tissue—to regain functional mobility and strength. The rehabilitation process would be the first step forward on his quest of exacting vengeance. He continued doing push-ups to the point of exhaustion. Then he went on to squats and calf raises. By the time he met Sister Arámbula for a breakfast of *menudo,* a traditional Mexican dish composed of tripe and hominy, he had worked up a reasonable appetite.

Sister López arrived at the usual time of 10:00 a.m. and greeted G with her usual, bubbly smile. "God be with you, G. I'm sorry I missed you yesterday." She then launched into the latest news about her patients at the hospital. Sister López stood four-feet-eleven-inches tall, weighed ninety-three pounds, and was gorgeous. The nun had a trim hourglass figure, full pouty lips, and lovely honey-brown eyes that sparkled radiantly against her porcelain skin. G was stunned by her beauty when they first met. Despite the pain of rehab, he looked forward to the feel of her hands on his body. It was one of the few bright spots of his days. Sometimes, despite the love he still felt for his deceased wife, he fantasized about Sister López. And he felt guilty about it.

The nun had not always been considered beautiful; she'd been obese as a child and teenager. During high school, she because so self-conscious she developed bulimia and it had destroyed much of her life. Despite her illness and anxiety, she graduated from high school and enrolled at the University of Texas at El Paso where she studied biology and became a fitness fanatic. The bulimia never fully went away, but her newfound obsession helped take the edge off the eating disorder. Yet much of her anxiety persisted, and she turned down numerous suitors who thought her the sexiest thing they had ever laid eyes on.

After graduating from the University of Texas at El Paso, she returned to her homeland to earn a degree in physical therapy at Juárez of Durango State University. She continued to reject the multitudes of advances from interested males. After a few years of working at a Chihuahua hospital, she had several religious experiences while working with her patients. She would fervently pray for each person she treated and discovered that the more spiritual she became, the less her eating disorder ravaged her life. Eventually, she decided to enter the ministry.

Now, the beautiful nun was a fireball of charismatic energy. Despite her mild anxiety, she loved to chat and could talk about anything. The nun seemed truly sympathetic to G's situation and his underlying wellbeing. After a few uncomfortable days, G learned to relax in her presence and the strange duo managed to get on with the rehabilitation business just fine. Today marked the twelfth day of their time together. Father Navarro had constructed a gym in one of the monastery's rooms containing an exercise bicycle, treadmill, and basic row machine. Sister López managed to supplement it with a couple of treatment tables, exercise mats, exercise balls, stretching aids, bands and tubing, and an assortment of other equipment.

G now sat down on one of the tables and, as the nun cheerfully talked about the academic achievements of her younger siblings, she extended G's knee with the force of someone twice her size. He grimaced at the pain. *Son of a bitch!* Because he never complained, rarely said a word for that matter, the young nun would sometimes forget that the stretching must be excruciating.

Despite her bubbly personality, Sister López didn't mind G's hours of silence and connected with him at an instinctual level, like the relationships she had established with some of her more incapacitated patients. She was secretly amazed at the progress he was making and the extent to which he let her torture his body. On her first physical examination, she had been flabbergasted that he could even walk. He was by far the best patient she had ever had, and the nun took a special pride in watching him improve his strength and recoup his muscle mobility and coordination. When talking about G's status with Father Navarro and Sister Arámbula, she sometimes had difficulty containing her enthusiasm. This morning she had decided to take him to the next level.

"G, today we are going to try something new. I think you could do with some fresh air." G had come to respect the nun's expertise and shrugged in compliance. Sister López seemed more excited than usual. "Great!" she replied. "Let's get out of here."

The nun led G out of the makeshift exercise room and through the main corridor of the monastery. G followed her, more or less, without difficulty. He still walked with a limp, though it was not quite as noticeable as two weeks ago. On the way, he encountered the usual cast of priests and nuns, along with more colorful individuals.

Running down the main hallway was a dwarf-sized man with Down's syndrome named Felipe. Felipe, who appeared to have been born with a large toothy grin engraved onto his round face, jumped up and down excitedly and yelled "G! G! G!" It was the only word G ever heard Felipe say and, as usual, G ignored him. At the end of the main corridor, near the cathedral, was an old woman in a wheel chair named Esmeralda. She constantly talked with herself. G had seen her a few times, always alone, and always talking.

Sister López politely greeted everyone she encountered but continued walking at her normal, brisk pace. G had to struggle to keep up. Around one of the corners he bumped into a bald man with a pencil-thin mustache and a nasty scar across his left cheek that ran up to the corner of his eye. He wore a black t-shirt. His lower arms were covered in tattoos. G had known many people like him in his days with the DEA: *cholos*—'gangbangers,' *sicarios*—'assassins'—most of them connected to the cartels in one way or another. G was astonished to see such an individual at the monastery. The man grinned, revealing two gold-plated front teeth, and greeted Sister López warmly. He looked at G, *"¿Qué onda, güero?"* G said nothing in return and simply stared at the strange man. The man shrugged, introduced himself as Javier, and faced the nun.

"Hey Sister López, I just got a new dog and you know what? He's a tri-sexual."

Javier waited for a few seconds with a perverted grin on his face. "He tries to have sex with everything!"

Javier burst out laughing and went about his business. Sister López blushed. G cracked a smile.

Eventually, Sister López and her patient reached one of the doorways near the cathedral and, as he surfaced into the bright sunlight, G realized he hadn't been outside since the night he planned to commit suicide just a few weeks ago. The outside of the building now appeared quite different from how he remembered it that evening. The building architecture was patterned after the complex at Tochimilco, one of fourteen original monasteries decorating the slopes of Popocatépetl, a volcano to the southeast of Mexico City. Those original monasteries were constructed during the sixteenth century by the Augustinians, Franciscans, and Dominicans, and considered a World Heritage Site.

The more modern monastery where G now resided consisted of a large rectangular atrium, relatively plain chapel with a single nave, and a few other monastic structures located to the south of the church. All the buildings were constructed out of adobe and painted in a dull sandy-brown color that strongly reflected the light of the powerful Mexican sun. The adobe edifices blended in perfectly with the rugged desert wilderness that went on for miles and miles to the south. A farmhouse, barn, and granary stood a few hundred yards east of the main complex, along with several acres of green fields that dramatically contrasted against the desert sands, ocotillo, palmilla, cholla, and sagebrush. A large pond, a few fruit orchards, and several pastures dotted the landscape to the west. Clusters of foothills and bluffs, streaked with hundreds of shades of whites, browns, and oranges, popped out of the desert several miles to the north. A range of purple mountains, sprinkled with green, rose from the bluff tops and ascended sharply to pierce the clear blue sky. G stared at the scenery for several moments before Sister López grabbed his left arm with both of her hands and tugged.

"Alright, tough guy—let's see if you can keep up." G watched in amusement as the nun ran twenty paces, turned around to jog backwards, and motioned for him to follow. He hesitated for several seconds, watched Sister López laugh at him, and then tentatively took off. He ran for ten yards, fell flat on his face, and scrambled back up.

"Damn it!" He wiped the dirt and pebbles off his clothes and skin and tried again. He made close to twenty yards. The pain and humiliation propelled him onwards and fifty minutes later, though falling thirteen times, he successfully completed the half mile run around the cherry orchard. After that first run, the odd-looking pair began each therapy session with a light jog. Within two weeks, G could complete a slow-paced mile without falling.

Although Father Navarro was impressed with G's physical rehabilitation, he knew that all other aspects of his progress were abysmal. G was invited to Bible study and prayer sessions each morning and evening. He would curtly refuse each invitation. Between therapy sessions, the priest would attempt to engage G in light-hearted athletic discussions. He was unsuccessful. Ventures to converse about fishing, hunting, and hiking fared likewise.

Any communication directed at Father Navarro from G was semi-cordial, but always terse. G would, however, speak a bit with Sister Arámbula and the two formed a bond. While he was incapacitated, Sister Arámbula had learned his favorite tastes and prepared meals accordingly. Oftentimes they would dine together. The good-natured nun continued to teach him Spanish as well as practice her own English. Sometimes they would read books together including *Don Quixote, Cantar de Mío Cid,* and *Lazarillo de Tormes.*

Internally, G was still emotionally unstable. He was depressed. Bitterness and cynicism warped his thinking. He craved vengeance, yet in some of his weaker moments still wished he had died in the desert. Most of the time he rejected the existence of this God that Father Navarro and the nuns so desperately wanted him to believe in, yet he cursed his name continually. In some of his more morbid moments he did believe in God. And he was sure this sadistic God was mocking him with a diabolical cruelty. That he lived in a place of worship galled him, as well as his constant interaction with the ubiquitous religious symbolism.

His rage-filled obsession drove him onward. The need for retribution had become part of him now and despite the occasional lapse, his chemical make-up would not allow him to surrender. He fantasized about the brutal way he would kill Vásquez—kill all his enemies. Those fantasies provided the fuel he needed to go on.

The nuns were deeply worried about him and prayed continually for his soul. Sometimes, they wondered if he could mentally recover. Father Navarro, however, somewhat more learned in the intricate nature of mankind, stressed the need for patience. "The Lord God has seen fit to bless us with one of the great remedies for a broken body and spirit: time. We must use it to our advantage. Trust in the Lord with all your heart and lean not unto your own understanding. Proverbs 3:5. I believe the Almighty has a plan for G, yet I do not pretend to know exactly what it is. The man has been through quite an ordeal; the effort to mend his soul will be considerable."

So the days went on. Six weeks into his rehabilitation, G performed his first pull-up. He was far from the physical specimen he had once been, yet even G recognized his transformation was remarkable. He remembered the priest's words about recovering his strength and grudgingly had to admit the old man was indeed correct.

One day, G discovered a chicken coop on the eastern edge of the monastery and began to start off each morning with a run towards the farm, where he would gather a dozen or so eggs. Afterwards, he would run back to the kitchen in the monastery. There, he separated the yolks with a couple of cups and a tablespoon. He swallowed down the slimy raw white material, resisting the urge to vomit. It was one of Mother Nature's best sources of protein. He threw away the yellow yolks for eight days straight before Sister Arámbula discovered what was happening and started saving the leftovers for the orphans.

Nine weeks into the training, G could jog nonstop for three miles as well as run some basic sprints with about 75 percent the speed of his former self. The sessions with Sister López were becoming less and less painful, and he sought for different outlets to break down his body. During some of the downtime he took to exploring the agricultural areas on the outskirts of the complex. The fields and orchards were well kept, producing crops to feed the inhabitants of the monastery, a few nearby villages, and some orphanage which G had heard Sister Arámbula talk about. He marveled at the sophisticated irrigation system necessary to grow such a quantity of food in this barren desert. When he discovered that Father Navarro was the architect, G once again had to be grudgingly impressed with the old man's skills.

One day he was inspecting the inside of the barn next to the apple orchard and found some old water buckets in a back corner. The buckets possessed iron handles and, when filled with stones, proved sturdy enough to serve as workout weights. With some tossed-out farm machinery and a little ingenuity, he created several different stations to perform bench presses, squats, and other basic exercises.

Occasionally he ventured into the desert hills and stared for hours at the multi-colored bluffs rising magically from the desolate sands and scrublands. In the evening, on the dark side of twilight, the fading sunlight irradiated the peaks of the mountain tops behind the bluffs and G wondered in awe what lay beyond them and what mysteries they held. And, every so often, howbeit for short periods of time, G would get caught up in the scenery for just long enough to forget his own miserable existence.

Sánchez sat on the edge of his seat without blinking. The beat of the music softened as the large-breasted woman slowly and methodically removed her black lace bra. Her hips continued to sway to the seductive rhythm. Both of Sánchez's elbows were on the table, arms propping up his large head. He leaned forward, mesmerized by the dancer's movements. As the woman's bra fell to the stage, the table jolted unexpectedly. Sánchez's nose plunged into the pitcher of *cerveza*. The other narcos howled with laughter.

"¡Putos cabrones!" Sánchez rose and sprayed his comrades with what remained of the pitcher of beer.

"Cálmese hijo de la chingada," said a lanky narco named Peralta. "What the hell do you want to do, marry the *puta* bitch?" He was sitting in the center of the booth between two prostitutes. Laughing, Peralta snorted another line of cocaine.

"¡Vete a la verga culero!" snapped Sánchez.

"Shut the hell up, both of you," growled Javier. "I'm trying to watch." Javier reached into his leather vest pocket and tossed another packet of cocaine onto the table. The cocaine was high quality. The best. The others knew Javier only brought the good stuff. And, as usual, he had hired the prostitutes.

"You want her?" Javier asked Sánchez, referring to the naked dancer. "I'll get her for you. Tonight."

"¿En serio?"

"Of course *cabrón*. What are friends for?"

Sánchez smiled and gazed lustily at the dancer. *"Gracias,* Javier. You're the best."

Javier smirked and signaled to the waitress. *"¡Señorita, más tequila para mis amigos!"*

Several hours later Sánchez took another swig of tequila, grinning like a *pendejo*. The large-breasted dancer was wrapped around him. When Sánchez started talking about the Ortiz woman and the stash house, Javier had the recorder running. Father Navarro never knew the exact details of his informant's work, but Javier always got the job done.

Three months from the day Father Navarro removed his casts, G decided it was time to leave the monastery. He knew he wasn't ready physically, but figured he was strong enough to strike out on his own.

He needed guns, ammo, and several weeks on the shooting range. His eyesight worried him, as did his reconstructed fingers; he needed to gauge his dexterity and accuracy. During his stint in Culiacán, he made several points of contact in the Mexican military and police force. Now, he would go to them. *They will provide me information I need and we will work together to bring the sons of bitches to justice. I will kill Vásquez and every single bastard involved. All of them.*

Living in the monastery and interacting with the residents was really weighing on him. He felt awkward; almost every person he met seemed happy—and it bothered him. He continually met new people—many of them had physical deformities and some were not quite there mentally—outcasts of society. But they seemed cheerful enough and smiled at G whenever they saw him. *These were good people here*, he reflected, *the laborers, nuns, priests, all of them, even Father Navarro.* They had healed him, fed him, clothed him—looked after his every need. He was sure the old man believed he had performed God's will by resurrecting him from the dead. Instead, he had created a monster. *Navarro couldn't possibly know the pain of losing everything; living with the knowledge your family was brutally slaughtered; deformed for life; nothing to hope for but the bloodshed of your enemies.*

On a cloudy Sunday afternoon, G performed seven pull-ups and then proceeded to blast all the muscles in his body. Afterwards he ran sprints until he puked, then collapsed in one of the green pastures. He watched the clouds float over the sky for more than an hour before running over to the vibrantly colored bluffs.

The bluffs drew him in like a magnet. He spent hours staring at the magnificent specimens. It was as if they had mystical properties, serving as borderlines between the welcoming green mountains and the savage desert. Where the desert imagery fueled his darkest ambitions, the mountainous scenery soothed his damaged soul. Now, as raindrops began to prickle his skin, he focused his gaze on the rocky mountain peaks above the bluffs and wondered again what lay beyond them. He would never know. He was leaving in the morning.

It was close to midnight, as G was preparing to sleep at the monastery for the last time, that he heard a soft knock at his door. *Strange,* he thought. *No one has ever come this late to my room.* He had not told anyone about his decision to leave, nor was he planning to do so. G walked over to the door and opened it. It was Father Navarro.

"G, I am sorry to bother you at this late hour but something urgent has come up. We need to talk for a few minutes."

G stared at the old man for ten seconds and then glanced towards the bag containing his assortment of meager possessions. It was zipped up and set alongside the bed. G watched the old man's eyes shift towards the bag and then shrugged. *So much for my silent getaway.* "I don't really have time right now, Padre. I'm leaving in the morning."

Father Navarro seemed strangely unconcerned about the announcement. His eyes narrowed and his demeanor became stonelike. "Just a few minutes, G, and I shall not hassle you further. If you intend to leave the monastery, you may do so in peace and I shall inform the sisters of your decision after your departure. But I am afraid I have to insist that you accompany me for a few minutes."

G perceived genuine urgency in the old man. *Something really must be up.* He looked back at his bed and his bag and then met the piercing stare of Father Navarro.

"Five minutes."

The priest led him into a room in the monastery in which G had never been. Inside was Javier, his skinny tattooed arms hooking up a VCR to an ancient Sony television. Javier completed the set-up, nodded curtly at Father Navarro, then left the room. The old man walked over to the VCR, inserted a video cassette, and hit the start button.

"I received the video a short time ago."

The television showed a girl sitting cross-legged on a gray carpet in front of a curtain. She looked to be in her preteens, all skin and bones. Large, dark eyes. Short brown hair. Slight cleft in her upper lip. She was naked except for bandages covering her forehead and nose. A black cord bound her hands. Tears streamed down her face. Her whole body was shaking. She slowly lowered her trembling head and a voice growled from behind the camera, "Start now!"

The girl started talking in a voice signaling a pain well beyond tears.

"Mama, take back the newspaper stories. Please. Please, or they are going to cut a finger off. And they know where Aunt Guadalupe lives. Please, now. I want to go home, Mama."

The gruff off-camera voice kicked in. "Are you suffering?"

"I'm suffering," the girl answered, in a tone begging for mercy.

Then the beatings began. First a masked torturer kicked the girl in the head and then whipped her across the back with a belt. He then kicked her, harder this time, in the stomach. The man turned the girl around to expose the bruises on her back and beat the wounds with the belt.

"No! No! No!"

The girl screamed as the beatings went on and on.

During the whole process the torturer was looking into the camera, "Is this what you want for your daughter, you *puta* bitch? This is the beginning of the end, I warn you. It depends on you, how far we are going to go. The next step is a finger. Do not publish again. Recant all your stories by Monday."

The video ended abruptly, followed by a long silence. The silence went on for nearly two minutes before Father Navarro spoke.

"The girl is the cousin of the boy who found you in the desert, Ignacio Jarabo, and her mother is Beatriz Ortiz. Ortiz is a journalist in

Culiacán reporting on police corruption. Her daughter was kidnapped in broad daylight the morning after her last piece came out. If nothing is done, the girl will be dead within three days, regardless of whether Ortiz publishes her latest piece or recants the previous stories. The honest and courageous journalists and reporters are key to victory in the struggle for Mexico. The cartels know this and have worked hard to suppress their voice."

There was an uncomfortable silence in the room for five minutes. It was G who finally spoke.

"Have you gone to the police?"

"No."

"Why not?"

The old man gave a deep sigh and spoke in a slightly frustrated tone.

"G, in the video there were two male voices. One belonged to the torturer in the mask and the other came from a man behind the camera. Did you hear them?"

G felt slightly insulted. "Of course."

The priest's voice softened. "The man behind the camera is Pablo Gonzales, the police chief in Culiacán."

How could the priest know this? G absorbed Father Navarro's accusation and instantly knew he was right. The voice on the camera had seemed strangely familiar. He had met Chief Gonzales before and the man had appeared to be a stand-up guy who would take care of business.

Sister Arámbula carried two glasses of ice water into the room. G downed one of the glasses in two gulps. It helped clear his mind.

G cleared his throat, "I know someone who can help—one of the top military commanders in Mexico."

Father Navarro slowly stood up. He sipped water and paced around the room. Finally, he spoke.

"You are perhaps referring to Colonel Ramón Acosta? Acosta might be the most dangerous man in Mexico. He is now the main negotiator between the drug cartels and the government. He is the man who ordered your torture and execution."

G went numb. He tried to speak but was hindered by what came close to physical shock. *Impossible. No way in hell.* Ramón was a friend. He was his first Mexican contact. Ramón spoke perfect English and they talked about everything. The man was a top member of Mexico's national anti-drug agency. He had opened up to Ramón Acosta and they had discussed their ambitions, their desires to rid Mexico of the cartels. *How could the priest even know who Acosta was, much less about their relationship?*

The priest continued, "G, Mexico's corruption runs deep, much deeper than anyone in your country can possibly imagine. But there are some of us who recognize the imminent danger to Mexico. There are some of us who fight for its very soul."

A sudden thought crossed G's mind and he regained enough composure to ask a question.

"Do you know General Jorge Huerta?"

"General Huerta is now dead. He was killed by Acosta."

It was too much for G. He rose from the table, physically sick. He left Father Navarro and walked back to his own quarters. The old man made no attempt to follow him.

G entered the bathroom, knelt in front of the toilet, and puked to exhaustion. Light-headed and dizzy, he crawled onto his bed. Closing his eye, he took deep breaths and cleared his mind. *I was right about Huerta.* No one in the DEA had listened to him. *Incredible—absolutely unbelievable—who exactly was this mysterious old priest, and how could he possibly have this information? How could it be true? Was Ramón Acosta really behind it?* He mentally assembled the pieces of his previous life and processed the events over and over. He considered all pertinent details of his time with the DEA, now taking into account the priest's revelation. He recalled all conversations, decisions made, and resulting ramifications. And then he remembered the night at the *cantina* in Guadalajara. He had asked Ramón something about General Huerta and he remembered the expression of sheer wrath on Ramón's face. It had only lasted for a few seconds but G found it bizarre, though at the time he attributed his own reaction to his overindulgence of tequila.

After ninety minutes, G opened his eye. *What Navarro revealed seemed plausible.* Rage erupted deep within him, helping to alleviate the cold shock. But with the fury came a sense of intrigue. *There was much more to the ancient priest than he let on. I've completely underestimated the old man—what else does he know?* G's thoughts went back to the video. *The sick bastards.* The girl's image burned in his mind, reminding him of his own daughter. He rolled off the bed and walked back to the room where they watched the video. The priest was still there, kneeling in prayer. G interrupted him without hesitation.

"Do you know where the girl is being held?"

The priest slowly opened his eyes.

"Yes."

CHAPTER 11

DOWNTOWN CULIACÁN, SINALOA, MEXICO

IT WAS 4:15 A.M. SILENCE blanketed the city. The sky was overcast, and east winds brought a slight chill to the dogs and cats wandering the alleyways. The silhouette of a large bronze cross belonging to a newly renovated cathedral could be seen a few blocks to the north. Two- and three-story homes, colored in shades of blues, yellows, and pinks, lined both sides of the street, interspersed with an assortment of liquor stores, restaurants, and dancing clubs. Much of the downtown area had been designed in such a fashion that two steps out the front door could get a careless person run over. Globes of orange light hung from streetlamps, illuminating a garbage truck that had been parked in the area for several hours.

Situated between a mom-and-pop taco shop and an unfinished apartment complex stood a pale-blue, two-story house. It was surrounded by a fifteen-foot wrought iron gate, controlled by an electronic security system. Four different cameras, two on each corner of the gate, the other two some twenty feet high on the rooftop, monitored the immediate area.

Giggling interrupted the early morning silence as a flock of scantily clad young women emerged from the blue house into the spacious car port. Shiny black and white boots wrapped around their lower legs and crept up just above their knees. Their dresses and skirts were short enough to provide ample scenery for interested male onlookers. It had been a good night for the girls: All were high on cocaine and wads of cash filled their expensive designer purses. An unshaven male chauffer escorted the prostitutes into a black Cadillac Escalade parked in the corner of the carport. The man was dressed in black jeans, tan alligator skin cowboy boots, and a white long sleeve dress shirt embroidered with images of Santa Muerte. Tattoos ran up to his neck. A pair of automatic Colt .45 pistols hung from holsters on both hips.

The man was agitated—there had been no heroin at the party and he was long overdue for his next shot. Anxious to get his fix, he yelled at the girls to get into the vehicle. With all the passengers finally piled into the SUV, the man got into the driver's seat and gave a thumbs-up to a narco colleague standing near the door leading from the carport to the house. The man at the door keyed in a code on the security panel; the metallic gate growled and started to open. Waiting a few seconds, the driver checked his rearview mirror for possible traffic and then hit the gas pedal fairly hard. The Escalade backed out of the carport and its rear tires rolled on to the open street before crashing into what seemed like an iron wall. The prostitutes erupted into new episodes of laughter. Cursing, the driver got out of the vehicle, slamming the car door shut.

Somehow the SUV had smashed its rear end directly into the broad side of a foul-smelling garbage truck. *I checked behind me, how the puto hell had it got here?* The SUV's front end never cleared the opening to the car port. The gate started to close and hit the right mirror of the Escalade hard. Fragments of shiny glass sprayed onto the driveway and sidewalk. Livid, the driver drew a gold-plated Colt .45 from his right hip. "*¡Pinche idiota!*" "I'm going to kill that *puto* bastard!"

They were the last words the man would ever speak. A nine-inch bowie knife flashed against the truck's headlights and jet streams of bright red blood misted its windows. The man's lifeless body hit the sidewalk and his golden gun made just enough of a clink to cause G to look down at it. For a microsecond he stared at the Colt .45 and then noticed an identical pistol, this one plated in silver, secure in the holster of the dead man's left hip. He spent three precious seconds replacing the archaic guns the priest had given him with the dead man's more modern pistols. *Javier was indeed correct,* G realized as he collected the weapons. *This is a narco safe house all right.*

The buxom passenger in the middle front seat was pulling out a crack-laced marijuana joint from her purse when she noticed the bizarre red artwork on the left window. She laughed loudly at the strange coloring until she rolled down the window and saw her driver sprawled across the sidewalk in a pool of his own blood. Laughter quickly morphed into screams. The intoxicated man controlling the gate at the house's entrance had the front door open and was about to go inside when the screams jolted him out of his stupor. Both his hands were going for the AK-47 when a bullet from the gold-plated Colt .45 drilled a hole in his mustache and exploded into his brain.

G blasted the security cameras to pieces, sprinted across the carport, picked up the AK-47 in midstride, and swung the shoulder strap over his head. He burst through the front door in a low crouch, both arms extended with hands gripping the golden pistol. Three shirtless men, skinny chests covered in tattoos, were waiting inside the kitchen. They were high on crack and their hands clung to AR-15s. Three bullets drove into each of their hearts before they could find the triggers. G immediately surveyed the household, looking for stairs leading upwards.

Speed and surprise were the only possibilities of success and those assets were fading quickly. He knew he had to take out everyone before he could even begin to look for the girl. Swiftly but cautiously, he exited the kitchen and entered the hallway of the living room area. *Stairs!* Bounding upwards, he pocketed the pistol and leveled the AK-47. He fired fifteen rounds as the stairway walls gave way to the visibility of the second story. Four men went down immediately. Upon reaching the top, G put a single bullet in the back of a naked man's head as the narco sprinted across the hallway.

G continued to move quickly. *One, two, three bedrooms and one bathroom.* He kicked in the door of the first bedroom, AK-47 ready to fire. The room was a pigsty but otherwise empty—likewise with the other two bedrooms. He kicked in the bathroom door and, in response, a bullet whizzed past his left ear. It infuriated him. He sent ten rounds into the gut of the unseen foe hiding behind the shower curtain. He then walked back to the staircase and scanned the surrounding area one more time. Relatively confident he was in the clear, G hustled back down the stairs, breathing heavy; a stark reminder that his days as a world-class wrestler were long past. And when G reached the ground floor, the giant narco slowly moved on the upstairs hallway.

Edgar Borja-Díaz squinted as blood streamed from his eyes, hiding the nine teardrops tattooed on his upper cheeks. Two rounds had hit him in the ribcage and another had ripped out the flesh on top of his head, grazing his skull. But Borja-Díaz had managed to put on a bullet-proof vest when he heard the gunfire. He had been knocked down, but not out.

It took him five minutes to breathe properly. But now, completely blown out on cocaine, he felt no pain from his bruised ribs or the scalp wound. Borja-Díaz was an ugly brute of a man. Large, pockmarked nose. Sunken, dark eyes of a killer. He was by far the biggest and strongest thug in the cartel, perhaps even the strongest man in Sinaloa. Just three days ago he had bench-pressed 500 pounds. And he was ruthless. He raped, murdered, and tortured at will and he was rapidly moving up the cartel ranks.

Now, listening intently to the fading sounds of staircase footsteps, Borja-Díaz slowly tried to sit up and discovered, to his relief, that he could do so. He wiped away the blood blinding his eyes and then inspected the smooth skin on his scalp. He had gone completely bald a few months ago due to years of steroid abuse. As he realized his head wound was superficial, he smiled morbidly and his eyes glowed with deranged fury.

Back at floor level, G knew that time was of the essence. There was a basement and he had to find it. He entered the kitchen and inspected the cabinets, dishwasher, stove, and surrounding walls. *Nothing*. He proceeded to the dining and living rooms and scanned the walls. He rummaged through destroyed sofas, chairs, and television sets—everything seemed normal. He thoroughly searched the master bedroom, bathroom, and guest room with no results.

Maybe the priest was wrong, he speculated. *Maybe this was the wrong stash house.* G thought again of the video and the girl, felt a short stab of pain and swore loudly. *Think. Who the hell knows if these guys have buddies on their way?* He cleared his mind and went back to the kitchen. And then he noticed the skid marks on the floor around the corner edges of the refrigerator. He smiled softly. *Someone had gotten lazy*. He put down the rifle, gripped the fridge, and pulled it out three feet. *Bingo*.

A trap door with a steel handle, clamped down by a large padlock, was built into the floor. G picked up the AK-47 and quickly demolished the lock. He ripped open the trap door and descended a narrow staircase leading to a dark cellar. Feeling around for a light switch, he eventually found a slight cord which he gently pulled. Light rushed into the basement revealing bricks of cocaine and cash stashed along the walls. And directly in front of him was the girl. She was bloodied, bruised, gagged, and bound to a heavy wooden bench. But she was alive. Flashbacks of his own torture flooded G's mind; he felt his adrenaline levels sink from fear.

He whipped his head back to pull himself together and ran over to the girl, unsheathing a knife strapped to his calf. Terrified, the young girl slammed her body backwards, trying to avoid his touch. G looked into her frightened, round eyes and reminded himself that his appearance probably scared her more than any of the narcos. He dropped to one knee and, in Spanish, spoke as gently as he could.

"Está bien, Claudia. I'm here to take you back to your *madre."* He removed the rope binding her mouth and cut the cords binding her to the bench. "Come now, *rápido!"*

Claudia hesitated. The man looked like the devil himself. *Go with him, it's okay.* The thought abruptly popped into her mind. Instinctively, with childlike trust and tremendous effort, she rose to follow the strange man. G clasped the girl's hand and led her across the cellar and onto the stairs. But she was having a tough go of it with her beaten legs. Midway through the climb, he put the AK-47 over his shoulder and reached down to pick up Claudia. He took ten more steps upward and popped his head back into the kitchen. He was starting to believe they would make it out alive when he felt the powerful arm wrap around his neck. He dropped Claudia as Borja-Díaz hauled him upwards onto the kitchen floor.

Borja-Díaz's wild-eyed face was purple with frenzy as he clamped down, determined to take out the intruder with his bare hands. G had been in similar situations in some of his jiu jitsu, but never against a man so strong, and never fighting for his life. And G was in serious trouble. He had managed to slip his left hand between the man's forearm and his own trapezoidal muscle but he was otherwise trapped. He slammed his head backwards and viciously kicked his legs out. Borja-Díaz held on like a steel lock. Five seconds passed, and then ten. G, already fairly worn out, was quickly reaching the limit of his own physical threshold. The only thing saving him was his left hand that provided half an inch of cushion from complete strangulation.

G continued to thrash his body. The hold around his neck remained tight. Fifteen seconds passed, then twenty. Borja-Díaz himself was surprised at G's resolve and resourcefulness. The narco thug had similarly killed other men instantaneously. G's resistance enraged him further and Borja-Díaz cursed and put renewed strength into his choke hold. In a final act of desperation, G made his whole body go limp. *Relax,* he told himself. *Focus. Think*. He reached down with his right hand and stretched his fingers towards his calf muscle. Thirty seconds passed and then forty-five. Feeling light-headed, he started to lose consciousness.

Claudia was crying hysterically. She had been so close to being rescued. She knew the gigantic man killing her rescuer—he was one of her torturers. She had scrambled up the stairs and now, from her spot on the floor. she looked up at the face of G. His expression was emotionless and his skin was sallow. Sobbing harder, her eyes flickered to Borja-Díaz and she imagined what he would do to her once he killed this man. In horror she saw G's single eye start to close. She screamed. And then, unexpectedly, she saw G's fingers grasping at something near his right boot.

What was he looking for? She quickly moved closer to G's right foot and discovered a knife strapped around his lower leg, the same knife that had freed her just a short time ago. With the nimble fingers of a child, she unsheathed the primitive weapon and put the handle in G's fingers.

Father Navarro will be disappointed, G concluded. He sensed he only had a few seconds left. He could feel his left hand slipping out of his enemy's grasp and he knew it would then be over. *So, this is how it will end? After everything I've been through and the unfinished business I have in this life. God is mocking me one final time.* And then he felt it. *Or am I imagining?* Finding strength from deep within his being, he forced his eye open and exerted enough mental focus to visualize a metallic blade protruding from his fingers. He made the most of it. With a superhuman effort, built from years of pushing his physical limits over the edge, he willed his right arm to swing upwards. It was a vicious stroke. Borja-Díaz toppled over backwards with an expression of victory across his face and a nine-inch bowie knife sunk into his left eye socket.

It took G two full minutes to gather himself off the floor. Breathing raggedly, he picked up the AK-47 and checked the status of his pistols. Then he gently wrapped his left arm around Claudia's waist. She had stopped crying and was looking up at G in amazement. Narrowing his eye once again, he scooped the girl up onto his left hip and moved the rifle into battle position. "Let's get out of here."

Concerned what he might find outside, G held the AK-47 steady to this shoulder. There was no visible threat. The prostitutes were huddled up in the Escalade and still screaming. Their noise subsided when they saw G with the girl. A few people had come out to the street to see what was going on. Most of the residents, however, had learned to stay indoors during such events. And such events were becoming more and more common in the city of Culiacán.

G ran to the garbage truck with Claudia, got in, and drove forward thirty feet before slamming on the brakes. *Wait a minute.* Grabbing the girl, he got out and ran back to the Escalade, waving the AK-47. He opened the driver door of the SUV and snarled at the prostitutes. "Out!" Screaming in fear at the sight of the bloody stranger, they wasted no time in obeying. G loaded Claudia into the SUV and started the engine.

"Hey, how are we going to get home?" shouted one of the braver prostitutes.

G tossed her the keys to the garbage truck.

Thirty minutes later, Claudia was huddled up in a mink fur coat she had found in the Escalade, left by one of the call girls. She clung to G from the passenger seat with wary, wide eyes focused directly on the road. A few minutes ago, she had found some tacos in the vehicle and quickly devoured them. She was still in physical pain but a bright hope was now spreading through her body, providing her with a happiness she had not felt since her kidnapping. They drove in silence for hours until G finally asked her a question, something that had been bothering him. "Claudia, how did the knife get in my hand?"

Her eyes still focused on the road, Claudia hugged G just a little bit tighter. "I put it there."

That's what I thought.

"When I saw the bad man trying to kill you, I said a prayer so God would help. I then saw you reaching for the knife and I knew just what to do."

A strange emotion overcame G, a feeling that was foreign yet vaguely familiar. He did not know what it was. They rode on in tranquil silence.

Beatriz Ortiz had been awake for the last ninety hours, a nervous wreck. She had paced every square foot of the monastery. In the cathedral, she was having bouts of hysteria between her prayer sessions. Her brother Alfonso was also at the monastery, as was his wife Aracely and their children Fernando, Gabriel, Ignacio, and Adela. Crying and praying for their niece and cousin, as well as providing comfort to Beatriz, each member of the Jarabo family tried to endure the difficult circumstances the best they could.

At 8:30 a.m., Beatriz was outside in the courtyard with Father Navarro when a speeding black Cadillac Escalade appeared on the incoming dirt road. Wailing, she grabbed the priest's arms and slammed her head into his chest, fresh tears filling her violet-red eyes. She ran from the courtyard to the front of the monastery, followed by the aged priest. The Escalade came to a screeching halt and Father Navarro breathed a titanic sigh of relief as Claudia, still bundled up in the fur coat, got out of the passenger side of the vehicle and raced into the arms of her overjoyed mother. G, feeling very uncomfortable, left his newly acquired arsenal in the truck and slowly, with a deal of hesitation, walked over to Father Navarro and the reunited mother and daughter. Claudia fought out of her mother's embrace and clung to G's leg with adoration.

"*¡Me rescate, Mami!* This man saved me from the bad guys!"

Now crying with joy, Beatriz joined her daughter and embraced G like a favorite brother. He took a few steps backward when she plastered his scarred cheeks with heartfelt kisses.

"*Gracias a Dios por conocerte*, G. Thank God for you."

Chapter 12

Culiacán, Sinaloa, Mexico

General Ramón Acosta was in bed with one of his newer girlfriends when his secure line rang. He stared at the pair of 50-carat Burmese star rubies inside the eye sockets of Don Pedro's skull. His eyes flickered towards the newer skull, the one adorned with two 50-carat Sri Lankan blue sapphires, the one belonging to General Huerta. With effort, he directed his eyes to the phone. The girl clinging to him, he picked up the phone and heard the distressed voice of Chief González. He softly pushed the girl away. "Leave me alone now, Anna. I have important business to discuss."

Anna laughed and stroked his chiseled chest muscles. Ramón's mood darkened upon learning the bad news: massacre at the safe house; Ortiz girl gone; no clue who was responsible; Ortiz woman disappeared, her latest piece, the most harmful, would go into print—nothing could prevent it from happening.

He ended the phone call abruptly. *Joder. And now I have to go into damage control.* Several of his men would have to die, including Chief González; this would set him back considerably. But it had to be done, and the sooner the better. He made a new call on the secure line and gave the recently promoted Colonel Vásquez precise instructions for his new assignment.

After the strange disappearance of Jorge Huerta, Ramón Acosta had been promoted to the office of general and took command of the third region in Mexico's ninth military zone. And now he had to clean up Huerta's mess. Huerta had never been able to fully comprehend the new landscape of the Mexican drug trade since the fracturing of Félix Gallardo's empire. The new, autonomous cartels found it much easier to bypass Huerta's heavy hand without the shackles of the monolithic hierarchy and they took full advantage of it. Commissions were not paid, and cartel leaders had started to infiltrate various government agencies without Huerta's knowledge. Deals went down with the Colombians behind his back.

General Acosta cracked down on the insubordination, torturing and murdering without restraint. Rumors of his exploits at the warehouse with Huerta had spread like wildfire in the Mexican underworld. Both his profits and prestige had risen accordingly. But it was not enough. He wanted more. And despite his ruthlessness, *el narco* was mushrooming out of control. The future seemed bleak. The AFO was going rogue, growing in power daily. El Chapo was in prison. The Gulf Cartel was in chaos after the arrest of Juan García Abrego. The Juárez Cartel, under the leadership of Amado Carrillo Fuentes and running the most valuable *plaza* in Mexico, was making a fortune and going independent. Carrillo Fuentes had recently flat-out refused Ramón's command to meet with him.

Anna smiled seductively as Ramón put down the phone, her fingers moved down towards Ramón's highly defined abdominal muscles. He backhanded her across the jaw, knocking her out instantly. Although Anna was beautiful, she was not Mónica. And he had grown to despise her for that. He had grown to despise most all people. Since the death of his family, his hatred and anger had exploded.

General Acosta got dressed and made travel arrangements with his bodyguards—he never traveled alone anymore. He would go to the compound and visit Tlaloc in person.

Two hours later, General Acosta's black armored Humvee was traveling through the streets of Badiraguato, a small city of 35,000 inhabitants widely considered to be the birthplace of Mexican drug-trafficking. Over 90 percent of its residents were thought to be involved in *el narco*, in one form or another. Ramón had personally recruited many of his men from these parts. He had key allies in all areas of the regional government. The Humvee passed by a government building and General Acosta instructed the driver to stop so he could have lunch with the city's mayor, Raúl Carrasco Guerrero. Ramón gave Mayor Carrasco an expensive bottle of Scotch and the two chatted amicably for an hour before Ramón's phone buzzed.

"Excuse me for just a minute Raúl—I have to take this call."

Mayor Carrasco, now fairly inebriated, smiled jovially as he nodded his head and poured himself another glass of Scotch. "By all means, Ramón. Please, take your time."

Ramón stepped outside the building and put the phone to his ear. It was Vásquez. "Talk to me."

Vásquez's voice was sober and cold. "It's done."

The man's a professional, Ramón reflected. "Good work, Héctor. Take the chopper and meet me at the compound."

General Acosta hung up the phone and went back inside to terminate his conversation with Mayor Carrasco. One hour later, he was gazing upon the military compound which would soon become his masterpiece. And make him one of the wealthiest men on the planet.

During the revolution, up in the lush mountains of the *Sierra Madre Occidental*, Pancho Villa established a military fortress. It had been abandoned, however, for several decades until General Huerta renovated it in the late 1980s. The fortress was built on one of the largest mountains in the area. The mountain itself was streaked with large deposits of granite which served as a natural barrier against military assaults and provided several locations for base development.

Currently, Tlaloc and Ramón were transforming the compound into a narco utopia which Tlaloc called Tamoanchan, named after the mythological Mexic/Aztec origin of all civilizations. Granite outcroppings had been chiseled away and tunnels were dug directly through solid gray stone to create a winding road leading to the peak. Huge amounts of soil, rock, and vegetation had been displaced to create a large field for tactical exercises and training. Overlooking the entire base, at the highest point of the mountain, a luxurious 45,000-square-foot Spanish colonial palace rose into the sky. It now served as Tlaloc's home.

The Humvee pulled into the driveway of the palace. General Acosta got out and let his bodyguards go visit the central base several hundred yards downhill. He entered the building and walked down the vast hallway, still decorated with Huerta's paintings. The hallway led to a 4,000-square-foot room that Tlaloc had been remodeling into something of a museum. Ramón walked through the entrance and stared at a gray statue until his vision blurred. The round, bulging eyes, hollow, inverted nose, and the wide, grinning mouth with prominent teeth combined to generate a mesmerizing image that had fascinated him since youth. He contrasted the appearance of Mictlantecuhtli with the adjacent life-size painting of Santa Muerte. There was a dark magnificence in the macabre art work; both pieces seemed to radiate power. For as long as Ramón could remember, Tlaloc had revered Mictlantecuhtli and preached the importance of this god in the resurrection of Mexico. In the last few years, he had been obsessed with Santa Muerte, convinced that the wife of Mictlantecuhtli, Mictecacihuatl, was manifesting herself in this ubiquitous being.

Ramón had known Tlaloc since he was thirteen years old, several months after he left Mónica and the orphanage. He had been traveling through Mexico and survived by his wits and thievery. Darkness and hatred built up inside of him as he fought to live on the streets. Eventually, he came to Mexico City and found a home among the colorful open-air markets in the barrio of Tepito.

In Tepito he discovered Santa Muerte for the first time, at a shrine at 12 Alfarería Street in Colonia Morelos. It galvanized him—the skull, the scythe, the globe, and, most of all, the power. The worshippers used marijuana smoke instead of incense, for purification. It was everything the Catholic Church was not. He visited the shrine, day after day, and stared at the brightly clothed skeleton for hours. And it was there he met Tlaloc.

Tlaloc befriended the young Ramón. The hunchback instructed him how to worship Santa Muerte and taught him of her true nature. Intrigued by the youngster's keen intellect, Tlaloc took Ramón to Chichén Itzá, Teotihuacán, Palenque, Uxmal, Monte Albán, and other pre-Hispanic ruins. He taught the teenager of the true gods, the ones that had ruled Mexico before the parasitical Catholics. And he showed him of their power.

Tlaloc invited Ramón to live with him. Together, the cripple had promised, together they would return glory to Mexico. And to Ramón, Tlaloc himself became a deity, his savior and his master. Under his guiding hand, Tlaloc had promised, Ramón would become the most powerful figure in Mexico. Together they would restore the old order and bring justice and retribution to the people. Mexico would rise from the ashes and become the most powerful nation on earth.

Ramón broke off the train of thought as he heard the hobbling steps of the ancient cripple slowly enter the room through a large oak door. Ramón knelt down.

"Greetings ... Ramón." Tlaloc spoke in Nahuatl. His voice was harsh and raspy. The tone of it suggested he had difficulty breathing. Save General Acosta, the voice tended to unnerve anyone he communicated with.

"Master Tlaloc," General Acosta replied, in the same language. Still kneeling, the general immediately brought up the issue. "We had an issue with the Ortiz woman. Her daughter was rescued and several of our men were killed."

Tlaloc gazed into the empty eye sockets of Santa Muerte. He remained silent for several minutes before facing Ramón. "I trust ... you have ... made ... arrangements?"

"Captain González is dead as well as several of the others. Pablo will be difficult to replace. It will set us back."

The old man turned back to the painting. He spoke very slowly and very deliberately. "The current ... events ... have been ... at the ... forefront ... of all ... my thoughts." He took a deep, ragged breath. "I believe ... that now ... is the ... time ... for us ... to move ... forward." The old man sucked in more air. "We need ... to begin ... our seeding ... operation ... immediately ... on the ... borderland. ... Send ... forth ... your ... best ... men."

Ramón nodded. They had discussed this for several years. They desperately needed more men. The seeding operation would involve breaking some of the more traditional Mexican drug-trafficking rules. Large quantities of drugs would be given directly to young teenagers. They would actively recruit foot soldiers in the slums of the border cities with free cocaine and heroin. To help fund the operation they would market the drugs to Mexican citizens. But the plan would have adverse consequences. For decades, key members of the PRI actively participated in *el narco,* overall the party had encouraged its success provided the toxic narcotics were consumed by the *gringos* north of the border. Distributing the poison among Mexican citizens was another story. There would be some who would object to the new plan. They would need to be dealt with.

Both Tlaloc and Acosta reasoned the plan was necessary. It was for the greater good of the country. Chaos creates opportunities. Both men understood the massive turmoil and casualties of war destined to occur in the short term. But the mayhem would provide wealth, manpower, and opportunities to restore glory to Mexico—and to demonstrate to the people the nature of the true gods. The terror unleashed upon Mexico would serve as a religious catalyst.

Tlaloc continued, "The AFO ... is a threat ... and they ... must be ... exterminated. ... ... The Gulf ... Cartel is ... in upheaval ... and there ... may not ... be a better ... time to ... take them ... out." The old man's nostrils flared. He coughed and then sucked in more air. His face transformed into a frenzied expression and his tone turned eerily violent, "And ... above all ... we need ... ... Juárez!"

The North American Free Trade Agreement (NAFTA), effective in 1994, was a drug cartel's dream, a deal made in narco heaven. Millions of trucks now flowed into the United States from Mexico annually. Approximately one billion dollars' worth of cargo was shipped across the border daily. The United States had been entirely unprepared for the chain of events; customs agents were overwhelmed. Only a tiny fraction of the trucks crossing the border were inspected for illegal substances. The number of methods for transporting drugs into the United States multiplied exponentially. No other organization profited as much as the Juárez Cartel.

"Ciudad Juárez"—"Juárez City" or just "Juárez," historically known as "Paso Del Norte"—"Gateway to the North," lies directly across the border from El Paso, Texas. It has been a smuggler's paradise for over a century. The entire city was built to transport goods and services across the border. Four international ports of entry connect the two cities. As NAFTA came into effect, the high demand for cheap Mexican labor caused foreign companies to construct more than 300 *maquiladoras* in Juárez. Thousands of these *maquiladora* managers commute across the border daily, along with huge quantities of their products. The city's infrastructure and the high volume of border traffic made it possible for Amado Carrillo Fuentes to rake in billions. Juárez was considered the crown jewel of Mexico by all the cartels.

Yes, Master Tlaloc is right, thought Ramón, *we've talked about this many times but we need a new angle.*

Tlaloc went on as if reading Ramón's mind. "We need ... to form ... an ... alliance. ... ... You will ... go to ... El Chapo ... and offer ... him your ... enforcement ... services ... for a ... percentage of ... his profits ... and his ... release from ... prison." He gulped more air. "You will ... propose ... to help ... him eliminate ... the AFO. ... ... And then ... we will ... together ... go after ... Juárez."

The words struck Ramón; he immediately knew the old cripple was correct. El Chapo had both the personnel and infrastructure in place. And the kingpin must be somewhat desperate. He continued Tlaloc's line of thought. "And when El Chapo Guzmán is sufficiently weakened, we will take him out. We will be in total control."

Tlaloc turned back to face the statue of the dark Aztec deity. "The ... old ... gods ... will ... rise."

Ramón's phone buzzed. Vásquez had arrived at the compound. Ramón stood up and walked over to Tlaloc. "I will leave at once for Puente Grande. By the way, I have a gift for you. Walk with me outside to the Humvee."

The ancient cripple scuffled alongside Ramón as they walked to the vehicle. Ramón popped open the trunk and Tlaloc gazed upon Anna, still unconscious. Her limbs were bound with cords, her mouth sealed with duct tape. The old man reached out and roughly examined her body with leathery fingers. "Yes, ... yes." He inhaled sharply. "She will ... do nicely."

☩

Puente Grande was one of three maximum security prisons in Mexico, equipped with state-of-the-art TV cameras and alarm systems. Every corner of the facility was monitored. Located just northeast of Guadalajara, in the state of Jalisco, it housed 508 prisoners, one of whom was Joaquín Archivaldo Guzmán Loera (a.k.a. "El Chapo"—"Shorty"). El Chapo was transferred to Puente Grande in 1995, two years after his capture in Guatemala. Here he reunited with Héctor Luis Palma Salazar (a.k.a. "El Güero"—"Blondie" or "White Guy"), a former gunman for El Padrino, and El Chapo's original mentor. Eventually, however, El Güero fell hard from El Padrino's grace; the bad blood helped fuel the brutal feud between the Sinaloa Cartel and the AFO.

Despite being in a high-tech, maximum security prison, life for El Chapo was far from strenuous. He still ran the operations of the Sinaloa Cartel. He possessed both mobile phones and laptop computers. Drugs continued to gush through the border tunnels he designed and became famous for. Cash poured into prison, sent by his loyal colleagues including El Mayo, Juan José Esparragoza Moreno (a.k.a. "El Azul"), and the Beltran Leyva brothers. The smooth-talking El Chapo, flush with cash, had bribed a significant number of guards and prison workers. He had relationships with a bevy of women, both in and outside of the prison—female and male inmates were unseparated in Mexican penitentiaries. Through his inside connections, El Chapo could summon his wives and girlfriends at will. He even had a steady supply of Viagra coming into his jail cell. El Chapo had also found a steady lover in a beautiful inmate named Zulema Yulia Hernández, a former police officer from Sinaloa seduced by the allure of *el narco.*

El Chapo and El Güero were playing basketball in the prison yard when Corrections Officer Fontes walked over and stopped the game. "*Señor* Guzmán, you have visitors."

El Chapo noticed the guard's trepidation; his visitors must be important for Officer Fontes to have risked interrupting the game. El

Chapo nodded and signaled for another inmate to take his place. He took a towel from Fontes, wiped beads of sweat from his forehead, and followed the prison guard into the central control location of the outside facilities. They passed several secure gates and eventually walked down a long corridor leading to the warden's office.

Warden Contreras was conversing with General Ramón Acosta. Standing next to Ramón was a giant of a man who El Chapo had never seen before. Five other men, dressed in military attire and armed with HK21 machine guns, were standing in the back of the room. Ramón smiled, walked over to El Chapo, and embraced him like a brother. "Joaquín, it's good to see you my friend. It's been a long time."

Ramón glanced at Warden Contreras, "Warden, leave us. Please show my men your facility and extend them every courtesy."

Warden Contreras was perspiring heavily, his fingers were trembling. "Of course, General, I would be delighted." The warden looked at Colonel Vásquez, then at the armed men behind him. "Please, if you will gentlemen, follow me."

The men followed Warden Contreras, leaving General Acosta alone with El Chapo. Ramón walked over to the warden's desk upon which he had previously laid out an assortment of goodies. He retrieved a bottle of Bacardi white rum, a six pack of Coca-Cola, and a handful of limes. He made a few glasses of Cuba Libre, El Chapo's favorite beverage, and handed him one. Ramón prepared a simple glass of ice water for himself and then sat down in one of the warden's plush chairs, inviting El Chapo to do likewise. He took a sip of water. "So, I hope they are treating you well here, Joaquín?"

El Chapo shrugged and took a drink of the Cuba Libre. "It could be a lot *puto* worse. We have women, alcohol, drugs—life goes on and business continues."

Ramón smiled, "Yes, I hear things are going well and the Federation is thriving—perhaps not quite like the AFO or the Juárez Cartel, but under the circumstances your success is impressive. Especially since certain politicians are working furiously to extradite you to the U.S."

General Acosta's words struck a nerve in El Chapo but his demeanor remained stoic. *The general's assessment of recent political developments is correct—hijo de puta.* Extradition to the Unites States was his worst nightmare. Life in Puente Grande was tolerable, it could even be entertaining, but life in a U.S. prison would be a *puto* nightmare. "*¿Qué chingados quieres?* What the fuck do you want, Ramón?"

Ramón's eyes narrowed. "We are more alike than you suspect, Joaquín. Our situations could have easily been reversed. I've followed your progress. You're one hell of ballsy bastard and I believe we can work together."

General Acosta looked the drug lord straight in the eye. "The AFO will take us down. Left unchecked, they will incur the wrath of both the U.S. and certain government officials here. I propose we exterminate them."

El Chapo's eyes lit up just enough for Ramón to perceive his interest.

"I've already got a plan in place, Joaquín. I just need your support."

Ramón edged closer to the kingpin.

"Trust me on this, Joaquín. Together we can do big things—great things. And I will prove it to you with the demise of the AFO. Help us kill the bastards and I will get you out of here, before the U.S. can get their hands on you. And then we move on to Juárez."

For the first time since he left the basketball game, El Chapo's lips loosened, forming the slightest trace of a smile. It was at that instant that Ramón knew he had him.

"Ah, Joaquín, I almost forgot. I have something for you." General Acosta stood up, walked over to the main door, and opened it. A dozen prostitutes flocked into the room. Ramón walked back to El Chapo, extending his hand.

"So Joaquín, do we have a deal?"

El Chapo looked longingly at the girls and singled out a sultry red head dressed in a provocative violet dress. He started to laugh and clasped Ramón's hand tightly. "Okay, Ramón, *hijo de puta*. I'm in."

Chapter 13

Catholic Monastery—Durango, Mexico

Nine hours after delivering Claudia Ortiz to her mother, G sat down face-to-face with Father Navarro in the old man's headquarters. It was the first time G had been in the room. Bookshelves decorated all interior walls save for a large portrait of Christ and his twelve disciples at the Last Supper. G stared at the books while the priest pulled the cork from a bottle of red wine.

"Have you read all of these books?"

The priest chuckled and took the first sip of wine. "G, in order for a shepherd to successfully tend to his flock, he must fully understand its history and its nature. To properly serve God, my country, and my fellow neighbor I must understand the fundamental ethos of mankind, their flaws, and their potential. History teaches us valuable lessons about the human soul—impossible to obtain elsewhere, save one's own personal experience."

G ignored most of Father Navarro's response as he took his own drink of the wine. His expression sobered. "Tell me everything you know about Ramón Acosta."

The priest drank steadily from his wine goblet. His demeanor did not change and he remained silent for several moments. "And what exactly would you do if I told you? Leave this very instant and go kill him?"

G did not answer the question. It was exactly what he would do. His single eye flickered to his pistols. He was obsessed.

Father Navarro went on, "You would not get very far in your venture. Ramón has spies and assassins everywhere. He travels with an armed escort at all times and takes the utmost precautions in all of his doings."

G grimaced in annoyance. He remained silent and took another swig of wine. It was not the response he was looking for. The priest discerned G's displeasure.

"Who was Maximilian Ferdinand?"

The hell? "What does that have to do with anything?"

"Just answer the question."

G kept silent. He had no idea.

The old man went on, "What was unique to the world about the Constitution of 1917?"

Again, G had no response.

"What is the origin of the Day of the Dead?"

G had no clue.

"Who wrote *The Art of War*?"

G finally knew the answer. "Sun Tzu."

The priest was unimpressed. "Then you might know one of the basic principles of warfare is this: To defeat your enemies, you must understand them."

G said nothing. Father Navarro gave a faint sigh of exasperation.

"You are completely ignorant of Mexican history, politics, culture, and religion. Your Spanish sounds like the braying of a constipated donkey. As you should be aware, Ramón Acosta is one of the most intelligent persons to have ever been born in Mexico. He has more connections than our current president. How can you possibly hope to defeat such a man?"

G gulped down his wine and contemplated the priest's words. *The son of a bitch had a point*. Father Navarro perceived G's internal reasoning; his own countenance brightened. "But, if you are willing, patient, and reasonable, we can educate you."

G sank into his chair, reflecting on everything this crazy old priest was telling him. He looked deep within Father Navarro's eyes. He felt a stirring in his soul, a sense of serenity that had been so foreign to him in the dark months since his capture. He decided instantly. He would stay here at the monastery. He would follow the old man's advice and see what happened.

"When do we start?"

The old man smiled warmly. "I am ready if you are."

G started interlacing his physical workouts with classes from Father Navarro and the nuns—to improve his broken Spanish. He spent hours trying to roll his 'R's with no success. "*Ferrocarril, Ferrocarril, Ferrocarril.*" He could not make his tongue generate the correct motor sounds. A native Mexican would peg him for a *gringo* from his first two or three words. But his vocabulary was expanding and he was picking up some of the nuances of the Spanish language and semantics. He struggled with verb conjugation and the distinction between preterit and imperfect usage. But the priest drilled him relentlessly and he progressed daily. Learning the slang proved difficult as well. Father Navarro enlisted his tattooed informant in G's education.

Besides gathering narco intelligence, Javier Rayón Valencia was the cook at the monastery. Rayón's knowledge of Mexican slang and gutter talk was extensive, as was his familiarity with both the narco dialect and culture. He was, by far, the most jovial and boisterous individual at the monastery. He knew thousands of jokes, most of them dirty, and he thoroughly enjoyed embarrassing the puritanical nuns, especially Sister López.

"Hermanas," he called out one day to a group of nuns at lunch time. "Who was the world's first carpenter?"

A few nuns glared at him; most looked on with feigned dread and attentive ears. "Eve," Javier said in English, "because she made Adam's banana stand!"

G enjoyed his company. Javier was always friendly; everyone seemed to like him, especially the dwarf Felipe. He spent hours educating his *gringo* student. One day, G asked Father Navarro how he met Javier.

"I met Javier Rayón several years ago in the Aquiles Serdán prison in Chihuahua," replied the priest. "He was one of a group of inmates who converted to Jesus Christ. Javier has proved himself a worthy ally. I trust him implicitly. So must you."

G expected as much but looked at the old man inquisitively.

"The narcos who sincerely repent and desire to come unto Christ will be instrumental in the fight for Mexico's soul. We must accept their return to the fold. But know this: One can commit sins that will wipe out one's conscience. For those, there is no turning back and justice must be served. A peaceful society can only exist with justice, and the balance between justice and mercy is a delicate one. Those who govern must themselves possess a certain moral rectitude to recognize and exercise this principle."

As the months went by and G advanced his linguistic skills, the priest began to alter the Spanish classes into history and cultural lessons. "If one is truly to understand the Mexican culture, as it exists today, they must understand its past." The old man paused for a moment and then went on. "As with other civilizations of the ancient world, the introduction of agriculture completely transformed Mexican societies. Populations grew exponentially; communities became dependent on successful crop harvests. Mexico's unique geography generates weather patterns much more unpredictable than other parts of the world. To help ensure a steady food source, the ancients worked relentlessly to understand the nature of weather, climate, and time. They used logic and science to develop the most sophisticated and mathematically precise calendars the world had ever known.

"Unfortunately, other techniques were introduced, not so rational, to understand the different weather patterns. Shamans emerged, claiming they could control rainfall through magical rituals. The shamans introduced gods in the form of revered animals to venerate the sun, fire, water, and fertility. As the shamans became more powerful, the nature and demands of their gods became evil and twisted. Eventually, they introduced the greatest scourge this land has ever known: human sacrifice."

G's physical workouts intensified between the tutoring sessions. He pushed his limits to regain former levels of physical strength and conditioning. The priest provided equipment he asked for—a modern weight set, punching bag, wrestling mat, and a very large supply of ammunition. Unburdened by the antiquated farm equipment, G could perform a multitude of new exercises to more effectively work out different muscles. He spent hours shadow wrestling on the mat; he pounded the punching bag until his arms ached. And he fired thousands of rounds with his pistols and rifles.

His favorite activity, however, was long distance running. He ran along the splendidly colored bluffs on the northern outskirts of the monastery and, as his endurance strengthened, he pushed himself farther and farther into the wilderness. He ran through the flat desert, scaled the rocky cliffs of the bluffs, and ascended the pine-covered mountains beyond them. He explored a plethora of various terrains, occasionally staying for a few days in locations that interested him.

G became captivated by both the earthly splendor of the forested mountains and the rugged beauty of the desert. The outdoors had a soothing effect upon his damaged soul. During his tenure in the military he received extensive wilderness survival training, and he used the skills he learned on his retreats. G discovered, not to his surprise, that Father Navarro possessed a deep knowledge of the Mexican terrain and G picked his brain for knowledge of the vegetation, wildlife, and geography. He learned how to find watering holes and efficiently extract water from a variety of cacti. He also learned how to find food and to hunt. One day, to the astonishment of the nuns, he brought back an antelope to the monastery. Father Navarro later claimed it was one of the best meals he had ever eaten.

G also spent time with the Jarabo family. Alfonzo and his sons showed him various hunting techniques. G taught Ignacio how to shoot. He discovered Ignacio was too tense and his breathing was too fast. "Relax, Ignacio—let your muscles soften. Take one deep breath before you shoot. Suck in all the air you can. Gently squeeze the trigger—never jerk it." G gave Ignacio a few exercises to work on daily, and in a few weeks, he was shooting as well as his brothers. Ignacio's horse, Blanca, developed a special affinity with G. Ignacio let him ride the pale-white animal in the desert and mountains.

G's Spanish became better and better. His American accent was fading and, through hours of practice, he even learned how to roll his R's. The priest began to introduce him to other academic disciplines including economics, politics, math, and logic. "Mathematics is a tool that will sharpen your mind," Father Navarro told him. "Your brain and your ability to use it will become your most powerful weapon. The battle against the narcos will involve intelligence. We must find a way to lift the impoverished out of their misery before the narcos can get to them."

Father Navarro would always find ways to teach more history. "During the ancient Mesoamerican Golden Age, mathematicians developed the notion of zero, a feat not accomplished by their Indo-European counterparts. Entire cities were constructed in correlation to the movements of our solar system. Scientists are just now beginning to understand the depths of their astronomical knowledge. Their intellectual achievements led to the creation of incredible architectural developments. The ancient pyramids at Cholula and Teotihuacán were the largest structures in the Western Hemisphere until a greater building was erected at Cape Kennedy to support the landings on the moon. At Chichén Itzá in the Yucatan, the Mayas constructed a temple with an extraordinary illumination technology to help the people know when to sow their crops."

The priest's eyes narrowed slightly. He rubbed his ancient thumb against the silver stubble on his chin and went on. "Despite their scientific knowledge, the Indians were never able to collectively root out their twisted magical thinking. During times of famine, large-scale human sacrifice was performed to appease their gods. But thankfully, as with all evil actions perpetrated on mankind, we do know there was opposition to it. Long ago, a man named Ce Acatl Topiltzin studied at the ancient center of Xochicalco, now located in the state of Morelos. Topiltzin became a high priest of Quetzalcoatl, the god of learning and the priesthood—the most important god in ancient Mexico. He fought to end human sacrifice and recommended substitutions of snakes or butterflies. Topiltzin's heroic fight against evil made him a hero for centuries to come."

G listened half-heartedly to the old man's lecture. The priest continued. "The battle of good versus evil has been raging since mankind first walked on this planet. Heroes such as Topiltzin occasionally come along during humanity's darkest hours. To a believer such as myself, it would seem as if these individuals were called upon by a higher power."

G's learning and physical development progressed, but bitterness and despair continued to dog his soul. He fought it by seeking solace in the wilderness and working out his body to the point of exhaustion. But it was really his longing for revenge that kept him going. He had become completely obsessed with killing Ramón Acosta, Vásquez, and every single one of his accomplices. It was his sole purpose in life—the only outlet, he believed, for self-respect and serenity. Most of the time he disbelieved in God. And during his more susceptible moments, where he suspected that some type of God might actually exist, he hated him.

But most of all, he hated himself. He hated himself for being captured and he hated himself for allowing his family to be destroyed. He hated himself for becoming the miserable creature who he now was. He forced himself to believe that the day of his redemption would come, that he would be ready for it. But other forces interfered with his singular purpose of existence. He still fantasized about Sister López. He could not suppress memories of his past life. Images of his family continued to oppress him. Sometimes he would let himself vividly recall every feature of both his wife and daughter. His daughter's sweet laughter would ring through his ears; his wife's intoxicating scent would rush through his being like an avalanche. The memories and imagined sensations were torture and he hated himself for his weakness.

G's mood grew so foul that Father Navarro perceived his inner turmoil. One morning after a Mexican culture class, the priest made an unexpected announcement. "We are going on a field trip and we will be gone for a few days. Go pack what you need and get in the truck. I'll drive." G casually shrugged and obeyed.

The Cadillac G brought back from Culiacán now donned a xenon-blue metallic coat and, much to G's amusement, had been rigged up with a ten-ton winch and set of monstrous tires. The priest had taken a special liking to the vehicle and gave his old jeep to a family in his congregation. G got in the passenger's seat and was mildly surprised at how fast the old man drove. They traveled southeast for hours through many states which G was unfamiliar with—Zacatecas, Aguascalientes, Guanajuato, Querétaro, and Hidalgo. The priest gave an intricate history of each state from pre-Hispanic times leading up to the Spanish conquest.

"When the Spanish arrived, the Aztecs were ripe for destruction. They had made bitter enemies among their neighbors. The extent of human sacrifice was at an all-time high; surrounding tribes were constantly raided to obtain fresh captives. Warfare tactics and training had become perverted; focus was placed on taking live prisoners. Aztec warriors were unprepared for the battle-hardened *conquistadores* and their brutal strategies. When the Spaniards did come, the Aztecs were annihilated, along with every other indigenous people in this land.

"However, it is important to not vilify all of the Spanish who came to Mexico and we must classify their actions in accordance with contemporary events and their own understanding of the world. Despite the injustices of the political policies, there were decent and noble Spaniards. Juan de Zumárraga was the first archbishop of Mexico City. He was known as the "Protector of the Indians" and fought relentlessly for their rights as well as their safety. He established schools and hospitals for the natives and sought to provide them with economic opportunities. Vasco de Quiroga was the first bishop of the state of Michoacán and founded Christian communities for the Indians based upon the writings of Sir Thomas More. Under his organization, the Indians were taught various crafts and industrial skills as well as the principles of self-government. De Quiroga was also instrumental in removing corrupt and vicious political leaders. He was beloved by the members of his flock and to this day he is considered a great saint in the area.

"Often, in the course of human events, thousands of kind and benevolent acts are overshadowed by the few vile and heinous ones. The nature of mankind is complex and inherently imperfect. Some reject Christianity because of the failings of the Spaniards and their ethical imperfections. While perhaps understandable on some level, I see this as tragic. My own approach is to accept the positive aspects of the Spanish while trying to understand the ramifications of their shortcomings. Such a strategy can help us take the necessary steps to remedy the wounds inflicted upon this nation."

G stared out the window into the countryside and remained silent for hours as the old man went on and on. Finally, after six hours on the road, G asked where they were going.

"Ah, one of my favorite places in Mexico: Pico de Orizaba, also known as Citlaltépetl from the ancient Nahuatl tongue. Citlaltépetl literally translates to Star Mountain, the name I have used since childhood. Star Mountain is actually a dormant volcano that stands almost 20,000 feet above sea level. It is the highest peak in Mexico and the third-highest peak in North America. Unfortunately, we are not properly equipped to get near the top, but we shall go high enough to accomplish our purpose."

G did not bother to ask what that was.

It was 2:00 a.m. when they reached the city of Orizaba. They pulled over into an isolated area and the priest said a quick prayer before leaning back in his car seat and dozing off. It was the first time G had seen the old man sleep. He had wondered if the priest was capable of the task. G himself slept soundly for four hours before waking to the light of dawn. Father Navarro was already awake, dressed in blue jeans, hiking boots, and a faded red flannel shirt. He was sporting sunglasses and was in the process of rearranging a few objects in his backpack. G silently groaned and then, with mental effort, got dressed and proceeded to follow the old man up an ancient hiking trail.

The trail originated from a lush valley point near the parked Cadillac. It slowly changed into a series of switchbacks on the side of a massive mountain heavily forested with coniferous trees. As their hike progressed, G was taken aback by both the beauty of the landscape and the stamina of the old man. He marveled how, despite Father Navarro's limp, the priest strode across the mountain side with strength and confidence. G figured after a mile or so he would be carrying the priest across his shoulders, but at noon the holy warrior was still going strong.

They had a light lunch of antelope jerky and then marched on for eight more hours before Father Navarro called it quits. G finally cracked a smile when he noticed the old man breathing heavily. They had made excellent progress and G could feel the dramatic change in elevation as he inhaled the thin mountain air and felt the coolness seep through his skin. It was a nice change from the brutal summer heat at the monastery. Off in the distance he could see a snow-capped glacier glistening against the red rays of the setting sun. The priest pulled out a canteen from his backpack and took a long drink of water. He then handed the canteen to G and joined him in taking in the view.

"Star Mountain: perhaps the most magnificent volcano in the world. Long ago, the Aztecs believed that the god of the night sky, Tezcatlipoca, defeated Quetzalcoatl by using divine fire from the volcano's crater. Quetzalcoatl then took the form of a man and sailed across the eastern sea, vowing to return and seek vengeance upon the Aztec nation as well as end all human sacrifice. The legend did not serve the Aztecs well when the Spaniards arrived."

Both men stared at the scenery for some time before setting up camp and starting a fire. The crisp, clear air brought back long-forgotten memories into G's mind. But they were good memories and he felt comfortable in the new environment. The priest warmed up *tortillas, frijoles,* and venison, and both men ate heartily, washing down the meal with sharp red wine.

Sitting against a pine tree, G felt good—better than he had for a long, long time. He watched the sky slowly change from midnight blue to jet black. The moon was full and its light reflected against the ice-capped volcano top to emit a fluorescent glow. Stars appeared everywhere and their radiant beams pierced through the darkness to illuminate the landscape and create a heavenly spectacle. Never had G witnessed such a marvelous exhibition. For several precious moments, he entirely forgot the injustices inflicted upon him. It was some time before the priest broke the peaceful silence.

"The accumulated advances in the field of astronomy, by both ancient and modern civilizations, are astounding. It is as if some unforeseen force binds us to the great unknown as we strive to understand where we came from, why we are here, and where we are going. Long ago, not far from this very place, lived a philosopher king named Nezahualcoyotl. Nezahualcoyotl ruled the Acolhua tribe, another Nahua people loosely related to the Aztecs. He is best remembered for his poetry and my favorite poem from his collection is translated something like this:

The obscurity of the night
Reveals the brilliancy of the stars.
No one has power
To alter these heavenly lights,
For they serve to display
The greatness of their Creator.
And as our eyes see them now,
So saw them our earliest ancestors,
And so will see them
Our latest posterity.

"Like Nezahualcoyotl, when I gaze upon such a breathtaking night as this, I cannot help be convinced of the existence of a supreme creator. G, I do not comprehend all things. I myself am both confounded and unnerved by the injustices in this world and the suffering of its inhabitants. There are unimaginable horrors and afflictions. I weep for my fellow brothers and sisters who endure such pain. Yet, despite such misery, I have come to understand and know that there is indeed a God and he loves each one of us. Our own potential is unlimited when we submit to his will."

The priest reached out to place his right hand on G's shoulder.

"G, there is one thing I know for sure: Bitterness is a cancer that will destroy a man's soul. There is no solace in the dark waters of atheism. Let go of your bitterness, G. Let it go. Only with God's help will you succeed in your endeavors. You will find no better ally. Trust me on this."

CHAPTER 14

CATHOLIC MONASTERY— DURANGO, MEXICO

THE PRIEST'S WORDS STRUCK G. He reflected on them again and again. One morning, Father Navarro invited G to visit the orphanage—the one the nuns talked about. Out of sheer curiosity he accepted the offer.

"Splendid," replied Father Navarro. "You shall accompany me there after breakfast tomorrow."

Later that day, G asked Sister Arámbula more about the orphanage. The rotund nun smiled jovially, "El Padre Navarro built many orphanages. Close where we live is the Esperanza de México orphanage. He start it forty years ago. Some of the most smart kids in the country live there and Padre Navarro hire best teachers."

The sister's face lit up with pride. "I'm a teacher at Esperanza de México. I also was student years ago, but not as smart as some. Many students from Esperanza de México now are *ingenieros* and scientists and political leaders. El Padre Navarro has many other projects too. He built many schools in Durango and Chihuahua. El Padre Navarro also built many hospitals and farms—this give work to many. He also give much food to the poor."

"How does he finance the operations?" G broke in, genuinely interested now.

Sister Arámbula explained, "El Padre Navarro come from one of most rich families in Mexico. He was very good businessman before joining ministry. He has made plan to spend all his wealth for benefit of Mexico."

G almost asked how much money the old man had left, but then decided to keep quiet.

The following day was cloudy and a bit cool, a nice change from the sizzling heat waves. G soaked in the cool air through the open window of the Cadillac. It helped sooth his muscles, still exhausted from his morning workout.

The Hope of Mexico orphanage was eight miles west of the monastery. G had run in the general vicinity, yet never in this particular area. It stood out nicely against the parched landscape: The grounds were well-kept and featured a unique assortment of blooming cacti, desert flowers, and palm trees. Several structures rose into the open air including a large red-bricked school, gymnasium, and children's dormitories. A number of crosses, freshly painted in gold, decorated each building.

Father Navarro parked the Escalade in front of the school, got out, and walked through the main door. G followed him. Most of the children were in their first class of the day. The priest led G up the main stairs to the second floor and into one of the classrooms. A nun was writing out math problems on a chalkboard. Twenty-two young children, male and female, sat in desks across the room, all dressed in matching black and white uniforms. A few children were copying the math problems; most were engaged in less noble pursuits.

As the classroom door opened, all eyes turned to Father Navarro. Twenty-two faces brightened with glee at the sight of their favorite instructor. The faces, however, quickly turned to unfeigned fear as G walked in the room. The priest handled the situation by introducing G as a friendly visitor who lost one of his eyes and was burned by fire. The children listened spellbound to Father Navarro and soon became genuinely interested in this unfortunate stranger. One of the boys raised his hand. Father Navarro nodded at him, "Yes, Jacob?"

Jacob looked directly at G, "Can you still see?"

"Yes I can," G answered. "In fact, in some situations my vision has actually improved."

The answer impressed Jacob and the other students. "Does your face hurt?" Jacob asked.

"No."

"How did it happen?" Jacob pressed.

"I let my guard down."

The answer seemed to satisfy the children.

"Can I feel your face?" Jacob asked again.

The teacher quickly scolded Jacob but G waved her off. He shrugged and then knelt down on one knee. "Why not?"

Jacob smiled and ran to the front of the classroom. He gently ran his fingers down G's scars. "*¡Chido!* Wow, your face is cool! Can I wear your eye patch?"

G thought for a moment and then pulled out a spare eye patch from his pocket. "You can have this one."

"*¡Chido!* Awesome!" replied Jacob. He put it on as fast as he could.

One by one, the other students came forward to feel the scars of the strange man. One of the girls remarked how pretty his blue eye was and how she wished she could have eyes of that color also.

The two men stayed for about twenty minutes before the priest announced, to the disappointment of the class, that it was time to return to their studies. As they made their way out the door, Jacob, still wearing his eye patch, shouted after G, "Will I see you again?"

Father Navarro answered with his charismatic smile, "Perhaps."

The priest was pleased with how G handled himself; he seemed to have a natural bond with the children. The two men visited several more classes and then went outside to inspect the playgrounds and soccer fields. The priest spoke each step of the way. "Some of the children had been abandoned and were found roaming the streets of various cities throughout the country. Quite a few are from Guatemala and other countries in Central America whose families died on their journey north. The children's minds are vibrant and full of life, as are their bodies."

Father Navarro led G to the outer edge of one of the three soccer fields. The fields were green and the grass had recently been cut. Father Navarro picked up an abandoned soccer ball. "Although we have leagues of soccer and softball, some of the more energetic youth could use other physical outlets. G, I want you to become a wrestling coach here and introduce the children to the sport."

The request came as a complete surprise. G kept silent for several minutes. "I'll think about it."

"Fair enough," replied the priest.

Later that afternoon, as G was wrapping up his afternoon workout, Sister Arámbula brought him a shake of strawberries, blueberries, and blackberries. "How was visit?" she asked.

"It went okay," replied G. He mopped up sweat from his forehead and graciously gulped down the beverage. "There were a lot more kids than I expected and they had a lot of questions."

Sister Arámbula smiled, "El Padre Navarro loves children. Working at orphanage has help him with pain he felt since deaths of his wife and family."

G was stunned. "Father Navarro was married? He had children?"

Sister Arámbula looked at G in surprise, "You not know?" She started shaking her head. *"Si,"* she said softly. Her voice was quivering. "El Padre Navarro was married and had *tres niños hermosos.* Two daughters *años* nine and seven *y un hijito* of five years. *Su familia* was killed in narco shooting—in Culiacán. Only oldest daughter *no fue matada.*" Sister Arámbula's eyes misted but she softly pressed on. "El Padre Navarro was *un ateo*—How do you say?—atheist—*durante algunos años* after killing—before he gave his *corazón al nuestro Señor y Redentor Jesucristo.*" Tears now flowed freely down Sister Arámbula's cheeks as she left a bewildered G to absorb the new information.

Several hours later, G put some light gear into his backpack and departed on one of his wilderness retreats. He needed to clear his mind. He set off on a brisk pace through the northern desert and made it to the mountains faster than he had ever done so before. G ran for twelve more miles before stopping for a drink of water. Forty yards to his right, a young jake turkey strutted into a small clearing behind a thicket of greasewood and dwarf oak tree. G whipped out a pistol and shot it cleanly through the head. He then constructed a small fire, quickly cleaned the turkey, and set it atop the open flames. He was hungry.

He consumed the last bit of meat near midnight, washing it down with several cans of Corona from his backpack. The blanket of clouds that had enveloped the valley just a few hours ago disappeared. The night was cool, crisp, and clear. The stars sparkled brilliantly against the darkness. The lobe-shaped moon lit up the desert landscape. The priest's words about God echoed throughout his mind.

In the morning, G experienced a small hangover. He extinguished it by running sprints up the mountainside, interspersed with hundreds of push-ups. He then headed further upwards and spent a full day climbing to the highest point of the mountains to see what was on the other side.

Bells chimed throughout the valley. The edge of the Mexican sun crept over the northern mountain tops. It was a gorgeous Sunday morning and families were pouring into the monastery's white cathedral which had served as the community's place of worship for 127 years. Little children laughed and giggled and frustrated mothers tried to organize their families. Religious paintings of Christ and various saints, plain yet powerful, hung expertly throughout the interior walls of the building. The cathedral was jam-packed, pews were limited, and many individuals were standing in the back.

As usual, the orphans were dressed in black suits and white dresses and sat in the front row. Their freshly washed faces beamed at Father Navarro, standing at the pulpit. The old man looked at his adoring audience and smiled warmly. He looked at his sermon and then, just before starting the service, glanced up at a group of stragglers trying to find standing space against the back wall. The ancient priest silently did a double-take upon seeing G in the back corner.

Five days later, the orphanage was abuzz with excitement. Today was the first day of wrestling practice. Thirty-two boys and five girls were rolling around the mat G had put in the orphanage's gym. G was trying his best to organize the chaos but appeared incapable. Sister López spent several minutes in silent laughter before blowing her whistle and getting the children in line. With Sister López's help, G managed to put the children in pairs, teach a proper stance and a basic double-leg takedown, and complete the first practice.

At the end of the week, G realized that most of the children would never prove to be wrestlers. But he did discover an athletic phenom in one of the younger boys: Jacob, the boy who had unashamedly asked to feel G's face several weeks ago. Late Friday afternoon after practice, G questioned Father Navarro about the boy's background. A look of anguish appeared on the old man's face. He remained silent for several minutes before answering. "You must know this, though it pains me to tell you. Jacob is the bastard son of Ramón Acosta. Ramón raped his mother who is now dead. A few years ago, Ramón's men massacred the entire family for vocally opposing the corruption sweeping over the community. Jacob survived the attack and was brought to the orphanage by some of his neighbors."

G felt revulsion creeping within him. Vomit rose to his throat. "Thanks for letting me know."

G continued coaching wrestling but completely ignored Jacob. He spent three consecutive practices teaching the importance of a stance, emphasizing that the quadriceps and glutes worked together in tandem to function as the human body's most powerful muscles. "A correct stance will allow you to move like a panther and defend takedowns like a bull elephant. Your first line of defense is your forehead." G had his team perform drills in which the kids could only use their stance and forehead to defend double-leg takedowns. "Your second line of defense is your hands." G held up his scarred hands to the team, palms outward. "Big hands. Big hands. Big hands. Should your opponent get past your head, your hands will turn into iron and stop any takedown."

Once G felt comfortable the kids were picking up the techniques, G went on in his progression. "Your forearms serve as the third line of defense. They will protect you like steel shields." G held up his forearms for his students to examine. They were thickly muscled now; veins bulged out unnaturally. "Should your opponent get past your head and your hands, your forearms will come down like sledgehammers. Outside of practice you must work hard to strengthen your bodies." G decided to have a push-up contest to encourage his team to work outside of practice. An eleven-year-old named Juan performed a record fifty-three push-ups and received heavy praise from both G and his teammates. The record stood until Jacob knocked out seventy-eight. G cancelled the contest without a word of congratulations.

The next day in practice, G taught the fourth line of defense. "Your hips are your final defensive attack—before you are forced to sprawl. Again, your upper leg muscles are the strongest weapons you have. They will provide you with the firepower you need for this skill. If your opponent penetrates deep in for a takedown, your hips must explode like a battering ram." G gave several demonstrations for five or ten minutes and then had the youth drill the techniques he covered. Despite himself, he glanced over at Jacob and his partner. Even with G's complete lack of attention, Jacob had mastered the defensive skills and was now successfully instructing his partner.

G concluded practice by having all wrestlers stand up against the wall and bend their legs in a 90-degree angle. After just a few seconds, as the burn ripped through their legs, some of the children started to complain. G simply stared at them. "We must forge your legs into steel. We are going to have another contest to see who can stay in this position the longest." After just a few minutes, 80 percent of the team gave up. After ten minutes, Juan and Jacob were the lone survivors. The team shouted encouragement at both boys but shortly after the eleven-minute mark, Juan's legs started shaking and he collapsed to the floor. G stared at Jacob without emotion as the kid burst into a wide grin. He looked capable of going another hour. G ended the practice unenthusiastically and returned to the monastery to perform his own workout.

Late Friday evening, the priest came by G's quarters with a bottle of wine. G had laid out his collection of weapons on his bed and had disassembled one of his .45 pistols. The old man watched from the doorway as G cleaned the weapon. He carefully wiped down the inside of the magazine well, ejector, and guide rails. He then plunged a bore brush several times through the barrel before re-assembling the gun. G stared out the window while spinning the pistol with his right hand and then his left. A religious-like song wafted through the air as G's fingers rotated the weapon at an incredible speed. "Good evening Father

Navarro." G spun the gun for a few more seconds before holstering it onto his left hip. He turned to face the old man.

"Good evening G. I trust all is well. Would you care to join me for a drink?" G shrugged and placed the firearms back into the gun safe stationed in the closet. He slipped on a white t-shirt and sandals and followed the old man into the outside corridor. As the two men walked, the priest casually launched into another history lesson, about the Spanish heritage of the conquistadores and the establishment of land grants to certain individuals known as *encomiendas*.

The two men finally walked into Father Navarro's room and G was listening somewhat half-heartedly to the priest's lecture. G looked at the painting of the Last Supper. The priest calmly filled two crystal glasses with crimson liquid and G watched in slight amusement as the old man brought the wine up to his lips and emptied the entire glass within a few seconds. "Despite his shortcomings, Cortés at least had a vision which included the successful establishment of a country in which the Indians would be integrated as positive contributing members of society. New Spain was envisioned to rise, flourish, and surpass its motherland in prosperity, implantation of Christian values, and dedication to the crown.

"I am convinced that the failure of Mexico to reach its enormous potential stems partially from one of mankind's most debilitating sins: the classification of an individual son or daughter of God based upon parentage or ancestry. Countless numbers of talented, intelligent, and motivated individuals were shut out completely from important professions and opportunities to construct what could have been a great and powerful nation. Instead, millions of people were shunned—left on the outskirts of a corrupt and incompetent hierarchy, ruled by despots from Spain who had no concern to better Mexico and no other goal than self-indulgence."

The priest poured himself another glass of wine, lifted the drink to his lips, and pointed the one-way conversation in a new direction. "I hear the wrestling practices are going well?"

G took a gulp of the wine and slowly nodded his head. In truth, he silently regretted his choice to coach the kids in the first place. As if he could read G's thoughts, the old man spoke softly as he lowered his half-full wine glass.

"One of the fundamental laws of the almighty is that man shall be judged according to his own sins. Spiritually and genetically, we are all part of the same family. Across the human spectrum we share the same disposition for greatness and weakness, heroism and cowardice, wisdom and foolishness, honor and corruption. Throughout history, some of mankind's most noble sons and daughters have risen from darkness."

The ancient priest then looked hard into G's eye. The intensity of his gaze surprised G; he had to steady himself to keep from flinching. "G, do not make the same mistake as the Spaniards. Do not reject Jacob because of his parentage. It was by no accident that your path has crossed with the boy's; God wanted this to happen for a reason. Your destinies are in some way intertwined."

On Monday, Jacob and his friends had come early to wrestling practice. He was in the process of pinning a boy named Gabriel in a half nelson when someone grasped him around the waist and tossed him up in the air. For a few moments Jacob's face showed panic before G broke his fall in midair and looked into the astonished face of the young wrestler. "That's a heck of a pin buddy. I'm glad you are here. You are going to be a fantastic wrestler."

It was all the motivation the young boy needed. Jacob smiled back lucidly, delighted to have his coach and idol talk to him again. Upon securing his release on the mat, he shot in for a double-leg on his instructor. His friends joined in on the battle. A six-year-old girl named Isabel, one of the five female wrestlers, set aside her oversized glasses and jumped on G's back. G even broke into some resemblance of a smile as he tousled with his young pupils. He eventually allowed himself to get pinned after giving the children a good workout.

After practice, G felt good, better than he had in a long time. He had struggled with his decision to accept Jacob—the priest had assigned him several Bible passages and G had spent all day Sunday studying the material from one of his favorite locations in the mountains. Ultimately he figured out what the priest was trying to convey—to move forward he must take a leap of faith; to survive he must purge the bitterness from his soul.

Chapter 15

Topolobampo, Sinaloa, Mexico

On the western shore of the Gulf of California, a foreboding fog smothered the small port town of Topolobampo. An army of AFO *sicarios* lined a secluded dock area. Behind them stood a collection of armored SUVs rigged with 7.62mm machine guns and 20mm automatic cannons. Several empty 18-wheelers were backed up to the dock. The AFO muscle was mostly composed of former gangsters from the meanest streets in southern California. All had spent time behind bars, and all were killers. Most of the *sicarios* were dressed in black, and all were armed with AK-47s and AR-15s. The Arellano-Félix brothers had picked them out carefully and made a substantial investment in training the hitmen with military-grade artillery.

One of the enforcers stood out among the rest. Manny Morelos Fernández was spearheading the operation. He had been with the AFO for three years and was already considered a legend. Recently, three of El Chapo's men were discovered constructing a border tunnel in Tijuana. Morelos beat all of them to death with his bare hands, decapitated each one of the corpses, then sent the heads back to El Chapo in an ice chest.

Morelos stood six-feet-three-inches tall, frame packed solid with raw muscle. He possessed a shaved head, large, sharp-looking nose, and a pockmarked face from years of adolescent acne. Tonight, he was wearing jeans, tennis shoes, and a thin white tank-top revealing a black hand tattooed across his right pectoral muscle. Inscribed in the center of the palm was the letter "M"—the "hand of death," the insignia of the Mexican Mafia (a.k.a. "La Eme").

Morelos had been born and raised in East Los Angeles. He was convicted of murder at the age of fifteen and spent eight years in Pelican Bay State Prison on California's remote north coast. There, he honed his lethal skills and gained a reputation as the most feared inmate in the penitentiary. Two years into his stint at Pelican Bay he was recruited by La Eme after murdering three of the more notorious black inmates on the prison yard with a glass knife.

La Eme was the most powerful organization within the California penal system, and Morelos quickly rose through the ranks to become one of the top commanders. His notoriety eventually attracted the attention of more sinister entities. With the help of a corrupt state senator and 600K, a cousin of the Arellano-Félix brothers offered to secure him an early release in exchange for a job south of the border. He accepted.

Morelos now took a long drag on his Marlboro cigarette and flicked it into the water next to the decaying dock. He stared long and hard into the foggy ocean, wondering how close the submarine was. It was rumored to have been the biggest narco sub the Colombians had ever built, capable of transporting seven tons of cocaine. There were other subs accompanying it as well. Tonight, they would deliver the single largest cargo of the white lady to ever arrive in Mexico; it was, for Morelos, a religious experience. Beeping broke through the night silence; Morelos lifted his mobile phone. It was General Ramón Acosta.

"It's me. You're all clear. I'll be there in five minutes."

Morelos grunted an acknowledgement and pulled out another cigarette. General Acosta had insisted on seeing the AFO set-up at the dock—said he wanted to visit the men, boost morale. There was something about Acosta that was disturbing. He didn't like it. No other man had induced anxiety within him before. But it was Acosta who had orchestrated the historic delivery. Benjamín Arellano-Félix had made the importance of this transaction abundantly clear to Morelos. And that meant he had to work with Acosta. Morelos had been there when Acosta made the proposal, an offer the AFO could not refuse; the chance to rake in such a large sum on El Chapo's home turf was an irresistible temptation. Only the pragmatic Eduardo Arellano-Félix expressed doubt. His concerns were swiftly alleviated when Benjamín Arellano-Félix pulled out a 9mm pistol and fired a shot two inches below Eduardo's genitalia. "Lost your *cojones,* brother? *¡Puto cobarde!* We're gonna *chingado* crush El Chapo and we're *chingado* gonna do it on his *plaza!*" The matter had been settled. Six weeks later, General Acosta announced he had all the arrangements in place.

Off to the east, an engine belonging to a dull gray Ford Bronco rumbled loudly. The men turned their gaze to watch General Ramón Acosta drive down the ancient cobblestone road to the dock. The Bronco came to a stop about ten yards away and Acosta stepped out of the vehicle, dressed in full military attire.

"Manny! *¿Qué onda, cabrón?*"

Morelos nodded cordially, "S'up *carnal.*"

The two men shook hands. Acosta cracked a few jokes about Morelos's latest bevy of girlfriends, causing laughter among the surrounding enforcers. Ramón proceeded to amicably greet each and every one of the other men. He had met half of them before and could recall each of their names as well as minute details of every trivial conversation. He passed out cocaine-laced marijuana joints and jovially talked about the new boundaries they were breaking, the money they would make from this evening's narco subs and the many more to follow. Thirty minutes later, the general was back in the Bronco, casually driving away.

An hour after Ramón left, Manny saw the metallic watercraft break the surface of the brackish ocean, piercing through the ominous fog. A red signal light flashed three times from the top of the periscope on the conning tower. In response, Morelos flashed his high-density spotlight twice. All men watched intently as the double-hulled steel vessel inched slowly out of the water and made its way towards the dock. With each passing second, more and more details of the mythical submarine materialized. It was bigger than any of them had expected, and, far more advanced. Many of the AFO enforcers had seen narco subs before; they now gazed in awe at this approaching technological marvel. The Colombian cartels had only recently started using the subs in route to Mexico. General Acosta had effectively convinced the Arellano-Félix brothers they were the way of the future.

When the vessel was within fifty yards of the dock, Morelos knew something was wrong. The sub was far too large and much too sophisticated. He lifted his spotlight to focus in on the oncoming hull and recoiled in horror as two huge gun turrets swung into action. Bursting into a full-speed sprint towards his armored Chevy Silverado, he roared at his men to take cover. He was within ten feet of the vehicle when the submarine opened fire.

The .50 caliber bullets were accurate and deadly. One-third of the AFO enforcers died within seconds. Some of the others reached their armored vehicles and returned fire with their own advanced weaponry. Morelos and a few of the braver gangbangers got in a few decent shots before they were blindsided. Three T-72 Russian battle tanks rumbled through the desert at thirty-five miles per hour and let loose a barrage of guided missiles from their 2A46 125mm main guns. Within a matter of seconds, most of the AFO vehicles were torn to shreds. General Acosta had brokered a deal with the Russian mob, and the T-72s had arrived just three weeks ago.

The tanks were his latest passion and he had been itching to test them out. They exceeded his expectations. Bullets from the AFO machine guns bounced harmlessly off the eleven-inch-thick composite steel and explosive reactive armor. Ramón grinned fiendishly as he plowed one of the tanks into a black Hummer H1 and felt it crumple to the ground like an aluminum soda can. The other two tanks rampaged on, demolished the remaining SUVs, and mowed down the bewildered AFO enforcers. Ramón's infantry followed up with M4A1 assault rifles and rounded up the remaining hitmen.

Eighteen AFO *sicarios* survived. Morelos and seventeen of his men were marched into a flat open sandy area near the docks. General Acosta slowly emerged from one of the tanks; Colonel Vásquez materialized from another. Ramón's lips were twisted, face flush with battle lust. His blazing eyes stared at the survivors with vitriol, openly displaying his contempt for the hitmen and muscle of all the cartels.

For years, General Acosta was trained by the most elite military squads in the world. *These AFO scum are third-rate gangsters.* Ramón had shot state-of-the-art weapons until his fingers bled. He had suffered through some of the most intense boot camps on earth. He had seen real combat on many missions and was himself a true professional. General Acosta now walked among the former gangbangers, examining each of them. He stripped them of their knives and other remaining weapons. Ramón then directed his own men to split the enemy into two groups and line them up horizontally. His own voice boomed with authoritative power. "I am giving you a chance to live. Each of you will have the opportunity to become part of a force that will revolutionize Mexico and the world. But you will have to earn it." He pointed to the first man in each of the lines: "You and you—fight—in the middle—now!"

The two men slowly marched out and looked at each other tentatively for several moments. "*¡Joder!*" Ramón swiftly pummeled one of them with a flurry of powerful punches. The AFO *sicario* went down and General Acosta expertly and brutally broke his neck with the right heel of his boot. The man died instantly. Ramón quickly turned his attack on the other. Within a few seconds, Acosta had the man on the ground and jabbed his right thumb into the man's left eye socket, driving it into his brain. The general then stood up, his uniform splattered with blood. He pointed to the next men in each of the lines. "You and you—in the middle—now!"

A five-foot-seven, 140-pound man named Fuentes came forward from the line closest to the ocean. He was bald and had a Fu Manchu mustache, his body littered with gang tattoos from the Logan Heights area in San Diego, CA. Another man named Murillos walked forward from the opposite line—one inch shorter than Fuentes, but much stockier. Murillos had an oversized nose partly concealed by a bushy mustache. La Eme tattoos were splattered across his arms and chest. Murillos threw the first punch but it fell a few inches wide and grazed Fuentes's ear. The fight was savage and ugly. Fists flew awkwardly and off-balance takedowns were attempted. Fuentes eventually got Murillos in a headlock, threw him on the ground, and put in a rear naked choke hold. Two minutes later a physically exhausted Fuentes snuffed out the life of his former ally.

The next fight went similarly and another AFO man was returned to his maker. The third fight lasted more than five minutes and reached a stalemate when both men, exhausted, bent down, and gasped for air as they vomited. Ramón drew a pistol and shot both of them through the head.

Morelos demolished his opponent in seventeen seconds with a series of brutal upper cuts and one roundhouse kick that knocked a skinny AFO thug out cold. While the man lay paralyzed on the sand, Morelos removed his belt and used the edge of the sharpened buckle to cut the man's throat. One of Ramón's men went to retrieve the makeshift weapon. The general waved him off and snarled, "Let him keep it."

The head AFO enforcer was soon the last man standing. He had barely broken a sweat; only his knuckles were wounded. Ramón stared at the big man long and hard. He had heard a bit about his exploits. "Take off your shirt," Ramón ordered. Although Morelos's expression was emotionless, the general could sense the underlying current of rabid anger. The AFO killer silently obeyed the command. His upper body muscles were pumped. Underneath the black hand tattoo of La Eme, etched into the skin of his abdominal muscles, lay a field of human skulls with beady red eyes. They represented his many victims. Ramón's eyes narrowed and his lips curled.

"Go ahead, Héctor."

Colonel Vásquez smiled violently. The evening's action had amplified his adrenaline levels. He was itching to spill more blood. He calmly handed his FN Minimi machine gun to the man next to him and took off his hat and shirt. His shredded chest and abdominal muscles were decorated with a ghastly image of Santa Muerte holding a serrated scythe. Vásquez cocked his head to the left and then to the right. He shrugged his shoulders, flexed his huge biceps, and stared at Morelos with a wicked grin. His gold-plated front tooth gleamed against the dull yellow globes of the dock's lampposts; the tattoo of Santa Muerte danced on his rippling muscles. Morelos stepped forward and stared right back at him, hatred and rage showing openly on his face.

For a full forty seconds the two killers slowly circled around the sand, sizing each other up. Vásquez continued to smile confidently at his opponent. He had trained in mixed martial arts for years, and he had never been defeated in battle. Morelos rightly took his perverted grin as a sign of disrespect and attacked first. He tried a series of front kicks and leg sweeps. They were countered expertly by the grinning Vásquez. The AFO enforcer then feigned a straight right punch and threw a left hook but again the colonel was ready for it. He blocked the hook with his right arm and threw a sharp left jab that broke his opponent's nose. Vásquez then came forward to clean up. He was a split second too late. Morelos shot in on a single-leg to his right, changed levels, and surrounded both legs to secure the takedown.

Vásquez's whole body hit the ground. He popped back up, but not before Morelos landed a solid left kick that knocked out his prized gold tooth. The fiendish smile on Vásquez's lips disappeared. Rushing forward, he threw a torrent of brutal punches. The AFO gangster defended them well until a left upper cut hammered his lower jaw. It rocked Morelos hard; his knees buckled and he started going down. Vásquez snarled. Spit sprayed from his clenched teeth. With bestial tenacity he went in for the kill. But Morelos, the wily veteran of a plethora of street brawls, recovered just enough to slam his head forward. Rotting, yellow-stained teeth clamped down savagely on Vásquez's right ear.

The colonel roared as bloody shredded cartilage spewed from his opponent's mouth. The pain launched him into an insane frenzy. His own head rocketed forward and smashed into Morelos's face, shattering his nose; blood erupted from his nostrils. But the blow failed to stop Morelos from discharging a wicked right elbow that pounded sharply into Vásquez's eye. The giant colonel went berserk. Machine-like, his massive arms blasted out a furious combination of punches and a right hook landed directly on target, knocking the AFO hitman out cold. Finally satisfied that Morelos was down for good, Vásquez wrapped his giant hands around his opponent's neck. Orgasmic joy rushed through his veins as he squeezed—right until a bullet ripped past his mutilated left ear.

"That's enough, Héctor." Ramón's voice bellowed loud enough to bring Colonel Vásquez back to reality. General Acosta turned to his medical staff. "Tend to the wounds of Colonel Vásquez." He then motioned to the unconscious Morelos. "And then take care of his injuries. He is one of us now."

Chapter 16

Catholic Monastery—Durango, Mexico

It was a beautiful autumn Saturday afternoon in Durango. Every child in the orphanage was present at the baptism. Most had never witnessed an infant baptism, let alone that of an adult. G, who had been fasting for the last forty-eight hours, came to the front of the cathedral dressed in funny-looking clothes. Jacob and most of the younger kids laughed. They were quickly silenced by Sister López and Sister Arámbula, the nuns themselves trying to suppress smiles. G looked stone-faced at the youngsters with a mock expression of anger; they laughed harder. The disfigured American had become a favorite at the orphanage; all the children adored him, Jacob most of all.

Everyone at the monastery was present. "G! G! G!" The dwarf Felipe was abnormally excited. G saw Felipe sit down next to Sister López. He reached for her left breast and his hand was immediately smacked by Sister Arámbula and Felipe recoiled in terror. G's face of stone softened; he bit his lip to keep from laughing.

The elderly Esmeralda was also in attendance and, strangely, remained silent. Father Navarro gave a brief sermon on the sacred rite and retold the biblical account of the baptism of Jesus by John the Baptist in a fashion that entertained the orphans. G was then baptized by the ancient priest and received the rites of Confirmation and Communion.

Late that evening, the priest invited G into his chambers. G stared once again at the familiar painting of Christ and his disciples while the old man perused the contents of a worn-down Bible. "I am worried about my country, G. Changes are occurring faster than anticipated." G looked at Father Navarro and perceived genuine disquietude. Undeterred, the priest went on. "The Adversary is powerful. From the creation he has worked tirelessly and ruthlessly to destroy the principles and ideals for which Christ stands."

Father Navarro remained silent for a few moments as he browsed through the Gospels of the New Testament. Eventually, he continued. "After the crucifixion, the original apostles and other prominent Christians were persecuted, hunted down, and horrifically murdered. Peter, deeming himself unworthy to be killed in the manner of his master, was crucified head down by Roman executioners. James was killed by Herod Agrippa with a sword. Andrew was hanged on an olive tree in a town in Achaia. Thomas was stabbed with spears, tortured, then burned alive. Philip was tortured and then crucified in Phrygia. Matthew was decapitated at Nad-Davar. Bartholomew was flayed and then crucified. James the lesser was cast down from a temple and then beaten to death with a club. Simon was crucified by a governor in Syria. Judas Thaddeus was beaten to death with sticks by pagan priests in Mesopotamia. Matthias was stoned to death upon a cross in Ethiopia. Paul was beheaded in Rome by the Emperor Nero."

Navarro's eyes moistened as he opened a bottle of wine and filled his favorite goblet. He took a small sip and looked at G, who was steadily drinking his Corona. "It was decided early on a certain level of protection was needed: to maintain the faith and defend the innocent. The protection would come in the form of Christian warriors—devoted to the cause of righteousness. An order was established for that purpose and enabled the founding of the church in Rome as well as the preservation of the Gospel.

"As the centuries progressed, the original order evolved into what today is commonly referred to as the "Knights Templar." The Knights Templar established elite combat units and many holy warriors fought in the Crusades and dedicated themselves to the defense of the Christians in Jerusalem and the Middle East. For a period after the Crusades, the Templars thrived. They founded important political connections and obtained lands and vast wealth. They created networks of military fortifications as well as sophisticated financial infrastructures. However, their prosperity did not last. Envy and greed raged in both the royal monarchies and the Church itself.

"In the early fourteenth century, the biggest conspiracy known to mankind took place in Europe. Starting in France, under the direction of King Philip IV, the knights were arrested, tortured, and murdered. In 1307, Pope Clement himself issued a decree instructing monarchs to arrest all Templars and seize their assets. Hunted to the brink of extinction, the organization splintered. Most knights fled to regions outside the influence of the Pope. Others joined smaller rival orders on better terms with the European monarchies. However, the organization did not die out completely. A group of devoted, top-tier military personnel was organized to maintain the sacred order of the Knights Templar. Under solemn covenant, these new knights were instructed to combat terror, torture, and all manner of heinous crimes against the innocent. The new order was to operate in complete secrecy and on a much smaller scale than the original, lest it should suffer the same fate. These new knights became known as the "Cruzados Rojos"—"Red Crusaders"—elite Christian warriors willing to spill their own blood, if necessary, in defense of the faith and ideals of our Savior.

"Operating undercover, the Red Crusaders flourished and became a successful unit in defending life and liberty across Europe. After the conquest of Cortés, a band of the Christian warriors was dispatched to the new world to defend the indigenous inhabitants against exploitation. They fought alongside Juan de Zumárraga and helped many of the Indians convert to Christ. Later, they stood with Miguel Hidalgo and José Marcia Morelos y Pavón in the struggle for Mexican independence. During the French occupation, they battled under the direction of Benito Juárez and later helped Emiliano Zapata Salazar amid the bloodshed of the revolution. They fought with the rebels in the Cristero War. Throughout Mexico's darkest hours, the Red Crusaders have served to combat tyranny and injustice. They have fought against the evilest people to have ever lived on this soil."

The priest took a copious drink of wine. His eyes bore down into the depths of G's soul. It was unnerving and surreal. G knew the old man well enough to understand where he was going with this. Without his experiences, G would have dismissed the priest as a loon. He now knew better. His mind had been expanded by orders of magnitude and strangely, one of the truths he had come to discover was the amount of knowledge he himself lacked. G trusted Father Navarro implicitly. Unconsciously, he found himself staring back into the ancient eyes of the holy man and nodding.

Father Navarro went on, "As you might have surmised, the Mexican order of the Red Crusaders has survived. We operate in complete seclusion. For perhaps the first time in my life, G, I am afraid for my country. An ominous darkness is clouding across the land. Faith is perishing and bloodshed is on the rise. The Adversary has grown powerful here, and he possesses many weapons.

"Long ago, an evil flourished upon this land which was so heinous I believe our creator saw fit to wipe out an entire civilization. The Aztecs worshiped a god of death they called Mictlantecuhtli. Thousands and thousands were brutally sacrificed on his behalf. The barbaric acts have left an unhealthy fascination with death that has been ingrained into Mexican society. A new symbol of evil has arisen which attracts narcos like a magnet: Santa Muerte—literally translated as "Holy Death." Paintings, statues, images, and lifelike representations of Santa Muerte, typically skeletons dressed in religious attire and armed with scythes, are ubiquitous. Altars of actual skeletons wearing wedding dresses and holding macabre weapons infest the roads of Northern Mexico. It is a representation of the same evil symbolized by Mictlantecuhtli and has existed since the dawn of mankind. Santa Muerte is simply the newest manifestation of this ancient evil. It has been sent forth by the devil and it has seduced some of the most powerful minds in Mexico. And now, the situation is unprecedented. I fear we are on the verge of destruction.

"You have seen what we are up against. Now I come to you as a brother in Christ to ask for your help and support. God has brought you here for a reason, I am absolutely sure of that."

The priest slowly rose to his feet. He turned around and walked to the back wall. For several moments Father Navarro gazed upon the painting of the Last Supper. And then, his fingers went to the frame. G watched in electric anticipation as the old man carefully removed the canvas and lowered it to the floor. In its place appeared a metallic safe box, solidly built into the wall. The priest reached into his black cassock and pulled out the cross which hung from his neck by an iron chain. For a few brief seconds his age-stained fingers fondled the cross before inserting it into a specialized key hole in the steel safe box. The safe door creaked open and the priest reached inside the box to retrieve a small leather bag. He locked the safe, hung up the painting, and returned to his desk. As he sat down, he lightly tossed the bag to G.

Carefully, G reached inside and retrieved a peculiar, two barred cross, constructed out of solid gold. The bottom horizontal bar was slightly longer than the one on top and the bars appeared to be evenly spaced. Centered across the top bar, a blood-red ruby was encrusted in the yellow metal. The metal and gem glimmered brilliantly. G's eye stared at the cross realizing his sole purpose in life, his quest for vengeance, had changed. He looked up at the priest inquisitively.

"What you now hold in your hand, G, has been the sacred symbol of the Red Crusaders since the order's conception, nearly 700 years ago. It is identical to the Cross of Lorraine, save for the presence of the red gemstone. The Cross of Lorraine had special significance among the original Knights Templar. To this day, though the original meaning has been significantly altered, the cross has been symbolic among various groups and nations. France, for example, used it to symbolize their freedom from the Nazis during World War II.

"The piece you now possess is one of 100 original crosses constructed in Rome, five centuries ago, to honor the founding members of the new order. Only a handful of the crosses now exist in the world; the one you hold is the last of its kind in Mexico. The ruby is meant to remind us of our own mortality, that our earthly life is but a small part in the eternal scheme of our creator, and if we should perish in the cause of faith and freedom then we will only be following our redeemer and others who have gone on before us."

G stared at the cross and remained silent for some time. "What do you want me to do?" The priest slowly got to his feet and walked over to where G was sitting. He removed the iron chain from his own neck and swapped the crosses. In solemn silence he meticulously draped the golden cross of the Red Crusaders over G's neck. He centered both his hands on the top of G's head and then proceeded, in Latin, to say the words of the ordinance that would create a new member of the ancient order. The ritual went on for thirty minutes as the holy man fervently called upon the heavens to guide and protect G in all his endeavors.

After what seemed like an eternity, G finally felt the hands lift from his head. He heard the priest's voice switch back to Spanish. "You are to go with God, defend Mexico, and unleash hell upon its enemies."

Chapter 17

Tijuana, Baja California, Mexico

The music was loud! Too loud, and it hurt G's ears. It was two in the morning and he had been here for five-and-a-half hours. He was growing restless. He arrived in Tijuana yesterday with orders to protect J. Jesús Blancornelas at all costs. Blancornelas was a journalist and Father Navarro considered him one of Mexico's greatest heroes. G could still hear the priest's words ringing in his ears: "The courageous journalists, reporters, and writers will help save Mexico, G. I cannot stress this fact enough. The people must know the whole truth of what is occurring. It is imperative we ensure their safety."

Together with friend Héctor Félix Miranda, Blancornelas had co-founded a weekly publication known as "Zeta" with the single purpose of covering organized crime and government corruption. And the corruption embedded within both the local and federal law enforcement agencies provided no shortage of material. In 1985, Blancornelas and Miranda ran a magazine cover story centering on a Tijuana police squad guarding a warehouse of marijuana. All 20,000 copies of the magazine were purchased by policemen dressed in street clothes. The pair re-published the story under the headline "Censored!" In addition, for the first time, the story introduced key players in Tijuana drug-trafficking, most notably the Arellano-Félix brothers.

Miranda was assassinated in 1988. In every subsequent publication after his death, Blancornelas printed Miranda's name on the masthead, overlaid by a black cross. Each issue also contained a full-page ad directed at Tijuana's politicians asking why he had been murdered. Blancornelas continued to relentlessly root out corruption and seek justice. The AFO shadowed his every move. When he published a photograph of Ramón Arellano-Félix, they put out a death warrant. A deadly hit squad was assembled, commanded by David Barron Corona, former leader of the San Diego-based Barrio Logan Heights gang and one of the top AFO enforcers. Barron was convicted of murder as a teenager, joined La Eme while incarcerated, and was later recruited by the AFO. Released from prison in 1989, he immediately crossed the border to work with the cartel. A few years later, he became of one the most notorious killers in Mexico.

On the morning of November 27, 1997, as Blancornelas was traveling to the airport, Barron and a band of AFO *sicarios* ambushed the journalist, riddling his car with 200 rounds of gunfire. Blancornelas somehow survived the attack but was shot four times in his abdomen. His bodyguard, Luis Valero Elizalde, was not so lucky. He died courageously performing his duty and even managed to take down an assassin while thirty-eight bullets pounded into his body. It was Barron's last venture. One of the rounds from his own men's rifles ricocheted off Blancornelas's vehicle and slammed into Barron's eye socket. The narco died instantly.

From an obscure booth in the ballroom, G now stared at the aging Blancornelas. The AFO was going the way of the dinosaurs; its enforcers had all been eliminated. El Chapo and the Sinaloa Cartel were the new kings in town. And Blancornelas had made new enemies. In a recent publication he made a vague reference about the possible link between General Acosta and El Chapo. The general went ballistic.

Blancornelas is treading in dangerous territory, G reflected, sipping water. He looked over at the honey-brown eyes and glowing lips of his date. Her long black hair was wound neatly in a bun which went well with her petite frame. She was wearing high heels, a modest blue satin dress, and a little too much makeup. Sister López looked dramatically different than G had ever seen her before and she was undeniably beautiful. This was, indeed, one of the times he regretted having taken a vow of chastity. Well, that, and the fact that she was a nun.

G was wearing a black cowboy hat, designer blue jeans, and a white denim shirt underneath a sheepskin vest. The eye patch he normally wore was gone, replaced with a prosthetic glass eye constructed by Father Navarro. His hair was dyed black. Sister López had covered his face with make-up to conceal his scars as well as to pass him off as Hispanic. He looked strange, to be sure, but only a few people at the *quinceañera* had looked at him funny.

It was Gabriela Guerrero Contreras's fifteenth birthday, and her father had spared no expense for the special occasion. He rented out a lavish multi-story ballroom complete with a modernized dance floor and bar. Hundreds of people were in attendance. Gabriela was the niece of J. Jesús Blancornelas and the weathered journalist had decided to attend the event, despite not usually going out in public. Blancornelas reasoned he would be safe at the *quinceañera*; eight bodyguards would accompany him and the governor of Baja California had offered to send in a squad of special forces agents. With the tightened security, it had taken quite a bit of ingenuity and a flirtatious Sister López to get G's pistols into the building.

A woman in Father Navarro's congregation was a distant relative of the Guerreros. She received a formal invitation to attend the *quinceañera*, despite losing touch with the family years ago. Father Navarro was concerned for Blancornelas: too many people were aware he would be going to the event. Father Navarro wanted G to attend and arranged for Sister López to show up as a long-lost cousin. The nun was enthusiastic about the endeavor, though G had argued vehemently against the proposal. But the matter had been settled when he could offer no better alternative for getting himself into the *quinceañera.*

Casually watching Gabriela select a handsome young man as a dance partner, G squeezed another slice of lemon into his water glass and attempted to block out the new tune sung by the *mariachis.* The music was getting old and he was ready to go. Sister López, however, seemed to be enjoying herself. She had not vomited since she first met G at the monastery and the remaining traces of her anxiety had evaporated. Her feet were tapping along to the rhythm of the Mexican folk music and she was smiling brightly towards the hordes of teenagers and various couples on the dance floor. The music changed into a quieter tune. G watched as a *guapo* cowboy, fondling the buttocks of his dance partner, was slapped in the face by a furious girlfriend.

G smiled at the encounter. *Maybe things will prove to be more interesting.* He once again looked up at the clock. The hands had not moved much since he last checked it three minutes ago. Nothing would be occurring at this *quinceañera,* he was certain of it. But Father Navarro had wanted him here. And so he would stay to the end and carry out his assignment—like he always did.

It had been three months since the old man initiated him into the sacred order of the Red Crusaders. With the intelligence provided by Javier, he had taken out nine narco *sicarios.* Three weeks ago, he prevented an assassination attempt on the new no-nonsense police chief in the border town of Matamoros by stopping four cartel henchmen in a heavily armed Chevy Tahoe. He killed two of the thugs with an AR-15, one with his silver-plated Colt .45, and the last one with his bare hands. He then thanked the shaken yet stalwart police chief for his service and warned him to take extra precautions in the future.

G took a liking to the Chevy Tahoe and, though it was scarred by bullet holes, he ended up keeping the vehicle. Later, at the monastery, he found a stash of cocaine, heroin, and 400,000 U.S. dollars in a hidden compartment in the back of the SUV. He trashed the drugs and gave the 400K to Father Navarro. The priest used it to provide food and shelter for a few groups of poverty-stricken Native Mexicans he had been working with.

As the rhythm of the *mariachis* picked up, G sighed. He considered replacing his water with a Corona but thought better of it. *I will complete the mission with exactness.* It was at that moment that he felt it. *The hell? Something is wrong.* His eye flickered to Blancornelas and scanned the immediate vicinity. Three of the special forces agents were missing. He grabbed Sister López's wrist and pulled her out of the booth.

"Time to dance!"

Despite his concern for the nun, he couldn't go on the dance floor alone—he would stand out like a damn sore thumb. Although prepared for this possibility, Sister López clenched her teeth nervously. Eyes on the journalist, she squeezed G's hand and followed him onto the dance floor.

While serving as an obstacle to the talented dancers, G zeroed in on Blancornelas and held Sister López tight. Amid the loud music, he heard commotion from the area of the missing agents. His mind raced, all senses on high alert. *It's happening,* he concluded, *and it's happening fast.* It was as if an invisible darkness was rapidly permeating the stuffy air. G then saw two bodies go sprawling to the floor. A group of armed men was walking towards him, roughing up anyone in their way. *They're coming for his niece,* he realized. It was unexpected and he had miscalculated their intentions. And, to make things worse, he had placed the nun in danger.

"Damn it!"

He quickly grabbed both of Sister López's arms and shook her. "Go to the bar and get behind the counter! Stay there till this is over! Go! Now! Run!"

G did not have time to watch the blue dress flow through the bar gateway. A group of seven armed men forcefully marched through the crowd and surrounded Gabriela. Without a word, one of them unsheathed a knife and slit the throat of her latest dance companion. Blood spouted upwards like a water fountain. Gabriela screamed and tried to run. She was immediately captured by two of the thugs. The *sicario* with the knife, a grisly man with beady brown eyes, placed the blade at the base of Gabriela's thin neck. He stared wolfishly at his prey. Gabriela was very attractive and he was excited. The girl was to become the latest victim of Tlaloc and the assassin would have first dibs on her. The tone of his voice failed to conceal his dark desires. "Move again, *puta* bitch, and I will cut you open like a ripe melon."

They were the last words the *sicario* would ever speak. Out of nowhere, a hand gripped his wrist with incredible strength. The brutish thug winced in pain as his fingers released the weapon. The agony he felt, however, was momentary. G caught the knife in midair and plunged it into the man's heart with a force that shattered several ribs. Before the other assassins could level their AK-47s, G drew his Colt .45s from the inside of his vest and splattered the brains of two *sicarios* into a group of dancing teenagers who were hitherto oblivious of the action. Several girls screamed in unison as jet streams of blood painted their beautiful dresses. Across the large ballroom, heavy gunfire exploded and two of Blancornelas's bodyguards went down to the weapons of the treacherous special forces agents. The entire building erupted in chaos.

G's left arm whipped around Gabriela's waist. Simultaneously, he dropped his silver Colt .45 and took off at full speed. Gunfire trailed his footsteps as he sprinted for the bar and he felt a searing pain as one bullet pierced through the edge of his left heel. Another round grazed the top of his right shoulder but without breaking stride he threw Gabriela through the bar gate and in one fluid motion he rounded on the attackers and fired two shots.

One bullet hit an assassin between the gap in his two rotten front teeth and the other hit a comrade slightly below the left nostril. G's eye darted towards Blancornelas. The journalist's remaining bodyguards were in a gunfight with the corrupted special forces agents and another team of narco assassins. G rapidly unloaded his golden Colt .45 and a torrent of well-placed bullets killed two of the corrupt operatives and two more *sicarios.* He quickly loaded another magazine into the pistol.

"Look out!" Amid the mayhem, G was still able to recognize the shrieking words. Sister López, unable to contain herself, had lifted her head above the bar counter to see what was happening. A flurry of gunfire came within inches of G's head as he dropped to the floor.

"To your right!" the nun screamed.

G grimly realized he had chosen the correct escort for the evening. He came up hard to his right in a standing crouch and aimed for the forehead of a narco gunman. But just as he squeezed the trigger, he noticed a wiry young cowboy, pushed into his line of fire by a group of stampeding teenagers running for the exit.

"Shit!"

G barely lifted his gun in time to direct the shot to the ceiling. It smashed into an expensive chandelier with a loud explosion and sent shards of glass spraying across the dance floor. Trying his best to see through the screaming multitudes of overdressed teenagers, G homed in on the hitman who had tried to kill him. He instantly put a bullet through the assassin's heart. But upon pulling the trigger, G felt fire slash across the skin and flesh of his right forearm. He dropped the pistol. Less than thirty feet away, to his immediate left, one of the thugs was shooting at him. G dropped to one knee while his left hand reached inside the right section of his sheepskin vest. The *sicario's* next shot hit the remnants of the chandelier as he toppled backwards with a bowie knife sunk into his throat.

G sprinted at full speed between a small break in the panic-stricken crowd. Protecting Blancornelas was now his only concern. Out of the left corner of his eye he saw the last standing bodyguard go down to the gunfire of the remaining four narco thugs. It appeared the special forces agents had all been killed, the good along with the corrupt. The four thugs had grouped together and were closing in on Blancornelas like a band of predators when one of them picked up on G's motion and shouted at his companions. But G had already accelerated to full speed and the powerful muscles in his legs converted his body into a torpedo.

As the narco hitmen swung their guns around, G's forehead plowed into the sternum of the nearest assassin. The narco killer was a giant, but the force of G's blow knocked him off his feet and the 9mm pistol came out of his hand. Both men landed violently on the ceramic tile floor and, upon impact, both of G's arms instantly launched outwards. His left elbow battered into the jaw of the huge *sicario* while the fingers of his right hand found the dislodged 9mm. Three AK-47s swung towards his head but G sunk a flurry of lead bullets into the foreheads of their owners before they could get off a shot. G quickly turned to finish off his attacker on the floor, but alarmingly discovered that the man was already on his feet. And the giant narco was in the process of delivering a powerful right kick.

The kick landed squarely on G's face, breaking his nose and snapping his head back hard. Ignoring the pain, G sprang to his feet and then watched in dream-like horror as the monstrous thug pulled out another 9mm and aimed it. It happened almost in slow motion. The pistol fired with the sound of a cannon and G knew he was a dead man. Yet he continued to move forward, expecting to collapse any second.

His eye flickered to his own chest. There was no blood. He then looked up to see the *sicario* backhand Sister López across the forehead. She flew several feet through the air, still tightly holding the whisky bottle she had used to free the pistol from the assassin's hand. She landed hard and her head cracked against the floor with a thud, knocking her out cold.

G ran at the thug like a raging Viking warrior. He got in a body lock while moving at full speed and slammed the giant hitman into some stereo equipment some thirty feet away. He underestimated his opponent. Upon recoiling from a large speaker, the *sicario* pounded his arms through G's grip while at the same time delivering a punishing headbutt to G's broken nose. Dazed, G was barely able to maneuver his head out of the path of another thunderous kick.

Grinding his teeth, G composed himself, readied into combat position, and came out swinging. None of his punches landed cleanly and they were well defended. He stared into the face of his foe and recognized the man immediately—from the collection of photos Javier had provided. He was Manny Morelos Fernández, the vicious and ruthless former leader of the AFO muscle. He stood a few inches taller than G, was well-trained in all aspects of combat, and his body was packed with raw muscle. *Is Morelos now working with El Chapo?*

He did not have time to answer his own question. The big man came forth with a barrage of kicks that sent G reeling backwards. The thug then threw a wicked right hook that found its target and crushed the prosthetic glass eye Father Navarro had so carefully crafted. Fragments of glass ripped through facial tissue and crimson blood spewed from the empty eye socket.

Snarling, G countered instantly and brutally. He dipped his own left hip and delivered a titanic left upper cut and followed it with a shot to the ribcage with his right fist. The stunned assassin stepped back for a moment as he felt his jawbone fracture and his ribs crack. Sensing victory, G went in for the kill and immediately threw another flurry of combinations. But Morelos recovered quicker than expected. The narco assassin countered with a right roundhouse kick that pounded G's left ear and sent him sprawling to the floor.

Though somewhat disoriented, G quickly rose to his feet and maneuvered into fighting position. Both men now circled each other, looking for weakness. Blood was streaming into G's eye and his vision was blurring. He fought the urge to panic and concentrated on the movements of his opponent. G threw a number of sharp jabs and feigned launching several haymakers before Morelos attacked with a straight left followed by an explosive right hook. Both punches missed their target and took the *sicario* slightly out of position. With the skill and power of a world-class wrestler, G ducked low and popped his foe's elbow upwards. It threw the big man off balance just enough to give him the edge he needed. G penetrated low and hard, his right hand reached out and snaked around Morelos's right calf.

In blinding fashion, G jolted the *sicario* to the left and came back hard to the right, cutting the corner and switching to a running double leg. G unleashed a guttural war cry as he yanked down on the huge legs of his enemy while accelerating to full speed. After seventeen yards, he had generated so much power that his murderous opponent was completely off his feet as the collision against the steel rail splintered the thug's spine. G expertly cupped his right hand under Morelos's fractured jaw and broke his neck with a single, savage thrust.

As life drained out of the narco killer, G's battle rage subsided and he fell back into the cold depths of reality. Both physical pain and apprehensiveness quickly consumed him, generating a wrenching knot in his gut. He blanked out his agony and ran over to Sister López in time to see the nun gain consciousness and slowly move her head. He quickly examined her and found no serious injuries. *Thank God*. G gently lifted her off the floor and they both returned to the bar where they found a weeping, yet unharmed, Gabriela. Slowly and tenderly, Sister López leaned down to comfort her. "God be with you Gabriela. *Ahora está bien*. It's over. Let's go see your family."

The entire Guerrero family was sobbing uncontrollably. A few of the females were attending to J. Jesús Blancornelas, alive, though shot in the left shoulder. All his bodyguards, however, had gone down in the line of duty. They were good, honest men, all of them, and they would be mourned by their families for generations. Several innocent teenagers had also been killed, murdered by the narco assassins, and their losses would have devastating effects on all those who knew them. G's heart went out to them.

As Sister López slowly guided Gabriela across the dance floor, her mother ran out and clung on to her beloved daughter. She was quickly followed by the rest of her family, along with the injured Blancornelas. Although G hurt like hell, he was not critically injured. Blood flowing freely from his wounds, he limped over to the old journalist. With effort, he placed his hand on Blancornelas's shoulder.

"I am sorry for the loss of your men." G's voice was hard, yet empathetic. "But you must continue on course and fight the good fight. Keep writing. Mexico desperately needs you."

With Blancornelas too stunned to reply, G hobbled over to the weeping Sister López who was trying to console the loved ones of the victims. "We have to go now, Sister. I'm afraid you'll have to drive." The nun helped him collect his discarded weapons and the odd couple made their exit from the chaotic scene of death.

Chapter 18

Badiraguato, Sinaloa, Mexico

The mountainous terrains of Northwestern Sinaloa are streaked with poisonous shades of red, disrupting the natural beauty of the area. It's been that way from the time the Chinese first introduced opium to the western hemisphere over a century ago. The bulbs of the poppy have steadily dotted the region now called Badiraguato ever since. Rape, child abuse, domestic violence, and alcoholism are commonplace in most of the rural areas, and the entire municipality is a narco breeding ground. Notorious for grinding poverty and disrespect for human life, Badiraguato has produced multitudes of major narco players and has helped fill the ranks of the Sinaloa Cartel with vicious killers. El Chapo Guzmán was from Badiraguato, born in the small town of La Tuna.

Vásquez was born in Batopito, Badiraguato, General Acosta reflected, as his Humvee, traveling in the middle of four armed VCR-TTs, drove up one particularly steep slope. Although Ramón did not know where he was born, he suspected it was up here in the rugged *Sierra Madre Occidental* Mountains. *Or somewhere in Sinaloa,* he thought.

The entire state had always had an aura of lawless independence, going back to pre-Hispanic times. It took years after the Aztec conquest for the Spanish to finally gain a foothold in the region, and even then they were in constant conflict with the indigenous inhabitants who fiercely detested the foreigners. A culture of rebellion and anarchy flourished in Sinaloa over the centuries and the accessible coastline and isolated mountains attracted some of the worst kinds of criminals Mexico has ever known. It was here that the legendary bandit and narco saint Jesús Malverde rose to prominence and attained a cult-like following among narcos and thugs around the country.

General Acosta soon found himself staring at the thick formations of granite weaving in and out of the forest as the armored Humvee slowed snaked around his mountainous fortress of Tamoanchan. He could see the tops of several newly erected watchtowers strategically placed around the compound. Off in the distance, through a clearing in the thick vegetation, he could see the T-72 tanks conducting military exercises. The Russians had exceeded his expectations with the quality of the tanks, and he was eager to do business with them again.

They were making good progress at Tamoanchan. A new state-of-the-art computer network had been installed inside the command center, flush with a host of sophisticated software applications that communicated with the T-72s and the plethora of other recently accumulated weaponry. At the edge of the command center stood an aircraft hangar and weapons storage facility housing three MBB Bo 105 helicopters and a wide variety of machine guns, rifles, pistols, RPGs, grenade launchers, howitzers, and mortars. A military-grade barbed wire fence surrounded the entire compound and armed guards patrolled the area constantly. The new watchtowers were constructed to assist in this regard.

On the opposite side of the command center stood Mexico's biggest heroin-producing laboratory. Under the protection of Ramón's soldiers, farmers transported thousands of pounds of poppy seeds into the lab where they were transformed into high quality heroin by sophisticated narco machinery. Adjacent to the heroin lab was a recently constructed methamphetamine laboratory, the largest of its kind in the world. Ramón had hired a team of Chinese chemists to automate and fine tune various procedures as well as create new chemical processes to increase output on a massive scale.

Both the labs connected to a series of warehouses containing thousands of bricks of heroin, cocaine, marijuana, and methamphetamine. The warehouses were impeccably organized; the merchandise was neatly stacked and ordered by production date and final destination. Each brick was assigned a unique barcode and the entire inventory was tediously tracked in a high security computer system. General Acosta had invested a fortune in the operation and was starting to see dividends.

Despite his success, Ramón was displeased. The Blancornelas fiasco hurt him, just as Morelos was proving to be an asset. Shipments had inexplicably disappeared—along with large numbers of his *sicarios*. For the past several months he had been operating in emergency mode. Working with Tlaloc he devised an aggressive surveillance and assessment strategy. They had interrogated twenty-three individuals, including some of his own enforcers, to obtain information. Ramón had tortured three men himself in the last five days—with no results. And the casualties were costing him.

General Acosta shook off the troubling thoughts as the Humvee passed through the security entrance of Tamoanchan and drove up the windy paved road towards Tlaloc's residence. The old man had called him early this morning. It was urgent, he had said, and they needed to meet in person immediately. *Joder, what does he know?* Ramón wondered. He knew it was something big but could not tell from the phone call whether it was good or bad news. *He's devoid of emotion,* Ramón reflected on his master. *He's funny that way, always has been.*

The Humvee pulled into the driveway. A few minutes later, General Acosta was wandering through the museum of the palace, admiring the new artifacts Tlaloc had collected. Towards the front of the exhibition area was a well-preserved statue, carved from volcanic rock in exquisite detail, depicting a female face of two fanged serpents, flabby breasts, and pointed claws on hands and feet. She was wearing a skirt of interwoven snakes and a necklace of hands, hearts, and skulls. *Coatlicue—"The Mother of Gods."* Ramón recognized the figure immediately, though he had never seen such a pristine specimen.

Hanging on the wall, to the right of Coatlicue, was a massive circular stone stretching out twelve feet in diameter. *Probably weighs twenty-five tons*, Ramón estimated. Special lighting encompassed the stone to accentuate the incredible number of figures and symbols, arranged in perfect symmetry, etched into the basalt with superb workmanship. In the center of the stone was a macabre face with an oversized tongue sticking out, propped up by clawed eagle hands clutching human hearts. *Tonatiuh,* Ramón thought, *"The Sun God"—the large tongue represents a knife signifying the sun requires perpetual sacrifice to maintain its movement across the sky.* The face was surrounded by depictions of four other suns, encapsulated by a band with twenty different segments, signs for the twenty days of the sacred Aztec calendar.

Left of the calendar stone was a glass podium holding the head of a gruesome-looking individual carved out of jade. It had two protruding yellow fangs and large goggle ring eyes. The contours of the eyes transformed into two serpents whose heads met at the center of the face to form a nose. *Tlaloc,* Ramón reflected as a smiled formed on his lips, *"The God of Rain"—the god to whom child sacrifices were made—the children were expected to weep to bring in the rain.* He knew his master must have been pleased to acquire the piece.

"My ... new ... specimens?" a raspy voice asked in Nahuatl. Ramón stared at the wicked goggle eyes for a few more seconds before turning around to greet the crippled old man.

"Magnificent," Ramón replied in the same language. "Where did you obtain them?"

"Monterrey." He sucked in air. "Kept by ... hypocritical ... elite. ... ... Never ... mind that ... now. ... Come." Ramón nodded and followed the old cripple. The old man spoke slowly and deliberately as he hobbled out of the exhibition area, gulping air. "Recent events ... have been ... deeply ... troubling. ... ... A surge ... of misguided ... faith has ... swept through ... the region." With effort, he inhaled. "Cathedrals ... are filling ... up. ... ... Some of ... the clergy ... have been ... preaching ... nonstop against ... government ... corruption ... and ... drug ... trafficking."

Ramón had learned long ago to listen to his each and every word. The disfigured old man was, save perhaps one other individual, the most intelligent human being with whom he had ever conversed. It was Tlaloc who had gotten General Acosta to this stage. They understood each other completely. And in their souls, they shared a thirst for power that could never be quenched.

Tlaloc led Ramón into an isolated hallway and kept talking. "The enemy ... is vast ... and powerful. ... ... They have ... a stranglehold ... on this ... land and ... they will ... not ... relinquish ... their grip ... without ... a fight." He paused and sucked in deep gulps of air. "Thus to ... save our ... country ... we must ... become ... ruthless."

On the right-hand side of the hallway was an elevator. Tlaloc keyed in a code on the security panel and the two men rode down to the lowest level of the palace. Inside the elevator General Acosta studied the face of the old cripple. The narrowing of Tlaloc's eyes conveyed a deep-seated hatred that only Ramón could grasp. "Our ... own ... people ... . are ... dying!" Tlaloc's tone was icy and his breathing was more ragged than Ramón could remember. When the elevator stopped, the general followed the old man into an elaborate chamber and he laid eyes upon the corpse of a man who had been tortured beyond recognition.

"His ... name ... . was .... Javier ... Rayón ... ... Valencia," Tlaloc hissed. Tlaloc was having difficulty breathing and his voice almost seemed to have a touch of emotion, something General Acosta was unfamiliar with.

"Master Tlaloc, I've never heard of him."

The old cripple forced himself to regain composure. His lips contorted strangely and he took deep raspy, metallic breaths. "His name ... came up ... during our ... last two ... interrogations ... and he ... apparently had ... some connections ... among some ... of our ... low-level ... enforcers. ... ... We ... apprehended ... him in a ... night club ... in Culiacán ... where he ... brought in ... eleven ... prostitutes ... for our ... men." Sucking in air, Tlaloc walked over to a small desk several feet away from the body and pulled out an electronic recording device. "Listen ... to the ... interrogation ... and ... listen ... very closely."

General Acosta did as Tlaloc commanded. He listened to Javier Rayón for more than an hour, right up until Rayón's body finally gave out. When it was over Ramón was left speechless. Instinctively he knew the man's confessions were true.

"The ... priest ... has ... been ... busy," Tlaloc whispered. "His ... work ... has inspired ... more people ... than even ... I could ... imagine. ... ... And now ... Ramón, ... the time ... has finally ... come for ... us to ... send a ... message."

A whirlwind of contrasting emotions scraped through General Acosta's mind: hatred, fury, but also a brooding type of excitement. He nodded at the old cripple in solemn agreement. He had waited a long time for this moment.

Chapter 19

Catholic Monastery—Durango, Mexico

G returned to the monastery at 1:30 a.m., exhausted and famished. He'd spent the last few days in Mazatlán preventing an assassination attempt on a judge who had put away several *sicarios* from the Sinaloa Cartel. Before hitting the sack he decided to raid the kitchen. Upon entering he discovered Sister Arámbula cooking chicken *tamales* and quietly singing a sad Spanish melody from days long past. Seeing her up this late was a surprise. She turned to face him and G immediately knew something was wrong. Her eyes were red, swollen, and tear-stained. *The hell?* "Are you okay, Sister Arámbula? What's wrong?"

"Nothing, G," replied the rotund nun, forming her best smile. "Everything is okay. How many *tamales* you want? What you want to drink with them?" G took seven tamales and a quart of orange juice. But as he ate he continued questioning, and thirty minutes later she broke down. "We're having money problems, G. I first learn some of it early this month and everything this afternoon. El Padre Navarro spent all his money to help others—schools, hospitals, orphanages, and other good things. But he has spent too much. For months we pay for everything on credit. But now we have bills we cannot pay. Some banks want to take our land and buildings. What happen if we lose Esperanza de México orphanage?"

Sister Arámbula burst into a fresh wave of tears. "El Padre Navarro is confident God will help us but my faith is not strong right now. Oh, G, what we going to do? The possibility of live without the children hurt—I cannot think about it." The nun ran over to G and hugged him tightly. It was the most awkward moment he had experienced since he set foot in the monastery. Sister Arámbula had not had very good luck with men in her life; G was one of only a handful she trusted. Her father was never around when she was growing up and she had been abused by an uncle for several years as a child and young teenager. Her former husband had beat her savagely until Father Navarro had threatened him both spiritually and physically; eventually she was granted the divorce she so desperately needed.

"It'll be alright, Sister. You heard the priest. God will provide." G's appetite disappeared but he quickly disposed of the tamales for the benefit of the nun. He crawled into bed fighting a bitter lump of anxiety within his gut. *This is what I am supposed to be doing.*

G was finally coming to grips with his new life as a Red Crusader. He had even experienced inklings of serenity. He was part of God's army fighting a war on multiple fronts. Father Navarro had done great things with his establishments—a direct assault on the cartels. *Every child taken care of means one less potential sicario. Every soccer game the kids play means less opportunity to be exposed on the streets. Every school graduate combats the narco weapon of ignorance. Access to health care promotes familial and social well-being and reduces the need to resort to criminal activity. We can't be shut down.*

G slept longer than intended and when he felt the sun's rays streaming through his window he silently cursed and rolled out of bed. His thoughts of last night's conversation with Sister Arámbula returned, bringing back the feeling of uneasiness. He ate some breakfast and then headed to the gym. Much to G's amazement, his current levels of strength and conditioning now exceeded the peaks of his previous life. Every muscle in his body was shredded. A few weeks ago, he bench-pressed 410 pounds and did fifty-one pull-ups. His legs had grown so powerful he had trouble finding enough weight to squat. Before his trip to Mazatlán, Sister López timed his mile at four minutes, fifty-three seconds.

This morning, G lifted weights for two hours and did a little shadow wrestling before packing some basic provisions for a journey. He craved the outdoors and the tranquility it would surely bring; he needed time to think. He was still being tutored by Father Navarro in various academic pursuits but today, he decided, those would have to wait. Strapping on his leather backpack, G walked out of the monastery and took off on a light run.

The desert air was crisp and clean; the sun dazzled the sands and painted the mountain tops a deep dark purple. It was a good day to get out. After jogging fairly slow for the first five miles, G picked up his pace, determined to burn off the troubling emotions about the finances. He now possessed a detailed knowledge of the surrounding miles of desert and mountainous landscape. Somewhere, deep down inside his soul, was a primitive instinct to explore, discover, and conquer the unknown. It burned bright within him. On this journey, he decided, he would go further than he had ever gone before.

One hour later, G reached the magical border between desert and forest that had always amazed him. The terrain grew more rugged and the ground rose steadily upward, but he kept up the grueling pace. Today he would travel northeast and he chose to climb a mountain he had hitherto avoided because of the steep incline. Up and up he went until his body betrayed him. Halfway to the top he suddenly stopped and vomited. He retched over and over, expunging toxic weakness from his body. Stomach empty, he took off again, increasing his previous pace.

Sometime later G made it to the mountaintop, not as exhausted as he had suspected he might be. He came across an ancient deer trail weaving through the mountain range and he ran it for hours before spotting a grouse that he killed with a pistol shot through the eye. It was dusk now. He stashed the bird inside his backpack and hiked for a few more miles, eventually discovering a stream and a place of refuge alongside it. He constructed a small fire and slowly roasted the grouse in the red-hot coals while relaxing on top of some freshly fallen pine needles. The cool stream water and juicy white bird flesh revitalized both his mind and body. As darkness fell, he stoked the fire and leaned back on the slope of a white pine. Looking at the stars, he contemplated the strange new direction that his life had turned. He reached inside his sweaty t-shirt and retrieved the golden cross that had now become part of him.

The cross gleamed against the waning firelight and the pigeon-blood ruby glittered brilliantly. He knew now the truth of the priest's words: He was indeed here for a purpose. This knowledge alone had helped him purge the feelings of shame and inadequacy inflicted upon his soul. It had given him a new sense of confidence and, a new life.

Existence was still painful. Thoughts of his family would occasionally bring tears to his eyes. For a few brief agonizing moments, he wondered what his daughter would look like now and then quickly concentrated on reality. He had been given a sacred calling and he had sworn to uphold it. And uphold it he would. The fire shed its last flame and with that he fell into a heavy sleep.

He awoke at dawn, refilled his canteens, and continued his journey. The mountainous terrain slowly switched back into flat desert and a few hours later he came across some yucca plants and harvested enough of the fruit to make a decent breakfast. Although he ran slower than yesterday, he still covered a lot of ground. The scenery was noticeably different than anything near the monastery and he was encountering unfamiliar plants, trees, and rock types. The vegetation became sparser; it struck him that water could be a concern. He ran for most of the day and eventually spotted a red-tailed hawk perched upon a juniper branch near some large granite hills.

G hiked up to the juniper and discovered a pool of rainwater in one of the natural rock basins. The water was cool and clear, and he soaked himself in it for more than an hour. Afterwards, he made a small fire on top of a stone ledge and dried out his clothes. He ate venison jerky from his backpack and found a place to sleep on one particularly smooth boulder.

G woke early the next morning feeling vibrant and refreshed. He shot a couple of doves for breakfast and then arranged his belongings, refilled his canteens, and continued his journey.

Five days later, G was running through a terrain he had never encountered. Blazing rays from the sun beat down against his back and around midday he stopped to rest for a few minutes. He glanced down at his watch. It was 8:47 a.m., as it had been about two hours ago. The second hand was motionless. *Funny,* he thought, *the batteries are new*. He sat down and studied the landscape in detail. Up ahead, to the north, he noticed some purple cacti, an oddity he vaguely recollected hearing about. G concentrated for a few moments and then realized where he was: "La Zona Del Silencio"—"The Zone of Silence."

The nuns had told him stories about the unusual properties of the area. No types of television, radio, or satellite signals would work in this land; batteries seemed to lose their charge inexplicably. There were widespread reports of mutated animals and fauna.

In 1970, a missile from the White Sands Proving Base, New Mexico, inexplicably veered off course and landed in the center of La Zona, some 400 miles off target. A few years later, an upper stage from one of the Saturn boosters used on the Apollo project broke up over the very same area. Interactions with strange beings had also been reported and La Zona Del Silencio was added to the urban legend list of UFO enthusiasts and conspiracy theorists around the world. Despite its notoriety, the region received very few, in any, outside visitors and local residents avoided La Zona like the plague. But G was not interested in supernatural encounters and scientific anomalies; he was just irked his watch wasn't working and ran on.

Towards evening he killed two rabbits and found a decent camping place near a pocket of nopal cacti. He spent several hours extracting two gallons of water from the plants and then cut up a large quantity of the edible portions. The fresh water quenched his thirst and the cool green flesh went down well with the charcoaled rabbit. He was feeling much better about the money issues now—and his future as a Red Crusader. The old man was the smartest person he had ever known. God was on his side. *Things would work out.* Sometime tomorrow he would head back to the monastery. Before shooting the rabbits he had noticed some unusual cliffs and rock formations a few miles away that he wanted to explore. He would go check them out first thing tomorrow and then be on his way.

G rose early the next morning and ate the rest of the nopal. He drank the cacti water until his belly ached, topped off his canteens, and set off on a brisk pace through the sand, cholla, and ocotillo. Prior to reaching the cliffs he killed three rattlesnakes, which he stuffed in his backpack for dinner. The cliffs stretched for a few miles across the desert, glistening radiantly against the sun to reveal a vibrant spectrum of colors ranging from orange red to bone white.

G spent forty-five minutes scaling one of the peaks and was delighted to discover a series of caverns a few hundred yards off to his right. He hiked to one of the larger entrances, climbed over a few boulders, and walked into the cool darkness. Although the difference in temperature was a welcome relief from the outside sauna, the thick blackness rapidly drowned out visibility.

As G fumbled around in his backpack for a flashlight he heard a strange noise. He quickly reached for his pistol. He was too late. An infernal scream pounded against the cave walls and G felt something feral and powerful slam into his chest. Knife-like claws penetrated his pectoral muscles; he staggered backwards into the dark unknown.

The beast roared again and delivered another punishing blow to G's body; the flashlight inadvertently turned on inside the backpack. He got a good look at the demon as he felt himself fall downward into obscurity. Before blacking out, the last thought crossing his mind was of the peculiar green eyes of the mountain lion.

G woke to a pounding headache and complete darkness. For a few brief moments he had absolutely no idea where he was. But memories of the cougar quickly returned, along with ripples of pain. He examined his body and discovered a sprained ankle, bruised ribs, and the aftermath of a slight concussion. His chest had been cut up pretty good, but it didn't seem too serious. He wondered how long he had been out and how deep he had fallen into the cave—it was pitch black and he could not see two feet in front of him.

Is it night, or is it really this dark? He unstrapped the backpack and pulled the flashlight out of a side pocket, pressing upwards on the power switch with his right thumb. Nothing happened. He moved his thumb to the rim of the flashlight and cut it on jagged glass. "Son of a bitch!" *The fall must have smashed the incandescent bulb*. He threw the broken flashlight into the unknown and heard it shatter against a rock wall.

G spent the next twenty minutes scrabbling on the ground before finding a medium-sized stick. He went through his backpack and eventually dug up some matches, an extra t-shirt, and some insect repellent.

He wound the t-shirt up on the end of the stick, lightly coated it with insect repellent, and wasted three matches before the crude torch lit up.

As the small flames gave the primitive gift of visibility, G surveyed his new surroundings. Deep violet ice crystals decorated the rock walls to his left. Several very small streams of water trickled from the walls onto the cave floor. Milky-white stalactites hung from the ceiling and, in some places, draped over the stalagmites to form collections of ghostly sculptures. Lifting the torch a tad bit higher, he slowly turned to his right and then snapped his head back in astonishment. He dropped the torch; it extinguished itself upon impact. He fell to the ground in disbelief.

G sat for a few moments trying to compose himself and then relit the torch; this time it generated a more powerful flame. The scene before him was surreal—a sight so incredible he could have sworn he was dreaming.

Bricks of gold and silver neatly lined the cave walls for as far back as he could see. Ancient masks, statues, shields, breastplates, mirrors, daggers, and other items, constructed out of gold and precious stones, were carefully piled up against the arrays of stalagmites. There were stacks upon stacks of large iron chests. G walked up and down the cave floor a few times and then opened one of the iron chests. It was filled with gold ingots. Another contained a life-size head of a jaguar, forged out of pure gold. Two large, brilliant emeralds had been carefully crafted into the face of the jaguar to serve as its eyes. He discovered various other golden animals including serpents, eagles, and butterflies, inset with jade, emeralds, turquoise, and other precious stones. There was also an astonishing assortment of collars, necklaces, bracelets, bells, earrings, and other types of jewelry.

Lying against a giant stalactite brushing the floor, G saw the sword. He walked over and picked it up. The first thing he noticed was the ruby, mounted within the sword's pommel. The ruby was positioned within a gold cross—identical in color and shape to the own cross he wore around his neck.

Bizarre. I wonder what Father Navarro knows about this?

G continued to examine the ancient weapon. The sword's blade was ice-blue and in its reflection, G saw a shimmering of gold. G gently returned the sword to its original position and turned around.

Standing upright against another stalactite was a golden disk, six feet in diameter and two inches thick. In the center of the disk was a face G recognized: *Tonatiuh,* the Aztec sun god. Father Navarro had given him several lessons on the Aztec culture and their gods. His mind flashed back to Star Mountain and the priest's nonstop lecturing on the Spanish conquest.

When the conquistadors entered Tenochtitlan, fueled by exotic gifts and rumors of vast riches, they were greeted as white-skinned gods. Smelling blood, Cortés took the Aztec King Moctezuma hostage and, under threat of death, the captive king directed his citizens to assemble one of the greatest hordes of wealth in the history of mankind. However, the conquistadors were in quite a predicament. Riches beyond their wildest dreams lay at their feet but they were heavily outnumbered and trapped in a city whose inhabitants were growing more and more restless by the day. To quell the unruly Aztecs, Cortés presented a chained Moctezuma to his people and commanded him to pacify the mob. The gesture backfired.

The Aztecs finally had enough and responded by launching a barrage of stones, arrows, and javelins. Moctezuma was struck in the head and killed. The Spanish were now in a fight for their lives. In what is known to this day as "La Noche Triste"—"The Sad Night"—the conquistadors and their native allies loaded up what they could of the treasure and fought their way out of Tenochtitlan. It was a debacle. Burdened with loads of gold, the Spanish were almost wiped out;

thousands of their indigenous accomplices perished. The bulk of the treasure was never to be seen again.

Was this the lost Aztec treasure? G decided it didn't matter. Whatever it was, it would save the orphanages, hospitals, schools, and charities one hundred-fold and Father Navarro would know exactly what to do with it. He loaded some of the gold in his backpack and searched for an exit. Forty-five minutes later, in exuberant spirits, G was running through the hot desert sand at a brisk pace—sprained ankle, bruised ribs, and all.

Chapter 20

Hope of Mexico Orphanage—Durango, Mexico

It was 10:40 p.m. on a Friday night. Most of the children had been in their beds for forty minutes. Sandstorms had swept through the area, and now the sky was dark and the stars were hidden. Only the moon released her light and it was an eerie shade of blood red.

Isabel was searching for her *tortuga,* 'Poky.' She had found it one day during recess and, unbeknownst to any of the nuns or priests, decided to keep it as a pet. Poky had escaped and Isabel had snuck out to find her beloved tortoise. Isabel sighed and looked at the dormitory. She hoped none of the nuns would discover she had gone out again. Returning her gaze to acacia, sagebrush, and ocotillo, she was distracted by vehicle headlights far off in the distance. The lights puzzled her—she had never seen that much traffic on Faith Road, especially late in the evening like this. Isabel ran through one of the desert trails she knew so well to get a closer look. A few minutes later she was hiding in a patch of creosote bushes some ways off from the school building, intently watching a train of armored SUVs speed down the dusty road. All notions of Poky aside, Isabel froze in disbelief as she watched a large group of men get out of the trucks. They were dressed in military uniforms and carried big guns.

Matías Armendáriz Carrasco struggled to keep from vomiting. His face had turned chalky white; he was sweating profusely. *This is unbelievable.* He snorted the last of his cocaine, foolishly hoping it would calm his nerves. He had been going through the white lady like there was no tomorrow and now he was paying for it. At first he thought the assignment must have been some sort of joke. Now, as he saw the orphanage only a few hundred yards away, he knew it was for real.

Just a few days ago he received an invitation to join one of General Acosta's elite squad units and he had jumped at the chance. In his one-year career with the military, Armendáriz had done some pretty bad things—rewarded with money, drugs, and women. Not an incredible amount, just enough to whet the appetite of an ambitious young soldier trying to erase the stain of being raised in abysmal poverty in the gutters of Guadalajara. Ramón himself had spoken directly to Armendáriz, commended him for his exploits, and promised him a bright future. The evening upon receiving the invitation he partied for forty-eight hours nonstop and went on the biggest cocaine binge of his life. It was when he learned what he was expected to do for the initiation rite that he started to lose it.

None of the other recruits seemed fazed by the task, however; most were openly joking about their mission and the brightness of the future. Like Armendáriz, the other recruits came from abject poverty. Almost all low-level narcos did. In a country with limited job opportunities, widespread poverty, and ubiquitous government corruption, it seemed like one of the only viable options for a decent life. Many of the Mexican narcos still had a set of morals which they adhered to; most had never taken human life. General Acosta was not interested in these individuals.

A young soldier named Rodolfo Marroquín Villanueva stood

next to Armendáriz. Marroquín was currently suffering from a brutal headache and desperately craving another heroin fix. He lit up a cocaine-laced marijuana joint and took a long, deep drag, hoping it would relieve the pain. Blue teardrop tattoos streamed down his face, symbolizing his prized status as a killer. At age fifteen he killed an entire family in their sleep as the result of a botched robbery and he was apprehended three days after the act. Prison life suited him well and there he was introduced to Ramón's network. Mexican laws prohibit prison sentences longer than seven years for minors, regardless of the nature or number of the crimes committed, and Marroquín was released at age twenty-two. After murdering the family of a troublesome news reporter, and this time getting away with it, the young killer was accepted into the military and stationed in a position under the command of General Acosta.

Among the new recruits, General Acosta's status had reached mythical proportions. Rumor had it that General Huerta once had him trapped—caught dead to rights; intending to have Ramón watch his family dissolve in acid. Acosta single-handedly blew Huerta's entire army to hell and then slowly dissected Huerta's body over the span of a week. The narco soldiers understood that all roads to wealth and glory went through General Ramón Acosta, and tonight was the opportunity of a lifetime. Now, on the verge of making it big time, Marroquín and the rest of the narco recruits stared at the general with awe and reverence.

General Acosta was well aware of his reputation and the power he carried over the soldiers. Right now, however, his thoughts were centered on the demons of his past. He felt both a strange exhilaration and long-suppressed hatred. Twenty years had passed since he last set foot here and the time had finally come to fulfill the vow he made as a teenager. Bitter memories surfaced as he stared at the orphanage and he allowed those memories to work himself into a wicked delirium.

The old man had both humiliated and bested him and now he would finally get the revenge he longed for. He looked back at the recruits. Though young and inexperienced, tonight they would prove their loyalty and bolster his army. Unexpectedly, Ramón thought of the deaths of Mónica and Rene. And then he thought of his other son—the one in the orphanage. His hatred exploded. General Acosta took one more loathing look at the golden crosses adorning the red brick schoolhouse and then cocked his AK-47. "*Joder.* Let's go."

Armendáriz forced himself to recognize the command. His cousin, Miguel Espinoza Piaggio, was a member of Ramón's upper echelon and on a few occasions, when they had been high on cocaine, Espinoza told him incredible stories—unbelievable, bizarre accounts of kidnappings, tortures, murders, and human sacrifice—modern re-enactments of ancient Aztec rituals. Armendáriz did not believe him at the time, really had never believed him. But as he processed the reality of what was happening, his unbelief faded. He gathered himself enough to take fifteen steps before bending over and puking. Some of the other men laughed but were quickly told to shut up and spread out. The operation was ready to commence.

Armendáriz felt even worse after vomiting and desperately tried to regain his composure. He tightened his grip on the rifle and marched forward into alignment. Midway between the main building and trucks, his clammy hands dropped the AK-47.

"*¡Carajo!*" He swore loudly and only took comfort in knowing he was spread out far enough from the others as to remain unseen. Before collecting his weapon, he stared at the looming crosses reflecting a strange glow against the red moon. Armendáriz reflected on his own childhood and his time at the orphanage in Hermosillo. The nuns and priests had always been kind to him and he knew he only had himself to blame for the life he had chosen.

It was while his hands rummaged through the dirt near some creosote bushes that he saw the small girl. The child stared at him in terror. *She looks just like my cousin,* thought Armendáriz. He went over to the girl and knelt beside her. "Look at me sweetheart. Something very, very bad is gonna happen here. You understand?" Isabel looked at the gun Armendáriz was carrying and, eyes filling with tears, slowly nodded her head. "Okay, now listen. In a few minutes you're gonna hear gunshots—loud booming noises. You stay right here in these bushes till you hear the guns. When the first shot is fired I want you to run as fast as you can."

Isabel's body was rigid. Armendáriz reached out with both hands and shook her. "Run to the mountains! As fast as you can! And run till you can't run anymore and then keep going! Do you understand? *¿Entiendes?"* Isabel did not reply and Armendáriz slapped her across the face. It woke her up. Tears streamed down her cheeks. Isabel nodded her trembling head. Armendáriz stood up with his assault rifle and slowly walked towards the buildings.

Isabel was sobbing hysterically when she heard the gunfire. The thunderous noise jolted her into action and she decided to do what the soldier told her. She ran like she had never run before. It was also the gunfire that sent Armendáriz into action. He threw down his weapon, made the sign of the cross, and ran like hell into the unknown desert.

Father Navarro was inside his office reading from the Gospel of Matthew. Sister López and Sister Arámbula had taken the Escalade and departed on a religious retreat earlier in the day. He had not seen G for over a week. He could sense something. Coils of darkness. Something very evil. It had been deeply troubling him and he had been unable to figure out exactly what it was. *Ominously reminiscent of the time before my wife and children...* When the priest heard the gunfire, he sprang up from his desk in a rush of alarm. Taking his first step forward, the door opened and five armed men slowly entered his room. They were followed by an old, crippled man with a gruesome, disfigured face. It was a face the priest knew. It was a face that haunted him during his darkest hours. And it was a face he had known since childhood.

Tlaloc spoke first. "Greetings ... brother. ... It has ... been a ... long time."

Hearing the raspy voice again brought back intensely painful memories. The priest's eyes narrowed and he gave a very slight nod of his head. It had been close to thirty years since he had last seen his younger brother. He had spent nights on end weeping and praying for his sibling. But it was all for naught. Father Navarro knew that any goodness his brother ever possessed had been purged from his soul, long before they had gone their separate ways.

It was now too late to wonder why, to beg his brother to return to the fold, to ask the questions that had plagued him for years. His brother possessed one of the keenest intellects he had ever known. He could have been a tremendous force for good. He could have gone on to accomplish great things. Instead, he had become a tool of the Adversary. He had become Evil and now posed one of the biggest threats Mexico has ever faced.

Father Navarro took a few steps backward and Tlaloc carefully studied his movement. His elder sibling still had the limp—the only trait they had ever shared. The throaty, disturbing voice continued to speak. "You have ... been busy ... brother." Nostrils flaring, he inhaled deeply. "Your ... accomplishments ... ... have far ... surpassed ... anything that ... even I ... could have ... imagined." Tlaloc's rage was growing with each passing moment. It was this man, his older brother, who had caused him so such torment and humiliation. He hated him. He had always hated him. He hated him for who he was, everything that he stood for, and everything which he had done. Tlaloc walked slowly over to his brother and glared into the deep-set, jet-black eyes. His grating tone hardened sinisterly. "But you ... could not ... leave well ... enough ... alone and ... now ... everyone ... you ... know will ... suffer ... for it."

Father Navarro's voice was deep, booming, and icy. "This is between you and me, Victor. Leave the others out of it."

Tlaloc coughed and then laughed wickedly. "The ... others ... are ... already ... dead." He gulped air. "Go ... ahead ... Colonel." Colonel Vásquez stepped forward and hit the old priest on the jaw with the butt of his assault rifle. It was a powerful, stunning blow and it knocked Father Navarro out instantly. "Take him ... with us," Tlaloc hissed to the other enforcers. "And then ... burn it ... down. ... ... All ... of ... it."

G's spirits were soaring as he made his way down the mountains into the familiar valley he now claimed as home. The sheer size and value of the treasure was unfathomable to him. Multitudes of new orphanages, food banks, homeless shelters, research centers, hospitals, and schools could be built. Father Navarro's dreams would come to fruition. G was nearing the rolling scrubland when he sensed it. Then he heard the noise. In a flash he drew his pistol and went to the ground. It took a few more seconds to register that the noise was human—the sobbing of a small child. G quickly holstered the pistol and ran towards the crying, voicing offers of assistance. It took a few minutes for the child to recognize who the man was.

"G!" sobbed Isabel. She burst forward from a pile of rocks, ran to G, and latched onto his leg with surprising strength.

Coming across the child at this time and in this place was a shock. "Isabel, what are you doing here?" G asked in a bewildered voice. "What happened?" Slowly, tearfully, and painfully, Isabel proceeded to tell the story. As the girl spoke, a morbid combination of fear, dread, and rage slowly started to resonate in G's soul. He shed his backpack and dropped it at Isabel's feet. "Stay here. There is some food and water in the pack. Someone will come back for you shortly." And he took off at full speed towards the orphanage.

G's worst suspicions were confirmed when he saw the unnatural patterns of gray smoke rising into the sky. Panic set in. Lungs burning, he forced onwards.

Upon reaching the orphanage he slowed down, fell to his knees, and screamed. The entire site had been reduced to a smoldering wreck of charred brick, rubble, and ashes. The majestic golden crosses that had ornamented the rooftop of the schoolhouse lay on the ground in a deformed pile of unrecognizable metal.

Fighting back the pain and horror, G rose to his feet and walked over to the destruction. Tears raced down his scarred face as he surveyed the damage. Just then he heard some commotion from the remains of the gymnasium. He drew both pistols and walked over to the main entrance. The steel-plated doors leading inside were scorched black but still stood upright. G smashed down both doors with one kick.

Sister Arámbula was kneeling down on the remnants of the gym floor, hands folded up towards the heavens. She was wailing in agony. Sister López was there also. Her eyes were puffed out and scarlet red. She was sobbing as hard as her friend and was in the process of covering a small body with a wool blanket. The lifeless bodies of other children lay neatly stacked against the partially standing west wall. The nuns had returned from the retreat just two hours ago.

Upon G's entrance, both women ran to him and clung onto his body. The inhumanity and evilness of the deed shocked them all. It was an unfathomable hell—much worse than anything they could have imagined. The sisters were incapable of speaking. G gently brushed the nuns aside, walked over to the body of the child that Sister López had just covered, and knelt on the floor. He slowly pulled back the top portion of the blanket and discovered the angelic face of one of the young girls that he knew—the one who wanted blue eyes. Her face was frozen in a terrified look of desperate pleading.

G broke down and wept. Memories of all the children he had known flooded into his mind, followed by his own wife and daughter. G cried until tears burned skin and agony turned to rage. After some time, when he finally composed himself, G stood up and faced the nuns. "We must go to the monastery." His voice was deathly quiet and void of emotion.

The monastery had been destroyed as thoroughly as the orphanage, and all the buildings had been turned into heaps of smoking rubble, burned beyond all recognition. Only the cathedral remained partially intact, yet it too had been incinerated, damaged without hope of reparation. The regal oak door serving so long as the church's entrance was now ashes and G and the nuns slowly walked unhindered into the wreckage. Anguish and torment swelled inside the souls of the nuns and a dark violent rage blazed within G. Streaks of blood painted the blackened wooden pews and corpses of nuns and priests were scattered throughout the rubble. Near what had once been the pulpit where Father Navarro gave his sermons was the body of Felipe the dwarf, a smile etched eternally upon his bloodied face.

G stared at the dwarf for a minute, still trying to come to grips with what had happened. *They rounded them all up, brought them into the cathedral, and butchered them.* Sister López and Sister Arámbula cried out in agony, made the sign of the cross, and fell to the floor. G, silently and stoically, went about collecting the bodies of the deceased nuns and priests as had been done with the orphans.

But where is Father Navarro? He searched the cathedral diligently for some time and then scoured the ruins of the other buildings and all surrounding areas. The body of the old priest was nowhere to be found. A few hours later G returned to the church and silently knelt beside the two nuns, still as the statue of Miguel Hidalgo that once rose prominently upwards in the courtyard.

More than three torturous hours crept by; the silence that flooded the air was deafening. It was G who first heard the faint noise of human footsteps. Without moving, his eye rotated up to the last piece of stained glass remaining intact. The glass portrayed an image of Saint Peter kneeling down in front of the Savior. In the image, G made out the reflection of a man dressed in military camouflage raising his hands.

Instantly, G's right hand reached down for his trusted bowie knife. And in one wickedly fluid motion, G's body turned towards the stranger and he whipped his right arm forward. The knife sailed through the air like a missile and penetrated through the man's left hand. The jagged steel weapon, piercing through mangled flesh, landed squarely in the center of a charred painting of the Virgin Mary, sinking itself deep into the remains of the adobe wall. The stranger was trapped and he let out a bellowing shriek of pain. It was followed by screams from the two sisters.

Without a word G walked over to the pinned man, grabbed him by the throat, and slammed him against the wall. G's eye had turned a bright shade of scarlet, bulging out unnaturally. Small bubbles of pink saliva frothed out of his lips. Adrenaline pulsated through his body at anomalous levels, giving him the strength to lift the man off his feet. The two nuns screamed louder at the shock of seeing G in such a frenzied state; both women rushed over and begged him to let the man down. Sister López reached up to grab G's arm with both hands and pulled it with all her might. It had no effect. It was Sister Arámbula who finally broke through. "G," she said peacefully and calmly, "he try to tell us something."

Forcing himself to relax, G slowly lowered the man and pulled the knife out of the wall. The man screamed again as G ripped the knife out of his hand. Blood spurted everywhere and Sister Arámbula quickly tore off a piece of cloth from her black habit and wrapped it around the hand to stop the bleeding. It took thirty minutes for the man to regain some control of his voice. He put together whatever was left of his courage and forced himself to look at the terrifying man with the eye patch. "I know who did this," he squeaked. "They came for an aged priest and a boy."

The story Armendáriz told was too incredible to be false. G listened intently and then questioned the man in detail for several minutes. He soaked up every piece of information that could be weaned from Armendáriz and let it imprint on his brain. Exhausting all avenues of questioning, G spoke to the sisters. "We are in danger. Get in the Escalade and drive straight through the desert and up and over the red-colored bluff a few miles southwest of here." Both the nuns knew the area he was talking about. "I will meet you there in two hours. Now go!"

The sisters stared at G for a few moments but then quickly gathered their wits and obeyed. G spoke directly to Armendáriz, "You are coming with me. If you cannot keep up, then I will kill you." G ran out of the cathedral and the panicked Armendáriz chased after him. Fifteen minutes later, the former narco soldier collapsed on the desert sands. G ran back to him; Armendáriz closed his eyes and prepared for death. G threw him a canteen. "Stay here. I'll be back for you."

One hour and forty-five minutes later, G arrived at the Escalade carrying Isabel across his shoulders. Armendáriz was lagging behind him. G told the nuns to get into the back seat and then gently placed the sobbing girl between them. He instructed Armendáriz to climb into the passenger's seat and he took over as driver.

Dawn was just breaking when they reached the Jarabo ranch. Isabel had curled up into a ball and was fast asleep. Both sisters carried her out of the vehicle and to the front door of the main house. Bursting into fresh sets of tears, the nuns were greeted by *Señora* Aracely Jarabo.

G, however, did not follow them. He got out of the vehicle and hooked up one of the Jarabo's horse trailers to the back end of the Escalade. Armendáriz stepped out of the truck and circled around G to see what he was doing. G briefly glanced over his way and snarled. "Get back in the truck and stay there!" G then walked into the horse stable and came out leading Blanca to the trailer. The horse neighed loudly as she walked up the ramp, causing the nuns to rush back outside. Screaming, they ran towards G.

"What are you doing?" shrieked Sister López. "Where are you going?"

G ignored her and walked to the front door of the vehicle. Sister López had gone down to her knees and was clutching at his ankles. Sister Arámbula wrapped both her arms around his waist to form a tight bear hug. With a gentle force, G freed himself and climbed into the front seat of the truck. He rolled down the window a few inches. "I'll be back in a few days." He floored the accelerator and only Armendáriz looked back to see the nuns chasing them.

Chapter 21

Tamoanchan—Sinaloa, Mexico

It was 8:00 a.m. on a foggy Sunday morning. Bellowing rings from the cathedral's massive silver bell echoed throughout the compound. Eleven narco guards were dead, their bodies strewn across the mountainside. All had died silently and all had been slain by the same blade. A sleeping Rodolfo Marroquín Villalobos manned a watchtower off in the distance. Marroquín had murdered the most children at the orphanage; he was rewarded with three prostitutes, stacks of cash, and ten grams of heroin. After the massacre, he went off on the customary binge and was still suffering from the aftermath.

Marroquín painfully lifted his jaw and looked out once again at General Acosta's latest prize—a T-90A tank acquired via a deal with the Russian mob. The T-90 represented the latest advances in Russian military armed vehicle technology. It was equipped with a 2A46M 125mm smoothbore tank gun capable of firing a variety of ammunition including 9M119M Refleks anti-tank guided missiles, was powered by an 830 hp engine, and featured next-generation explosive armor on its hull and turret. General Acosta was immensely proud of his new toy.

Six men surrounded the tank, outfitted in traditional Mexican military camouflage and armed with AK-47s and AR-15s. All were still fairly high and drunk from last night's partying. Four of them had participated in the latest sacrificial ritual exactly one week earlier; the other two were new initiates involved in the massacre at the orphanage. The men were discussing the female victim of the death ritual—the new members expressing desire and enthusiasm to be present at the next event.

"Hey Ramírez, toss me another cigarette, *cabrón,*" a narco soldier named Rivera exclaimed boisterously, amidst the chiming of the bell. As Ramírez fumbled through his jacket he noticed a strange apparition emerge from the fog and cross onto the training field. His snake-like eyes narrowed as he focused in on what seemed to be a farmer peasant riding a pale horse. The man was wearing a red poncho and a wide-brimmed *sombrero.* The horse was pulling a cart of recently harvested opium poppies. A chilling emotion billowed within Ramírez. But the sight was not that unusual. Hundreds of farmer peasants would show up at the gate of the compound to sell their crops. Nevertheless, they were not supposed to be allowed inside. Ramírez watched the horseman slowly march forward for several seconds before informing the others.

"What the hell do you think that old *puto* bastard is doing here?" asked Ramírez.

All the men turned to see what Ramírez was talking about. The horse continued to trot forward, directly towards them.

"The stupid *pinche puto pendejo baboso* must have gotten lost," answered a particularly brutish thug named De la Vega. "Want me to shoot him?"

"Then we have to move the *chingado* cart ourselves," answered Rivera, "you stupid *pinche* dumb-ass. Let him move the cart—then you can shoot him. And then you can screw his horse."

The narcos burst out in laughter, all except Ramírez. He remained silent as he tried to decipher the strange sensation that was now devouring him. And as the pale horse continued to trot forward, each of the others felt the sensation as well. When the horse came to within thirty yards of the tank, all laughter ceased. The atmosphere turned ominous. The chiming of the silver bell was now haunting. Dark currents of electricity surged through the air.

The soldiers were now able to visualize the details of the farmer's appearance and they did not like what they saw. The poncho was streaked lucidly with crimson blood. A patch covered one eye on the man's face and the bright red scars accentuated an underlying rage that none of them had ever witnessed. The hardened gaze of his single steel-blue eye introduced the first tremors of genuine fear. The men gripped their weapons tighter. Rivera finally broke the silence. "Hey *cabrón!* Where do you think you are going?"

The response was instantaneous and chilling. "In that tank."

In one single moment, the accumulation of their evil deeds came back to crucify each one of the narco soldiers. Ramírez finally identified the crippling sensation. It was the premonition of death. And it was his turn to die. Four of them had enough instinct to level their assault rifles. But it was too late. Two pistols appeared almost magically into G's hands. It was fast. Inhumanly fast. Six shots fired, three from each pistol. All six soldiers crumpled to the ground, each of them bleeding from a single bullet hole in the center of their forehead. G dismounted from the mare, ripped off her harness, and slapped her backside. The pale horse galloped back into the forest and G walked on unfazed and slipped into the tank.

The gunfire brought Marroquín out of his slumber. It took a few seconds to process what had happened. Six lifeless bodies lay on the training field in thick pools of blood near the T-90. A man wearing a red poncho had just entered the tank and a pale-white horse was racing across the training field. His eyes fiercely dilated for a few precious seconds before opening fire. He fired round after round and despairingly watched the .50 caliber bullets bounce off the tank's armor. He continued to fire as he watched the tank's turret rotate and the main gun rise and take aim. It was then that the faces of the screaming orphans flooded into his mind. Right before a Refleks missile exploded into his body, pulverizing him.

Some 400 yards away, upon hearing the gunfire, Armendáriz detonated the military grade C-4 plastic explosives that had been strategically placed around the watchtowers, power grids, and radio masts. A group of armed soldiers hurried out of the command center. It was not an intelligent decision. G took command of the tank's PKMT 7.62mm coaxial machine gun and squeezed the trigger—mowing the soldiers down like grass.

He then jumped into the driver's seat, turned the vehicle 120 degrees counterclockwise, and slammed the gas pedal with his right foot. Fifteen seconds later, at maximum speed, the tank crashed head-on into the heroin laboratory, spewing chunks of brick and concrete in all directions. The tank's speed remained constant as it plowed through workbenches, demolished expensive machinery, and splashed acetic anhydride and chloroform everywhere.

When the T-90 bull-dozed through the opposite wall, flames had taken root across the main processing center, engulfing the entire building. G continued to floor the accelerator and smashed into the side of the meth lab. The tank splattered plastic drums of acetone, anhydrous ammonia, and sulfuric acid across the facility and the flames from the heroin lab quickly spread to wreak havoc upon General Acosta's expensive investment capital. The tank eventually rocketed out of the other side of the meth lab and, after steering the T-90 clear of the fire, G took control of the main gun. A few moments later he had annihilated a warehouse and, shortly afterwards, another one. He fired again and again until every warehouse in sight erupted into fiery infernos and smoke clouded his vision. His teeth clenched down in rage and a primordial battle cry burst from his lips.

G was positioning the turret to fire on the command center when an explosion rocked the T-90 and sent him sprawling onto the metal floor. He got up immediately, peered through the gun scope, and cursed. Five tanks were bearing down on him fast. Another missile smashed into the armor of the tank and G braced himself and made for the driver's seat. He floored the accelerator, swerved the vehicle to the right and felt another missile collide with the Kontakt-5 explosive-reactive armor lining the sides of the battle tank. A few seconds later the T-90 was again at full speed and heading towards the security fence on the easternmost perimeter of the compound.

By the time G smashed into the military fence, the T-90 had sustained a number of direct hits. Several track treads had been damaged and slowed him down considerably. His facial muscles formed a contorted grimace and he clenched his teeth down so hard he tore a ligament in his jaw.

The five tanks were still on his tail and picking up speed. All thoughts of his duty as a protector were gone, replaced by an obsession to destroy the enemy. And if he died in the process, then so be it. In complete battle mode, fueled by his desire to win, G continued to accelerate down the mountainside. He was fifty some yards away from a road when an armor-piercing discarding sabot projectile hit just above his left track and took the T-90 down to almost half its full speed capacity. After demolishing a large pine tree, G brought the tank to an ugly stop and rushed to man the main gun. The turret swung around fast and he fired three Refleks missiles into the lead tank. For a brief instant G watched the enemy T-72 burst into fire before feeling another blast that rocked the T-90 hard. Instinct told him his own vehicle had just about endured its maximum punishment; at any instant he could be blown to hell.

By destroying the lead tank, G had gained a few seconds of precious time, and he barreled down the winding road in the semi-functional tank as fast as it would go. He had gone about a quarter of a mile when he abruptly did a 180 degree turn and went to man the turret. It was here he would make his stand. The remaining four T-72s had all reached the road and were rapidly approaching; the T-90 would be in their firing sights within seconds. Eye boring into the crosshairs, G locked onto his target and took a deep breath. He squeezed the trigger. He fired again and again and again until he was dangerously short on missiles. Out of breath, he stared in anticipation through the periscope. His target was not a tank. It was a massive stone ledge embedded in the mountainside a few hundred yards above the road.

The shots rang true. The expert placement of the missiles dislodged a huge granite deposit composing the overhanging ledge, triggering an avalanche that obliterated everything in its path. For a few seconds, G watched a series of huge boulders pulverize the four tanks. He breathed deeply and performed a brief inventory of his own assets. The T-90 was severely damaged but functional. The machine gun was working; so was the main gun. And he had three remaining missiles.

Colonel Héctor Vásquez was stationed in the main communication quarters at the command center, bellowing profanities into the radio. A short time ago he spilled coffee over his enormous chest and took out his anger on the radio controller, pistol-whipping him repeatedly. When the controller crumpled unconsciously to the floor, Vásquez crushed his windpipe with his left hand. The colonel was teetering on the verge of insanity. General Acosta had entrusted him with command of the compound while on some spiritual retreat with Tlaloc, and Vásquez knew full well of the pending consequences should Tamoanchan fall.

None of his tank commanders were responding. The intercom systems were offline. All the IT and communication personnel were very nervous; none of them knew what was happening and when Sergeant Portillo asked, Vásquez shot him through the mouth, dropping him instantly. A dozen troops rushed into the room upon hearing the pistol shot and were greeted with violent, threat-laced orders from a crazed, blood-splattered Colonel Vásquez to get to the choppers. The troops scurried off and a few minutes later were inside the aircrafts when the T-90 crashed through the security fence once again and crept up onto the training field towards the command center.

The rotors of the choppers were just starting to swing into full speed when the pilots and gunners saw the tank. Even from the long distance, they could see the turret rotate into position. A split second later the southern helicopter was destroyed by a 9M119M Refleks projectile. The gunner in the remaining chopper hastily fired off an AGM-114 Hellfire missile but it fell wide. In response, a second Refleks missile from the T-90 pounded the remaining helicopter into oblivion and set the entire air hangar ablaze. Swinging the turret to the left, G fired the last missile directly into the command center. He then got back into the driver's seat and punched the tank onward at top speed.

The tank slammed into the steel and concrete wall and penetrated thirty yards into the command center before grinding to a halt. On initial impact, G had taken control of the coaxial 12.7mm Kord Heavy machine gun and was now taking down every man in sight. Upon clearing the immediate vicinity, he quickly made for the driver's hatch and jumped out of the tank. Dozens of bloodied bodies were strewn across the room amid the mess of concrete fragments, smashed communication equipment, and other debris. The wall to his far left was lined with an array of machine guns and seeing a M60, G ran to the wall, holstered his pistols, and seized control of the massive weapon.

Dozens of olive-green steel ammunition cases lay near the stockpile of machine guns, and G quickly pulled out three belts of 7.62mm

NATO cartridges and wrapped two of them around his chest in a crisscross pattern. He was interrupted by a deafening explosion that slammed him against the wall and onto the floor. Pain registered into his brain as he rose and he looked downwards and behind him to discover a cluster of shrapnel had hit his right hamstring. He looked back at the tank. They had obliterated it.

Wincing, G managed to remove several of the larger pieces of metal from the bloody flesh of his leg muscle. His eardrums, slightly damaged by the blast, were still functional enough to pick up the sound of footsteps coming from beyond the remnants of the concrete wall the T-90 had punctured. Forcing his mind to block out the pain, his fingers loaded the third ammunition belt into the machine gun. Out of habit, his muscles flexed as he prepared for battle.

Twelve narco soldiers moved forward into the disaster area. Four were armed with rocket-propelled grenade launchers. G took these men out first. The shots from the M60 were expertly timed and placed. By the time the eight other men discerned the origin of the gunfire, G was running for cover behind the smoldering remains of the tank. Gunshots trailed his footsteps and he felt a searing pain in both his left calf muscle and upper right arm as bullets drilled in and out of his skin and the edge of his flesh. He dove hard and fast behind the fragmented metal and came up firing between a large rupture in a sheet of the tank's armor. The dismantled heap of metal served as an ideal shield and in less than fifteen seconds he picked off the remaining soldiers one by one. Blood was gushing from his wounds and he swiftly cut strips of cloth from his poncho and bandaged the worst of it.

Fueled by adrenaline, he walked over to the fresh corpses and collected the rocket-propelled grenade launchers. They were Russian made RPG-29s and he fired off two rockets towards a pair of fuel tanks near the adjacent air hangar. Thunder deafened the air and massive billows of fire erupted from the hangar and streaked through the toxic ground soaked with the spillage of broken gas pipes and combustible material. G watched the flames dance to the middle of the command center and then fired off the two remaining RPGs towards the swarm of soldiers fleeing the blazing inferno. Clamping down on the M60, G adjusted the cartridge belts around his chest. He then rushed into his fiery, nightmarish hell.

Another four narco soldiers appeared from behind a burning computer server rack and the M60 cut them down like rag dolls. Flames raged on across the rubble, concrete, and melting communications equipment as G went from room to room, hunting his prey. Blood, flesh, and mutilated bodies covered the ground and were being consumed by sporadic volleys of fire. G scoured the entire complex and killed nine more men before feeling reasonably confident that he had destroyed the enemy. Pain returned with a vengeance and the obscene levels of adrenaline pounding through his bloodstream started to subside.

And it was then he felt the murderous blow to the back of his head.

G sensed his body crash into the concrete floor while hopelessly watching the M60 free itself from his hands. His head bounced up from the impact just in time to see a metal pipe racing towards his face. It was only a primitive, spiritual-like impulse that allowed him to avoid the deadly thrust. As his eye gazed towards this new adversary, he snarled savagely, trying to erase the numbness in his mind. And, though the fiendish face staring back at him possessed charred flesh covered in blood, he recognized the owner. It was a face etched into his soul for eternity. It belonged to the monster who had tortured him: Vásquez.

All G's pain departed. The cloud in his brain vanished. Replacing it was a deep, hellish fury only a few men have ever known. Before Vásquez could strike again, G was up on his feet—left hand clenched in a steel-like fist; right hand wrapped around a razor-sharp bowie knife. Vásquez swung the copper pipe, directly towards G's head, with an incredible force. G slightly ducked before the moment of impact and the pipe shattered a computer monitor a foot behind him. He sprung up hard with the knife and launched it towards the giant thug's gut. Vásquez came back fast. Before the blade could penetrate flesh, the pipe slammed into G's forearms; he dropped the knife. But the strength behind the blow moved Vásquez off balance and G's forehead snapped forward and crushed the colonel's jaw. G's left hand struck out cobra-like, clasping his adversary's wrist while his right fist pounded the inside of Vásquez's elbow, forcing the colonel to relinquish the copper weapon.

The narco giant roared. He countered with a vicious left hook that landed solidly against the top of G's right ear and sent him sprawling once again to the concrete floor. Vásquez followed the punch with a violent right kick that hit nothing but air as G rebounded from the fall like a panther. G was now on his toes, circling his opponent warily. Vásquez threw a wild right hook. G blocked the punch with his left forearm and threw a wicked straight right that smashed into his enemy's nose. He followed the strike with a flurry of body shots; they slammed into Vásquez's midsection, bruising his ribs and liver. The colonel let out a guttural scream and responded with a head butt that pounded against the left side of G's head, directly on the temple.

G felt himself go lightheaded and desperately put up his arms in defense. As Vásquez went in for the kill, G lowered levels and, going on instinct, shot in hard for a double-leg takedown. But the narco colonel sprawled surprisingly fast and jammed in a right-handed guillotine from a front head-lock position. The guillotine was tight and Vásquez, sensing victory, squeezed savagely. He looked up to see fires raging amidst the myriad bloody corpses of his fallen men and he focused his entire wrath on this mysterious demon who had come from nowhere to unleash hell.

G fought fiendishly to relieve the deadly pressure with both hands.

The lock was too tight. He tried everything he knew to counter the murderous choke hold and failed. Precious seconds passed, accumulating into minutes. G started to slip into unconsciousness when he saw the orange blaze flare to his left.

Fighting back the darkness, G pivoted on his left foot, planted his right toes, and drove Vásquez back—directly into the oncoming flames. The colonel screamed and finally relinquished his death grip. Both men caught on fire and G felt the flesh on his left arm sizzle. He saw the remnants of his poncho light up but quickly stripped off the burning cotton with minimal damage.

Vásquez was not so lucky. The skin on his back and shoulders started to melt and his hair emitted a strange combination of luminescent smoke and embers. He let out a brutish cry and it was at that instant he recognized his one-eyed enemy. His pupils dilated freakishly. His melting skin quivered.

"¡Pinche gringo culero!"

The colonel came at his nemesis in a fury. G was ready for him. His right fist rocketed forward, knocking out two of the enemy's teeth. G followed the monstrous strike with a brutal combination of punches that sent the big man reeling backwards. Vásquez, breathing heavy now, snarled bestially and lunged forward with his own takedown attempt. G countered with an expert sprawl. His right forearm smashed into the narco's left trapezoidal muscle and he slammed Vásquez's head down towards the concrete.

G rapidly circled around and went in for a choke hold. Vásquez slipped out of it and came to his feet. With the deranged eyes of a lunatic, Vásquez came at G in a mad bull rush. Leveraging the big man's momentum and, with impeccable skill and balance, G positioned himself for an arm-throw. Generating an awesome amount of torque and force, he threw the narco colonel across his left shoulder and Vásquez crashed down onto a slab of fallen concrete. For several seconds, before he collected the machine gun, G stood still as he gazed upon the splintered iron rebar that pieced through the giant's chest and jutted out of his rib cage. There was an utter look of terror and disbelief within the narco bastard's eyes.

Colonel Héctor Vásquez desperately tried to move his arms and legs. He was unsuccessful. He stared at the scenery around him and realized he had finally entered hell. He knew it had been coming—the murders, tortures, and rapes would eventually catch up to him. He just didn't envision it would be like this. His own soldiers were there, too. Their lifeless bodies were everywhere and they were being eaten up by demonic bursts of fire.

And now he was staring at the devil himself. It was the most frightening creature he had ever seen—worse than anything he could have ever imagined. It had one single eye and the flames of hell blazed behind it. The eye was set in a hardened face streaked with glowing scars. Its red clothes were shredded to pieces, exposing a chiseled body and pair of intensely muscular arms gripping a wicked-looking machine gun. And, to mock him, the devil wore a golden cross attached to a chain around its neck. Vásquez focused in on the strange metal cross. It was stained with blood, pierced through its heart to reveal a peculiar color of red. He watched the cross intently as the devil picked up a bowie knife and ran on, leaving him alone to burn in the flames attacking his immobile body.

G limped out of the burning command center and looked towards the palace—the only edifice in the vicinity remaining unscathed. Pain returned. Brutally. Wincing, he renewed his determination to endure. He had lost a lot of blood and spent a few minutes redoing his crude bandages. The task was difficult. His forearms had swollen up like balloons and his leg muscles were cramping.

He forced himself onwards and commenced the hike to the mansion. He was about halfway up when he saw movement to his right.

Making the air sing, the M60 swung around and then G held up. It was Blanca and she was galloping towards him. He greeted the horse warmly and mounted her. She trotted straight up to the mysterious palace, right to the main front doors. G dismounted the mare and obliterated the doors with the machine gun.

The inside of the building was silent and impregnated by a dark aura, a deeply disturbing presence of evil. Macabre statues and figurines of ancient Aztec gods were everywhere. For thirty-five minutes he searched for the boy and the priest on the first floor of the mansion and discovered no one. Eventually, however, he came across an elevator, protected with some kind of security system. He pressed a few buttons on the outside panel. Nothing happened. He pressed a few more buttons and obtained the same results. G swore, lifted the machine gun and decimated the security panel. The elevator opened. G stepped inside, pressed the single down button and went to the lower level of the narco palace.

Proceeding cautiously, the M60 held tightly against his naked, blood-soaked shoulder, he slowly advanced down the corridor and opened the first door he came to. Inside, in a spacious room filled with food, water, and toys, was Jacob. He was sitting down on a bed cradling a jaguar cub. Although the boy's face was puffy, red, and tear-stained, he appeared unharmed.

"G!" the boy sobbed.

My God, he's still alive.

Jacob let go of the jaguar cub, rushed over to G, and latched onto his leg.

"Where is Father Navarro?" G asked.

Jacob responded by running out of the room and down the length of the corridor. His small fists pounded on a securely locked, thick steel door. G rushed over to the boy.

"Get behind me Jacob!"

Jacob obeyed and G annihilated the door's lock with seven rounds from the M60. Machine gun leveled, G entered what could only be described as a torture chamber.

On the far end of the chamber was a huge wooden inverted cross. And the brutally tortured body of Father Navarro was hanging upside down from it. An iron stake, covered in dried blood, protruded from the top of the vertical beam. It pierced through the centers of both the priest's feet, right foot overlaying the left. Another set of iron stakes were drilled through his wrists into the horizontal beam. G tossed the M60 aside and scrambled to the cross, delicately removing the sharp metal from Father Navarro's feet and wrists while helping him down.

G examined the body of the ancient priest and checked his vitals. The old man was alive—barely. He was unconscious, probably in a coma. Pink frothy saliva coated his lips. He was having difficulty breathing. His skin, where not covered in blood, was a deathly shade of yellow. G gently gathered the priest in his arms and, together with Jacob, removed him from the evil place.

Sister López and Sister Arámbula had not slept since the massacre. They spent Saturday and Sunday inside the ranch house with Aracely Jarabo and her daughter Adela, reading from the Bible, praying, and sobbing. Isabel, still in a state of emotional shock, asked the nuns a few times where G had gone. They ignored her questioning. After G left the ranch, Alfonso had gone to inform the upper level clergy of the mass murders. A volunteer team was dispatched, led by Alfonzo and Ignacio, to collect the bodies and make the necessary funeral arrangements.

It was shortly after midnight when Sister Arámbula, finally, fell asleep. It was only for a few minutes. At 12:38 a.m. she was wakened by a screaming Isabel informing her that the Cadillac Escalade just pulled into the driveway. Members of the Jarabo family were also wakened. Sister López dropped her Bible and everyone in the house raced outside after Isabel. Armendáriz jumped out of the driver's seat. Simultaneously, Sister Arámbula rushed over to the passenger side of the SUV, opened the front door of the vehicle, and pulled a sobbing Jacob, cradling the jaguar cub, into her arms.

"We need a doctor, now!" Armendáriz shouted frantically. "And I need help!" Aracely ran into the house to make phone calls. Everyone else followed Armendáriz to the back of the SUV. The horse trailer was still attached and Ignacio rushed to unload Blanca. Alfonzo quickly unhitched the trailer and Armendáriz opened the back door of the Escalade to reveal G: bloodied, battered, ashen and holding the seemingly lifeless body of Father Navarro. The nuns screamed.

"He's still alive," croaked G. "Help me."

Alfonzo scrambled to take the priest from the rapidly deteriorating G. Gingerly cradling the priest in his arms, and with the support of his sons, Alfonzo strode into the house. G rolled out of the vehicle, onto his feet. Sister López clung to him. He followed the Jarabos for twenty yards, the nun at his side, before slowing down, stopping, and passing out on the dirt.

Dr. César Fuentes examined Father Navarro for fifteen minutes. He then took Alfonzo aside and declared the priest's wounds were fatal. "His internal organs are damaged beyond repair and he has lost an unfathomable amount of blood. To be honest, it's a miracle he's still alive. I don't know how much time he has left. There is really nothing more we can do at this point except ease his suffering." The words were another blow to an already-devastated Alfonzo. He thanked the doctor nonetheless and asked him to not yet say anything to the nuns.

G remained unconscious. He was hooked up to an IV and had received a liter of red blood cells. Dr. Fuentes discovered twelve pieces of jagged metal in G's right hamstring and delicately removed the flesh-tearing metal in a process lasting four hours. Bullet wounds were detected in his left calf and right tricep, along with a multitude of lacerations. He also had two broken ribs and a hairline fracture in his skull. The doctor treated the injuries the best he could.

A private funeral was held on Tuesday, lasting seven hours. Sister Arámbula and Sister López gave beautiful, though excruciating, eulogies for each and every child, as well as all the other priests, nuns, and personnel at the monastery. Isabel, weeping and whimpering, sat through most of the funeral with her head bowed and her tiny hands covering her moist face. Jacob was also present, appearing confused and stonefaced the entire service. At the Jarabo ranch, he spent every waking minute at the bedsides of G and Father Navarro. Aracely had taken the jaguar cub to an animal sanctuary in Chihuahua.

It was late Wednesday afternoon when G regained consciousness. He opened his eye to stare into the face of a wide-eyed Jacob. "How is Father Navarro?" The boy didn't respond and ran out of the room. G's eye followed the boy and then surveyed his own surroundings. He was lying on his back in a comfortable bed. He attempted to sit up and winced in pain. His legs, head, and ribcage were heavily bandaged and he seemingly had stitches everywhere. He moved his legs off the bed.

"No, No! You mustn't get up! *Por favor, por favor*, lie back down." Jacob had returned with Isabel and a thin, middle-aged man wearing steel-rimmed spectacles and carrying a medical bag. A stethoscope wrapped around the man's neck. He introduced himself as Dr. Fuentes and tried to stop G from getting out of bed. He failed.

"Where is Father Navarro?" G demanded. "I want to see him, now!"

Dr. Fuentes sighed. "Isabel and Jacob, can I talk alone with the patient for just a minute please?" The children slowly walked out of the room. The doctor turned his full attention to G. "Father Navarro is in a coma. I'm afraid he's in bad shape and has been worsening swiftly. He could pass at any moment and there is no chance of his wakening."

The doctor stared at G for a few moments and saw the deep look of pain and agony on his countenance. And a steely determination etched into his jaw. "Follow me. I'll take you to his room."

The old man lay in bed, eyes closed, hands over his heart. His leathery face had turned several shades lighter since G had seen him last. The nuns were at the priest's side and, upon seeing G, rushed over to latch onto him. G, cringing in pain, hugged both nuns and kissed each of them on the cheek. He then knelt beside the bed and reached out with both arms to clasp the old priest's right hand.

Eleven hours later, everyone at the ranch was asleep. Except G. A thick blanket of clouds had swept into the valley and a rare thunderstorm was ravaging the desert. Lightning flashed, illuminating the dark rooms inside the Jarabo home. And G felt the priest's fingers squeeze his right hand. He looked up to see Father Navarro's open eyes and grim smile.

"Thank you G. Thank you for coming to get me." The old man's voice was hoarse. Barely audible. The room became unnaturally silent. G leaned in closer until his own face was within a few inches of the priest's mouth. He felt a gentle tug around his neck as Father Navarro's fingers wrapped once more around the golden Cross of Lorraine. "You must go to El Paso," the priest said. "There you will meet Padre Quezada and you will continue with your mission."

Tears filled G's single eye. The old man coughed violently and then went on, slowly, deliberately, and with obvious effort. "G, listen to me carefully. It is essential that you look after the boy. It is in your destiny. Promise me now that you will care for Jacob." Father Navarro stared intensely at the scarred face. G's tears streamed down onto the priest's body. G softly nodded his head.

"Good," whispered the old man, thoroughly exhausted. "From this point forward he shall be called Israel. Do you understand?"

G nodded his head once again.

The priest coughed and then remained silent for several minutes. His breathing worsened. His muscles convulsed strangely. G watched Father Navarro's face religiously as the old man summoned the last bit of energy remaining within his mortal husk. "Agent Dan Kasper—you must press forward with a steadfastness in Christ, having a perfect brightness of hope, and a love of God and of all men." With his last words of wisdom, the ancient disciple then passed through the veil, on to the other side.

Part II—Prologue

It is 2010. The Mexican drug cartels are in all-out war and the levels and nature of the violence is unprecedented. Heinous acts of barbarism, never before seen in Mexico, are committed daily. Approximately 50,000 people have died. The level of government corruption is higher than ever. Entire police departments have been disbanded and startling numbers of military personnel have deserted to the cartels. Heroin, cocaine, and meth, once reserved solely for foreigners, have been effectively marketed across Mexico to create an epidemic. Addicts compose staggering percentages of city populations and drug houses known as *picaderos* plague the nation. Cartels have expanded their operations to include kidnapping, racketeering, government theft, murder, and all manner of crime.

Nowhere in the country is the bloodshed more pronounced than Ciudad Juárez. A stone's throw from the United States, Juárez has been dubbed the murder capital of the world. It is, statistically, the most dangerous city on the planet. The judicial system has collapsed and the rate of convictions is between 2 and 3 percent. Citizens have lost faith in all government officials and processes; they no longer contact police. Eighty thousand jobs have been lost within the last two years, and extortion is ubiquitous. President Felipe Calderón has deployed the Mexican Army to Juárez as a stopgap measure. The effectiveness of the military, however, is questioned. Reports of army atrocities are widespread and the motives of the troops are highly suspect. But amidst the chaos and carnage, a small band of individuals fights desperately for peace and justice...

Chapter 22

Ciudad Juárez, Chihuahua, Mexico

Yvonne Siqueiros Murguía shivered; she wrapped her jacket tighter around her petite body as she walked home from the bus stop. The air was cold and crisp in the neighborhood of Villas de Salvárcar and Yvonne was anxious to get indoors. For the last fifteen years, she had worked her fingers to the bone in the nearby SW Electronics *maquiladora,* and through the grace of God, she finally had a home of her own in a decent, though modest, neighborhood.

And, if things worked out, she thought, *I might even save enough money to put Esteban through college. Perhaps he could even go to an American school.*

Esteban, Yvonne's son, was very smart and very good at math. He'd always received accolades from his teachers and passed all his classes with the highest marks, even the honors courses. Yvonne thanked God every day that he was not using drugs or involved with the cartels and myriad gangs that had turned Juárez into a hell on earth. She glanced down again at the newspaper in her left hand, *El Diario*, and shook her head in outrage and disbelief. Another twenty-one people had been killed yesterday via three different assaults. *"The Murder Capital of the World"—that's what people are calling it now*, she reflected. It was said to be the most dangerous place on earth and Yvonne was inclined to agree with the assessment. *¡Qué carajo! What is wrong with this city?*

Things had been bad in Juárez ever since she arrived here in 1994, seven months pregnant. She had left her home state of Campeche after her abusive husband tried to end her life in a fit of drunken rage. With his bare hands he had strangled her for half a minute before she managed to kick him in the groin and smash an empty bottle of tequila across his forehead.

At the time, she had no family, no job, and no one to turn to. But it was said there was plenty of work in the northern border city of Ciudad Juárez. The rich Americans were constructing enormous factories everywhere and they preferred women workers to assemble their products. So, desperate, Yvonne packed her meager belongings. She stole a handful of cash from her unconscious husband and got on a bus to travel as far north as it would go. She arrived at her destination destitute and she hated Juárez from the first moment she laid eyes on it. The blanket of desert dust strangling the city never seemed to go away and the noxious fumes of burning trash, tires, chemicals—anything that would set ablaze—constantly made her sick to her stomach.

She survived her first few weeks on the streets begging for coins from American GIs and tourists—back then they would come to the city. Eventually, however, she met an older man who also hailed from Campeche, and he knew her long deceased uncle. The man was insane, though not violent, and he kindly let her stay in his home, an incapacitated school bus in the impoverished Granjas de Chapultepec neighborhood. Just a few weeks later she gave birth to Esteban in one of the back seats.

Yet Yvonne was a survivor. Eventually she landed a job at SW Electronics, Inc. making electrical components for modems at fifty U.S. cents per hour. She worked nights, despite her terror of traveling through the city at dark, so she could be with Esteban during the day. And with the help of a kind elderly woman in the neighborhood, willing to watch over Esteban in the afternoon, Yvonne managed to get the sleep she desperately needed.

Those were dark times as well. Young women working in the *maquiladoras* were disappearing left and right, and the femicide was notoriously putting Ciudad Juárez in the world spotlight. Despite the outcry, the killings continued and no reasonable explanation was ever offered by the government or the media. Yvonne had known four women at SW Electronics who had vanished, including one close co-worker named Ofelia. She shuddered at the thought. Not a day passed by that Yvonne did not think of her friend.

I should have left this dismal, Godforsaken city long ago. But where would I have possibly gone? She had no one to go back to in her home state and now, despite her meager salary of thirteen U.S. dollars a day, she probably could not do much better financially anyways. *But it might be safer,* she admitted.

Things had gotten bad. Real bad. Everyone was dying now, not just the young women. Three weeks ago, on her bus trip to work, Yvonne witnessed a group of men traveling in a Chevy Silverado pull up alongside a Honda Civic and attack it with assault rifles. When the SUV sped off, the corpses of both passengers in the Civic—a young man and his girlfriend—fell to the street through the shattered doors of the car in a viscous pool of blood. The expressions of the youthful couple had haunted Yvonne these past few weeks, especially in the last couple of days. But perhaps even more disturbing was the complete indifference and nonchalance of the bystanders. It was as if the murderous events had become so common that no one even cared anymore.

Yvonne shivered once again. *At least I have Esteban and he is doing well.* Esteban's future was indeed bright, and Yvonne dreamed that he would become a well-paid *científico* or *ingeniero. Perhaps he will even find a job in America and he will take me there.*

Every day, Yvonne looked across the border at the majestic skyscrapers, fine homes, and straight, paved streets of El Paso and she wondered what it would be like to live there. Three years ago, when several members of Los Aztecas threatened Esteban's life after he refused to join their gang, a kindly nun helped them secure a small home in the government-subsidized neighborhood of Villas de Salvárcar, an area somewhat shielded from the ever-growing chaos ravaging the city.

Upon moving away from the influence of the violent gangbangers, Esteban flourished. He was a jovial, good-natured boy with a natural talent for music and he made several friends at his new school, including his current girlfriend Daniela, whom Yvonne liked and thought was a good fit for her son.

Perhaps I could even become a grandmother? Yvonne wondered. Daniela came from a strong Catholic family and Yvonne did not mind that Esteban was spending a lot of time at her home. *Was he going over there again tonight*? *Ah, no*. She'd almost forgot; there was a birthday party for one of the kids in the neighborhood—Jesús Enríquez—celebrating his eighteenth birthday.

Jesús's mother worked at SW Electronics, also; virtually everyone in Villas de Salvárcar worked at the *maquiladoras*. Despite the insulation from the violence, times were tough in the neighborhood. The recession had affected the *maquiladoras* especially hard and there were layoffs. Many of Yvonne's neighbors had been evicted; there were numerous vacated houses. It was at one of these houses, just a few blocks from where Yvonne lived, that the kids were celebrating Jesús's birthday.

Yvonne had almost made it to the doorstep of her own humble abode when she first heard the loud booming noises. For the first couple of seconds she wanted to believe they were firecrackers. Reality then crushed her delusions. And the gunshots were close. Scary close. Yvonne's heart chilled as she mentally connected the origin of the gunshots to somewhere in the proximity of the party. She wailed wildly and took off running at full speed.

Yvonne was panting when she saw the group of armor-plated SUVs lining the perimeter of the house where she knew her son was at. She screamed and ran faster. She was within ten yards of an SUV when a heavily tattooed man pointed an AK-47 at her head. "Stop, *puta,* or I will blow out your brains. This is an *operativo.*" The man's voice was icy and strangely calm. Yvonne stopped in her tracks for a split second and then decided to ignore the man's warning and try and help Esteban. But just then, she saw a woman race across the street. The woman was gunned down instantly. Helpless, Yvonne froze in her spot and, as the gunfire intensified, she began to sob uncontrollably.

Ten minutes later the *sicarios* packed into the SUVs and left the neighborhood of Villas de Salvárcar in disturbingly slow fashion. Yvonne and a group of other desperate, weeping parents immediately ran into the house. Not one of them was prepared for the unbridled carnage they would find.

Bodies of teenagers were everywhere, expressions of unearthly fear and horror upon their youthful faces. Grieving parents marched through blood-soaked carpet, hoping against all odds that their children had somehow survived. These kids were not narco gangbangers; their bullet laden skins lacked the telltale tattoos of the Los Aztecas, Artistas Asesinos, or one of the other violent gangs plaguing the city.

Yvonne, not sure now if this was real or some demonic nightmare, went from room to room, searching frantically for her beloved Esteban. Finally, after searching through the aftermath of the massacre for forty minutes, but still before the arrival of the police or military, she found her son in the corner of the upstairs bedroom. He lay on the floor, holding hands tightly with his girlfriend Daniela. Each one of them had been shot at close range with a bullet to the forehead.

It was only two hours later when Sister Arámbula received the phone call from the office inside the cathedral in El Paso. Upon hearing the news, she collapsed to the floor in mind-numbing grief. Her good friend Yvonne, the woman whom she had known for years; the woman whom she had prayed for so fervently; the woman whom she had helped obtain housing and provide mental, physical, and spiritual support, had just hung herself.

Chapter 23

El Paso, Texas, USA

It was cool outside. The autumn air was crisp and a hunter's moon shone down ominously onto the back alleyway of the high school. A crowd had gathered to witness the event. Some of the onlookers would be willing participants in the activity. Others were simply bystanders too terrified to do or say anything. A few were eagerly looking on with morbid curiosity. It had happened before, just five months ago at nearby Socorro High School. The victim had an abortion, was treated for several venereal diseases, and spent months at a psychiatric hospital before resuming her education at an unnamed charter school in another part of the city.

The perpetrators were never apprehended. Instead, they were initiated into the prestigious Barrio Azteca gang. The ringleader was José Luis Elizondo, and tonight he was again leading the assault. José Luis was a shaven-headed *cholo* with a thin mustache and skinny upper body covered in tattoos. He wore black pants and a white tank-top with a thick golden chain draped around his neck. Attached to the chain was a brightly colored pendant of Santa Muerte.

José Luis was street-smart, ambitious, and one of the more heinous members of the Barrio Aztecas. He'd spent most of his teenage years in and out of juvie. On a Halloween night, at age thirteen, José Luis opened the front door of his home in the projects to see his father, drunk yet again, punch his mother across the teeth. He decided it was time. He, and his mother, had had enough. José Luis pulled out the recently stolen Beretta pistol and shot his father through the heart four times. The memory of the event still ravaged his thoughts.

His time in youth prison drained his respect for humanity. At age fifteen, when some nazi skinhead insulted his mother, he slit the bastard's throat with a shard of glass. And he got away with it. Eight months ago, he received an invitation to go to Jefferson High School in South-Central El Paso as a parolee. He took the offer and thus far avoided trouble. Or, at least, he had never been caught doing anything. Three months ago in Juárez, while hanging out with his older cousin—a member of the Los Aztecas, José Luis melted some rival gangbanger with a Smith & Wesson 686. José Luis was eager to kill again, but it was gang rape that consumed his every thought. The wait had been unbearable, and tonight he had the perfect victim.

The victim's name was Mayrín—the most beautiful girl that any male at Jefferson High School had ever laid eyes on. When approached by José Luis in the cafeteria with a crude and vile proposal, she promptly slapped him across the face and walked off, leaving the *cholo* thoroughly humiliated amidst a significant percentage of the student body. And when José Luis discovered she would be attending the homecoming dance at Ysleta High School, he immediately put together the plan.

Mayrín was a Spanish national with family in El Paso. She had been invited to participate in a student-athlete exchange program and was currently attending Jefferson High School as a senior. She was a star volleyball player as well as a highly-ranked sprinter, and she was hoping to receive scholarship offers from an American University. But tonight, her athletic dreams were gone; replaced by pure terror. She screamed once again as she stared into the hideous face of José Luis—straddled over her with a ruthless look of lust.

Israel awkwardly moved his feet to avoid being stepped on by the toes of his overly ambitious date. Yet another slow song wafted through the gymnasium—he had lost count of the exact number some time ago. He normally loved to dance. Tonight was a different story. Israel took a deep breath and prepared for the next python-like squeeze from the large girl. Feeling her plump arms wrap around his neck, he looked over at his best friend Sergio, who shot him a mischievous grin. Sergio, as usual, was with his girlfriend Lucía and, to taunt Israel, started a make-out session.

Israel's date Bárbara asked the handsome, popular athlete to accompany her to Ysleta High School's homecoming dance several weeks ago. He didn't have the heart to turn her down. Israel gently tried to place his arms around Bárbara's ample midsection, inadvertently took a whiff of perfume, and wondered how many songs this interminable dance had left. He was exhausted. After the big football game last night, he blasted out his legs in the weight room at 10:00 p.m. He then woke up at 6:00 a.m. to get in some wrestling and conditioning before spending the next ten hours in Juárez. He normally went to Juárez on Saturdays.

Today, he put in drywall for a house in a new neighborhood being built in the outskirts of the city. Drywalling was tedious and one of the least favorite of Israel's tasks. He'd participated in a range of construction jobs in the border city for a few years now and could perform basic tasks as a plumber, electrician, and carpenter. He enjoyed working with the kids the most—he coached a variety of sports teams at the youth clubs. He worked as an academic instructor as well and taught an assortment of subjects at a number of different levels. Israel himself was a straight 'A' student; the importance of education had been instilled within him since childhood, and luckily, school came easily to him—it always had.

Bárbara's fingers started to caress Israel's muscular neck and then stealthily moved to fondle his triceps muscles.

What the freak?

Israel stiffened sheepishly and glanced over at Sergio, whose grinning had morphed into open laughter. Even the normally reserved Lucía could not hide her smile. About half the attendees, however, were far too romantically involved to notice the odd spectacle. All the females in the other half were wishing they were Bárbara. And the males watching the drama respected Israel far too much to say anything, except perhaps, for some good-natured ribbing that would surely come in the locker room on Monday.

He almost single-handedly won the game last night with nineteen bone-crushing tackles. The sports writers at *El Paso Times* were saying he was the hardest-hitting linebacker to have ever come out of West Texas, and there were rumors he was interested in staying in town to attend school at the University of Texas at El Paso. He was also a three-time State Wrestling Champion, and he hadn't lost a match in over three years. But his peers respected and liked him for his humility and kindness. He was always willing to make those less fortunate feel good about themselves and he possessed an overall jovial nature. Most everyone always wanted to be around him, except, of course, when he was on the mat or on the football field. In those instances, both his friends and opponents were absolutely terrified. And, despite his many valued traits, there were other times when his intensity frightened those around him.

It was towards the finale of the painfully long song that Israel's state of awkwardness was interrupted by a pair of frantic arms trying to separate Bárbara from her date. With premature relief, Israel looked down at a pair of familiar feminine eyes covered by Kazuo Kawasaki designer glasses. He acutely observed the turquoise tortoise necklace Isabel wore at all times. The two teenagers had become foster siblings ten years ago. Isabel's narrow eyes were darting left and right.

"Israel, come with me. Now!"

Israel stood stupefied for a moment, looked at his bewildered date, and then watched Isabel take off at a full speed sprint across the dance floor. His sister turned around one more time, still running.

"Hello? Run, you idiot!"

Mayrín screamed. She lay spread eagle on the concrete next to the torn remains of her once beautiful lavender dress. Her fingernails clawed into the face of one the four *cholos* attempting to subdue her. Momentarily freeing her right leg, she kicked one of the bastards in the groin. She caught a glance of her date, roughed up by the young Barrio Aztecas. He was now standing motionless—too scared to do or say anything.

Unable to move her limbs, Mayrín spit into José Luis's face and, in return, received a vicious back-hand. The gangster's expression turned livid. "I told you you'd regret it, *pinche puta*. No one turns me down. You hear that! Nobody!" José Luis hit her again and stared wolfishly at her flawless, glossy skin and long, silky black hair tumbling onto the shoulders of her perfectly shaped figure. She was sobbing convulsively and finally seeing her so humiliated made José Luis go crazy with lust. He grinned fiendishly, reached down with both hands to rip off her pink lace bra, and felt his nose crush into his skull.

Before anyone could comprehend what was happening, Israel knocked out two of the thugs trapping Mayrín with two laser straight punches. He attacked the other gangsters in a hellish fury. Mayrín freed her limbs and sprung to her feet, desperately trying to cover herself. Isabel quickly wrapped her up in Israel's suit jacket and then hugged her. Five Barrio Aztecas now lay on the ground immobile and another came at Israel with a knife. Israel adeptly dodged the thrust and threw a wicked left hook that broke the gangster's jaw and laid him out. A dazed and weary José Luis crawled to his knees and reached inside his baggy pants for his Smith & Wesson 686 pistol.

"Israel, look out! He's got a gun!" screamed Isabel.

Before the befuddled gangster could pull the trigger, Israel's right foot shot out and knocked the gun out of his hand. Sergio scrambled to pick up the weapon as one of the larger thugs came at Israel with both fists swinging. Israel adroitly sidestepped the attack, crouched down low, and went after the gangster with a running double leg that left him flat-backed and knocked out on the concrete. The commotion was interrupted by a deafening blast from the pistol. Sergio had fired it into the night sky.

"If any one of you bastards moves the next shot will be through your gut," yelled Israel's skinny friend with as much tenacity as he could muster. Sergio stood five-feet-five-inches tall and barely weighed one hundred pounds soaking wet. Although he could not throw a punch for the life of him, holding the gun gave him confidence. Israel looked at Sergio and then over at the few Barrio Aztecas who remained standing. José Luis was just coming to his feet and glared at his new enemy with a look of murder in his dark sullen eyes. Israel ignored him.

"Isabel, call the cops," he said calmly. "And no one moves till they get here."

Isabel winked, made a clicking sound with her tongue, and pointed her right index finger at him. "Hello? I'm way ahead of you, big brother. They're on their way."

Two skinny *cholos* tried to slink off into the darkness; Sergio fired off another warning shot towards the moon. Lucía smiled at her boyfriend of two years and clung onto his right arm adoringly. Sergio attempted his best snarl. "You heard him," he growled. "No one moves!"

Despite herself, Isabel looked over at Sergio. She felt a twinge of envy as she watched Lucía wrap her arms around Sergio's waist. Isabel had had a crush on Sergio since she was ten years old.

José Luis spit out a glob of blood onto the concrete and lifted his right hand to examine his broken nose—blood was gushing from it. His venomous eyes locked onto Israel with a savage brutality and he stepped forward. "This is not over, you son of a bitch. I will kill you and I will come back for her."

Israel's lips quivered. The edges of his nostrils twitched. His narrowing dark eyes turned cold. He walked towards the vile gangster until he was within mere inches of his bloody nose. "Anytime you think you can work yourself up for it." And before the gangster could see it coming, Israel's left hand rocketed upwards. It smashed into José Luis's jaw with a force that broke it and sent the *cholo* thug crashing down onto the concrete once again. Israel rushed over to his enemy and hit him again and again and...

"Israel!" Isabel wrapped herself around her brother, desperately trying to hold him back. "It's over!"

His sister's voice brought him back to reality. With effort, he willed the rage to subside.

Israel had no tolerance whatsoever for these rapists. He believed they all deserved to be put away for a long, long time. From as early as he could remember, the importance and need to respect and care for women and children had been ingrained within him. Israel glanced over at his sister Isabel, whom he loved so much. He still remembered when Isabel destroyed some of his favorite football cards. He was ten years old at the time and was so upset he hit her on her arm so hard she cried. The priest found out about the incident—his look of disappointment still bothered Israel to this very day.

Israel quickly dismissed the memory and, as police sirens started to blare, walked over to his little sister who was still embracing Mayrín. He quickly hugged Isabel and looked into the red-eyed face of Mayrín. And did a double-take.

What the heck?

The girl was stunningly beautiful. He couldn't recall ever seeing such an attractive girl. Her velvety eyelashes fluttered to reveal a pair of dazzling green eyes that majestically contrasted against her full lips and dainty button nose. She had an hourglass figure possessing the toned definition of an athlete. Israel looked into the green eyes and felt his stomach drop. "Are, are you good-looking?" His face turned scarlet. "I mean, are you okay?"

Mayrín looked at her handsome hero and, though Israel was completely oblivious to it, her watery eyes sparkled. Ever so gently, without realizing it, she threw back her hair. "I am now," she replied. "Thank you."

She spoke perfect English, with a slight Spanish accent. It was the sweetest voice Israel had ever heard. "Don't worry about the jacket," he stammered. "You can keep it."

Mayrín wiped away a tear. "Gracias." Her lips parted to form a small smile; a strange sensation swirled within Israel's chest.

It was at that moment that the police car showed up. An officer got out of the vehicle. "Uh, well, I guess I have some splaining to do," Israel said, not taking his eyes off Mayrín. "I really do hope you are okay."

Mayrín, now feeling eerily elated despite the harrowing ordeal, smiled a little wider to reveal a set of white teeth. "I really think I am, thank you. For real." And then, without warning, she reached up to give Israel a long, hard embrace and kissed him on his cheek, strong enough to leave a perfect replica of her lips imprinted onto his skin.

Isabel, who had been watching the exchange with amusement, smiled at Mayrín as a bewildered Israel walked towards the policeman. "He likes you," she said. "I've never seen him like that around a girl."

But Mayrín was too busy staring in the direction of the police officer to hear what she said. After a few moments, however, Mayrín awoke from her stupor and smiled warmly at Isabel. "I'm so sorry," she said.

"I just got a little, um, distracted." Mayrín reached out with both her arms to delicately grasp Isabel's left wrist. She looked directly into Isabel's eyes. "Thank you so, so much. Like—how can I ever make it up to you?"

Isabel winked, made a clicking sound with her tongue, and smiled. She decided she liked this girl.

Chapter 24

Ciudad Juárez, Chihuahua, Mexico

Raúl Soto Borja-Díaz adjusted the FN Five-Seven pistol in the front of his jeans. The weapon was known as the "cop-killer" for its ability to pierce through bulletproof vests—ironic, given that Soto was a police officer. Taking a long sip of tequila, he stared once again at the scantily clad women making their rounds in the bar. Soto was a big and burly man with a full, bushy mustache and thick, black hair shagging down in the back. Born and raised in the border city, never had Soto loved Ciudad Juárez as much as he did so right now.

Juárez was a city at war and it presented him with the opportunities of a lifetime. He was good—a certifiable killer. The cartel knew it and rewarded him handsomely. Soto reached down and felt the bulge in his back pocket. Flush with never-ending cash, he kept partying harder and faster.

Soto had steadily risen through the ranks of La Línea since 2005; he was now a top commander in the organization. La Línea was the enforcement wing of the Juárez Cartel, composed almost entirely of active duty police officers. Just a few years ago, the police held the real power in the border city—before Amado Carrillo Fuentes (a.k.a. "El Señor de Los Cielos"—"The Lord of the Skies") transformed the Juárez Cartel into, perhaps, the wealthiest crime syndicate on the planet.

Carrillo Fuentes became head of the cartel in the early 1990s after arranging the death of its original founder, Rafael Aguilar Guajardo. Aguilar was a federal police commander of the National Security and Investigation Center and leveraged his position and influence to create a model drug-smuggling infrastructure. Carrillo Fuentes expanded the empire by transporting large-scale shipments of Colombian cocaine to Mexico in hollowed out cargo jets. With the people in place, on both sides of the border, he amassed billions and flooded the border city with narco cash. It was estimated that the business of *el narco* composed well over 50 percent of Juárez's economy. By 2004, the cartel had grown so powerful the police were forced to play a subservient role to the criminal organization, thus marking the birth of La Línea.

El Señor de Los Cielos was gone now—he died during a plastic surgery operation in Mexico City. Power transferred to his brother Vicente. And the Juárez Cartel was in the bloodiest turf war ever seen in Mexico with El Chapo and the Sinaloa Cartel. Just four days ago, Soto led a successful assassination in which he took out Eduardo Valdéz Jiménez, a major player for the Sinaloa narcos. Three weeks before that he led a group of enforcers in armored Chevy Silverados that ambushed an army DN-XI personnel carrier and killed eleven soldiers.

The putos bastards, Soto reflected. Everyone knew the army was working for El Chapo and Soto would kill every man in military uniform he could find. In 2008, the Mexican Army was deployed to the murderous city to restore some semblance of order. But the number of killings continued to skyrocket and the nature of the violence grew more and more barbaric. School children routinely came across severed heads. All citizens were exposed to an onslaught of bodies, hanging from telephone lines, with mutilated genitalia and bloody messages engraved on skin. All faith in any sort of justice system, besides the perverted justice of the cartel, had been lost. Widespread whispers of army atrocities circulated throughout the region but the stories were never official. Those who filed official complaints or grievances vanished under mysterious circumstances. Most people avoided both the police and military at all times.

The bartender caught Soto's attention and raised an empty glass. Soto nodded his head in acknowledgement. *"Sí, señor,"* the bartender said with wide grin, "coming right up, Sergeant Soto." He used Soto's official title of rank in the Chihuahua State Ministerial Police Department, though the lines between La Línea and the police were somewhat blurred. Until recently Soto had been a captain in the Juárez Municipal Police. He resigned his post upon discovering that all municipal police officers would be subjected to "Confidence Tests" administered by the *federales*. The "Confidence Tests" were designed to assess the honesty and reliability of the officers and included polygraphs, drug tests, and psychological evaluations. Three hundred thirty-four police officers ended up failing the tests and were summarily dismissed from the department.

For more than a decade, the wealthy Juárez Cartel had been recruiting young men from both the state and municipal police who would unquestionably do their bidding. In Soto, they found the type of man they were looking for. El Chapo's strategy to overtake Juárez hinged on infiltrating and controlling the municipal police. Sinaloa assassination units had been ordered to abduct key police officers and torture them for information. It was Soto who led the first retaliation efforts six years ago when he collected the mutilated corpses of six members of "La Gente Nueva"—"The New People"—the name of the Sinaloa Cartel in Juárez.

Soto had been involved in the narco blood bath from the beginning. In 2004, the Sinaloa Cartel executed Rodolfo Carrillo Fuentes, the brother of Vicente and Amado. Vicente went ballistic and demanded the head of El Chapo from longstanding ally, Ismael Zambada García (a.k.a. 'El Mayo'). Carrillo Fuentes was denied. In response, the kingpin of the Juárez Cartel ordered the murder El Chapo's brother, Arturo. Soto had been part of the hit squad.

Soto lifted the new glass of tequila to his lips, turned slowly to his right, and found himself staring into the ample bosom of a voluptuous brunette. The girl's eyes sparkled and she gave him a mischievous grin. "How are you doing, *guapo?*" Her tongue gently ran across her upper lip. "My name is Elena. Looking for some company, *papacito?*" The police sergeant quickly downed his beverage and studied the sultry woman carefully. She had blue eyes covered by thick, provocative eyelashes. The white of her knee-high acrylic boots seductively contrasted against the copper skin of her thighs and stomach. He was instantly aroused. He'd never been with such an attractive woman.

Soto turned his attention to the bartender: "Mario, a bottle for the road."

"*Sí Señor*, Sergeant Soto!" the bartender replied, studying Elena with a smirk.

Soto pulled out a wad of cash and left the bartender a generous tip. He grabbed the woman's hand and looked at her lustily, "Let's get out of here, *mamacita.*"

Forty-five minutes later, Elena was passionately ripping off Soto's police uniform inside a motel room. The bottle of tequila lay on the floor, mostly empty, next to the clothes dresser. To his surprise, Soto had discovered she could drink almost as heavily as he could. It was only a few moments after she pulled out the FN Five-Seven pistol from his pants that the door crashed onto the floor. Four men dressed in military fatigues burst into the room, FX-05 Xiuhcoatl assault rifles extending from their arms like bodily appendages. A half-drunk Soto went for the pistol. Elena was pointing it at his heart, a deviant smile upon her beautiful face.

A tall, sinister figure strode through the soldiers, his impressive military insignia contrasting sharply against the dank motel room. Sergeant

Soto's hands trembled; his muscles became weak; he felt an icy chill in his gut. The police officer knew this man, though he had never seen him in person: Ramón Acosta—the Mexican Secretary of Defense. Dark, disturbing rumors about the secretary abounded in La Línea and the Juárez Cartel. He was intensely feared in all quarters of the city.

Standing next to Secretary Acosta was a man standing five-feet-six-inches tall with tough, leathery skin and a jaw of granite. He possessed a thin, athletic frame, once making him a standout on the Mexican national soccer team. His silver hair was cropped short in military style and his eyes were hard and cold. Sergeant Soto knew who this man was also: General Ortiz.

Ortiz was a fifty-seven-year-old military veteran with a reputation for brutal efficiency. The man was as ruthless and intelligent as he was effective, and Secretary Acosta had given him command of all military operations in Juárez. General Ortiz displayed the faintest traces of victory on his hardened face and Secretary Acosta gave the commander a nod of commendation. Soto's body stiffened. Still smiling seductively, Elena walked over to Secretary Acosta and gave him a kiss on his lean cheek. "Greetings, Sergeant Raúl Soto Borja-Díaz." The secretary spoke in a powerful voice that was eerily calm. "We've been looking for you for some time."

Sergeant Soto awoke to the strange, ominous rhythm of beating drums. He was in handcuffs, chained to the wall of a primitive, dimly lit jail cell, and wore only a loincloth. His skin had been painted blue. As the wicked drum beat reverberated throughout the structure, Soto noticed other men inside the dwelling, semi-naked and blue-skinned. The men were silent, faces emanating an emotion Soto was intimately familiar with: fear, paralyzing fear.

The chilling music reached a feverish pitch. A door creaked open to reveal the fiery rays of an afternoon sun. Two large men entered the chamber, robed in *ichcahuipilli*—ancient Aztec armor composed of braided cotton, hardened by brine. Bright red feathers adorned the outside of one man's armor; vibrant green feathers decorated the *ichcahuipilli* of the other. Stylized eagle helmets, strikingly realistic, covered both of their heads. The red eagle warrior carried a *macuahuitl*—a sword-like weapon constructed from steely oak, lined with prismatic blades of razor sharp obsidian. The early conquistadors reported the *macuahuitl* could decapitate a horse with a single stroke.

"Who's *chingado* next?" The red eagle warrior spoke in a gruff voice. No one answered. The green eagle warrior unchained one of the men sitting closest to the door. "You! *¡Levántate cabrón!* Get the hell up!" The blue-skinned prisoner remained on the ground, petrified. A stream of dark yellow urine flowed down his leg to form a puddle on the stone floor. In a flash, the red eagle warrior swung down his *macuahuitl* towards the prisoner's head. It hacked into his left shoulder and sunk deep into his body, all the way to his gut. Bright red blood sprayed across the walls of the chamber. The green eagle warrior ignored the bloodshed and unchained the next prisoner. *"¡Levántate, hijo de puta!"* The prisoner slowly rose, hands still chained behind him, and followed the two large men into the sunlight. The door closed and a few minutes later Soto heard the faint rumblings of a roaring crowd. Twenty minutes passed before the eagle warriors re-entered the chamber and proceeded with the same process, taking another blue-skinned prisoner into the foreboding unknown.

Two hours later, Soto was the last man in the room. The entire ordeal was surreal and a sensation of dread and nervousness racked his body, mind, and soul. When the eagle warriors finally came, his hands were shaking and his legs were weak. Somehow, he found the courage to stand and follow the eagle warriors to his death. *At least let me die like a man.*

"They've all been waiting for you, Sergeant Soto, *hijo de puta,*" whispered the green eagle warrior mockingly. "Don't disappoint them."

Soto did not reply and tried to calm his growing terror. He desperately craved some heroin. *Or maybe just even a little coke,* he thought. He had always been high on some type of drugs when doing his duty as a *sicario,* and he now tried to force the agonizing desires out of his mind. *Let's just get on with it.* The overwhelming probability of an early, violent death had always been part of the lifestyle he had chosen. He had no regrets. *Women, drugs, money, I've had more than my fair share.* Still, he could not shake off the blanket of fear enshrouding him.

Soto was led through an ancient limestone corridor. Though his brain was numb, he gazed in morbid fascination at the intricate carvings and murals adorning the walls: All featured death. Depictions of Aztec warriors, donned in outfits like his captors and armed with bloody *macuahuitls,* covered the stone wall to his left. The wall on his right displayed a gruesome figure, half-man/half-beast, with an obsidian knife in one hand and a human heart in the other. Human bodies, painted in blue to honor the Aztec rain god, lay scattered at the feet of the macabre individual in the artwork. Empty red cavities were depicted on the left sides of their chests. The wicked rhythm pounded into Soto's ears with each step he took and reached a climax as the two eagle warriors led him out of the corridor and into the open air. The crowd erupted.

Soto gazed at the scene before him with shock, awe, and disbelief. He was in an ancient arena lined with myriad spectators standing up on their stone seats. In the distant background he noticed a vibrant red pyramid overlooking the arena. And directly in front of him was the most terrifying man he had ever seen.

The man was wearing jaguar skin and the beast's fanged teeth dazzled against the orange-gold rays of the afternoon sun. Bulging muscles protruded from the man's huge body to stretch his *ichcahuipilli* armor to the limits. The jaguar warrior held a *macuahuitl*, its embedded obsidian soaked with human blood. Scattered about the arena were the blue corpses of the former inmates. The green eagle warrior unlocked Soto's handcuffs and, as the red eagle warrior slid the handle of a *macuahuitl* into his hands, Soto's eyes quickly and nervously scanned the arena. Off in the distance, towards the pyramid, Secretary Ramón Acosta was seated alongside General Ortiz in the section of the arena reserved for royalty. Seated nearby, engaged in animated conversation with General Ortiz, was El Chapo.

In 2001, El Chapo had escaped from Puente Grande under mysterious circumstances. All surveillance video from the evening of his departure had vanished. And, ever since his escape, with the aid of Acosta, the drug lord had gone on a bloody rampage to take over the most valuable *plazas* in Mexico. He left a wake of carnage across Mexico and, in the process, made himself one of the most wanted men in the world.

The Sinaloa narcos were smart, vicious, and numerous but the battle for Juárez was proving to be difficult. The extent to which Vicente Carrillo Fuentes and the Juárez Cartel had infiltrated the city and its people had surprised even Secretary Acosta. El Chapo had learned just how difficult it was to uproot that infrastructure. It was not until 5,000 military troops arrived in Juárez under direct command of Secretary Acosta that El Chapo began to have his first inklings of success.

Secretary Acosta stared for a few seconds at Soto, wondering how long he would last, and then glanced at El Chapo. He envisioned gutting the narco kingpin with a *macuahuitl*. He hated the infamous drug lord, hated him with a passion. But right now he needed him, and therefore would extend El Chapo every courtesy and feign to strengthen their relationship. It was the kingpin's first time at the spectacle and he really seemed to be enjoying himself. He cheered loudly at each of the brutal victories of the jaguar warrior. The Sinaloa Cartel kingpin turned from General Ortiz and directed his attention to Secretary Acosta. "*¡Joder!* Where did you find this guy?" El Chapo asked, referring to the Aztec fighter.

"Nuevo Laredo," replied Ramón casually. Six years ago, he had taken 150 *sicarios* from the Gulf Cartel hostage. In a gladiator-style tournament, the jaguar warrior emerged as the lone survivor. The man's strength, tenacity, and ruthlessness had so impressed Ramón that the defense secretary quickly immersed him within the organization. "We call him Tehuantl," Secretary Acosta continued. "To date he has over 200 kills in events such as this. No one has come close to stopping him." Although El Chapo remained outwardly enthusiastic, the mention of Nuevo Laredo caused him to flinch. He had launched a relentless campaign against the Gulf Cartel several years ago but was eventually forced to retreat. And, though he hated to admit it, the Sinaloa Cartel might have succumbed to a similar fate in Juárez had not Secretary Acosta intervened. The stocky drug lord shook off the troublesome thoughts and watched with pleasure as Tehuantl, to the delight of the spectators, slashed his *macuahuitl* through the air.

Soto's legs wobbled as he gripped his own *macuahuitl*. He shakily stepped forward to put up a fight. The entire scene seemed like a bizarre nightmare from which he desperately hoped to wake. Somehow he managed to steady himself. Clenching the handle with both hands, he lifted the weapon above his head and swung it as hard as he could at his opponent. Tehuantl easily sidestepped the awkward attack and countered with a slight thrust that sliced open Soto's left ear and gashed his left shoulder.

Soto felt his head buzz and, although he felt no pain, saw a jet stream of blood shoot out from his wounded flesh. He looked up into the face of the jaguar warrior and felt another wave of fear. The man was smiling at him. His face was broad, painted in gold, and featured a prominent, hooked nose. His eyes were a strange shade of hazel; the sclera was streaked with red and Soto could not differentiate the pupil from the iris. His countenance reeked of death.

Somehow, Soto forced himself onward and jabbed the *macuahuitl* towards the deadly face. Laughing, Tehuantl parried the blow with the flick of his wrist and struck down with his own weapon in a quick arching motion. Soto saw half his nose drop to the ground as his own brain registered the pain. It was the pain that finally woke Soto from his frozen stupor. He howled like a wounded animal and swung the *macuahuitl* in a long, sweeping motion to his left and then to his right. The crowd cheered in response to his defiance. And, for just a split second, the hardened killer emerged from beyond his blanket of fear as his *macuahuitl* collided into that of the jaguar warrior. As his legs buckled, the police sergeant felt an icy spray of tiny obsidian daggers penetrate his face and chest. Sergeant Soto would not live to hear the clamor of the crowd when they saw his head rocket through the air in a trail of crimson blood.

Chapter 25

Ciudad Juárez, Chihuahua, Mexico

The fingers of Officer Gustavo Portolatin Alamán y Escalada were trembling. He tried to pick up a cigarette and failed. His wife Flor was shaking worse than he was but, not driving, managed to retrieve the cigarette off the floor mat. She lit it and put it between his lips. Officer Portolatin took a deep puff of the burning tobacco and blew out a cone of bluish smoke. Trying his best to appear calm, he drove the 1992 Buick station wagon past the Benito Juárez monument on Avenida Vicente Guerrero, wondering what the man behind the city's namesake would now think of this mayhem.

For more than 200 years the city had been called "Paso del Norte"—"North Pass" until, in 1888, it was renamed to honor the revered president who expelled the French from Mexico and overthrew the Second Mexican Empire. The French invasion of Mexico in 1862 had forced President Benito Juárez to flee to the northern border city while his republic forces regrouped. Eventually, in 1866, under U.S. Mexican sympathy and a growing threat from Prussia, the French left Mexico. Emperor Maximilian I of Mexico, backed by France and Napoleon III, was executed. President Juárez was seen as the great liberator of Mexico.

Officer Portolatin took another glance at the Benito Juárez monument and then looked at his three children through the rear-view mirror. Anita, the eldest, was extremely intelligent and, though only eleven years of age, had picked up on her parents' emotions even before they hurriedly grabbed their most valuable possessions and scrambled into the station wagon. The pupils in her soft brown eyes were fully dilated. She was not blinking. She had not spoken since sitting down in the station wagon. Anita's sister, Anabel, was playing with her favorite doll and quietly singing an old Spanish melody that caused her father's eyes to well up in tears. *Nine years old and the voice of an angel*, thought Officer Portolatin with choked-up pride. His five-year-old son, Alejandro, was scribbling in a Disney coloring book. Alejandro had inherited his mother's round face. He loved to play soccer. He wanted to be a police officer when he grew up, just like his father. Officer Portolatin was fiercely proud of all his children. And watching them now was shredding his very soul.

He changed lanes, made a quick right hand turn to get onto Calle 5 de Mayo and, through the corner of his eye, saw once again the strange man on the motorcycle. Officer Portolatin's right hand fingered the pistol holstered on his hip and his head whipped around backwards. No one was there. *Or am I imagining things?* Beads of sweat trickled into his eyes and he put on the brakes, wiping away the perspiration with his shirt sleeve.

It was the third time this morning that he had seen, or perhaps imagined seeing, the ghostly apparition. Fighting back hellish anxiety, he drove south down Calle 5 de Mayo and then veered to his left onto Avenida Reforma. Flor put another cigarette into his mouth and he gratefully sucked in the calming nicotine while reaching for his wife's hand. He continued driving until reaching Avenida Sanders and then took another left. A few minutes later he was staring at the bronze statue of a sober and solemn-looking policeman. The statue stood atop a cone-shaped pedestal constituting the centerpiece for the Monument to Fallen Police in Ciudad Juárez.

It was said that Sergeant Alejandro Portolatin, Gustavo's father, was the inspiration behind the statue. His name was engraved upon one of the plaques on the semi-circular wall standing in the background. "The Last Honest Cop," they had called him—"The Untouchable." He had gone down in the line of duty when Gustavo was seventeen years old. Although Officer Portolatin was unaware of the details of his father's death, he had made a vow at his funeral that he would follow in his footsteps and serve with honor. And, though he was persecuted and made an outcast within the police department, he had done so. He had lived on the edge and survived—at least so far. But the bell had finally begun to toll and the angel of death was coming for him. *And this angel,* he thought, *will also take the lives of my family.*

Three days ago, a well-groomed man in a dark business suit approached him in a coffee shop. The man introduced himself as one of the Gente Nueva and handed him a pouch of money and a list of tasks. Officer Portolatin refused to take it. And now a big part of him was regretting it. *Plata o plomo.* Take the bribe or be assassinated. He had refused bribes in the past and, through his reputation and connections, had gotten away with it. It was not until he received the ominous phone call that he finally realized the Sinaloa Cartel was an entirely different animal. He looked again at the statue of the policeman. *What would my father have done?*

The Monument to Fallen Police, inaugurated by Mayor José Reyes Ferriz in 2002, had become infamous in January 2008 when El Chapo and the Sinaloa Cartel announced their presence in Juárez with a bold and calculating message. At the monument they delivered a simple narco message written on a poster board. At the top of the poster were the words "For those who did not believe"—followed by the names of the Juárez Municipal Police officers whom they had killed. On the bottom of the poster were the words "For those who do not believe"—followed by more names of police officers—those who were next. The disturbing message struck fear through both the police department and La Línea. Every so often the "unbelievers" list was updated and early this morning, Officer Portolatin received word the list had been refreshed again. And that his name was on top of it.

Officer Portolatin had just taken his first sip of coffee when he received the telephone call. Within four minutes he was backing the station wagon out of his driveway and looking up at the humble home he would never again see. He immediately headed towards the Ysleta International Bridge to see if he could perhaps plead his case and get into El Paso. But the military had set up checkpoints on all routes to the border. Running into them would be certain death. A huge percentage of the soldiers were either members of the Sinaloa Cartel or working for them. Going south was not an option. Two years ago, checkpoints were installed in the exit routes of the city.

Officer Portolatin reflected on his dilemma. He was trapped. He had nowhere to go and no one he could trust. They would kill him and, worse, they would kill his family. His eyes watered up again and his wife inserted another cigarette. He inhaled deeply and blew out a cloud of smoke. *Think. Clear your mind.* But the only thing he could think of was to keep driving, and his gut was telling him time was limited.

Now driving east down Boulevard Municipio Libre, he looked into the rearview mirror and once again, for just a fleeting moment, could swear he saw the strange man on the motorcycle. The beads of sweat flowed stronger. His eyes darted in all directions. He took a sharp left turn down Calle Monterrey, then a quick right onto 21 de Marzo. Officer Portolatin now knew where he was going. Though agnostic, he would go to Santisimo Sacramento, the church where his father's funeral was held some fifteen years ago. The streets were empty at this hour and for just a moment he felt rays of peace burst through the chains of fear and despair. The serenity quickly evaporated as he turned the station wagon onto the street Fernando Montes de Oca.

The strange man on the motorcycle appeared out of nowhere. And this time, it was no apparition. His wife and children screamed. They saw the haunting figure also and he was coming right at them. The motorcycle moved fast, much faster than Officer Portolatin could ever imagine a machine moving. The police officer slammed on the brakes and still had his gun in the holster when the cycle's thick black tires pounded on the hood of the station wagon. The collision generated a massive spider web on the front window, spraying shards of broken glass everywhere. Through the shattered window, just before hearing the fusillade of gunfire, Officer Portolatin saw a shimmering flash of gold and silver.

What strange colors to see before we die, he pondered. His wife and children sobbed hysterically as the sounds of battle echoed throughout the neighborhood and into their station wagon. The thunderous noise pulsated into his eardrums, wreaking havoc upon his sense of hearing. The explosive chaos was over almost as soon as it had begun. As if in a nightmare, Officer Portolatin examined his own body, expecting blood and carnage. He was unharmed. In a trance, he turned his head to the right and looked upon his wife. She appeared petrified and in shock but likewise uninjured.

Simultaneously, both parents turned around to check on the children. There was no blood on the backseat. Though crying convulsively, the children were safe and healthy. Through the back window they saw two armor-plated SUVs, engines running, surrounded by a growing puddle of blood. Amidst the gray fog of gun smoke, five narco bodies were humped over on the street. In the inside of the SUVs, Officer Portolatin could see at least two more *sicarios*, tattooed bodies torn to shreds.

In relieved confusion, Officer Portolatin failed to notice the mysterious man on the motorcycle pull up to the driver's side of the station wagon. The policeman was not aware of his presence until the shrill, high-pitched scream of his wife pierced through his momentary deafness. With newfound dread, his eyes aligned with his wife's.

Officer Portolatin felt his heart try to jump out of his chest. His stomach sunk. Ice scraped through his blood. He stared into the hard, lean face of the most terrifying man he had ever seen. Black and white stubble dotted the protruding jaw of the stranger and bright red scars outlined his features, giving the man an unearthly complexion. But it was his single, steel-blue eye that frightened Officer Portolatin the most. It glistened with electric intensity. It took the policeman several dream-like seconds to confirm he really was alive, and that the man on the pale motorcycle was not some imagined ghost.

"Take this," the strange man said, handing Officer Portolatin a leather pouch. His voice was hard and deep, but surprisingly friendly. "In it you will find directions to a place where you and your family will be safe. Go there quickly. They will soon find out what happened and come for you again." The strange man revved up the motorcycle's engine. "Thank you for your honest service. Your father would be very proud." The motorcycle blasted off and the man was gone before Officer Portolatin could say a word.

In the early morning hours after midnight, the pale motorcycle emerged onto Avenida 16 de Septiembre from the street of Santos Degollado and cruised in a northwesterly direction. Verifying he was alone, G drove the cycle from the vacated parking lot of Plaza de Armas onto the now secluded grounds of the Cathedral of Our Lady of Guadalupe. For a few moments, he gazed up at the ornate towers.

Silently, G dismounted the motorcycle and unlocked an obscure entrance of the black iron fence delineating the religious complex. He pushed the machine past the two pairs of fluted columns framing the semicircular entrance arch of the cathedral. Just a few seconds later he was walking the motorcycle onto the grounds of its more ancient counterpart: The Mission of Our Lady of Guadalupe of the Meek Paso del Norte. The Franciscan mission, founded on December 8, 1659 by Fray García de San Francisco, was the first in the area and is the oldest structure in the Ciudad Juárez/El Paso metropolis. Up until 1692, it was the northern most outpost of Colonial Spain in the new world. G wheeled the motorcycle up near the bronze sculpture of Fray García and then into an aloof corner behind the ancient building.

The thick adobe walls emitted a dim, burnt-orange glow against the lobe-shaped Mexican moon. For just a split second, a section of adobe collapsed into darkness as G walked the motorcycle into the back of the edifice. Immediately, the missing section of adobe re-appeared as if nothing had happened. In a secluded chamber in the mission, behind the log staircase near the choir loft, G wrapped his right arm around a hand carved oak beam. He pressed his right index finger against a metallic button inside one of the intricate floral designs. A section of the flagstone floor gave way and G, both hands gripping the motorcycle, descended into a more modernized construction of steel and concrete. The makeshift elevator traveled one hundred feet downwards before coming to a halt. The motorcycle's engine growled into the cool air of the soundproof tunnel and it sprung forward onto the black asphalt lining the ground.

Only a handful of people knew of the existence of this particular border tunnel, and it was far more advanced than any of the narco tunnels that had proliferated in the last few decades. It was constructed inside the mammoth cavern system deep underneath the El Paso/Juárez metropolis. Though rivaling the caverns of nearby Carlsbad, New Mexico in both size and scope, the subterranean labyrinth remained hidden to most of the outside world.

The paved street lining the largest natural tunnel was secretly created in 1927 in response to the Cristero War by a number of concerned Red Crusaders from around the globe. With its construction, desperately needed war supplies flowed freely into Mexico through El Paso apart from the oppressive eye of President Plutarco Elías Calles's anti-clerical government. On June 27, 1929, after the deaths of more than 90,000 people, including 30,000 Cristeros, a truce was established and the bells on Mexican cathedrals rung once again. The anti-clerical "Calles Laws" remained on the books, though not enforced, until 1992, in which the constitution was finally amended.

The engine of the motorcycle rumbled and the twin throttle body blades opened as G accelerated the vehicle up to sixty miles per hour. He thoroughly enjoyed riding the machine. It had been built to his exact specifications seven years ago and over time, Alma, his mechanic, had made numerous ehancements. G unconsciously nodded his head in admiration.

Alma was good. Damn good. She was also a former Air Force engineer. She came with G to mass every Sunday, despite being a self-proclaimed atheist. When Alma was sixteen, her mother discovered her with another girl. Much to the devastation of her younger brother, she was kicked out of the home in El Paso. Alma moved in with her girlfriend and, partly for the money and partly to spite her parents, worked as a topless dancer in Juárez for two years before enlisting in the U.S. military.

In 2002, G rescued her little brother from a hit squad in Chihuahua City and, despite his initial reluctance, she had been bound and determined to help him in whatever he needed. Alma had a master's degree in mechanical engineering from the University of Texas, and G soon recognized her skill set as well as her brilliance. She worked with him on a variety of projects, but the motorcycle was by far her favorite. It was G's also.

The machine had an 8.3 liter, ten-cylinder, 90 degrees v-type engine that could produce 500 horsepower @ 5600 rpm. Alma claimed its top speed was well over 300 mph and G believed her, though he had never traveled that fast. He'd gotten it close to 190 mph once, up near the White Sands Missile Range in New Mexico, right before the U.S. Army spotted him, forcing his high-speed return to El Paso. The vehicle had two front and two rear wheels, each wheel separated by a few inches. The four wheels were necessary to handle the engine's power: It could reach sixty miles per hour in less than two seconds. Projecting from the middle of the two front wheels was the barrel of a Browning .50 caliber machine gun operated through a customized button panel on the handlebars of the cycle. The motorcycle was designed using a monocoque construction and its body was originally made from billet aluminum, which Alma plated with several composite layers of titanium and depleted uranium armor. Alma called it the "pale hog." G referred to the motorcycle as the "white chopper."

It only took a few minutes for G to reach the opposite end of the tunnel. He slowed down the white chopper and pushed it into a freight elevator, like the one he had used on the Mexican side of the tunnel. He pressed a green button on the operating panel and the elevator slowly ascended out of the tunnel and into a large hidden chamber inside the Ysleta Mission Church. There were three people anxiously waiting for him inside the chamber. One was Alma, dressed in her typical jeans, black t-shirt, and leather motorcycle jacket. A smile played across her lips as she visually inspected the pale hog and decided it was unharmed.

"Mi mamacita," she purred, stroking the right side of the armor-plated gas tank.

A set of high-resolution computer monitors were situated on the north wall of the chamber and, directly underneath one of the larger screens, feverishly typing away on a keyboard, was Matías Armendáriz. Armendáriz was wearing a tank-top and baggy jeans. His head was shaven and his arms, chest, neck, and face were covered in fierce-looking tattoos. He spun around in the swivel chair, looked at G, and nodded. Armendáriz's loyalty had never wavered over the years; his contribution to the war had been invaluable. He had numerous connections within all the cartels and was willing to do whatever was necessary to help G and to help the cause. Determined to make amends for his former life, Armendáriz worked relentlessly to obtain intelligence.

G also discovered Armendáriz had a sharp mind and was very adept at working with computer hardware and software. Although G himself hated the vile machines, he encouraged Armendáriz to extend his talents and the former narco became the administrator of their sophisticated computer network. He had installed an extensive complex of clandestine cameras and sensors throughout Juárez and had written data mining software to scour through the plethora of license places and facial features of the suspected enemy. At the turn of the century, the cartels began to employ the use of information technology to broadcast torture and murder across the internet. To help counter the effort, Armendáriz began to dabble in the dark arts of computer science. He was now established hacker and his skills had provided the necessary intelligence to help save numerous lives.

Standing near Alma was a man who stood five-feet-two-inches tall and weighed well over 300 pounds. He was dressed in faded blue jeans and a navy blue Notre Dame football jersey. A baseball cap embroidered with the golden letters "Fighting Irish"' covered his mop of gray hair. He tipped the lid of his cap and grinned boyishly. G parked the motorcycle inside a small garage within the secret room and took off his grease-stained gloves and dusty black leather jacket.

"Hello, Padre Quezada."

"Hello, Father G."

Chapter 26

Ysleta High School—El Paso, Texas, USA

Israel, using his left hand, swiftly pulled back his opponent's right arm as if combing his own hair. He quickly changed levels and penetrated with his right leg and arm to attempt a high-crotch takedown. As his opponent reacted to the attack, he masterfully changed directions and went in for a sweep-single on the other leg. In the split second that his knees touched the mat, Israel wrapped his right forearm around his opponent's left ankle, rapidly hauling the leg to his chest. Simultaneously, he gripped the left ankle with his left hand and reached out with his right arm to grab his opponent's lower right leg. Squeezing the legs together, he drove forward hard on his toes to secure the takedown. It was explosive, perfectly executed, and the first time in his life that Israel had taken the priest down. The priest, dressed in solid black shorts and a gray t-shirt, slowly got up to his feet.

"Impressive. Very nice, Israel. You are definitely improving."

Israel smiled with obvious pride. His confidence was boosting daily now. Yesterday he did forty-three pull-ups, a new record for him—only ten less than the priest. "Thanks, G. I mean, Father G," he replied boisterously. He was still getting used to the "Father" part.

Israel was setting up for another takedown when Father G dove in onto his own foot with incredible speed and took Israel down with an ankle pick. The priest then proceeded to pummel Israel over the course of the next hour, as usual. But Israel wrestled hard and he wrestled aggressive, every single second. At one point, he got in a deep gut wrench on Father G and almost, though not quite, came close to turning him. And he also came close to getting another takedown with an underarm-hook/leg-trip combination.

"Well done Israel," Father G said, after they finished wrestling and prepared to do green berets and other conditioning exercises. *The boy has come a long way.* Just a few years ago, during his freshman year in high school, the priest had taken him to participate in a competitive open tournament with collegiate wrestlers. Israel had never lost a match in his life and Father G had felt he was getting just a little too big for his britches. In his first match, Israel came out onto the mat terrified. He was just fifteen years old and his opponent was a twenty-one-year-old NCAA All-American out of Arizona State. Israel lost the match, his first loss ever, by technical fall in the first period. Father G had been disappointed and scolded him after the match, not because he lost but because he allowed himself to succumb to fear.

"It's okay to lose, Israel," the priest had told him. "If you give it everything you have. But it's never okay to be intimidated. You lost the match before it even started. You may get physically dominated, but you can never be afraid of your opponent. If you show courage and give it all you got, that is everything anyone can ever ask of you. Throughout your life you will run into opponents who are bigger than you, stronger than you, and faster than you. Those factors are out of your control. But whether they are tougher, well, that's up to you." It was a harsh lesson but an important one, and Israel took it to heart.

The pair trained until 6:00 a.m. and then showered. Israel went to Bible study and Father G to Juárez. Although the morning workouts were intense, Israel was used to them; he had been wrestling and working out with the priest for more than ten years. Today was Monday and after Bible study he would go to school. Saturday mornings they would wrestle for thirty minutes and then train in various hand-to-hand combat situations, knife fighting, and even fencing. Afterwards, they would swing by to pick up Isabel and go to Juárez to work on the housing projects or help the kids at the youth centers. Sunday was the only day the two did not work out.

Father G had progressively increased the intensity of Israel's workouts every year. Israel could still remember the morning of his fourteenth birthday in the mountains of New Mexico. He had been excited. Father G had told him they would do a little birthday run and then go fishing. Isabel was there too, along with their black lab. Isabel usually went on all the outings with Father G and her foster brother. She had developed a unique bond with Israel and they shared each other's dreams and secrets. Nothing was off limits except for the massacre at the orphanage—the one thing never discussed.

Upon their arrival in El Paso, Israel and Isabel were both official adopted by Santiago and Rosa Quezada. Santiago was the elder brother of Padre Quezada and there was no one the priest trusted more. He and his wife were both decent folk with big hearts; they tried their best to provide the children a loving home. But the couple was advanced in years and both had health problems. Padre Quezada checked up on the family regularly and Father G stepped in as the eccentric uncle, providing both children an avenue to pursue their more adventurous interests.

Isabel was kind of ambivalent to the fishing stuff and she preferred reading romance novels to physical training, but she loved the outdoors and she loved to spend time with the priest, Israel, and the black lab whom she had named Poky. Israel loved to fish. The priest took the siblings often. Fishing was probably Israel's favorite past time. Father G had taken him hunting once, when he was twelve, and he had shot a doe deer. But the boy was devastated upon seeing the face of the animal he killed.

They had gotten in the mountains early for the birthday celebration and Father G picked out a steep slope by the lake. "Okay, Israel. There are some nice rainbow trout down there just waiting for us to catch. We just have to do a little conditioning and we can fish for the rest of the day."

"No problem," Israel had replied.

Father G did a little stretching and lined up at the base of the slope. "Alright," the priest said, "full speed and keep up with me." Father G took off up the mountain. Israel followed him, as well as the exuberant Poky. They ran hard, further up than Israel had expected, and when Father G finally stopped, Israel was out of breath and Poky was panting. Father G immediately turned around and jogged back down to the base of the mountain. Israel and the dog followed him. After five sprints, Poky quit and went to the lake for a drink before joining Isabel who was picking some Indian Blanket flowers in the nearby meadow. After ten sprints, Israel thought he was reaching his physical limits and he mustered up enough courage to ask the priest how many they were running.

"Fifty," Father G had answered. At first, Israel didn't believe him. His lungs were burning and his legs were blistering with pain. *What the heck? No one can actually run that many*, Israel had thought, *not at this freaking speed*. But after twenty sprints, as Israel thought he surely must be on the verge of death, he started to suspect the priest was telling the truth. With his hands on his knees, gasping for air, Israel had asked what happened if they couldn't do it.

"Then we die trying," the priest replied. And the hardened look on his face had told Israel that he was dead serious. But in the end, though never believing his body could take such punishment, Israel had made it. Just like he always did. "Happy Birthday, Israel," Father G had told him, as they both lay down in the meadow near Isabel. "Your body is capable of much more than your mind believes. You must train your mind to correct such defective thinking."

There were twenty-three students inside the classroom in the Ysleta Mission Church, the first and oldest mission established in the state of Texas and the second oldest continuously operated parish within the United States. In 1680, in what is now called New Mexico, a group of Pueblo Indian tribes revolted against the Spanish and drove about 2,000 Spanish settlers, as well as a number of more assimilated Indian tribes, out of the region. One of the fleeing Indian peoples that followed the Spanish was the Tigua tribe. The Tiguas followed the Spanish southward and eventually settled in El Paso del Norte, just north of the Rio Grande. In 1682, the Tigua people built a permanent church in the area—the Ysleta Mission Church.

Israel had attended the early morning classes since he was twelve, Isabel as well. Other regular attendees included Israel's friend Sergio and the black lab Poky. Despite being an avowed atheist, though the priests suspected she was agnostic, Alma sometimes attended the classes also. Today was one of those days. She was sitting in the back of the class, dressed in black leather embroidered with Harley-Davidson logos, legs stretched across her desk. She was browsing through a copy of *Easyriders*.

"Buenos Días," said the round priest, entering the classroom with a smile and tray of *pan dulce*. He nodded suspiciously at Alma and his eyes homed in on the magazine. Two years ago, he caught her with a "Playboy" while he was preaching from Galatians. The aftermath of the event had been the most talked-about topic among the students for the next year. Padre Quezada also carried in a pitcher of orange juice and a good-sized bone for Poky. At this early hour, despite objections

from his higher-ups, the priest was not dressed in his clerical clothing, instead wearing gray sweat pants and a navy blue hoodie of his beloved alma mater, Notre Dame.

All in all, he had spent twelve years at the university before receiving a Ph.D. in theology, despite struggling with dyslexia. At age fifteen, his high school counselor told his parents that he would never graduate from high school, much less college, and would be better off dropping out. But Padre Quezada was a scrapper—always had been. After a stern and solemn discussion with his father, he took his studying up a few notches. With the help of a supportive nun who made the diagnosis, he received a library of textbooks with special fonts enabling him to distinguish Latin characters.

Padre Quezada was born and raised in El Paso. His paternal grandparents migrated to Juárez from Villahermosa sixty years ago. His own father had been born in Juárez and spent the first seven years of his life in one of the more poverty-stricken *colonias* before his grandfather obtained a green card to work in El Paso at ASARCO, the copper smelting and refining company. Padre Quezada thoroughly understood the culture, landscape, and politics of the region, on both sides of the border. He had made it his mission in life to better the conditions for the people he served, especially in Juárez. The destruction and madness ravaging the city over the course of the last two decades had been harrowing. When his little sister Daniela disappeared while partying across the border in 1994, it nearly destroyed him.

Shortly after the loss of his sister, Padre Quezada became a Red Crusader. Tackling the violence and corruption had become personal. When Father Navarro approached with the offer, he eagerly accepted. He was more than willing to devote his life to the protection of his beloved country and people. He became fascinated with the origins of the ancient sect and within a few years had developed a knowledge and breadth of the order that rivaled Father Navarro's.

Padre Quezada had worked tirelessly and obsessively during the infamous Juárez femicide. He had photos of more than 300 of the missing girls and women up in his office, with detailed notes on the circumstances of their disappearances. He had spent thousands of hours interviewing and consoling grieving family members and had organized over 200 *rastreos* (combings of the desert badlands and garbage dumps in a cumulative effort that combines forensics, political activism, and a search for psychological healing). And this was before the drug wars. Before the violence was to escalate tenfold and make the Mexican border city the murder capital of the world. But the priest had attained some level of peace with his efforts. In general, he enjoyed working with the Mexican people and their propensity for hospitality and kindness. He especially loved working with the youth and knew that it was this generation of his people that could perhaps, under the right circumstances, turn things around.

The hefty priest took a swig of coffee and walked over to the corner of the room, picking up his Great Highland bagpipe. During his time at Notre Dame, he had become infatuated with the legendary Celtic instrument and had become quite an accomplished musician. For a few months he had been practicing 'The Foggy Dew' and while the students munched on their *pan dulce*, he played the tune masterfully. The class gave a tremendous applause for his effort and Alma demanded an encore. The priest simply smiled and grabbed a piece of sweet bread.

"*Híjole*, tomorrow," he said with a smile. Then came the daily joke. "What kind of car does Jesus drive?"

Normally, Isabel answered the punchline before Padre Quezada could deliver it. This one had her stumped.

"A Christler!" the priest answered himself, roaring in laughter. "Get it?"

The class moaned at the lame joke while the round priest laughed for another fifteen seconds.

"Isabel," Padre Quezada said with a chunk of *pan dulce* in his mouth. "Please tell us your favorite story of Christ in the Bible."

Isabel thought for a moment and then made a clicking sound with her tongue. "It's from the Gospel of Luke, I think. I believe it's somewhere in the end of the book. Anyways, Jesus had just returned from the Garden of Gethsemane. Well, Jesus suffered incredibly in the Garden. In fact, I think the Bible tells us that he was bleeding like sweat was coming from every one of his pores. I wonder if that is really true?"

Isabel, looking inquisitive, caressed the turquoise tortoise attached to her necklace, and then continued before anyone could answer. "Anyways, the Romans had come for Jesus to take him away to his death. But some of his disciples fought back. Peter, the Bible says, took a sword and cut off a soldier's ear. But Jesus told his disciples not to fight back. And, despite just having suffered so much and now knowing he was going to his death, Jesus reached out and healed the man's ear." Tears filled Isabel's eyes and she wiped them away with one of the napkins next to the *pan dulce.*

"Thank you very much, Isabel," said Padre Quezada. "That is one of my favorite stories also. Israel, would you like to share one of your favorite stories of Christ?"

Israel remained silent, casually nibbling on the sweet bread and staring off into the stained-glass window of the Virgin of Guadalupe.

"Ahem," the priest cleared his throat. "Israel?" *Híjole, the boy has been distracted lately,* he thought. And Padre Quezada did not know why. Normally he listened to his every word. The round priest knew the boy was kind and had a good heart. Despite the rigorous physical training, Padre Quezada knew Father G had taken extreme precautions to make Israel understand the importance of following Christ. They had taught him for years that no amount of victories on the mat or tackles on the football field could compensate for spiritual and moral failure.

Israel quickly turned around. *What the freak?* "Yes Padre?"

The priest slowly shook his head with mock disappointment. "Israel, who is the mother of our Lord and Savior?"

"Mayrín," he replied instantly.

The class burst out in laughter. Padre Quezada studied Israel carefully. The boy's face reddened. He had not seen the girl since the night of the homecoming dance, ten days ago. But she was all he thought about. "I mean Mary," he stammered.

The priest just shook his head and joined in the laughter. *¡Ay, caramba! Who in the world is Mayrín?*

"Anyways," said Padre Quezada, "one of my favorite stories of Jesus is found in the Gospel of John. The scribes and Pharisees, looking to trap our Savior, brought unto him a woman accused of adultery. Now students, though incomprehensible to us in this day, remember that for over a thousand years the practice of stoning adulterers had been common among the Israelites. But what did Jesus say to the scribes and Pharisees? 'Let he who is without sin cast the first stone.' The mercy and symbolism behind the simple phrase is astounding. Christ was about love. He was about giving people second chances. He sought to promote the best within all of us."

It was 6:00 p.m. Football practice had ended at 5:30 p.m. and Israel was alone in the weight room performing triceps extensions. He grunted loudly, as if to alleviate the pain, and completed the final repetition. He turned to face the barbells and froze in astonishment.

What the heck?

It was Mayrín. She appeared just like the inerasable memory in his mind, except her hair was different; her eyes were no longer red and tear-stained. She was wearing black jeans and a modest white blouse.

And lookin' all mind-blowing beautiful.

"What are you doing here?" Israel asked, face reddening.

Mayrín just laughed. "Well, I wanted to like, see you again and they told me I might find you here." She hesitated momentarily. "Um, if that is alright with you?"

"Yes," Israel blurted out, way too fast. "Uh-huh, I mean, of course it's alright—just surprised to see you, is all. You doing okay?"

Mayrín casually studied Israel's sweat soaked gray t-shirt. She stared at his bulging biceps and abdominal muscles, the t-shirt revealing the outline of a solid six-pack. "I'm doing fine, thanks to you. Um, but, well, I'd be doing totally better if we were chatting over dinner."

It took a few seconds for Israel to register what she saying and his eyes widened.

What the heck?

"Are you asking me out?" he replied awkwardly. "I mean, yes I would love to make out with you." *Freak.* "I mean go out to dinner with you."

Mayrín smiled fully, revealing more white teeth. "Great. Go take a shower and we'll go."

"You mean tonight?" he asked, genuinely surprised. "Now? For real?"

"Yeah—why not? I'm totally hungry. Why wait?"

Israel thought for a moment. "Well, I still need to finish my workout and then drive Isabel home. She's waiting for me in the lobby doing her homework and our parents will be expecting us for dinner."

The girl gently laughed at him. "Isabel already drove home. She said she would smooth things over with your parents."

On Israel's sixteenth birthday Father G had given him a 1988 white Volkswagen bug. Israel drove the car back and forth to school and Bible study, usually taking Isabel with him. But Isabel recently acquired her driver's license. She had been sixteen for six weeks now and Israel usually let her drive the car when they were together. And then Israel remembered she had asked for the car keys at lunch time.

Wow. Israel thought. *¡Chido! This girl is full of surprises. And Isabel too, apparently.* He looked over at the barbells and then back at Mayrín. So beautiful it almost hurt looking at her. *Yeah, okay. I can skip the weights tonight and do some extra push-ups when I get home.*

"Yeah, okay—let's do it. You have transportation?"

Mayrín reached into her pink leather purse and pulled out a keychain. "Ever driven a Jeep?"

¡Chido! Israel grinned. "Not yet," he replied. "Gimme ten minutes."

Israel started up the cherry-red Jeep Wrangler and fell in love with the vehicle immediately. His friends jokingly referred to his own set of wheels as the "Love Bug" from the Disney movie series *Herbie*. It was a source of amusement among the football players and wrestlers. *Just like Father G probably had in mind,* Israel thought, as a wry smile came to his lips. *He gave me the car most difficult to pick up girls with.* Mayrín, however, came from a well-off family in Spain and they had arranged for her to purchase a car in El Paso. Israel drove the Jeep to *Chico's Tacos* and was shocked to learn Mayrín had never eaten a taco before coming to El Paso.

"So, what kind of food do you eat in Spain? What's your favorite?" Israel asked her, munching on a chicken soft taco soaked in spicy salsa. Tacos were his favorite food and he could not imagine a life without them.

Ever so softly, Mayrín shook her hair. "I dunno—maybe paella," she answered, nibbling on her own steak taco, completely devoid of hot sauce. "It's a rice dish made with onions, tomatoes, peas, seafood, and chicken. When you come over to my house I will make you some."

¡Chido! "You're on," he said, laughing. "Hey, see that cook—he looks like Severus Snape!"

"Who is Severus Snape?"

Israel stared at her, flabbergasted. "Professor Snape? From Harry Potter?" Both he and Isabel had read all the *Harry Potter* books three times and had seen each movie twice.

"Um," mumbled Mayrín sheepishly. She pursed her lips thoughtfully. "Yeah, well I had a friend in Spain who really loved the books. I just never got into them."

"What the heck? You sound just like a one-eyed priest I know. Everyone loves HP."

She pursed her lips again. "Yeah, well, I'm more of a Stephenie Meyer fan."

"Who the freak is Stephenie Meyer?"

"C'mon, really? The author of *Twilight*?"

Uggh. Isabel had forced him to watch *Twilight* and he was not a big fan. Yet he was really enjoying himself and starting to feel comfortable around Mayrín. She told him about her family in Spain and her relatives in El Paso. He told her all about Isabel, his foster parents, Padre Quezada, Father G, and the nuns. Mayrín listened, spellbound, as Israel told her stories of his father figure and mentor. He casually left out, however, all tales from his early childhood at the orphanage.

"I can't wait to meet all of your friends! Father G sounds like a really, um, interesting individual." Mayrín giggled and blushed. "I hope he won't make me confess. It's, um, been a while since I've been to mass."

"Yeah well, then you must come with me one of these Sundays. Mass is one of my favorite times of the week. And afterwards we can watch *Harry Potter and the Sorcerer's Stone*."

"You mean *Twilight*?" she laughed. "Um, I'm thinking more Easter or Christmas. Sunday is the only day I get to sleep in." Then, abruptly, she put her taco down, grabbed Israel's hand and probed his eyes. "So tell me, Israel, where is your favorite place to go in El Paso?"

Israel's face reddened once more as he felt a calming numbness from the touch of her hand flutter through his body. He felt confused and excited at the same time. "Uh, Mount Christo Rey, I guess, though it's actually in Sunland Park, New Mexico. It's a mountain with a large limestone statue of Jesus Christ at the top. Spectacular view."

Mayrín's eyes brightened. "Wow," she said, "Let's go there. I wanna learn everything about this area. We must go there sometime—um—check that. Will you take me this Saturday?"

Israel looked into her dazzling green eyes and felt paralyzed. *Freaking chido!* "Yes," he replied. "Totally. Yes, I will."

Chapter 27

Ciudad Juárez, Chihuahua, Mexico

For a city of 1.5 million residents, though some estimates place the number much higher, the ratio between the sixty-two drug rehabilitation centers and the *picaderos* (drug houses where users can get hits of cocaine, heroin, meth, or any other drug) was dangerously low. The number of *picaderos* in Juárez was now close to 3,000, helping make the murder capital of the world also claim the highest concentration of drug addicts in Mexico. Many of these drug addicts came from 'Los NiNi,' the nickname given to the young generation of Juárez residents who neither study nor work.

Reynaldo Balcázar was one of the 100,000 or so drug addicts in the city, a member of Los NiNi, and a rising leader in Los Artistas Asesinos, also known as the "Double A's," the ruthless gang multiplying exponentially across the region. They worked directly under the Sinaloa Cartel and were currently at war with the Barrio Aztecas. Reynaldo's face was now so heavily covered in tattoos that his own family, had they been alive, would be incapable of recognizing him. Reynaldo's family was killed by La Línea when he was thirteen years old and the youngster had sworn revenge. And in so doing eviscerated his conscience: he had become one of the most vicious murderers in Juárez.

Defense Secretary Acosta, constantly searching for recruits, discovered Reynaldo Balcázar. Ramón recognized Reynaldo's potential. The kid was ruthless yet displayed a charismatic leadership attracting many aspiring gang members. Secretary Acosta decided to take him to the next level. "I have an assignment for you Reynaldo," Ramón told the young gangbanger. "You will choose seven comrades and accompany me on an important mission." Reynaldo, in awe of the revered defense secretary, had agreed enthusiastically.

General Ortiz was driving the Sedena-Henschel HWK-11 Infantry Fighting Vehicle, listening to the soccer match on the radio. Mexico was playing Argentina. The general, however, couldn't fully concentrate. Accompanying him in the passenger seat was Secretary Acosta, and General Ortiz had developed a strange sort of anxiety in Ramón's presence. The general regretted his decision to command the occupation of Juárez. And, despite his vast wealth and power, wished he had never met the defense secretary.

He's a psychopath, General Ortiz thought grimly, as Argentina scored another goal. *Brilliant, yes, but absolutely deranged—possibly the most dangerous man Mexico has ever known.*

"We are not doing well, General," said Secretary Acosta.

General Ortiz's mustache twitched. "What's that, Secretary?"

"The match," Secretary Acosta said. "Argentina is now leading 3-0."

"Yes," replied General Ortiz, relieved. "Not our best outing."

"I trust we are doing better on other fronts," said Secretary Acosta. "The problem we face, General. I am counting on you to take care of it."

General Ortiz took a deep, long drag from his cigarette.

"Cómo no, Secretary Acosta. Everything is coming together as planned."

"Good," Ramón replied. "I do hope so."

Reynaldo Balcázar was again high on crystal meth as he drove the armored Humvee through downtown Juárez, following the camouflage HWK-11. The music from the armored Humvee blared loudly; the station was playing yet another one of the *narco-corridos*, the Mexican drug-trafficking ballads that had become ubiquitous across the country. They were played at weddings, *quinceañeras*, bars, discotheques, and most anywhere there was dancing or partying. The *narco-corridos* were big business and aspiring young narcos would fork out big bucks to get a song written about their exploits. The current song on the radio was called "Los Sanguinarios del M1" by the group El Movimiento Alterado:

With goat horn [AK-47] and bazooka at the nape
It flew heads who atravieza
We are bloodthirsty, crazy good wavy
We like killing
Pa 'give levantones, we're the best
Always caravan, all my plebada
Well empecherados, armored and ready
To run
With a private call is activated
High levels of hasten
From torturaciones, bullets and explosions
To control
People get scared and never question
If you see commands when they pass
All enfierrados either masked and well Camuflash
They are possessed, well commanded
Ready to order, pa 'make a mess
To suffer and die cons to agonize
Go and do pieces, people with bullets
Continuous bursts, which are not terminated

Sharp knife, atravezado horn
To slay...

Nodding his head to the tune, Balcázar parked the Humvee twenty yards behind the HWK-11 in the Bellavista neighborhood, an area to the west of downtown Juárez close to the border. He pulled a mask over his head and checked his AK-47. The other seven gangbangers did likewise. They casually got out of the truck and walked over to Secretary Acosta.

"Stay here and listen to the match," said Secretary Acosta to General Ortiz. "I will be back shortly."

"Bueno," said the general. The defense secretary readied his FX-05 Xiuhcoatl assault rifle and nodded at Reynaldo. The secretary walked across the street to 1243 Uranio, home of the Casa El Aliviane drug rehabilitation center. Reynaldo and his group of gangbangers followed him and Secretary Acosta broke down the front door of the residence with his right foot.

Six unarmed individuals were inside the living room watching the Mexico-Argentina soccer match. Among them was Ernesto Lozano, once an elite warrior for Secretary Acosta. He had been pushed over the edge: the tortures, the murders, and especially the human sacrifice rituals. Realizing he was losing his sanity, he deserted and went into hiding. Lozano looked at his former commander and his heart chilled. His bowels loosened, causing him to soil himself. Secretary Acosta calmly walked over to Lozano and fired nineteen rounds into his skull. No one else moved.

"Kill them," said the secretary to Reynaldo, quietly, strolling back to the front door. "All of them."

Reynaldo Balcázar ever so slightly nodded his head in acknowledgement.

"Into the hallway, *putos cabrones,* now!" shouted Jesús García Guerrero, Reynaldo's second in command. Jesús stood about six feet tall and weighed 113 pounds—the crystal meth had taken its toll on his body. The tattooed skin on his face stretched tight around his skull, giving his dark, sunken eyes a murderous edge. Staring down the barrels of two assault rifles, the drug rehab residents did as they were told. The other Artistas Asesinos went from bedroom to bedroom, rounded up every person in Casa El Aliviane, and forced them into the hallway. There were twenty patients in all, ranging in ages from seventeen to fifty-one—seven of them Barrio Aztecas. Reynaldo Balcázar stared at them all with cold gray eyes. Without a word he leveled his AK-47. The other gangbangers followed suit and they fired until they were out of ammo. Just a few minutes later the Artistas Asesinos swiftly departed the rehab center. Eighteen of the patients had been killed and the other two were not so lucky.

Months after the massacre at Casa El Aliviane, Reynaldo Balcázar and his posse were on a different kind of assignment: They were going to get rich. Reynaldo felt the smooth, steel barrel of his AK-47 and peered around the corner of the cardboard shack. They were in the heart of "Los Reyes Ciegos"—"The Blind Kings," one of the more poverty-stricken areas in Juárez. Jesús García swore as he stepped in a pile of fly-covered human excrement.

"*¡Cállate, hijo de puta!* Shut up, you son of a bitch!" Reynaldo was not in a good mood. It was hot outside, close to 100 degrees, and being led into this vermin-infested hellhole was not making anything better. He looked at the pitiful cardboard house and spit on it. The abysmal neighborhood was even worse than the gutter where he had been born and raised. The smell of goat, chicken, and human feces, combined with the toxic aroma of burning tires, was making him nauseous. Makeshift dwellings of rotting plywood and ancient cinderblock, covered by dirty tarps and cardboard, lined the crooked, dirt-paved streets for as far as he could see. Fifteen feet in front of him was a sickly greenish-yellow pool of water, urine, and a plethora of discarded chemicals.

But even the unknown solution of noxious chemicals could not prevent the liquid from being a fertile breeding ground for flies and mosquitoes. Three chickens and a goat were drinking from the strangely colored pool, and a caravan of cockroaches was marching back and forth from the putrid liquid to the cardboard shack. Garbage was everywhere and a family of rats could be seen in the distance, searching for food near a glossy-eyed woman dressed in tattered rags attempting to breastfeed an infant.

"What in the hell are they doing here?" whispered Pablo, a beady-eyed gangster with a hard, pockmarked face and shaven head.

All the Artistas Asesinos remained silent. Most had been thinking the same thing. Clemente, a rough-looking, beefy *cholo* with a gruesome scar across the left side of his face, took a long drag on his cigarette. Finally, he broke the uncomfortable silence. *"Se dice,"* replied Clemente, "that Las Dos Vírgenes visit the poorest regions in Mexico." Clemente spoke slowly. The tone of his voice had a portentous edge to it. "They take the people away to live in better conditions. Las Dos Vírgenes are tireless in their efforts and have been doing it for years. No one really knows who they are, where they come from, or *por qué lo hacen."*

Reynaldo faced Clemente with narrowing, gray cold eyes. His tattooed face quivered. "And it is also said that their *putas* pockets are lined with gold. Some say they have more money than fucking El Chapo himself."

Clemente stared back at Reynaldo, his rising fear providing enough outward courage to challenge the vicious gang leader. "It is also whispered that the Las Dos Vírgenes are untouchable. They cannot be killed, raped, or robbed, for they are protected by an angel, sent directly from God. Some call him the 'Angel of Death.' Others say he is one of the four horsemen of the apocalypse. The 'Pale Horseman,' they call him. They say he appears out of nowhere on a pale-colored steed, forged in the fiery pits of hell itself. They say he kills anyone who dares interfere with the business of Las Dos Vírgenes." Clemente narrowed his own eyes. "We should not be here, Reynaldo. I have a very bad feeling about this, *cabrón*. Let's get the hell out of here while we still can."

It was too much for the gang leader—he had been second-guessed by Clemente one too many times. A knife appeared in his hand and, before Clemente had a chance to react, he plunged the blade into the lungs of the burly *cholo*. Balcázar turned around to face the other gangbangers while Clemente fell to the ground, gasping for breath as blood rushed into his throat.

"And it's also said that one of the *putas vírgenes* is good-looking," said Reynaldo calmly, "very good-looking. And we'll all have a go at her before we break her neck and take the gold." Balcázar sheathed the bloody knife and walked on.

Twenty minutes later, they discovered the Las Dos Vírgenes, dressed as nuns and handing out water bottles to the masses of Los Reyes Ciegos. Some of the people were kneeling in the trash-strewn dirt, their arms folded and their teary-eyed faces looking up towards heaven in the act of praising their God. Others were scrambling to touch the clothing of the nuns, as if the feel of the sacred cotton would instantly heal their pain and misery. Still more people were marching into the train of school buses that could be seen in the background.

"There they are," exclaimed Reynaldo. "And there is no one to stop us. Remember, we take both alive and we kill anyone who gets in our way." His tattooed face broke into a fiendish grin. "And I get first dibs on the *flaca*."

Reynaldo cocked his AK-47 and walked out into the open, directly towards the nuns. The other gangsters leveled their assault rifles and followed him. Screams pierced through air, followed by what sounded like infernal thunder. Reynaldo's chest exploded into bloody chunks of flesh and bone before he could aim his assault rifle at the horrifying figure blazing towards them with incredible speed.

Jesús García got off a shot. The bullet ricocheted off the uranium armor of the roaring motorcycle and hit one of the rats scurrying around a pile of trash. García watched in amazement as the rat squealed and died just before he himself crumpled to the ground, adding to the tangled mess of blood and filth.

Out of the seven assassins, only Pablo was left standing. A .50 caliber bullet had pulverized his forearm. He stood upright in shock, staring at the fountain of blood erupting from his elbow and spraying onto the bodies of his fellow gangsters. He remained motionless until the terrifying figure walked over to him and outfitted his arm with a crude wire tourniquet. When the bleeding subsided, Pablo stared into the face of the terrifying man; his lungs froze.

The rumors are true! It is the Pale Horseman and he has come for me!

Pablo's arm no longer hurt; he did not feel the stream of urine trickle down his left leg. He stared with morbid fascination into the single, steel-blue eye of the horseman and felt iron fingers wrap around his throat. The horseman single-handedly lifted him into the air and tightened his grip.

"The nuns are to be left alone! Do you understand me?"

Pablo did not answer. The horseman's voice was deep, loud, and powerful. Pablo's face went white and the macabre tattoos on his neck turned a strange shade of purple. He felt dizzy—on the verge of unconsciousness. The roaring voice jolted him back to reality.

"Answer me!"

With death enveloping his soul, Pablo mustered his strength and blinked his eyes. The horseman threw him savagely to the dirt.

"Now go back and tell them," bellowed the horseman, as Pablo struggled to bring his left hand up to his throat, "the nuns are to be left alone. Or else I will come for them. Every single one of them."

Pablo nodded his head, unable to look at the hellish nightmare in front of him, and crawled out of sight.

Seven hours after the failed assault, both priests and the nuns, inside a rundown white van, returned to observe the neighborhood of the Los Reyes Ciegos. They were followed by Alma and Armendáriz, both riding black Harley-Davidson motorcycles. All the residents of Los Reyes Ciegos, close to 2,000, had been shipped out on buses to a newer part of the city, one with electricity, running water, and clean, though modest, housing complexes. They would be given medical examinations, drug tests, and psychological evaluations—and then be dealt with accordingly. Those who could work would be offered jobs per their skill sets and everyone would be provided with educational classes. Children would be able to play on sports teams and pursue opportunities in art and music. All would be shown the various houses of worship and would be encouraged to attend services weekly as well as be involved with their congregations. But there was no compulsion.

Padre Quezada stared at the miserable shacks and filth and shook his head in disgust. Even after all these years the abject poverty, especially so close to the United States, shocked him. Sister Arámbula and Sister López were traveling across Mexico and going through the same routine over and over and over. But even with the nonstop efforts, it never seemed to be enough. He walked over to one of the shacks, taking care not to step in a pile of goat feces, and casually tore off the roof. Sister López bent over to pick up a family bible dropped by one of the families. Alma watched her intently. Padre Quezada, upon witnessing the event, silently shook his head and then turned to Father G.

"Híjole. And what shall we do with Los Reyes Ciegos? The usual?"

"Yes," replied Father G, smashing a cockroach with his left toe, "The entire place is a biohazard. Burn it, sanitize it, and then we will start again."

CHAPTER 28

EL PASO, TEXAS, USA

WITHIN DAYS OF THEIR INTRODUCTION, a few months after Father Navarro's death, G led Padre Quezada, along with Sister López and Sister Arámbula, to the mysterious cave in La Zona Del Silencio. Upon seeing the Aztec treasure for the first time, the husky priest's legs buckled; his breathing went erratic. Sister Arámbula simply passed out in disbelief. More than thirty minutes went by before the nun obtained consciousness and Padre Quezada regained his physical composure. The priest then spoke so rapidly his companions had difficulty understanding him. "*¡Ay, caramba!* It is a blessing from God in this dark hour." The priest hopped around the ancient Aztec gold and artifacts like a large child.

Yet Padre Quezada was most interested in the sword that G had described to him. G led the stocky priest to the exact stalagmite where he had originally found it and lifted up his lantern. Padre Quezada grasped the sword and carefully held the weapon's hilt into the lantern light. He carefully studied the strange metal for a few minutes before wrapping the ancient sword in a spare cloak and setting it next to their supplies.

In the next several days it was decided, unanimously amongst the four, the historical artifacts would remain hidden until the time was right. They represented Mexico's cultural heritage and were to be preserved at all costs—except for the sword: Padre Quezada insisted the sword go with him. The bulk of the treasure, the gold and silver bars and ingots, the precious stones, would be used to help Mexico. Plans were made to build housing projects, hospitals, welfare centers, youth recreational facilities, schools, research complexes, and a host of other institutions designed for the progress and social well-being of the country.

"The people need hope for their future," said Padre Quezada. "They need the basic necessities of life. They need healthcare and education. They need good-paying jobs. Otherwise, they will simply join the narco ranks. The fight for Mexico's soul will take place on several fronts. And you," Padre Quezada looked directly at G, "will continue your military tasks in defense of the innocent. Part of the treasure will be used for this purpose. But a Red Crusader is truly a fearless knight, and secure on every side, for his soul is protected by the armor of faith, just as his body is protected by the armor of steel. He is thus doubly armed, and need fear neither demons nor men."

"What are you talking about?" asked G.

"To fulfill your mission, you must be complete—doubly armed, so to speak. You must go into the ministry."

The hell? The request left G stunned, almost as much as Sister López. He argued vehemently. But Padre Quezada was adamant and, in the end, G acquiesced. Over the next few months Padre Quezada instructed him in the ways of the faith. And in the sacred order of the Red Crusaders.

"Come with me," Padre Quezada said one Saturday night to G, as the pair finished a dinner of steak fajitas. "There is something I need to show you." G shrugged and climbed in the passenger seat of the round priest's beat-up Ford pickup. After a brief pit stop at *7-11*, where Padre Quezada purchased a Double Gulp Dr. Pepper, the two men drove to Ysleta Mission Church. G was shown the secret border tunnel for the first time and Padre Quezada led him into a hidden chamber, deep within the tunnel.

It was dark and the priest spent a few minutes lighting various candles. Upon illumination, G observed the chamber was decorated with ancient artwork of Red Crusader insignia. Next to a particularly colorful painting of the Cross of Lorraine was a marble mosaic featuring two knights, armed with spears, riding on a single horse. Encircling the horse and two riders were the Latin characters SIGILLUM MILITUM.

"That is a strange picture," said G, staring at the horse with two knights.

"It was the seal of the Knights Templar," replied Padre Quezada, "and is the current seal of the Red Crusaders. The two knights depicted are Hugues de Payens and Godrey de Saint-Omer, heroes of the First Crusade and two of the founders of the Knights Templar."

The priest looked thoughtful for a few moments and then, tossing aside his straw and chugging the Dr. Pepper, walked over to an iron safe in a dark area of the chamber. He opened the safe and retrieved the sword Sister Arámbula discovered among the Aztec treasure. He held it up to the candlelight.

"I have confirmed the sword's authenticity. We have searched for it diligently—for a very long time. Here, have a look." He handed the weapon to G. "It is called the Sword of Aragon."

The blade was double-edged and sharp. G ran his left thumb against one of the edges and drew blood. The blade's color was a strange shade of ice blue—he couldn't discern the composing metal. There were no signs of rust. The hilt however, was gold-plated, and imprinted near the hand guard was the seal of the Red Crusaders. A blood-red ruby was mounted within the pommel. G examined the ruby and noted it was positioned within a gold engraving of the Cross of Lorraine. He gripped the hilt and raised the tip of the blade into the air.

The metal glittered eerily against the candlelight. As his single eye studied the ancient weapon he was reminded once again of the sole, unique purpose of his life. He still had nightmares; thoughts of his dead wife and daughter tormented him; he struggled to understand. But he had to keep going.

"The metal alloy of the blade is unknown," Padre Quezada continued. "The Sword of Aragon was one of the few Templar artifacts transported to the New World. And it is perhaps the most important. Legend has it the blade was part of Solomon's Treasure."

"Solomon's Treasure?" asked G.

"Yes," replied Padre Quezada. "Nine hundred some years ago, a band of French noblemen, led by Hugues de Payens and Godrey de Saint-Omer, was sent to Jerusalem—with specific instructions. It is said the French noblemen possessed a copper scroll: a map confirming the location of Solomon's Temple and an extensive and intricate tunnel system built underneath it."

"Intricate tunnel system?" enquired G, "In Jerusalem?"

"Yes," Padre Quezada answered. "The ancient Israelites accumulated massive amounts of wealth, along with a horde of sacred religious artifacts. They were extremely wary of an attack and pillage by the Babylonians or any one of their enemies. What were they to do? They built tunnels, passageways leading to secret underground chambers where their treasure would be safe. Even today, vast subterranean labyrinths exist under Jerusalem and archaeological discoveries are still being made. But, I digress.

"The ancient French knights occupied a wing of the royal palace on the Temple Mount, in the captured Al-Aqsa Mosque. The Templars were very aware of the importance of the Temple Mount: The copper map divulged it was built upon the ruins of Solomon's Temple. Using the copper scroll, Hugues de Payens, Godrey de Saint-Omer, and their companions created a secret excavation site from their headquarters in the palace. At some point during their decade-long tenure, the French knights discovered the greatest treasure in the Old World. Besides the incredible tonnage of gold, silver, and precious stones, the Templars retrieved the Arc of the Covenant, the Holy Grail, and the Lance of Longinus."

The priest paused for a moment, studying the blade in his hand. "And this sword."

"Then the seal was engraved upon the hilt after it was discovered?" G asked. "And the Cross of Lorraine was added after that?"

"Yes, very good observations, G," replied Padre Quezada. "Legend has it the sword was used by various prophets and kings in Israel before Christ was born. King Solomon was said to have possessed the sword until his death. It was passed down to the Savior himself, though, of course, as purely a symbolic gesture. He never used it for violence. Before his crucifixion, however, Christ passed the sword on to Peter."

G looked at the sword suspiciously. He remained silent.

"Remember the scripture found in the New Testament: 'And I say to you, that you are Peter, and upon this rock I will build my church, and the gates of Hell shall not prevail against it.' Now Peter, if you remember, was crucified some thirty years after the death of Christ, in the Neronian persecution. But, it is said, before his death he hid the sword in a secret subterranean chamber under the Temple Mount. The weapon remained hidden for more than 1,000 years. Recognizing its importance, Hugues de Payens took custody of the sword. Before his death, he passed it on to Robert de Craon, the second Grand Master of the Knights Templar. For almost two centuries, the sword remained in the hands of the Grand Masters, until the dark times, until the complete corruption of Pope Clement V and King Philip IV of France.

"Sensing the imminent danger, Jacques de Molay, the last Grand Master of the Knights Templar, traveled to the Kingdom of Aragon in Spain. There he met with a family who for generations had been staunch supporters of the religious order. Numerous family members served faithfully and courageously during the Crusades. Many were veterans of the legendary Battle of Montgisard."

"What was the Battle of Montgisard?"

"A fight in which 500 Templars defeated the famous Muslim military leader Saladin and his army of 26,000 soldiers. But that is beside the point. This Spanish family whom Jacques de Molay trusted was committed to God, truth, justice, liberty, and the advancement of the Christian faith. They were the Navarros, of whom our recently deceased dear friend and brother is a direct descendant."

The round priest gently took possession of the sword, lifting the pommel to the candlelight. "It was during this visit to Spain, that Jacques de Molay, together with Ordoño Navarro, patriarch of the family, developed the organizational framework for the Red Crusaders. The sword was passed into the hands of the Navarro family. To protect its true identity, the weapon became known as the Sword of Aragon. For more than 200 years, the sword remained in Spain, in the possession of the Red Crusaders, and it was used to help repel the invading Moors. Then in 1535, Pelagius Navarro, under the direction and counsel of his father, traveled to the New World with a small group of Red Crusaders. They were commissioned to protect the indigenous peoples and they took the Sword of Aragon with them."

Padre Quezada lifted the ice-blue blade into the air once again. "The sword is somehow intertwined into your destiny, G. It was by no accident that you discovered the cave in La Zona Del Silencio."

G simply shook his head and smiled. "I don't want the sword, Father. I don't even know how to use it. We need guns. We need RPGs. We need advanced weaponry."

"And we shall get them," answered Padre Quezada calmly. "But the sword is part of your destiny. I shall maintain possession of it until the proper time."

CHAPTER 29

XIUHCOATL—JUNGLES OF OAXACA, MEXICO

TLALOC WIPED THE THICK BLOOD off his *macuahuitl* as the two priests carried the female corpse down the limestone steps of the pyramid. The wicked beat of the drums subsided. The hunchback watched with anticipation as the four blue-skinned prisoners entered the arena and were instructed to pick up the *macuahuitls* lying on the stone floor. They did so with shaking hands and wild eyes, unable to hide their mounting terror. The blue-skinned men were muscle for the Beltran Leyva Cartel, a splinter organization of the Sinaloa Cartel that had rebelled and gone to war against El Chapo. Secretary Acosta had just rounded up Carlos Beltran Leyva, the current capo and third Beltran Leyva brother to be captured or killed within the last two years.

Tlaloc's weathered lips formed the slightest trace of a smile as he watched the blue-skinned captives clumsily and frantically collect the weapons. He looked across his kingdom of Xiuhcoatl. The entire city had been restored in painstaking detail. Vibrantly colored murals of Aztec gods decorated building walls. Carved images of jaguars, eagles, and serpents, features etched in exquisite craftsmanship, could be seen everywhere. Tlaloc had designed an elaborate canal system within the confines of Xiuhcoatl and most travel was performed via watercraft. On the south side of the city stood another, smaller pyramid restored to its former glory. Tlaloc could see its outline from where he now stood, its brilliant scarlet color standing out majestically against the setting sun. The pyramid was his home now. Not long after the destruction of Tamoanchan, some ten years ago, Secretary Acosta closed the Sinaloa military compound permanently and began rebuilding here at Xiuhcoatl, in the South. Tlaloc had decided they needed a more clandestine location for their forces.

The tragedy at the military base hurt us deeply, Tlaloc pondered. What exactly happened there remained a mystery to both him and Secretary Acosta. There were rumors, however, some of them so strange that the ancient hunchback perceived they may contain a bit of truth. Disturbed by the train of thought, Tlaloc's eyes locked onto the muscled figure of Tehuantl as the champion warrior gracefully and confidently entered the arena. He carried his favorite *macuahuitl* in his right hand and wore *ichcahuipilli* armor covered in a tan-yellow pelt with black spots. On top of his head sat the fearsome face of a jaguar. The crowd erupted and Tlaloc felt a surge of adrenaline rush through him. He shook off the irritating thoughts of Tamoanchan. *Look to the future.*

They had put a huge effort into the resurrection and development of Xiuhcoatl. The heroin and meth labs had been rebuilt and were producing at twice the capacity of their predecessors in Tamoanchan—with higher-quality drugs. Several new arsenals had been constructed, filled with a wide variety and large quantity of weaponry—including some of the latest advances in RPGs. And Secretary Acosta had been back in business with the Russian mafia. On the outskirts of Xiuhcoatl, hidden deep within the jungle, they were constructing a highly sophisticated aircraft hangar to house Secretary Acosta's latest prize: the Mikoyan MiG-35—praised by the Russians as the most advanced fighter jet to have ever been built.

We are indeed powerful, Tlaloc contemplated, *and back on schedule. We're winning in Juárez. We will wreak havoc in the Gulf and we will soon have complete control of the border. And of Mexico. And then...*

Tlaloc unconsciously grinned and then focused his attention on the more immediate conflict. One of the blue-skinned captives lunged awkwardly at Tehuantl with his weapon. Tehuantl retaliated with a brutal swing of his *macuahuitl* that sliced through both of the man's forearms, unleashing a fountain of bright crimson blood. A nefarious roar pierced through the applause of the crowd and a live jaguar, driven to frenzy at the sight and smell of the blood, raced across the stone floor of the coliseum. It sank its fangs deep into a bloody arm of the blue-skinned captive.

The man's companions recoiled at the sight of the yellow-spotted beast; Tehuantl seized upon the opportunity to move in on his opponents. With two strikes he slashed open the ribcage of one man and crushed the skull of another. Focusing all his attention on Tehuantl, the man never saw the yellow beast pounce onto his left shoulder and sink its fangs into his throat.

Later that evening, Secretary Acosta disembarked from the dugout canoe in front of the dark pyramid at the city's edge. He climbed up eleven limestone steps on the south side of the structure and entered a corridor leading into the heart of the ancient building. In the middle of a large chamber, lighted by candles, was Tlaloc. The cripple was on his knees, eyes closed and arms folded.

In front of the ancient cripple was a life-sized female skeleton, standing upright, clothed in the turquoise robes of the Virgin Guadalupe and wearing a flamboyant Aztec headdress composed of brilliantly green quetzal feathers. The headdress was mounted on a base of gold studded with precious stones. It sat perfectly upon the crown of the white skull. The left fingers of the skeleton were attached to a seven-foot-tall scythe, crafted out of silver; its serrated blade glimmered hauntingly against the candle light.

Next to the representation of Santa Muerte was another skeleton, this one male and a few inches taller. It was splattered in blood and on top of its head sat a headdress of owl feathers. Two large, circular emeralds protruded from the eye sockets of the skull and an array of gold teeth had been inserted into its mouth. A chain of bloody human eyeballs, taken from the corpses of the recently deceased blue-skinned captives, draped around the neck of the male. Tlaloc had gone to great lengths to obtain the skeletons. Four years had now passed since he desecrated the Navarro family gravesite and dug up the sacred remains of his parents. *And now they are immortal, powerful, and completely under my control.*

He remembered the lies that his parents and other had instilled in him as a child—back when he was young Victor Navarro. About how Jesus Christ loved him and if he had enough faith, he might even be healed from his infirmities. He remembered the blatant hypocrisy of the priests and the nuns, and wondered once again how his family could become prey to such a ludicrous religion. By age twelve, Victor had discovered the pre-Hispanic history of his country and became obsessed with it. It was at this time he realized his destiny: He would obtain vengeance for the true people of Mexico. He would return glory to his country. He became convinced the Aztec gods would assist him in his quest for vengeance—against the church and against anything European.

Tlaloc reflected upon his teenage years and recalled his first murder. At age sixteen, he witnessed a priest sexually abusing a young boy in the cathedral. He stabbed the priest through the chest with a large hunting knife and dedicated the kill to Mictlantecuhtli. He remembered the thrill flowing through his mind and body as he glared at the lifeless body. It gave him a confidence he had never known and it gave him power.

Secretary Acosta gazed at the skeletal couple for several minutes as Tlaloc continued his silence. Tarantulas covered the stone floor and bats hung from the walls and ceiling—Aztec associations of Mictlantecuhtli. Fifteen minutes passed before Tlaloc acknowledged Ramón's presence. He slowly rose to his feet and opened his eyes, sucking in air.

"Welcome ... Ramón. ... I was ... just finishing ... up. ... How is ... the progress?" Tlaloc spoke in Arabic.

The defense secretary waited a few moments before speaking. "Master Tlaloc—It seems things are in order and we are ready for the next stage."

Secretary Acosta also spoke in Arabic. He spoke perfectly, without traces of any accent. The pair had been speaking exclusively in Arabic for the last five years, and Secretary Acosta had become quite adept in the language.

Tlaloc inhaled deeply. "The problem ... in ... Juárez?" His voice was dark and raspy; his breathing hard and ragged and metallic.

Secretary Acosta flinched for a brief second and his lips twitched unintentionally. The rumors were disturbing, and both of them could not quite discern the truth of the events. Especially unnerving was the possible connection between the recent killings and the destruction at Tamoanchan. But one thing was for certain: His men were dying and they were not all being killed by La Línea. His mind quickly analyzed his long list of enemies. Again, somewhat disconcertingly, he remembered DEA Agent Dan Kasper. *Impossible. He is dead.*

Secretary Acosta quickly composed himself. "General Ortiz assures me the problem will be eliminated shortly, Master Tlaloc. All is in place."

Tlaloc slowly nodded his head and brushed off a tarantula crawling up his leg.

"Everything ... is ... arranged ... for your ... travels ... overseas?"

"Yes, Master, I depart next month."

Tlaloc nodded, closed his eyes and knelt once again. Both men understood the importance of the Secretary Acosta's upcoming journey. They had been planning it for ten years.

The radiant El Paso sun was shedding its last hour of light when Israel and Mayrín reached the top of Mount Cristo Rey. "Oh my gosh! It's beautiful!" exclaimed Mayrín, gazing at the twenty-nine-foot-tall white limestone statue of Jesus Christ. The statue rose from the center of a huge cement crown atop the peak of the mountain formerly known as the "Cerro de los Muleros"—"Mule Drivers Mountain." A former lookout peak for the Apaches, it provided one with a panoramic view of two U.S. states and two countries. Mayrín skipped around the cement crown like a little girl, enjoying the spectacular scenery. She then focused her attention on the Mexican landscape. Even from this distance she could see the crooked streets and impoverished neighborhoods of Juárez. The contrast between the neighbors was striking. She slowly shook her head. "How is it that two countries can be so close together and yet be so different? I mean, come on!"

Israel assumed a businesslike air. "Yeah, well, it's a very complex question, Mayrín, and somewhat of a divisive one. One possible theory is that the Spanish colonists came to the New World with the intent of enriching and glorifying themselves as well as Spain. They were not so concerned with the foundational development of the new lands and individual rights, a primary goal of some of the English colonists who settled North America."

Mayrín narrowed her eyes just a bit while pursing her lips and stared at him for a few moments. "Well, that was certainly an intellectual explanation."

Freak. Israel blushed. *Whatever.* "Well, you asked the question." Unlike Father G, he was very interested in politics. And history fascinated him. Despite Father G's indifference to the theoretical, he had always encouraged Israel to pursue his academic interests.

"Um, wasn't the U.S. really established on the backs of Africans and the thievery of land from the Native Americans?"

What the heck? Israel took a deep breath. "Mayrín, over the course of America's history, there is no doubt that mistakes have been made and atrocities were committed. Remember, though, that Americans fought one of the bloodiest civil wars ever recorded to end slavery. People often forget the great sacrifice of hundreds of thousands of brave Americans willing to die to achieve justice. So, from a certain perspective, one can say great strides have been taken since the conception of the United States to attain what the founders envisioned."

Mayrín looked out again upon the Mexican scenery. "Uh-huh. Yeah, well, how come it's not doing something to fight the poverty and suffering of its neighbor?"

"Another good question. It could, and perhaps should, do more," Israel answered. "Just earlier today, in Juárez, we came across a malnourished fourteen year-old girl whose three month old baby was on the verge of starvation. It is heartbreaking. If we could get more people involved in humanitarian efforts and increase their faith in general, we could totally do so much more."

Mayrín stepped back, shocked. She studied Israel's eyes. "You went to Juárez? Like, today?"

"Yeah, well, I go every Saturday. I've been doing it for years now. The priests and the nuns are continually building new neighborhoods, medical centers, schools, youth sports complexes—things like that."

"Um, isn't it dangerous? My aunt and uncle have forbidden me to cross the border. They tell me it's the most violent place on earth."

Israel smiled. "True—I guess I'm used to it by now. My people are over there, desperate for any kind of help. I gotta go over there. I have to—especially during these horrible times and their greatest hour of need."

Mayrín stayed silent for a few moments, contemplating all that Israel had told her. It was getting darker now. A sudden gust of wind caused the skin of her forearms to break out into goose bumps. She then gazed at Israel once again and looked deep into his eyes, much more softly now.

"Will you like, do something for me?"

Israel looked at her and, once again, felt the strange emotions swell with in him. *Lookin' all mind-blowing gorgeous.* The striking green eyes made him powerless.

"Yeah, of course."

"Will you take me with you over there, to Juárez? So I can see what's going on and what you are doing?"

"What about your aunt and uncle?"

"They don't need to know."

Israel thought for a moment as he watched Mayrín's hair flutter in the wind. She was so beautiful it made him ache.

"We'll see. I'll talk to Padre Quezada."

And then, without warning, Mayrín stepped up on her tiptoes, wrapped her arms around his neck, and kissed him hard on the lips. She kissed him long, deep, and passionately. It was Israel's first kiss.

Chapter 30

Ysleta Mission Church—El Paso, Texas, USA

Father G rapidly changed clothes inside the secret chamber of the cathedral and holstered his pistols.

"Damn it!"

He swore loudly, forgetting for the moment that someone may hear him behind the closed walls. He then quickly strapped on his other weapons and moved the motorcycle into the elevator. Beads of sweat accumulated on his forehead while he checked the fuel level. It was full. He inserted new magazines into both Colt .45s and ritualistically checked the number of rounds in the machine gun. It was at max capacity. When the elevator reached the bottom floor, Father G jammed the start button; the white chopper rumbled to life and took off at high speed. The priest traveled through the tunnel at record pace. He had just learned of the assassination plans on Mayor José Reyes Ferriz—scheduled to occur in thirty minutes.

Mayor Reyes was currently doing everything in his power to mitigate the violence and clean up the city. Padre Quezada considered his leadership essential in the fight to restore order to Ciudad Juárez. After Reyes' family received death threats, he moved them across the border to El Paso. Mayor Reyes was now living alone in Juárez, protected constantly by armed guards. But he was vulnerable, especially during public appearances, and today he would be giving a speech at a human rights convention.

Father G arrived at the basement of The Mission of Our Lady of Guadalupe in just a few minutes. It was the first time he would drive the pale hog out of the Mission in broad daylight. As he ascended the freight elevator, he briefly hoped for minimal cathedral attendance and then turned his attention back to the task at hand.

Focus. Stay calm. Think clearly.

The ten-cylinder engine erupted as the white chopper burst from the thick adobe wall into the outside air. It raced onto the mission grounds and then onto Avenida Vicente Guerrero. Three old couples, four women, and six children, coming to pay their daily respects to the Virgin Guadalupe, stared dumbfounded at the incredible sight. Padre Quezada would be along shortly to convince them they had seen a religious vision.

The priest rode eastwards down Avenida Vicente Guerrero, fast but calm, mapping out his plan of attack. *They'll have at least two armored vehicles and a few dozen hitmen,* Father G reflected. *A few of them will have been stationed at the university for some time.* He made a sharp left onto Avenida Adolfo López Mateos and glanced down at the newly designed control panel on the pale hog. Alma had recently engineered a few enhancements into the motorcycle, features he had been asking for, but he hoped he would not be pressed into using them any time soon. Father G swerved the white chopper to the right and headed east down the street Anillo Envolvente del Pronaf. He could now see some of the buildings of Universidad Autónoma de Ciudad Juárez, considered to be the most prestigious university in the city, where he had been told Mayor Reyes would be speaking.

Father G took a left, heading north, on one of the side streets leading to the campus and drove the pale hog through a parking lot. He then headed to the middle of the college. *Here,* he thought, *I'll be able to scout around for a few minutes and see what I'm up against.*

Passing the Biomedical Research Institute, he slowed down and observed his surroundings. *Mayor Reyes will be speaking at the amphitheater, just up ahead to the northeast.* Cruising through the sidewalks and back alleys of the university, Father G saw two camouflage-covered Sedena-Henschel HWK Infantry Fighting Vehicles off to the distance in the west. He paid them no notice. Military vehicles and personnel were ubiquitous throughout Juárez yet never seemed to be around narco violence when it occurred. And it would be normal for them to be seen around any appearance of a public official.

It was when he surveyed the amphitheater that he felt the first twinges of apprehension. *Something is wrong. There are not enough people here.* His uneasiness grew as he approached the multi-storied edifice. The parking lot was virtually empty.

Perhaps Armendáriz was misinformed.

He continued to drive up to the entrance. Within a few hundred yards of the building his earphone buzzed; a frantic voice pounded against his eardrum. It was Padre Quezada. "Reyes is in El Paso! There is no human rights convention today–we've been set up! They were spreading misinformation! It's a trap, G! Get out of there!"

The hell? The priest turned the white chopper around on a dime. Over half a dozen camouflage HWKs were closing in on him from all angles and they were moving fast. Sunlight reflected against the subtle insignia on the furthermost right vehicle. It was the morbid icon of Mictlantecuhtli, and Father G was one of the few people in the world who understood its significance. These military vehicles were commissioned by Secretary Acosta. The soldiers inside were in bed with the narcos and corrupt up to their armpits. And they were coming to kill him.

The priest swung the white chopper around again to face the amphitheater. Over two dozen narco troopers, armed with FX-05 Xiuhcoatl assault rifles, stormed out of the front entrance. Father G quickly analyzed the situation and instinctively made a decision. His left thumb hit the top yellow button on the control panel. A clear concave shield, constructed using industrial diamond, rose in front of him. The thunderous growl of the powerful engine ripped through the air and the pale hog rocketed forward, directly towards the amphitheater. Father G opened fire on the narco soldiers with the hog's .50 caliber machine gun and as the motorcycle went from 0 to 80 mph in 2.5 seconds, the deadly weapon rotated from the far right to the far left, mowing down every narco fighter in its path.

The white chopper crashed through the front doors of the building, showering glass shards and twisted metal fragments into half-dozen or so narco troopers on their way outside. Father G launched two hand grenades into the crowd of soldiers still positioned inside the building and made for the staircase.

He hammered the throttle and the pale hog soared onto the main hallway of the second floor just as the stairs collapsed from the incoming fusillade. The 20mm automatic cannons and 7.62mm MG3 machine guns of the HWKs were now firing without restraint. Cacophonous screams reverberated throughout the amphitheater as the first floor narcos were crushed to death by slabs of concrete falling from walls and ceilings of the crumbling auditorium.

The priest crunched the throttle and swerved maniacally around the hallway of the demolishing building. And, just as the second story of the amphitheater collapsed to the ground in a pile of rubble, the motorcycle exploded out of the upper north window like a cannon ball.

The white chopper traveled seventy yards through the air before crash landing near the street of Hermanos Escobar. As the motorcycle bounced against desert terrain, Father G was thrown in the air and his body smashed against a telephone pole before falling to the ground. Ignoring the bruised ribs and sprained ankle, he sprung to his feet and sprinted back to the pale hog. The machine seemed undamaged. *Thank God.* He threw his right leg over the seat, started the engine, and jammed the throttle wide open.

The front two wheels of the pale hog jumped nearly four feet off the desert sand before finding the black asphalt of Hermanos Escobar. It zipped onward and flashed between trains of cars traveling in both directions. Father G leaned hard to his left and all four tires gripped asphalt as the motorcycle wickedly spun northwards onto Avenida Plutarco Elías Calles.

Taking a deep breath, he prepared to speak into his microphone before noticing the black HWK racing towards him head-on. He slammed on the brakes and the pale hog skid a considerable distance, leaving a trail of burning rubber in the middle of the street. Father G then yanked on the handlebars and swung the motorcycle back towards the south. Another HWK had come onto Avenida Plutarco Elías Calles. He was cut off.

The priest cursed and turned the white chopper back to the north, simultaneously hitting a side control button with his right index finger. One portion of his left eye stared at the tiny computer monitor above the control panel while both his arms adjusted the handlebars. The oncoming HWK opened fire and one shot from the 20mm cannon ripped up a huge chunk of asphalt and dirt just up ahead of him. Ignoring the storm of debris, G adjusted the handlebars until the crosshairs on the computer monitor turned red. He fired. And then, microseconds later, he once again accelerated the pale hog northwards at breakneck speed.

The black HWK exploded as the FGM-148 Javelin anti-tank missile pierced its heart. Father G bristled at the intense heat of the flames as the motorcycle jetted through the fire, molten metal, and charred pieces of human remains. He hated to use the Javelin missile; it was the only one he had, but he had been left with no alternative. Off in the distance he saw a convoy of olive-green Humvees, coming directly at him.

How many of them are there? It appeared that both the defense secretary and General Ortiz were coming after him in full force. The priest cursed again and then abruptly turned the white chopper down a side street to the west and weaved in and out of the familiar back roads and neighborhoods. After clearing a few miles, Father G's earphone buzzed again and, now confident he was in the clear, pulled over in a small dark alley behind a grocery store.

He spoke softly in the microphone attached to the underneath collar of his bullet-proof jacket.

"Talk to me." He grimaced as he spoke and circled his arms to try and diminish some of the pain. His ribs were throbbing.

"G!" exclaimed Padre Quezada on the on other end of the line. "You made it! Thank God, Listen..."

"Yes," Father G broke him off, "I'm heading back to..."

Padre Quezada bellowed into his ear, "G, Listen to me! They've got the mayor's son! They kidnapped him right here in El Paso! Just a few minutes ago!"

G's heart stiffened. All thoughts of his aching body vanished. The new development was unexpected and disturbing.

Padre Quezada continued speaking in a frantic voice, "They're in a red Chevy Tahoe and close to crossing the border!"

"Which bridge?"

"Puente Libre," Padre Quezada responded, referring to the "Free Bridge," also known as the Bridge of the Americas.

Father G looked down at the computer monitor. 11:37 a.m. He quickly made some mental calculations. He had kept up with the daily math regimen Father Navarro had forced upon him at the monastery and his mind was sharp. Hoping nothing on the white chopper had been damaged, the priest leaned his face into the microphone.

"I'm going for him. Make the necessary preparations."

The powerful ten-cylinder engine roared once again and the pale hog fired out of the alley with a force that caused a grocery store clerk to drop a case of Corona onto the floor.

Carlos Herrera was on his daily commute back to El Paso from the Flextronics *maquiladora*. He was traveling northwards on MX 45 in his navy-blue Honda Accord. He took another bite of his chicken *flauta* and washed it down with a swig of Pepsi. He then looked back up at the traffic and decided he probably should have taken the Ysleta Bridge—Puente Libre looked like a parking lot. As he reached for another *flauta*, his upper body slammed into the car seat from the launch of the air bag and he heard a colossal crunching noise as the hood of his Accord smashed into the engine. And, at the same time, from the corner of his right eye, he visualized enough of the incredible sight to register shock waves to his brain. The most amazing driving machine he had ever seen had just landed on his car and jumped to the other side of the Mexican Federal Highway.

Father G spotted the camouflage Humvee before seeing the Tahoe. The Tahoe was heading straight for the Humvee, the narco gangbangers inside were eager to hand off their cargo and collect the reward money. Weaving diabolically through the traffic, the priest got within thirty yards of the military vehicle. He then drew his silver Colt .45 and took out the Humvee's upright gunman with a single bullet to the forehead.

As the gunman crumpled into the vehicle, and before the other narco soldiers knew what was happening, G launched a grenade. It landed directly on top of the gunman's corpse. Without waiting to see the fiendish explosion, he turned the white chopper northwards and sped towards the Tahoe.

There was now complete pandemonium on both sides of the highway. A burst of orange-red flames erupted from the remnants of the Humvee and screams could be heard from all directions. Traffic was at a standstill. A few people had taken cover on the side of the road but most were doubled up inside their vehicles, heads down with fingers fumbling for mobile phones. Father G had pistols in both hands and was blazing away by the time the narco thugs got their AK-47s out of the Tahoe's windows.

He took out the driver, gunman in the passenger seat, and a narco gangbanger in the back before feeling the left side of his chest cave in—three rounds from an AK-47 pounded against the body armor covering his left pectoral muscle and ribcage. The force of the shots against his bruised ribs knocked the wind out of him and he fell off the motorcycle onto the dirty, worn down asphalt of the highway.

The back of his head smashed against a slab of concrete. It jolted him back into action. He rolled hard against the gray surface of the highway and then rolled again and again as the lone remaining narco tore up asphalt with AK-47 gunfire. Two shots hit G's lower back before he managed to crawl underneath the Tahoe. The narco gangster continued to fire away. Round after round demolished the floor of the vehicle. In a fit of psychotic rage, the narco assassin went cyclic for twenty seconds straight before the assault rifle dropped from his lifeless hands and his corpse collapsed onto the bloody back seat with an eleven-inch bowie knife sunk deep into the back of its torso.

Father G ripped open the right back door, quickly freed his knife, and jerked the two narco corpses out of the Tahoe and onto the rough edge of the highway. In the far back of the SUV, curled up in a ball with his wrists and ankles tied, was a sobbing Pedro Reyes, the mayor's twelve-year-old son. Seeing the boy in such a state caused the priest to freeze for a few moments as the recollection of his own torture dominated his mind. The boy cried louder upon seeing Father G, and the noise brought the priest out of his stupor. He cut the cords that bound Pedro and then grabbed the boy's wrist. In return, he received a vicious kick to the chin. Pedro's purple and bruised eyes were unnaturally round and sweat was running down his forehead. Blood was flowing from his mouth and nose. The narcos had beaten him up pretty bad.

Father G released his hold on the boy and probed his eyes. "It's okay, Pedro. I'm not one of them. I'm here to take you back to your family. You must hurry now. There will be more of them coming for you."

Pedro continued to stare at the strange man. His appearance frightened him much more than any of his narco kidnappers. The man had on an eye patch and his face was streaked with glowing crimson scars underneath the stubble of facial hair. His jaw was rock solid. There was a barbaric intensity in the single steel-blue eye that sent an icy chill slashing through Pedro's gut. But the man did not look like a narco.

Pedro's eyes fell to the strange golden cross dangling from the man's chest. The cross gleamed majestically against the afternoon sun and the brilliant red jewel seemed to hypnotize him. Slowly, the boy crawled out of the Tahoe and onto the edge of the highway. And then froze in fear at the growl of a rapidly approaching black Hummer.

I'm a dead man, thought Father G. *And Pedro is dead also.*

Sicarios were shooting AK-47s from the Hummer. He had no weapons and there was no time to escape the line of fire. His single eye homed in on the enemy and his brain went numb. *It will be a relief,* he realized. His mind was constantly in torment and turmoil. He lived for a single purpose and his existence was painful. He had no woman, and he yearned to see his wife and daughter again. Almost in slow motion, he prepared for his death. And then, out of nowhere, he saw a blur of yellow and it violently smashed into the black Hummer. In a daze, as he rushed to collect his weapons, the priest saw Alma get out of the yellow Mack truck and pepper the demolished Hummer with a machine gun.

Pedro watched Alma in amazement as she fired from the machine gun again and again. His fascination was interrupted, however, upon observing the convoy of camouflage HWKs approaching from the north.

"Get in the Tahoe Alma! I'll draw them off!"

Alma fired a few more shots and then rushed into the SUV.

Father G took the boy's wrist again, more gently this time. He forced his voice to soften. "Pedro, you must listen to me. The men that are coming are bad guys. They are not good soldiers and they wish to harm you. You must come with me. Now!"

Pedro stared into the strange man's single eye for several moments. His eyes then went back to the train of HWKs. They were coming in fast. He heard gunfire and saw another squadron of black Humvees approaching from the south. Pedro nodded his head and let the strange man help him up onto the seat of the white chopper.

Father G quickly outfitted him with a spare bullet-proof jacket and locked him onto the back with a customized seatbelt Alma had constructed. And, as the gunfire became louder and the enemy vehicles came dangerously close, the powerful ten-cylinder engine thundered to life and the pale hog took off at a speed that froze Pedro's lungs.

Any hope of getting Pedro to the U.S. border using the bridge was snuffed out. The HWKs had sealed off the return lane of MX 45. *And most probably,* the priest reflected, *all other bridges.* The white chopper surged down the Mexican Highway, southwards, directly towards the oncoming Humvees. At the last possible second Father G veered right hard and made for the Benito Juárez monument.

The white chopper blazed past the statue and veered southwest down the trails and dirty flatlands of Chamizal Park. Fairly confident they were now in the clear, G traveled some of the side roads and eventually made it to Avenida 16 de Septiembre. They were now just a few blocks from the mission and the tunnel leading to safety. It was a mistake. The entire street was crawling with military HWKs, Humvees, and armored SUVs. He cursed.

The whole damn operation has been compromised. I must have been seen and reported somewhere near the church.

Sprinkled between the military vehicles were shiny black motorcycles, mounted with riders outfitted in jet-black clothing and dark visored helmets. Pistols hung from their hips and FX-05 Xiuhcoatl assault rifles clung to their shoulders. Lines of armed infantry were stationed on both sides of the street and their assault rifles and machine guns were in shooting position. On the left shoulder of the troops' olive-green uniforms was the subtle insignia of Mictlantecuhtli. They were narco soldiers, all of them. And they spotted the pale motorcycle instantly.

Father G drew both pistols and took out four of the nearest infantrymen and one of the black riders. The pale hog's shield rose and the .50 caliber machine gun unleashed a torrent of bullets that tore into the lines of soldiers. A cannon shot from one of the HWKs ripped into the pavement just a few yards away and FX-05 Xiuhcoatl gunfire riddled the diamond-plated shield. One shot from the rear hit G's right forearm. The silver Colt .45 fell to the street and G's right hand grabbed the handlebar and hammered the throttle. The ten-cylinder engine screamed and the pale hog launched forward like a heat-seeking missile, .50 caliber machine gun bullets mowing down any narco soldier that got in its path. Gunfire tailed the pale metallic machine, shredding the concrete asphalt and cement sidewalks of Avenida 16 de Septiembre.

The priest turned hard right, rammed the throttle, and the motorcycle crashed through the metal doors of Mercado Juárez, the city's historic shopping plaza. Nonstop gunfire continued to follow the pale hog as it rifled through the hallways of the *mercado* and plowed through cowboy boots, wool blankets, ceramic pottery, guitars, and an assortment of other merchandise that used to be sold to the tourists before they stopped coming. Two of the black narco motorcycles rumbled forwards and followed the white chopper into the large building. As G darted in and out of plaza corridors he raised his voice into the microphone near his chest.

"Quezada—We're in trouble! Lucy, I repeat, Lucy!"

"Confirmed." The reply was instantaneous.

"And talk to Alma—Charlie, I repeat, Charlie!"

"Confirmed," Padre Quezada said once again.

"Pedro!" Father G yelled in a guttural voice. "Are you okay?"

Pedro squeaked out something that sounded like no.

At that moment a black motorcycle materialized and Father G felt a rush of gunfire blast past the left side of his body. He violently spun the white chopper around and demolished the narco rider with three direct hits from the .50 caliber machine gun. Five seconds later the pale hog had bulldozed through the northwest exit door of Mercado Juárez and hurled onto Calle German Valdez.

An olive-green HWK was traveling eastwards down Calle German Valdez, only thirty yards away, and the priest had to swerve like a lunatic to get out of its line of fire. The HWK's cannon exploded and demolished the corner of the shopping plaza. The pale hog spurred forwards with incredible acceleration; the front two tires lifted three feet off the ground and Father G took out the HWK's vertical gunman with the machine gun. He drove the white chopper to within just a few feet of the narco vehicle and expertly tossed another grenade into the open hatch to join the dead gunman. The priest felt the heat on the back of his skull from the heinous explosion and he hoped Pedro did not get burned.

All thoughts of immediate injuries left his mind as an enemy motorcycle launched through the smoldering remnants of the back corner of the Mercado and three more black riders and a camouflage Humvee approached from the southwest. The pale hog made a wicked 90 degree turn and raced southeast through a narrow back alley near the shopping plaza. Another enemy motorcycle was stationed at the end of the alley and Father G used the last of the machine gun ammo to annihilate it. He gunned the throttle and the pale hog ripped through the wreckage and vaulted onto one of the side streets at a velocity of 150 mph.

The priest remained oblivious to Pedro's terrified screams as he continued to accelerate to obscene speeds. The enemy was everywhere and seemingly multiplying around every corner. And the black motorcycles were fast, much faster than he originally anticipated. Five of them were on his tail when he jetted onto the dirt road delineating two decaying neighborhoods. Thick walls of concrete and stone, standing nearly seven feet tall, lined the edges of the dirt road. And, coming in the opposite direction some distance away, was a squadron of HWKs and Humvees. It was a death trap and Pedro's screams intensified as the boy perceived the imminent danger.

Yet Father G gunned the throttle. The white chopper had reached a velocity of 180 mph when the priest brutally slammed on the brakes. The wheels skid for a considerable stretch but he controlled the machine brilliantly and at the last possible moment, torpedoed through a narrow gate through the left stone wall. A steel trapdoor slammed shut behind him and, as the pale hog blazed southwards, a series of deafening explosions rocked the ground like an earthquake.

Three HWKs, four Humvees, and seven black motorcycles were instantly incinerated from the immensely powerful high-tech landmines set off three seconds after G passed through the trapdoor. It was "Lucy"—one of the emergency plans put in place for extraordinary circumstances. Padre Quezada had successfully cleared the surrounding area of any lingering civilians just a few minutes ago.

G raced southeast at breakneck speeds. Enemy vehicles still swarmed the streets and he recognized any chance of a successful getaway depended on getting out of the city. A black HWK was stationed on one of the southern intersections of Avenida Manuel Talamás Camandari, a major road near the outskirts of Ciudad Juárez. The HWK gunman spotted the pale motorcycle as Father G zoomed back onto Blvd. Independencia and opened fire. Feverishly, the priest threw himself to the right and lowered the white chopper just enough to avoid being hit before quickly finding another route.

They were getting close to the city exit now; the priest could visualize the outlines of the HWKs at the military checkpoint. And then, finally, he saw the dirty-white Ford pickup parked on the edge of the road.

Thank God.

Father G leaned down and spoke into the microphone on a different channel. "Alma?"

The response was immediate. "Yes?"

"Now!"

He thrashed the throttle, ignoring the barrage of bullets tearing up the road ahead. One second later a massive explosion silenced the entire area as two HWKs turned into billowing clouds of neon-orange. The gunfire stopped and two seconds later three camouflage Humvees burst into flames as a second FGM-148 Javelin anti-tank missile, also launched from the back of the Ford pickup, smashed into its target. There was no need for Alma to fire a third Javelin missile.

The pale hog barreled through the molten wreckage of the checkpoint and for a few hundred yards in the open desert highway, they were home free. Until the ominous hum of the Kamov Ka-52 "Alligator" helicopter broke through the unnatural tranquility. The priest cursed. The helicopter was completely unexpected. And now both he and the boy were in serious trouble.

The white chopper jumped from asphalt onto the sunbaked flatlands of the Chihuahua desert. The Alligator veered closer and the fire from its 2A42 30mm machine gun intensified. The pale hog snaked in and out of the light creosote brush, spinning off storms of dirt and sand into the air, desperately trying to avoid the Alligator's line of fire. They came into a stretch of open terrain and Father G's right hand slammed open the throttle. The white chopper rocketed forwards with an intensity that caused Pedro to pass out.

Completely psyched up, yet with his mind focused on the number crunching, the priest continued to accelerate the motorcycle as it broke 195 mph and then 210 mph, putting a little space between them and the helicopter. It was the fastest speed he had ever attained. He pushed harder.

As the pale hog's velocity passed 225 mph, Father G roared and, alarmingly close to passing out himself, prayed Alma had done her job well and that he himself was up to the task. Now, going purely on instinct, he pounded the brakes and masterfully controlled the white chopper as it ripped up dirt, brush, sand, and rocks—eventually coming to a forceful halt. Simultaneously, the priest's right toes unlocked a metal lever in the front right of the pale hog and both his hands reached down to firmly grasp the weapon that appeared from underneath the uranium plating near the kickstand. The Alligator was close now, dangerously close, and the deadly gunfire was rapidly approaching. As the bullets came within several yards of the motorcycle, Father G got the Alligator within the crosshairs of his FIM-92X Stinger missile launcher. He pulled the trigger. And blasted the enemy narco helicopter to hell.

A few days later, in the wealthy suburbs of Mexico City, Pablo and Pedro Ortiz were playing soccer in the front yard of their vast mansion. The five-year-old twins loved to play soccer, just like their famous father. Their father, General Ortiz, the wily commander of all military operations in Juárez, had once been a star on the Mexican national team some twenty-five years ago, before beginning a successful career in the military.

General Ortiz had become wealthy in the last decade, very wealthy, and he married his trophy wife named Angélica, a former beauty queen from Guadalajara, to prove it. Angélica had born the general twins five years ago and, though he was rarely around, General Ortiz was immensely proud and fond of the boys.

From the French glass window on the second floor of her lavish palace, Angélica looked out upon her handsome sons with a smile. They were playing soccer on the freshly mowed lawn in the brilliant sunlight. A few minutes later, the doorbell rang. Angélica happily hummed one of the tunes from her favorite *telenovela* as she made the long walk down the spiral staircase, across the Italian marble floor, and to the front cedar door. Both her sons were racing across the well-kept front lawn to meet her.

"What is it *Mami?*" Pedro excitedly asked, his eyes staring at a spherical-shaped object wrapped up with fine gift paper and decorated with ribbons.

"Looks like a *futbol!*" exclaimed Pablo. "Open it, *Mami!*"

"¿Quien dejó esto aquí?" Angélica asked.

"Andrés Mami" answered Pedro. Andrés was one of the security guards. "Please, *ábrelo!*"

Angélica smiled, picked up the beautifully wrapped gift, and gently opened it. She then felt her heart plunge to her stomach. She screamed harder than both her sons could ever imagine. She screamed until she passed out. Her sons had been correct: the gift was indeed a *futbol.* And the skin of her husband's face was stitched into the leather—the price paid for failing to kill the pale rider.

Chapter 31

Matamoros, Tamaulipas, Mexico

"Bienvenido, cabrón," said Secretary Acosta, as Antonio Ezequiel Cárdenas Guillén (a.k.a. "Tony Tormenta"—"Tony the Storm") entered the reception area.

"Vete a la verga culero—Screw you, asshole," answered Cárdenas with a smile.

The two men embraced like brothers.

"Enjoy yourself, Antonio," continued the defense secretary. "I have spared no expense."

Cárdenas looked around lustily at the hordes of beautiful women. All were dressed in lingerie and all were high-quality, the best in Mexico. Cárdenas realized Acosta must have dished out a small fortune for them.

Secretary Acosta was dressed in fully military attire. Cárdenas, a top drug lord in the Gulf Cartel, wore a western dress shirt with embroidered roses, designer blue jeans, and ostrich skin cowboy boots. Strapped across his shoulder was a gold-plated AK-47. Cárdenas's famous brother, Osiel Cárdenas Guillén, was extradited to the United States in 2007 and forced to relinquish control of the cartel. Tony Tormenta, along with sibling Mario Cárdenas Guillén—a.k.a. "El Gordo" or "Fatso"—, and Jorge Eduardo Costilla—a.k.a. "El Coss"—, filled his void.

Tony Tormenta strolled across the marble floor of the reception area, eyes flicking up at a giant high-definition TV screen showing the movie *Scarface*. Near the TV screen was his brother Mario, his vast gun hanging over his gold belt buckle as he snorted cocaine and whooped in laughter. He was accompanied by two voluptuous prostitutes who were also eagerly snorting the white powder.

There were fifty-two high-ranking Gulf Cartel members at the party, and a slew of low-level drug-traffickers hailing from all over Tamaulipas—all connected to the Gulf Cartel in some shape or form. Some drank tequila; some snorted cocaine; some shot heroin. The prostitutes outnumbered the narcos about two to one; many of them on their knees, openly performing fellatio.

Aloof from the temptation of drugs and women were twenty-five members of Los Zetas, the enforcers of the Gulf Cartel. Los Zetas—"The Z's," named after a Mexican military code for high-ranking officers, were composed of some of the most highly trained and ruthless soldiers in the Mexican Special Forces. In 1997, Osiel Cárdenas Guillén, head of the Gulf Cartel at the time, was introduced to Arturo Guzmán Decena, a high-ranking member of the Mexican Army's elite Grupo Aeromóvil de Fuerzas Especiales (GAFE)—Special Forces Airmobile Group. Lured by money, more than thirty members of GAFE deserted from the Mexican Army to found the armed wing of the Gulf Cartel. Most had gone through extensive training conducted by both the United States and Israel. Guzmán Decena became known as "Z-1." His two chief deputies, Rogelio González Pizaña and Heriberto Lazcano Lazcano, were known as "Z-2" and "Z-3," respectively. Within the organization, Secretary Acosta was known as "Z-0."

For Cárdenas and the Gulf Cartel, the alliance appeared to be a stroke of genius. Los Zetas were the best trained assassins to ever fight for a cartel, outside of course, the "informal" involvement of Secretary Acosta and the Mexican military. Los Zetas also had access to weaponry and equipment never before used by the cartels. Recently, they broke into a prison in the state of Zacatecas with twenty heavily armed men, a dozen vehicles, and a helicopter. They freed fifty-three prisoners with ties to the Gulf Cartel.

Los Zetas, stoic and armed with AK-47s, took no part in the festivities. It was 4:15 a.m. when Secretary Acosta approached Lazcano, the commander of the mercenary squad for eight years—since Guzmán Decena went down in 2002. The party had quieted down considerably. A few of the Gulf Cartel members were still busy with the prostitutes, but the majority was sleeping or passed out.

The secretary's face was hard; his lips twitched. "It's time," hissed Acosta. "Finish them. Leave no witnesses. You are now in control of the *plaza,* Z-2."

Commander Lazcano nodded, slightly startled at the ruthless tone of the defense secretary's voice. Ramón Acosta was the only man he truly feared. But his fear evaporated as the defense secretary left the building and Z-2 gathered his troops. Los Zetas would now be in control of the Gulf.

It was 11:00 a.m. on the outskirts of Ciudad Juárez and an anomalous dark cloud provided a moment of respite from the fiery rays of the desert sun. Slanted across the dusty hillside, the giant painting of the white horse turned a strange shade of gray and El Pastor—"The Preacher," gazed for a few seconds at the mysterious artwork. He had no idea who created the portrait of the white animal or when it had been done. *Before the insane evil struck this Godforsaken city?* wondered El Pastor. Ultimately, he decided, it did not matter. The depiction of the white steed provided a tranquility that soothed his soul during his most trying times. It was the strange painting which made him choose this particular location to go forth with his work.

El Pastor wiped the perspiration off his forehead with the sleeve of his plaid shirt and gazed back at the sun-bleached concrete building housing 102 patients. *How am I going to feed them all?*

In truth, sometimes he regretted taking so many of them in. *But they had nowhere else to go,* he contemplated, trying to relieve his anxiety. *Most of them would probably be dead already.* The official death toll of the narco wars failed to include those who had overdosed on the venomous heroin, meth, and cocaine that had infiltrated every level of Juárez society. Not to mention those whose lives had been destroyed by the ubiquitous violence.

El Pastor decided some time ago that this was his calling in life; this was his own way of making amends—helping those whose bodies and minds had been ruined by the bloodshed, drugs, poverty, and disease which were so endemic to his side of the border metropolis. It was the least fortunate of the unfortunates whom the Lord had called him to serve; those who had no family and no social services; those to whom he himself had once belonged when he lived as a drug-addicted illegal immigrant in Los Angeles, California. But he had been saved by his Savior and Redeemer and thanked God every day for the miracle that occurred in his own life. He had been broken well beyond the point that those who had known him had ever thought he could recover. But by the grace of God and the love and mercy of Jesus Christ here he was, healthy, alive and, most of the time, at peace with himself. And on a mission to help save as many souls as he possibly could.

A twenty-two-year-old man named Marcos, insane by any account, walked into the backyard of the asylum. El Pastor had still not decided if Marcos suffered from schizophrenia or his brain had been permanently damaged by drug abuse and glue sniffing. Marcos saw El Pastor walking up the mountain trail and yelled at him with a toothless grin. El Pastor waived at Marcos and continued his journey.

There were many like Marcos at the asylum; lost spirits wandering around blindly in a cold world of darkness; rejected by all save for a precious few. For a while, the asylum housed Miss Sinaloa, a former beauty queen who came to the border city seeking fame and fortune. Instead, she was gang raped until she lost her mind. The police, not knowing what to do when no other facility would take her, dumped the beauty queen at the asylum several years ago, where she became a legend among her co-inhabitants.

El Pastor walked a few more hundred yards up the steep slope of the desert mountain and knelt beside the wooden cross he constructed years ago. On the crest of the barren ridge he could see miles and miles of the desolate landscape. Below him he could see the tiny bodies of his patients walking the grounds of the primitive asylum.

After being born again in 1985 and freeing himself from the heavy chains of substance abuse, El Pastor became an evangelical preacher on the dirty streets of Juárez—preaching to the drug addicts, the impoverished, the physically handicapped, and the mentally insane. Eventually, he and his wife ended up out here in the desert outskirts and somehow carved out a home in the inhospitable terrain. And, in those areas in Juárez where few respectable persons dared tread, El Pastor continued to preach the Gospel of Jesus Christ to all those who would listen.

In 1998, a freak snow storm ravaged the border city. As El Pastor was driving downtown through the blizzard, he swerved around a huge mound of snow in the middle of one of the streets. To his shock, the mound came to life and a half-frozen, brain-damaged man stood up shaking the snow off his body. El Pastor put the man in his vehicle and took him back home. He returned to the storm and rounded up as many homeless people as he could find. He took them back home also. And, slowly but surely, brick by brick and block by block, he converted his home into a shelter for the outcasts and the rejects of Juárez. He had been taking care of them ever since.

El Pastor folded his arms, looked up at the sandy sky, and prayed—as he had been doing for the last several months. He worked tirelessly on the radio to raise money for the ever-increasing expenses of the asylum. It had not been enough. He was deeply in debt and now at his wit's end. In these last few weeks he had prayed and fasted relentlessly, harder than he had ever done so before. It all seemed to be for naught. Tomorrow, he would begin rationing food and medicine. In a few days. he would send his patients back on the streets.

It was after El Pastor was done praying, when he had trekked about halfway down the mountain, that he saw the shadow on the rocky hillside. It was a strange shadow—a black stallion; an identical reciprocal of the painting of the white horse. El Pastor looked for the source of the mysterious shadow and saw, atop of an adjacent barren mountain, the silhouette of a motorcycle. Disturbed, El Pastor picked up his pace down the mountainside.

A few minutes later, in the crudely made parking lot of the primitive concrete building he called home, the preacher saw a dark blue minivan. The driver of the minivan, upon seeing El Pastor, got out of the vehicle. He was a bowling ball of a man, dressed in the clothes of a Catholic priest, smiling jovially, and carrying a tan leather bag. Two nuns, one heavyset, the other slim and petite, also got out of the minivan. A few of the patients had been watching the vehicle drive across the barren desert and pull into the parking lot. One of them, Reynaldo, a forty-nine-year-old white-haired man with Down's syndrome, recognized the visitors. "*¡Las Dos Vírgenes! ¡Las Dos Vírgenes!* They have come to rescue us!"

El Pastor looked at the grinning Reynaldo and then back at the nuns. He, too, had heard the rumors of Las Dos Vírgenes but dismissed them as Mexican folklore. He watched the nuns walk over to Reynaldo and hug him like a brother. The heavyset nun retrieved a Butterfinger candy bar from a brown bag and offered it to Reynaldo. El Pastor knew

Reynaldo loved Butterfingers. *Strange,* he thought, *they must know him from somewhere. They must be familiar with the forlorn streets of Ciudad Juárez.*

"El Pastor!" exclaimed the Catholic priest as he unashamedly walked up to the evangelical preacher and clasped his elbow. "It is indeed an honor, *Hermano!* My name is Padre Quezada and I have been looking forward to meeting you and seeing firsthand the great work you have done here. And let me say, El Pastor, it is great work you are doing. A marvelous work! And, upon a few conditions, we wish to help you."

El Pastor looked shocked. He scrutinized the round, fleshy face of his curious visitor. He had run-ins with Catholic priests before and harbored a slight resentment for them, and for their religion.

"You want to help me?" El Pastor asked. "You do understand, don't you, that I am an evangelical preacher? I do not believe in La Virgen de Guadalupe, and baptism by immersion is essential to one's salvation..."

Padre Quezada, still clutching the preacher's elbow, roared with laughter. His entire body shook like a massive chunk of jello and he laughed until tears came to his eyes. "*¡Ay, caramba!* Forgive me, El Pastor," he spoke in a jovial voice, "but I doubt very much that the Good Lord is as concerned in the mode of baptism as he is in how well we treat our neighbors. And I don't have to tell you that these people," he motioned to the crowd of patients flocking to witness the commotion, "—these people are our neighbors. Come," the priest continued, tightening his grip around El Pastor's arm, "walk with me."

El Pastor shrugged and did as Padre Quezada requested while the two nuns handed out goodies to the patients. Walking into the desert, the priest spoke again. "The Adversary has grown powerful in this land, El Pastor, and our society and culture is teetering on the brink of collapse. The level and nature of the occurring violence is unprecedented. To achieve victory, all followers of our Lord and Savior Jesus Christ must come together. There can be no infighting or disputations among us. Tell me, El Pastor, do you agree?"

The preacher stopped walking and studied Padre Quezada. The priest's features had sobered; there was urgency within the man's eyes El Pastor had not perceived before. And he felt something, too. Immediately he knew the truth of this strange-looking priest's words. The preacher nodded his head.

"Bueno," said Padre Quezada. "It is settled. We shall labor together."

The dark suspicions returned to El Pastor's mind. "Wait a minute. Before, you spoke of some conditions?"

"Ah, yes," replied the round priest. "How many patients do you currently have?"

"102."

"You must expand. This location is well capable of housing thousands of patients. The work of the narcos has destroyed the minds and lives of countless individuals and the effort to heal them will be considerable."

For the first time that day, El Pastor laughed. "And how do you propose we finance your vision of expansion?"

Padre Quezada handed the tan leather bag to the preacher. "Take it. It is yours."

El Pastor took hold of the leather bag and almost dropped it. It was surprisingly heavy. He looked inside at its contents and then fell to his knees, flabbergasted.

"It contains one million U.S. dollars' worth of gold and three million in cash," said Padre Quezada. "To quote the words of our Savior: 'Be ye therefore wise as a serpent.' Always take heed of the Adversary, for he will rob you blind and destroy all that you have built. Work with the right people and expand, expand, expand. There are innumerable souls counting on you. Do not burden yourself with finances. The sisters and I shall check in from time to time to see how you are progressing and we will provide whatever you need."

Tears filled El Pastor's eyes. His knees sunk deeper into the desert soil. He tried to speak but found himself incapable. He looked up at the painting of the white horse and knew then that God had finally answered his prayers. And as his eyes went from the white horse to the wooden cross on the mountain top, he again saw the motorcycle. Its pale metal glistened eerily against the sun's rays and the oncoming dust storm. Upon the motorcycle he could see a man and amidst his joy, El Pastor felt a tremor of fear. El Pastor could still hear the echoes of Padre Quezada's departing words: "And fear not the pale rider that shall come among you. For he shall be your protector."

Chapter 32

Al Wajh, Saudi Arabia

Sheik Mahdavi Haqqani was having difficulty breathing. His jaw was trembling and his beige *bisht* was drenched in sweat. As Mokhtar walked into the bedroom, the old man tried to compose himself. Mokhtar was also wearing a *bisht* and both men had black flags of jihad embroidered onto the left breast of their robes. Mokhtar slowly ran his fingers through his beard while observing the coal-colored eyes of his revered grandfather. Sheik Haqqani was the supreme religious figure in the province of Al Wajh. His power in the region was unparalleled. But something was wrong. Mokhtar knew his grandfather had been suffering from nightmares for the last several months, though the old man obstinately refused to talk about them.

Sheik Haqqani was among the oldest men alive in Saudi Arabia and he was also the richest. No one, not even Mokhtar, knew for certain how much the ancient sheik was worth but it was suspected he was one of the wealthiest men on the planet. Sheik Haqqani had been his father's favorite son and at the time of his father's death, forty-seven years ago, Mahdavi inherited over 80 percent of the family's fortune. The thirteenth of twenty-one children and the fifth of eleven sons, Mahdavi left a trail of familial destruction in his rise to power. He was shrewd, calculating, and ruthless. After two of his older half-brothers died in an operation in Jerusalem, Mahdavi successfully convinced Nasir, his semi-sane older full brother, to carry out a suicide mission in Yemen. He then killed his oldest male sibling, Hassan, in a duel over the honor of one of their half-sisters.

For the last four decades, Sheik Mahdavi Haqqani had been in total control of both the economic and religious aspects of the land. He married any woman he desired and when he tired of any wife, she was conveniently disposed of. Anyone in the community who dared oppose him was dealt with swiftly, and Sheik Haqqani became incredibly adept at overtaking the assets of individuals and families put to death under Sharia Law.

Mokhtar was fiercely proud of the old man and had striven to gain the affections of his grandfather since childhood. On the evening of his thirteenth birthday, during his family's visit to France, he killed for the first time. Mokhtar remembered the incident well. His victim was a seventy-one-year-old Jewish woman; he stabbed her thirteen times with his pocket knife in downtown Paris. He had always been taught that Jews were to be destroyed. Before making his getaway, Mokhtar ripped off a golden necklace from the woman's throat. Later that night he presented the gold Star of David, painted in the Jewess's blood, to his grandfather. Tears filled Sheik Haqqani's eyes as he embraced his young grandson. "Praised be Allah," the old man had told him. "You will grow to be a great warrior, Mokhtar. You will be the sword sutured to Allah's hand and you will be instrumental in carrying out his justice!" Mokhtar could still visualize the gritty determination etched within his grandfather's watery eyes.

Mokhtar, now forty-seven years of age, had fulfilled his grandfather's prophecy and had proven to be every bit as clever, ruthless, and ambitious as the old man. Working in the shadows of several terrorist organizations, his power and influence had grown exponentially in the Islamic underworld. In 1996, he had been involved in the Khobar

Towers bombing in Saudi Arabia that murdered twenty individuals, including nineteen airmen from the U.S. Air Force, and wounded 372. In 1997, he helped carry out the Luxor Massacre in Egypt that murdered sixty-two people. In 1998, he worked in conjunction with al-Qaeda and the Egyptian Islamic Jihad to orchestrate the bombings of the U.S. embassies in Tanzania and Nairobi that murdered 224 people and injured more than 4,000. In 2000, Mokhtar helped command the attack on the USS Cole that murdered seventeen U.S. sailors and injured thirty-nine. He worked with Osama bin Laden and key Al-Qaeda operatives in planning the suicide attacks on 9/11 responsible for the murder of 2,977 people. It was Mokhtar who commanded the attacks in Istanbul in 2003 that murdered fifty-seven individuals and wounded 700 others. He masterminded the train bombings in Madrid in 2004 that murdered 191 people and injured another 2,050. In 2005, he planned the bombings on London's subways that murdered fifty-two individuals and injured over 700 others. And then, going on five years now, Mokhtar had gone silent. He had been planning an attack that would engrave his name into Islam for centuries to come. And, tonight, he would meet in person with the man he hoped would help make that happen.

Secretary Acosta cringed at the heat as he stepped out of his private plane in a small airport near the outskirts of Al Wajh. He wore a black *bisht.* A white turban was wrapped around his head. His black beard was thick; the skin on his jaw irritated him. He had not shaved in two months and would not do so until he returned to Mexico. The failure at Juárez still enraged him and, with effort, he pushed the thoughts out of his mind—he needed to concentrate now on the mission at hand.

There were several black Rolls-Royces stationed nearby the plane, surrounded by men in cream-white *bishts*. The men's arms were folded, faces bearded and hard. Each wore a crimson turban and dark sunglasses. A red 2008 Ferrari FXX Evolution was parked in between the Rolls-Royces and Mokhtar got out of the vehicle with a smile on his face. He walked over to the plane's stairway and held out his hand.

"Secretary Acosta, welcome to Saudi Arabia. You do not know how long I have been waiting for this moment." He spoke in English with a heavy accent.

Secretary Acosta bowed, reached out with both arms, and shook Mokhtar's hand. "Please, Mokhtar, call me Ramón. It is an honor to be in this great country. I, too, have been anxiously anticipating this journey." He spoke in perfect Arabic. Mokhtar was visibly impressed.

"Excellent," replied Mokhtar in Arabic, smiling wider. "Praised be Allah. You both look and sound like a true follower of Muhammad, peace be upon him. Come," he motioned to the Ferrari, "I shall introduce you to Al Wajh."

Secretary Acosta got in the passenger seat of the Ferrari. Mokhtar floored the accelerator. He paid four million U.S. dollars for the vehicle and it was his favorite sports car. Mokhtar brought the Ferrari to a speed of 130 mph and casually observed Secretary Acosta as he swerved around a bend. A wry smile appeared on Ramón's face. "When you come to Mexico, Mokhtar, you will accompany me for a ride in my MiG-35. I will show you the true definition of speed."

Mokhtar laughed. "I like you, Ramón. I see we are going to get along just fine."

The size and elegance of the palace complex surprised Secretary Acosta. Immaculate paradisiacal gardens surrounding residential structures covered two square miles. Thousands of palm trees stood among dolphin ponds and tropical birds of all varieties could be seen flying in and out of emerald leaves. Outside the central palace, Mokhtar parked the Ferrari in a massive garage housing 107 other such sports cars. On the opposite side of the garage, some 200 yards away, was a mosque with a solid gold dome and façade in fine polychrome porcelain. The palace itself possessed a classical Islamic architecture and was built on top of a rolling hill overlooking the Red Sea. Mokhtar and Secretary Acosta entered the palace via a monumental archway above an elaborate stone doorway with a pagoda-shaped roof.

Inside was a vast reception room with walls and ceilings covered in intricately carved and painted wood, embellished with Arab calligraphy. The mosaic floors were constructed from fine Italian marble and glimmered brilliantly against the elaborate crystal chandeliers hanging from the ceilings.

"Remarkable," said Secretary Acosta.

Mokhtar smiled. "The palace was originally constructed in the eighteenth century by one of my ancestors, the great Sheikh Saif Muhammad Haqqani. My grandfather, praised be Allah, inherited it in 1968, and since that time the palace has gone through several renovations. Most recently we have installed several new security systems including a unique labyrinth of bunkers and tunnels designed to withstand biological, chemical, and nuclear attacks. We've also put in state-of-the-art computer networks and artificial intelligence software to fend off cyber-attacks as well as perform our own virtual espionage. But first I shall take you to the second floor and the museum. My grandfather, praised be Allah, owns the most impressive collection of swords and daggers in the world."

The collection was impressive. Podium after podium displayed multitudes of metallic blades from all different time periods, some dating back to the Bronze Age. There were thousands of Arabic daggers and swords with hilts of gold, ivory, and rhinoceros horn, inset with precious stones of incredible quality. There was one weapon Mokhtar was especially proud of: a strange, split-bladed sword, appearing as giant shears with serrated edges. It had a hilt of gold studded with precious stones. It lay across tablets of bronze engraved with ancient Arabic characters.

"The sword has a name and it is Zulfiqar," said Mokhtar reverently, his eyes moistening. "It once belonged to the Prophet Muhammed, peace be upon him. In the year 625, Muhammed, peace be upon him, gave the weapon to his cousin and son-in-law, Ali ibn Abi Talib, at the battle of Uhud. Using Zulfiqar, Ali slew the strongest warriors in Mecca—the blade destroyed both shield and helmet of the enemy. It is the most powerful weapon ever made. It is our most prized possession, praised be Allah." Ramón could not contain his skepticism. Mokhtar keenly observed his expression.

"You do not believe?" Mokhtar asked. Secretary Acosta said nothing.

"I will show you," said Mokhtar. He picked up Zulfiqar with his right hand and swung it through the air. He then extended his left hand towards the collection of weapons and looked at Ramón. "Go ahead. Choose one." Ramón shrugged. He selected one of the bigger swords, two-handed hilt, thick blade—double-edged and sharp.

"Swing it," said Mokhtar. "Hard."

Secretary Acosta obliged. The thick blade sliced through air and was greeted by the sting of Zulfiqar. The large blade held by Ramón shattered.

"Impressive," acknowledged Secretary Acosta.

Mokhtar grinned.

Late that evening, close to midnight, Secretary Acosta was introduced to Sheik Mahdavi Haqqani. The old man was alone in a secluded area of the palace, staring at a huge portrait of the Dome of the Rock, a shrine in Jerusalem standing out as one of the oldest works of Islamic architecture. The sheik was smoking guava-flavored tobacco from a gold *hookah.*

Secretary Acosta slowly walked towards the old man. "Greetings, Sheik Haqqani. It is indeed an honor." Ramón knelt down at the feet of the old sheik and presented him with a gift. Sheik Haqqani mumbled something in response and glanced at the offering. It resembled a long club with a two-handed grip, about four feet in length, decorated with blades of black glass.

"In our native tongue we call it a *macuahuitl*," Secretary Acosta said in English. "This is an original and is believed to be over 600 years old. Officially, there are no such specimens in existence today—the last publicly known *macuahuitl* was destroyed during a fire in 1884 at the Royal Armoury of Madrid."

The ancient sheik studied the weapon. "It looks flimsy," he said. "It would be no match for any of the contemporary swords of the time period."

Sparks of rage flickered behind Secretary Acosta's eyes. *¡Hijo de la chingada!* He pictured cupping his right hand underneath the sheik's jaw and twisting it in one brutal motion—hearing the crunch of bone and the rush of blood...

He quickly composed himself. "I'm not so sure, Sheik Haqqani. The prismatic blades can be sharpened to a much finer edge than any metal, and the weapon was engineered in such a fashion that the obsidian is impervious to destruction. There are many tales of its effectiveness in warfare from the Spanish Conquistadors. Even today, the weapon is compared to a chain saw."

Secretary Acosta spoke in perfect Arabic and his mastery of the foreign language threw Sheik Haqqani off guard for just a moment. The old man frowned but did not press the issue. "You are the first

Mexican I have ever met in person, Secretary Acosta, though I have studied the history and culture of your country. So, tell me something of your religious beliefs, you are a Catholic I assume?"

Secretary Acosta eyeballed the old man. "No, Sheik Haqqani. I am not."

"Then a Christian of another denomination?"

"The vast majority of my countrymen are indeed Christians, Sheik Haqqani, but I am not among them. The scourge of Christendom on my country is a tragic ramification of the conquering of a magnanimous and noble people through treachery, deception, and disease." The answers took the sheik by surprise and he stroked his long white beard in silence for a few moments before speaking again. "My grandson tells me, Secretary Acosta, that you are the most powerful man in your country."

"Yes. That is true."

"He also tells me that you will soon be in control of the United States border."

"I will own the most valuable ports of entry by year's end."

"And what will you be able to transport into the United States?"

"You name it. Men, supplies, vehicles, weapons—in any size or quantity you can imagine."

The sheik stroked his beard and remained silent for forty seconds. "Very well, Secretary Acosta. Welcome to Saudi Arabia and to my home. Enjoy your stay here. First thing tomorrow, you shall accompany us as an honored guest to one of our more traditional events here in Al Wajh."

Secretary Acosta bowed once again. "It will be an honor, Sheik Haqqani."

The old man smiled for the first time. "It is settled then. My servants shall show you to your quarters. Good evening, Secretary Acosta."

After Secretary Acosta left the room, Mokhtar walked over to the sheik's side. "What do you think, Grandfather?"

The old man sucked in the guava flavored tobacco from his *hookah* and exhaled. "I don't know yet, Mokhtar. We cannot rush this. Did you confirm the plans with Bahirah?"

"Yes, praised be Allah."

Secretary Acosta recognized the girl immediately. She was dressed in black lace lingerie and lay sprawled out on the purple satin bedspread in a provocative pose.

"Hello, Bahirah," said Secretary Acosta with a wry smile.

The girl was genuinely shocked. Secretary Acosta had met the girl briefly, along with Sheik Haqqani's other wives, and she had been wearing a black *hijab*—her head and face fully covered by a veil.

"How did you know it was me?" the girl asked, wide-eyed. She was the youngest of the sheik's wives at eighteen years of age and she was beautiful. Her long dark hair stood out lustrously against her smooth olive skin.

"By your eyes, Bahirah. I could never forget such pearls. They are truly the eyes of a princess. Tell me Princess, does Sheik Haqqani know you are here?"

Secretary Acosta acutely observed the flicker of fear—her husband did know she was here; he had commanded her to be here under the threat of family violence.

"Yes, Secretary Acosta, he knows I am here and he wants your experience at the palace to be as pleasant as possible."

Secretary Acosta smiled unashamedly as he disrobed and took the girl into his arms.

At 9:00 a.m., the small arena was crowded with spectators, some of them screaming in fits of madness and others crying for mercy. Two men, guards of some sort, dressed in black *bishts* and black turbans, marched an eight-year-old boy into the middle of the arena. The boy went willingly with a strange grin on his face. Secretary Acosta, sitting between Sheik Haqqani and Mokhtar in the front middle section of the arena, observed the boy had Down's syndrome and was suffering from malnutrition.

In the middle of the arena was a large man with a thick beard, dressed in olive-green fatigues. He wore a black mask and was carrying a scimitar, a traditional Arabic curved sword, in his right hand. The two guards marched the boy up to the executioner and tied his left hand to his right ankle. The executioner looked directly at Sheik Haqqani. The old man nodded his assent.

"For the crime of thievery," the executioner bellowed, "you are sentenced in accordance with the writings of the Prophet." The crowd went into frenzy. Many of the spectators clamored for leniency; others shouted for justice. "But alas, the almighty Sheik Haqqani has decided to show mercy. The boy shall keep his right hand." The executioner put down the scimitar.

"But," he continued, "it is the will of Allah that justice be served." He reached down to pick up a sledgehammer. "May you never again rob from another."

The young boy was still smiling as a guard grasped his right wrist and stretched his arm out on a large stone. The child had been caught stealing a loaf of bread in the market place of a nearby village. The executioner smirked sadistically against the noise of the crowd. He lifted the sledgehammer above his head. It was only then that the child recognized his fate; his facial muscles contorted to display the expression of raw terror that Secretary Acosta was so familiar with. The boy's screams echoed throughout the arena as the sledgehammer slammed into his arm. A few spectators shouted their approval; most looked on in dread. The child blacked out and was carried back outside the arena to be dumped on the streets from which he came.

Two young teenage girls, sisters, were marched into the arena, hands bound behind their backs. Unlike the boy with Down's syndrome, they were visibly terrified and shaking uncontrollably. Their father, a man named Ibrahim, had made the error of speaking out against Sheik Haqqani on a crowded bus and the incident was reported. Ibrahim, as usual, was present in the arena. Everyone was required to go. Upon realizing the two captive girls were his daughters, Ibrahim went into a crazed panic. He was silenced immediately by the cold metal of dagger blades at his throat.

The sisters were forced onto their stomachs. Several guards stomped on their lower backs. The executioner, now holding Sheik Haqqani's *macuahuitl*, spoke in a booming voice that carried throughout the arena: "For the heinous crimes of homosexuality and incest, you are both hereby sentenced to death." The girls had been spotted holding hands on their walk home after school. Ibrahim wailed and serrated steel cut into his jugular vein as he tried to stand up. The guards carried away his corpse and the two sisters were summarily beheaded by the ancient weapon.

Mokhtar grinned as he faced Secretary Acosta. "You are indeed correct, Ramón," Mokhtar said with a chuckle. "The weapon is indeed sharp—never before have we had such a clean cut." He pulled out a cigarette, lit it, and took a deep drag. "You will enjoy this next session. I've added my own little twist to it."

Eight men were led into the arena, dressed in dirty rags, hands tied behind their backs. "Apostates," said Mokhtar, "the worst kind of scum. The man in front is the leader and has been secretly preaching Christianity."

The Christians were forced on their knees. The executioner exchanged the *macuahuitl* for the proven steel of the scimitar and came forward with blade in hand. "You are swine! You have betrayed your family, your country, and Allah! But Sheik Haqqani is merciful and, in his intelligence and grace, has allowed you to die honorably!" A section of the crowd erupted. The guards placed eight scimitars near the kneeling Christians and, one by one, the cords binding the Christians' hands were cut.

The leader, Bilal, remained kneeling. His eyes were closed, his head was bowed, and his hands were clasped together in prayer. He was promptly beheaded. The executioner killed three more men before one of the Christians challenged him with a series of strong blows.

The lone Christian attacker was an experienced swordsman and within a few minutes, to the stunned silence of the crowd, he drove his scimitar through the executioner's gut. Sheik Haqqani frowned and looked at his grandson. Never had such a thing happened. "This is unexpected," Sheik Haqqani said, in a subdued tone. "We must now make different..."

Before he could finish the sentence, the ancient sheik watched open-mouthed as Secretary Acosta jumped into the arena, walked to the center, and picked up the *macuahuitl*. He approached the Christian warrior holding the bloody scimitar. With previously unseen speed and skill, Secretary Acosta sliced the *macuahuitl* through the Christian's arms, expertly avoiding the flashing scimitar. Then, with one incredible back-handed thrust, he slashed the weapon into the Christian's ribcage, killing him instantly. Within a few seconds, Secretary Acosta disposed of the survivors. The spectators applauded, expressing respect for the display of swordsmanship. But as Secretary Acosta returned to the arena's edge, Sheik Haqqani stood up and raised his right hand. The crowd went silent.

"Ramón, we have one more punishment due, and I would ask that you be the executioner," said the sheik.

Secretary Acosta slightly nodded his head in assent.

"Good," said the old man. "Now trade me weapons."

Secretary Acosta dropped the *macuahuitl* and Sheik Haqqani threw down a round stone the size of a baseball. On the south side of the arena, a gate opened and two guards marched a woman inside. She had long, dark hair, smooth olive skin, and was wearing nothing but black lingerie. It was Bahirah. A cacophony of catcalls, hisses, and whistles spewed from the stands. Sheik Haqqani immediately silenced the spectators. A wicked grim formed upon his aged face. "For the crime of adultery," he announced, "I sentence this harlot to death."

Secretary Acosta walked back to the middle of the arena, face as hard as the stone he carried. Upon recognizing her would-be executioner and former lover, Bahirah screamed for her life with newfound hysteria. "Help me, Ramón! Please help me! I had to come to you! I had no choice! They said they would kill my family if I did not!"

"Don't worry, Bahirah," Secretary Acosta replied calmly. "Everything will be fine."

For just a split second the girl's face relaxed in relief, right before Secretary Acosta crushed her skull with a perfect throw of the stone.

It was well past midnight when Mokhtar visited his grandfather on the palace's rooftop. The old man was smoking intensely from his gold *hookah.* The moonlight eerily reflected off his long white beard. "You have done well, Mokhtar. Secretary Acosta presents us with the opportunity we have been waiting for. I give you my blessing to work with this man. Give him anything he asks for."

This Mexican is the key to victory. The thought elated him. The ancient sheik stared at the full moon like a wolf and dug his fingernails into his own flesh, drawing blood. His next words hissed venomously out of his cracked lips. "And we will bring the Great Satan to its knees!"

Just before sunrise, when he could no longer fight the urge to sleep, Sheik Haqqani found himself in a fiery dungeon—one which he knew very well. He was naked and his wrists and ankles were bound to glowing orange chains. He could see the faces of the people whom he had murdered during his lifetime. And they were many. He recognized the vengeful screams of Bahirah. She had now come to haunt him in his dreams.

Another voice, one he was intimately familiar with, was shrieking in his ear with an intensity that racked his brain. But it was the image that caused his soul to quake. It was the same image that had tormented him so thoroughly, driving him to the edge of insanity these last few months. He tried desperately to close his eyes and wipe away the terrorizing sight. But it was to no avail. And, despite himself, his eyes focused in on the scene that shook his ancient bones to the core....

Chapter 33

Juvenile Detention Center—El Paso, Texas, USA

José Luis Elizondo stared at the hollow eye sockets of the black skull and let the hate thrash through his blood. His right eye was permanently damaged and he wore sunglasses continually to hide the deformity. Fists clenched in rage, he stepped back from the mirror and his own eyes flickered from the reflection of his latest tattoo of Santa Muerte to the newspaper clipping posted on the wall.

The caption read "Four-Time State Champion" and below it was a photograph of the individual José Luis had become obsessed with. The leader of the Barrio Azteca gang now hated Israel more than anyone and his quest for vengeance had become all-consuming; he could think of little else.

Although José Luis's time at the juvenile detention center had seemed like an eternity, he would be out in two weeks. And the new contacts he made here were invaluable. There was a sharp rap on the door and Adolfo, a tall, lanky gangster with a morbid tattoo of a female devil draped across his back, entered José Luis's cell.

"*¿Qué onda, cabrón?*" chirped Adolfo. He was grinning like a *pendejo* and the two gold teeth in the front of his mouth popped out at a strange angle that José Luis found tremendously annoying.

"¿Qué chingados quieres? What the hell do you want, Adolfo?" José Luis growled, unclenching his fists and rotating his eyeballs into an awkward position. He disliked being interrupted at this hour and Adolfo knew it. His eyes went back to the newspaper clipping.

"We got some good news, *vato.* Your homeboy goes to Juárez—a lot—every Saturday." Adolfo spoke English with a thick accent.

José Luis removed his sunglasses and turned around to face Adolfo. *"Joder*—what did you say?"

"He goes to Juárez every Saturday *ese*—all day. He does volunteer work in the *colonias* and youth centers, stuff like that. He works with some Catholic priests and nuns."

A gruesome smile stretched across José Luis's lips. It had been a long time since he had smiled. He could do anything in Juárez and get away with it. He had killed there before and he would do so again. Still smiling, José Luis turned around to again face the mirror. A brand-new set of ugly and vicious images, centering on the murder of his arch nemesis, ran through his brain as he worked on a plan. He imagined himself raping Mayrín while Israel was forced to watch. And then he envisioned himself slowly slicing Israel's throat with his favorite knife.

"Gracias, Adolfo. You shall be *puto* rewarded for this."

"¡Buenos días!" Padre Quezada beamed as he entered through the classroom doorway of the Ysleta Mission Church. As he passed out *pan dulce* to his early morning students, two nuns entered the classroom. "We have two special guests with us today," said the husky priest. "Please welcome two of my dearest friends, Sister López and Sister Arámbula."

Overjoyed, Israel got to his feet, rushed over to the nuns, and embraced each one of them like a mother. *"¡Chido!* Where have you all been hiding? I haven't seen you in over a month."

Sister Arámbula hugged the boy with obvious pride and her eyes moistened, "Sorry Israel—we been very busy."

"And Father G?" Israel asked. He hadn't seen the priest now for a few weeks, since the State Wrestling Championships.

"God be with you Israel. Father G sends his regards," Sister López answered. "He's had some unexpected work but he plans to return to El Paso as soon as possible."

"We hear you have new *amiga,*" Sister Arámbula said in a coquettish tone, eyeing Mayrín with a coy grin. "Perhaps after the lesson we can sit down and talk a bit."

Freak...

After Israel sat down, Padre Quezada noticed Mayrín sitting next to him. "*¡Ay, caramba!* I see we have a visitor with us today. Welcome, child, welcome!" Padre Quezada extended both of his arms to warmly shake Mayrín's hand and offered her *pan dulce*.

"Thank you very much, Padre," replied Mayrín, taking one of the sweet rolls. She unashamedly reached down to take hold of Israel's left hand. Padre Quezada slightly arched his eyebrows. "Israel, would you please introduce us to your friend?"

Freak. Israel blushed and slowly rose to his feet in concert with his friend. Once standing, he gently tried to unlock his hand from Mayrín's grasp. She wouldn't let him. "Yeah," he stammered. "This is my, uh, girlfriend, Mayrín. She is from Spain and is spending her senior year in high school here in El Paso with her aunt and uncle."

There were good-natured chuckles throughout the classroom. Isabel was all smiles and Israel's friend Sergio was pinching himself to keep from laughing out loud.

"It is a pleasure to have you here, Mayrín, and I sincerely hope we will be seeing more of you," responded Padre Quezada, ignoring the amusement of his students. "What do you call it when Batman leaves church early?"

"Hello? Christian Bale," answered Isabel instantly, amidst the groans of the class. She had heard that one before.

The stocky priest laughed for a few seconds and then consumed one of the sweet rolls and took two gulps of black coffee from his Fighting Irish mug. "This morning, students, we will have the privilege of hearing from Sister López."

The petite nun finished a glass of orange juice and then faced the group of young students. "God be with you." She smiled brightly. All the male students stared at her in awe. "Can anyone tell me," she asked, "what are the three virtues Paul writes of in his epistle to the Corinthians?"

Mayrín remained quiet for thirty minutes as she listened to the back-and-forth discussion on faith between the nuns and the class. Finally, she spoke.

"Yeah well, but in such a world of pain, suffering, and chaos, how can we like, find faith in the first place? Um, and with so many religions and varieties of faith, how can you be sure that I should not put my faith in Muhammad or Buddha?" Everyone turned to stare at Mayrín. She continued unabashed. "Weren't the atrocities committed during the Inquisition and Crusades due to the unwavering faith of Christians goin' all fanatic?" After the outburst, more than a few individuals thought Sister López might become upset. But the nun remained smiling and continued speaking in her gentle tone.

"God be with you, Mayrín. Thank you for your thoughtful comments. You raise important questions that people have been struggling with for thousands of years. Let me start out by saying that I do not pretend to understand all of life's mysteries. No one on Earth does. This is where the notion of faith plays such a vital role—to believe and hope without a full understanding."

For another forty minutes, Mayrín listened intently to everything the nuns had to say. She was still embroiled in intense conversation well after class had ended. Padre Quezada had just gone to Juárez and Israel had left for school some time ago. Mayrín had not moved from her chair—she found herself completely engrossed in what the nuns were telling her. It was only the abrupt chiming of the mission bell at 8:00 a.m. that startled her back into reality.

"Oh my gosh," she exclaimed, springing to her feet in a flustered panic, "Like, I am sooo late."

It was just then that Sister Arámbula noticed the silver pendant dangling around the girl's neck, escaping momentarily from the white blouse holding it captive. A strike of déjà vu blossomed in the nun's mind. Mayrín saw the rotund nun staring at the piece of jewelry and quickly tried to stuff it in her blouse. It was too late.

"That is beautiful jewelry, Mayrín," said Sister Arámbula. "Where you get it?"

Mayrín's full lips formed a smile but both nuns sensed an undercurrent of pain behind it. "I've had it for a very long time," she answered quickly. She abruptly stood up and gathered her belongings. "Yeah, well, I have enjoyed our discussion. Who'd a thunk, huh? I will think about everything you've all told me."

Chapter 34

Coahuila Desert, Mexico

Livia squeezed her thirteen-year-old sister's hand tighter as they marched over the crusty desert sand. "It will be okay, Yadhira. We're almost there now—I can feel it." Despite her big sister's brave words, Yadhira could sense the doubt in Livia's voice. Yadhira's mouth was so dry it was difficult to swallow. She fiercely craved water. She looked at her sixteen-year-old sister with drooping eyelids, glistening with tears, and nodded her head. It was clear to Livia from her sister's heartbreaking expression that she did not believe her. Livia stared up ahead at the backside of César, the "coyote" of their ragged band, and silently cursed him. *¡Hijo de puta!*

She had never trusted César, not since the group of Honduran refugees first met him in the Mexican city of Minatitlán seven days ago. But her fellow countrymen had become enamored with the smooth-talking Mexican and his supposed, vast intimate knowledge of the Mexican/U.S. border. César had told the group he would guide them through the most trusted railways and through the safest desert trails. He said they would be in the northern promised land before they knew it. He said that good-paying jobs would be waiting for them. He said that there would be all the food they could eat and enough clean hot water to take ten showers a day. And all he required was twenty-five

U.S. dollars, from each member of the group, paid once they reached their destination. Livia sensed something fishy about the agreement from the beginning. She also disliked the way César looked at both her and her sister and she argued tenaciously against following him.

Despite Livia's protests, the group of forty-three Hondurans had collectively overruled her. They decided to place their trust in this charming, beady-eyed Mexican who claimed he could lead them to paradise. Livia unconsciously clutched at the ragged purse where she kept her 443 U.S. dollars—the life savings of her parents that she and Yadhira had collected upon their deaths. The familiar agony of her parents' memory caused Livia to stumble in the lifeless scrub and it was only the sturdy arm of Yadhira that kept her from falling. None of the group paid any attention to her.

Almost everyone was out of water and most were starting to suspect their faith in César had been misplaced. But there was nothing they could do now but march on. The group disembarked the train two days ago when it stopped unexpectedly in the most barren land any of the Hondurans had ever seen. But César had claimed they were close now, very close, and their new lives of bliss were just a day's hike away.

The sun was just starting its descent into the pink western sky when César abruptly stopped walking and raised his brown arms into the air like a desert Messiah. "*¡Amigos!*" he exclaimed triumphantly. "We have made it! *¡Miren!*" César pointed off in the distance to the northwest and everyone's eyes rotated in that direction. And, for the first time in seven days, a spark of hope flickered inside Livia.

Perhaps I have been wrong about César, she thought, squeezing Yadhira's hand in earnest. Sure enough, several hundred yards to the northwest, just like the charming Mexican had promised, a group of vehicles could be seen surrounding the perimeter of a green mass of creosote bushes. "See!" César exclaimed jubilantly, "The vehicles that will take you to your new homes!"

"They're coming," grunted Gonzalo Geresano Escribano, a.k.a. Z-18.

"*Chingado* finally," responded Galdino Mellado Cruz, a.k.a. Z-9.

Mellado opened his eyes. "*¡Joder!*" His head was throbbing. He picked up the microphone to inform the others. Despite his misery, the Zeta forced his senses to come alive and he checked the weapons one more time. His training demanded it. Not that he expected any trouble from the docile Honduran immigrants. But like all missions, he would be thorough and prepare for anything.

Los Zetas had made Secretary Acosta a fortune through theft, extortion, kidnapping, and human trafficking. And they were helping bring the terror and bloodshed in Mexico to a new level. It was necessary, Tlaloc had insisted. Ramón was in agreement. The weak must be culled to achieve their vision and the soil must be plowed for the people to receive the true gods. The terror inflicted by Los Zetas would serve as a catalyst for the religious conversion of Mexico.

Secretary Acosta had instituted a DNA biometric laboratory within the military and developed a sophisticated DNA database. Los Zetas would use the database to strike fear in their enemies by killing family members—spouses, children, siblings—even aunts, uncles, and cousins.

Many a mutilated corpse was found with the letter 'Z' engraved into its flesh. Los Zetas were notorious for robbing migrants from Guatemala and Central America, traveling north with all their cash and worldly possessions on hand. And Los Zetas would kill them—women and children included—indiscriminately. In 2008, a female body was found in a car trunk outside Mexico City. The deceased victim had a bullet wound to the head and 'Z's slashed into her chest, stomach, and buttocks. It was later discovered the woman was Zulema Hernández, the lover of El Chapo.

Mellado and Geresano met five years before the founding of Los Zetas while serving in the Mexican Army's First Special Forces Airmobile Group. Both were transferred to a unit in the attorney general's office for counter narcotics operations. There, they met General Ramón Acosta and became two of the thirty-four founding members of Los Zetas who deserted the Mexican Special Forces to become enforcers for Osiel Cárdenas Guillén's Gulf Cartel. Those days of indentured servitude were long gone. Supervised loosely by Secretary Acosta, Los Zetas had become their own independent crime organization.

In addition to Mellado and Geresano, thirteen other Zetas were waiting for César to bring them the goods. All were trained killers and most displayed complete disregard for human life and dignity. The fifteen Zetas had been stationed at this dismal spot in the wilderness for seventeen hours and were anxious for their next assignment. Some were eagerly anticipating their introduction to the Honduran females before heading back to Nuevo Laredo.

Central American refugees were easy targets, and a group the size César was leading would have about 50,000 U.S. dollars in cash and at least eight or ten young women that would make nice profits in the sex trade. The rest of the migrants—the males, elderly, and undesirables—would be summarily executed.

As César led the migrants to the vehicles, turning out to be military Humvees, thirteen Zetas disembarked. They were dressed in military fatigues and heavily armed with AK-47s and FX-05 Xiuhcoatls. A handful of the exhausted migrants, sensing the trap, started to make a run for it. The deafening sound of assault rifle gunfire stopped them in their tracks.

"*¡No corran!*" yelled César, brandishing his own pistol. "Your lives will be spared. All they want is a toll for their services. You will all be safe and these men will help you get across the border. Now everyone kneel and take out your wallets and purses."

Her worst suspicions now confirmed, Livia made the decision within seconds. She quickly surveyed the immediate landscape and noticed a distinct difference in ground levels far off to her left. Her eyes homed in on several large boulders and a series of rocky outcroppings guarding an ancient cliff. The cliff seemed to draw her in like a magnet.

"Run," she whispered to Yadhira, "follow me and run as fast as you can. It's our only hope." She did not tell her sister their only hope was dying at the bottom of the cliff before the soldiers could get to them. It would be less painful than what the Zetas had in mind.

Livia had lived long enough in this dark, harsh world to understand what these men would do. She clenched her sister's hand so tight that Yadhira whimpered in pain and both stumbled out into the open desert as fast as their wearied bodies would take them. César aimed his pistol at the escapees and then swore loudly upon realizing the runners were his most valuable commodity.

Two Zetas broke into a sprint and followed the girls like rabid predators whose very lives depended upon catching their prey. The sisters made it to within twenty yards of the cliff's edge when they were tackled down onto a bed of jagged basalt behind a wall of reddish volcanic rock. One of the Zetas, a tall, lanky bastard, hit Livia hard across the mouth and stared wolfishly into her eyes. Men had always found her desirable. Livia stared back at the soldier and felt her heart chill. She knew what he wanted.

"You were smart to run," the lanky Zeta growled, intimately observing both Livia and her sister. The other Zeta, a short muscular man with a gruesome scar running down the left side of his face, clawed at Yadhira's clothes while the girl struggled desperately to clasp the metallic cross around her neck and pray to her Creator for deliverance.

The scarred Zeta laughed at Yadhira's feeble attempt. "There is no God and there is no hope for you now."

The lanky Zeta hit Livia again and slowly removed his own belt, staring salaciously into her eyes. The fear and panic in her face aroused him tremendously. It always did.

"You will experience suffering that you cannot possibly imagine," the tall narco continued. "And when we are done, we will consume the flesh off your bones."

The muscled soldier's fingernails dug into Yadhira's flesh and she screamed with an intensity that pierced through the desert's very soul. It sent terror into the hearts of the other Hondurans who wondered in horror what was happening behind the ominous rocky terrain. Yadhira's screams persisted as the stocky Zeta's lifeless body toppled over her head and his partner's skull was crushed against a mass of obsidian.

"*¿Lo ven?*" yelled César. "You see what will happen if you run?"

César raised his pistol above his head and walked forward ten steps before a 175-grain bullet from an M24 sniper rifle ripped a crater in his heart. As César's corpse hit the ground, the entire desert wailed like a band of demons and for a few precious seconds, both Los Zetas and the Hondurans thought they must be experiencing an earthquake.

It was Álvaro, a.k.a. Z-59, who first saw the wicked machine torpedoing through the desert. Despite his extensive military training, the incredible sight immobilized the Zeta for just a moment while he watched thunderous neon fire erupt from the pale beast. As Álvaro regained his wits, he aimed his FX-05 Xiuhcoatl at the unknown enemy. He almost managed to pull the trigger when three rounds from a .50 caliber machine gun sprayed his brains out the back of his skull.

Now hiding safely behind a reddish-brown boulder, Livia and Yadhira watched in shock as the camouflaged killers went down, one by one, to the rapid gunfire of the pale machine and 175-grain rounds from two M24 sniper rifles stationed 500 yards away. And then Livia screamed. A deafening explosion rocked the surreal scene as the strange motorcycle burst into billowy clouds of smoke and flames. Both girls saw their black-clad rescuer violently eject from the smoldering remains of the motorcycle and crash onto the desert floor near the Humvees.

"Look!" yelled Yadhira, pointing in the man's direction. "He's still alive!"

The man crawled thought the smoky dirt and sand like a crazed lizard. Neither sister could take their eyes off the strange figure as he came to his feet. Geresano got out of the Humvee with another RPG-7 shoulder-fired launcher, scanning the open desert for more enemies. His laser-like vision was so intense he failed to see the haunting devil emerge from the smoke. And he failed to see the fist crush his own jaw. As Geresano's unconscious body crumpled to the sand, a round from the FN Five-Seven pistol of Mellado seared the left side of the black-clothed man's scalp. It grazed his skull before exiting a tangled mess of hair and blood to bounce off the armor plating of one of the Humvees.

Still completely fixated on the dream-like scene, Livia screamed once again. And one more time, against all odds, the strange man in black got to his feet. Yadhira, as completely fascinated as her sister, again pointed at the mysterious stranger.

"He's still going!"

Neither of the girls blinked as they watched the man level the RPG-7 launcher and pull the trigger. A second explosion, much bigger than the first, lit up the desert landscape and sent another founding member of Los Zetas back to his maker in a mess of charred lacerated flesh and bone fragments. He was quickly joined by Geresano.

Ignoring the blood streaming onto his face, the man in black drew his pistols and searched for Zeta survivors. After twenty arduous minutes, he concluded there were none. "It's all clear," he spoke into his microphone. From a blue shaded hill, 500 yards away, he saw Alma and Armendáriz stand up and give the signal of acknowledgement. Father

G looked at the shredded remains of his motorcycle and sighed. Then, opening a Corona he found in one of the Humvees, he sat down near some ocotillo while the blood from his head wound continued to flow. After a few seconds, he felt the unexpected coolness of a wet cloth. Instinctively, his hands went for his pistols.

"It's okay, *amigo,*" whispered a soft voice. "You are hurt. Let me help you." Livia soothingly cleaned off the blood from the man's face and wrapped a makeshift bandage around his head. "You are lucky, *Señor*. It looks like the bullet just missed your skull."

Yes, Father G thought to himself. *I always seem to be lucky*. With the blood flow stopped and his eye clean, Father G looked up into the face of his helper and attempted to smile. "Thank you, *Señorita.* You are very kind."

Livia laughed nervously, trying not to stare at the strange man's scarred and disfigured face. "Please, *Señor.* You have saved all our lives. This is the very least I could do for you. My name is Livia."

"My name is Father G," the priest said, extending his arm and ignoring the stares he had become so accustomed to. "But don't thank me yet."

His steel-blue eye flickered to the left and then to the right. Most of the Honduran refugees were huddled together behind Livia, not knowing quite what to do. A few had discovered some cases of beer and water in the Humvees and were tentatively refreshing themselves.

"You are a priest?" asked a young teenage girl with large brown eyes standing next to Livia. The shock of disbelief was evident in her tone.

"Yadhira!" blurted out Livia, embarrassed at her sister's bluntness.

Father G smirked. "Yes, I am."

Ignoring her sister, Yadhira continued her questioning unabashed. "What kind of priest are you?"

"A different kind," replied Father G, more stoically. He was staring due north. He stood and quickly ran back to the nearest Humvee, retrieved a pair of high-tech binoculars and surveyed the northern landscape for fifteen seconds. His booming voice then startled the mass of migrants.

"Listen to me. You are still in danger. There are more men coming who wish to do you harm. Your only chance at survival is to follow me and do exactly what I say. My name is Father G and I am a Catholic priest. Quickly gather whatever water and food you can find. Ready yourselves for another journey."

Father G then spoke into the microphone. "There are more coming—no time to make it to the truck—we'll meet you on the south side of the hill."

The priest noticed a few of the migrants collecting guns from the fallen Zetas. "No!" Father G shouted. "Leave the weapons where you found them. Now let's go! Move it!"

Many of the Hondurans looked confused and a few of the young men started to complain.

"Listen to him!" yelled Livia. "He saved your lives! He is a man of God and we must trust him!"

The murmuring reluctantly ceased and the migrants obeyed. A few minutes later they were traveling southwest through the desert waste in the waning sunlight. They were soon joined by Alma and Armendáriz.

"It's a damn *puto* shame about the motorcycle," lamented Alma. "Don't expect me to build you a new one any time soon."

"Nice," replied Father G. "Let's get out of here."

The priest led them on a frantic pace and he abstained from hiding any of their tracks. On the contrary, he had the Hondurans hike side by side, and in the sand and soft dirt wherever possible. Several hours later, under the white crescent Mexican moon, the ragged band was walking down a steep trail leading to the bottom of a large, wide open canyon whose floor was dry and dusty and displayed the remnants of an ancient river. The group walked for more than an hour between the steep canyon walls before finally coming to another trail leading to higher ground.

Several of the migrants suffered leg injuries and one was bit by a rattlesnake. But Father G forced them onwards through the wee morning hours. One young girl named Marisa fainted from exhaustion and the priest carried her upon his shoulders. Finally, at 4:11 a.m., Father G led them to a large rock ledge near a beige-colored bluff and let the weary migrants rest. He gently unloaded the weakened girl from his shoulders and put her in the possession of Armendáriz. Alma immediately lit up a cigarette.

"Watch over them," the priest said to Armendáriz and Alma. "I will be back soon."

"Where are you going?" Livia asked. She looked suspiciously at Armendáriz. With all his tattoos, he looked just like one of Los Zetas.

Alma exhaled a cone of bluish-gray smoke and walked over to comfort the girl. *"Está bien, Mija.* He is okay—just an ugly *hijo de puta."*

"Stay here," Father G commanded, amidst the laughing of Armendáriz and some of the other Hondurans. "I will be back."

And with that he secured the M24 sniper rifle from Armendáriz and took off at a full-speed sprint back the way they had just come.

It was forty minutes after daybreak when Father G saw the first Zeta step into the confines of the canyon. He was followed by fourteen others. As the priest suspected, the squadron was moving fast and intently tracking the dusty footprints of the supposedly unarmed migrants. The Hondurans, Los Zetas had decided, would be able to tell them exactly what had happened to their comrades. The canyon walls were steep, rugged, and sparsely populated with ironwood and desert willow trees. Golden rays of sunlight bounced upon the barren bottom floor to reveal the wide variety of colored rocks forming the escarpments.

Up high, on top of one of these rocks, Father G had the first of the fast-moving Zetas in the crosshairs of the M24 sniper rifle. Not yielding to the temptation to shoot too early, he waited until all the narco soldiers were visible. He then calmly pulled the trigger. He shot accurately and he shot fast. Exactly fifteen times. For Los Zetas, there was no cover and none of them discerned the location of their unknown enemy. Within a manner of seconds, fifteen corpses lay strewn out on the canyon floor.

Within the first three shots, Z-99 had pinpointed the location of the enemy. He felt no remorse for his dead comrades. Only four Zetas had listened to him, the others had obstinately refused and now they were paying the price. And for Z-99, he would move up the ranks again. A wave of elation flowed within him at the thought and a wicked grin formed upon his tattooed face. He was smart, *pinche* smart, and he would soon be in charge. After he killed his target. And his target was big, *muy puto* big–Los Zetas public enemy number one, the man known as the pale rider. Z-99 knew the man they were dealing with. He had studied his tactics for a long time. He had listened to the rumors among the cartels for years and he had followed up on them meticulously and obsessively. And today, when he would return with the head of the pale rider, he would become a narco legend.

Z-99 turned to face his comrades and pointed up at the rose-colored rocks with his right index finger. The other Zetas, Z-84, Z-91, Z-110, and Z-119, nodded in comprehension. Z-99 had been right once again. The enemy was close, just a few hundred yards away, perched between an assortment of boulders serving as an ideal sniper location. Z-99 would have chosen it as well. The five Zetas were highly trained killers: cold, calculating, and ruthless. Z-100 was thirty-one years old and spent eight years in the Mexican Special Forces before surrendering to Los Zetas offers of unlimited drugs, money, and women. He was a lethal marksman, perhaps the best in the cartel, and he had a legion of kills under his belt. A few weeks ago, on a bet with Z-18, he killed twenty-one migrants in the deserts of Nuevo Leon at a distance of 500 yards. Now, the bald Z-110 silently snarled as he spread out and stealthily made his way up through the canyon rocks, followed closely by his cousin, Z-119. Z-110 wanted to kill the pale rider almost as much as Z-99. As his dead black eyes scanned the canyon rocks for abnormalities, he gripped his FX-05 Xiuhcoatl tighter and picked up his pace.

Z-84 spread out to the left, moving slower than his younger companions. He was the biggest of the group, standing six-feet-two inches tall and weighing close to 230 pounds. Z-84 had served over four years in prison for the murder of six men, three women, and a child. Two years ago he escaped during a jailbreak orchestrated by a squad of thirteen Zetas and a heavily armored helicopter. They had killed the prison warden and over twenty-seven guards. Z-84's time behind bars had transformed him into a ruthless and cunning psychopath. He, too, badly wanted this kill, though his plans were more devious. Once they had killed the man, he would dispose of Z-99 once and for all.

The young hijo de puta is smart, Z-84 thought grudgingly. He had prospered within the crime syndicate by following Z-99. *But he is too smart for his own good and he is way too ambitious.* And he had been given direct orders to eliminate him.

Ten minutes later Z-110 fired the first shot from his FX-05 Xiuhcoatl, followed by Z-119. Both Zetas unloaded their weapons, firing again and again at the black-clad figure lying down in prone position with a large sniper rifle extending from his upper body. Exuberant, both Z-110 and Z-119 bounded across the jagged rocks like mountain goats to admire their trophy. Z-110 was only eleven feet away from his target when he realized something was wrong. He felt the first sensations of panic.

There's no blood.

Studying the scene, Z-100's muscles stiffened. He had shot at a decoy, a collection of vegetation and rocks wrapped up in a black cloak to resemble a man. His eyes were still focused on the strange decoy when the metal blade pierced through his ribcage. It ripped up into his heart with a force that lifted him off his feet. Z-119 screamed, whipped his assault rifle into position and pulled the trigger. He was too late. Blood erupted from his tattooed throat as he toppled over backwards into a lifeless cluster of flesh and bones.

Z-84 fired next. In contrast to his younger comrades, he only fired a single round from his rifle. He then casually watched the fountain of blood explode from his enemy's head. Microseconds later he observed the black-clad body tumble down the slanted, rocky surface of the canyon wall slope. Eerily calm, Z-84 lit up a cigarette as he scaled over the rough boulders to examine his kill. He was contemplating how and when he would destroy Z-99 when his lungs went numb. His eyes slowly flickered from the blood-soaked torso to the mutilated head. It took several seconds to comprehend he had shot the head of a dead Z-110. It was not until his FX-05 Xiuhcoatl was dislodged from his hands that he finally felt fear. As his body was lifted and thrown violently into the air, he screamed with an intensity to rival that of his many victims. He screamed for four complete seconds before his bones were crushed on the rocky bottom of the canyon floor.

Z-99 was sweating profusely. His trembling fingers dug inside his pocket for more cocaine. He was gazing at the fifteen bodies at the bottom of the canyon. And it had sunk into him how much skill was required to kill all those men in such a short period of time. Just nine minutes earlier he had watched in disbelief as Z-84 sailed hundreds of feet downward to meet his bloody demise. He turned to look at the mutilated remains of Z-91. And then at the corpses of Z-119 and Z-110.

Z-99's bulging eyes darted right and left. Slowly, he turned around to study the landscape behind him. There was no one there. Various sounds of wildlife resumed. The normalcy was disturbing. As the first molecules of cocaine stimulated the dopamine levels in his brain, Z-99 fired several rounds from his assault rifle into the open air. He then yelled with a surprising force and intensity.

"Where are you?" The words reverberated loudly and ominously through the canyon.

The response was immediate, calm, and it chilled Z-99's blood.

"Here."

Out of nowhere, the pale rider emerged and one round from his Colt .45 drilled into Z-99's left eye and exited out the back of his skull.

At 10:00 a.m., Livia saw the priest approaching from the east. Her relief was evident to all around her. Father G was moving much slower than when he had abruptly left. He still had the rifle and was carrying something large across his broad shoulders. A few minutes later all the Hondurans were intently watching this strange priest return to their camp.

"He's got some kind of animal!" exclaimed Yadhira. "It looks like a, a..."

"A pig," answered one of the men excitedly. "It's a javelina! I hear they are very tasty!"

"And better-looking than Padre G and Armendáriz," chirped Alma.

The Hondurans laughed. They had all become enamored with Alma.

Before cooking the javelina, Father G showed the Hondurans how to extract water from both the *agave lechuguilla* and prickly pear cacti. He also taught them the basics of desert survival and led them in prayer before reading two chapters from the Gospel of Luke.

After the group devoured the charred flesh of the javelina, Father G slept for a few hours while the Hondurans rehydrated and regained some of their strength. Upon waking, the priest assembled the migrants together for a meeting. "You had the misfortune of meeting Los Zetas, one of the most evil and vicious groups of thugs to have ever walked in Mexico. They will send more soldiers to try and discover what happened. You are safe for the time being, but it would be unwise to return in the direction that we came. I will not take you to the northern border but I do have an alternative plan." The Hondurans listened attentively to the priest's proposal and every one of them accepted it. The migrants packed up their meager possessions and followed Father G as he headed west.

Two days and many miles later, bone-tired but bellies full of the flesh from a desert bighorn sheep, every one of the migrants was asleep near a Mexican pinyon tree in the high plains. At 2:00 a.m., Yadhira awoke from a particularly vivid nightmare. She stood up in the cool breeze to clear her mind. In the waning firelight, she saw Father G and Alma sitting down upon a flat rock. Alma was staring up at the crisp night sky and the priest's single eye was looking at some type of object in his hands. Yadhira stepped forward upon some dry pine needles, making a slight crackling noise that got Alma's attention.

"*¿Cómo estas, Mija?* What are you doing up at this hour?"

Yadhira had developed a bond with Alma during their short time together—both had shared the stories of their lives.

"*No puedo dormir,*" replied Yadhira.

Alma nodded in understanding and Yadhira looked again at the priest and the strange object he had in his hands. From the glowing light of the embers, Yadhira could tell it was some kind of cross, made of gold. She looked closer at the yellow metal and was startled to see a glimmering blood-red jewel. Curiosity getting the better of her, Yadhira walked over to the strange priest and gently touched him on the shoulder.

"Why are you still up Padre G? And what do have in your hands?"

The priest did not move. His eye looked up at the stars, reminding him once again of his unique and focused mission. Finally, after several moments of silence he spoke. "Hello, Yadhira. A good friend of mine once showed me the virtues of gazing into the night sky. The Lord's creations are truly amazing, Yadhira. Take time to appreciate them."

Yadhira looked up into the cool darkness and singled out the Big Dipper, the only constellation she knew about. She then focused her attention back on the priest's hands and the strange piece of jewelry. The priest could sense Yadhira's gaze and he handed her the cross.

"It looks very old," she said, caressing the yellow metal. "Where did you get it?"

"A friend gave it me."

"Why?" asked Yadhira.

"It is a symbol of the oath I have made."

"What oath?" the girl persisted.

Father G sighed. "I have sworn to follow Christ and protect the people of this land."

"Until the end of your life?" Yadhira asked.

The priest nodded in the affirmative.

"Do you have any family?"

Father G flinched. "Not on this earth."

"You're not scared of dying, are you?"

The priest kept silent for several moments. Finally, he shook his head. "No."

Yadhira perceived a great deal of pain behind the strange priest's rough exterior. With the tenderness of a thirteen-year-old girl, she fastened the gold cross back around Father G's neck and kissed his scarred cheek. "Thank you for saving us."

Five days and an unknown number of miles later, as the group descended the rocky slope of a pine covered mountain, it was the young Marisa who first spotted the human settlement. "Look!" she shouted, pointing to the faraway group of cattle from atop of Father G's shoulders. The Hondurans were hungry, thirsty, and exhausted. There had been many injuries, including several broken bones and three rattlesnake bites—treated by Alma's antivenom—but the refugees remained together and all were alive. Over the course of the last few days, Father G had let those who wanted to shoot the sniper rifle. A few of the migrants, including Livia, killed their own food for the first time.

As the ragged band walked down onto the flat green valley below the mountain, they were approached by a man from the west riding a pale-white horse. The man wore a white cowboy hat and a gray poncho flowed from his shoulders onto the pale mare. He was unshaven, had a thick black mustache, and carried a rifle.

The horse trotted to within twenty yards of the group and every one of the Hondurans stopped walking. Father G, however, let Marisa down from his shoulders and walked up to the mare undeterred. To the migrants' amazement, the mare neighed in warm recognition and her rider broke into a wide smile. He turned the horse broadside, revealing a huge set of antlers belonging to the biggest deer the Hondurans had ever seen.

"That's quite a buck," said Father G, returning the smile and extending his own right arm. "I hope it took less than seventeen shots to bring him down."

Ignacio Jarabo laughed heartily. *"Sólo una bala,* Padre G."

"How is Blanca doing?"

Ignacio gently stroked the mare. *"Está bien,* Padre G. *Y sus amigos,* new additions to the Saint Navarro settlement I suppose?"

Father G looked back at his new friends and nodded in the affirmative.

Chapter 35

Las Vegas, Nevada, USA

Israel inhaled deeply as he put on the headphones and let Sammy Hagar's "I Can't Drive 55" shake out his nerves. Again, he renewed his determination to not be mentally defeated.

There were 207 athletes at the annual U.S. Open Freestyle Wrestling Championships, twenty-three of whom were in Israel's weight class division of 211.5 pounds. He was the only high schooler among them and a few pounds short of the weight limit. He had not particularly wanted to wrestle in this tournament—he felt unprepared for the step up in competition, but Father G had encouraged him to do so. Israel had wrestled in national tournaments before—last year he won the championships in both Greco-Roman and Freestyle at the prestigious Fargo tournament. But that was at the youth level. Now, it was time to turn into a man.

Time to change from Clark Kent into Superman.

It was what the priest told him before every match. Taking off his gray sweatshirt, Israel stared at his opponent, a 2008 NCAA Champion from Oklahoma State, and then handed his exterior clothing to his high school coach Francisco. He wished for a moment that Father G was here, then quickly dismissed the thought.

He would want me to concentrate on the match at hand.

Squatting down low, Israel ground both red Asics wrestling shoes into the blue mat and sprung up three feet into the air. Walking to the center of the mat, Israel soaked up the thrill of adrenaline and crouched down into his stance. His opponent looked at his coach with a smile and lowered into his own stance. The Oklahoman was not unduly concerned. He'd gotten the best draw in the division, some no-name high school kid from Texas, and it would be good to get the first match out of the way.

On the sound of the whistle, Israel fired out of his stance and went in for a low-level single-leg takedown on his opponent's right ankle. The speed of the shot surprised the Oklahoman but he quickly adjusted and moved his foot back before Israel could secure the takedown. He immediately countered with his own shot, a straight on blast double-leg, but was greeted by a pair of powerful forearms that stopped him cold.

Undeterred, the former NCAA Champion's left hand quickly grabbed hold of Israel's right triceps muscle. He smoothly pulled his opponent's right arm behind his left ear while penetrating in with his right leg to masterfully pull off the high-crotch takedown. Israel went to the mat, belly first, and the Oklahoman went in for a leg-lace. But Israel spread his legs and pushed his hips back hard; he would not be turned. The referee put both wrestlers back up on their feet.

Instantly, Israel changed levels and faked a low-level shot. His opponent lowered his head and Israel's right hand hammered down on the back of his neck. He followed it with a brutal left forearm and went in for an ankle pick with his right hand. The Oklahoman moved his left foot back in time to avoid being taken down, but it forced him off balance. Israel performed an arm-drag in the opposite direction and managed to secure a tight body-lock from the backside position. In one fluid motion, Israel exploded his hips, arched his back, and lifted his opponent into the air with a perfect suplex.

Both the Oklahoman's back shoulders slammed into the mat simultaneously. The referee signaled a pin. The match stunned everyone watching it and a wave of silence swept over the arena. It was followed by a surge of electricity. Even Israel's coach, Francisco, who had seen him do amazing feats on the mat, was incredulous.

Oblivious to the commotion, Israel put his sweatshirt and sweatpants back on and prepared for the next match.

On Saturday night, the crowd was buzzing with anticipation. The talk in the arena was the high school Hispanic kid from Texas who had taken the tournament by storm. He would be wrestling in the finals against a three-time NCAA Champion and Olympian from Iowa and many a spectator was eager to witness the event. Mayrín, however, though a spectator, was not interested in the competition. Though she had happily traveled from El Paso to the tournament with Padre Quezada, Sister Arámbula, Sister López, and Isabel, she was more interested in sitting with Israel than watching him wrestle. And, to the dismay of the nuns and the priest, she unashamedly displayed her affections in public.

But the sisters and Padre Quezada had bigger concerns—they were worried about Father G. They had not heard from him in over a week. Ultimately, they had decided to come and support Israel at the tournament because they knew it was what Father G would have wanted. Besides, Padre Quezada had told the nuns, it would be good to take a road trip for a few days and get to know Mayrín better.

At 6:15 p.m., Israel kissed Mayrín and scurried down the cement steps of the stadium to prepare for the championship match. It was soon thereafter that Padre Quezada's cell phone buzzed. He picked it up anxiously and the nuns watched him with nervous anticipation. His expression oozed with relief upon hearing the voice on the other line. Both sisters made the sign of the cross and said silent prayers of gratitude.

"He's okay," whispered Padre Quezada to the nuns, shoving the phone in his pocket. "He's at the Jarabo Ranch and will be in El Paso as soon as possible."

"God be with him," said Sister López. "What is he doing over there?"

Padre Quezada answered by shrugging his shoulders, which they knew meant Father G marched to the beat of his own drum.

"Isabel," called the husky priest jovially. "Let's go get some more nachos."

Isabel was engaged in conversation with Mayrín while watching Israel down on the practice mats. "More?" she asked. "Hello? This will be our third serving."

The priest just laughed and rubbed his ample belly. "*¡Ay, caramba!* I'm a growing boy," he answered with a twinkle in his eye. "Besides, I'm out of Dr. Pepper."

"Alright," she answered with amused exasperation. She winked her left eye and made a clicking sound with her tongue. "Make sure I don't miss anything, Mayrín."

Alone in the stadium corridor, Padre Quezada took Isabel gently by the hand. "I need you to deliver a message to Israel," he said. "Tell him Father G just called and wishes he could be here but something urgent came up. Tell him Father G says to go all-out."

Isabel nodded in understanding and went down to deliver the message.

The whistle blew and both Israel's arms pummeled in hard as he circled to his left and attempted to secure the underarm hook. He felt good. Strong. Fast. Relaxed. All his opponents up to this match had been outstanding wrestlers, light-years ahead of the competition he faced in high school and junior national tournaments. But no one had been tougher than Father G in the practice room, and that bit of knowledge had boosted his confidence tremendously.

Israel jacked up the Olympian's right arm and simultaneously positioned his left foot down on the mat behind the Olympian's right heel. Then he brutally slammed his open right palm against his opponent's ribcage to send him sprawling downwards. In midair, right before his opponent's body hit the yellow portion of the mat, both Israel's hands locked around the Olympian's lower abdomen and his elbows clamped together. Israel arched his back and heaved his opponent over his left shoulder to score the two-point gut wrench. The maneuver electrified the crowd, and both Isabel and Mayrín screamed in delight. Israel immediately attempted another gut wrench but was unsuccessful as his opponent dug his right hip into the mat and turned his body to stone. A few seconds went by and the referee set both wrestlers on their feet.

The Olympian savagely surged forward. Both his ears looked like ripe cauliflowers and his upper body muscles were shredded. The speed of his shot surprised Israel, as well as the intensity. Israel countered hard but his opponent changed levels and directions to take him down with a blast double. As Israel hit the mat, the Olympian secured his left ankle, jerked it upwards and turned him over with a Suzuki. It was now Israel's turn to defend himself in bottom position. He did so for eleven seconds before the referee finally blew the whistle and set both wrestlers on their feet. The athletes then proceeded to go to war.

At the end of the first period Israel walked over to the corner with Francisco and spit a gob of blood onto the floor. Mayrín squirmed, nervously clutching Isabel. The match was tied 4-4 and thus far had been a brutal affair. The Olympian wrestled every bit as physically as his much younger opponent.

Israel's left eye had swelled up like a balloon. The Iowa coaches were hastily bandaging up the Olympian's head to stop the blood from gushing out of a deep cut in his ear. Francisco tried his best to encourage Israel but refrained from offering any technical advice. He had learned several years ago that the boy's skills were far more advanced than his own.

"You're wrestling a hell of a match, Israel," said Francisco, rubbing down the boy's arm muscles. "Just go out and give it all you can for three more minutes."

The Olympian furiously started the second period and delivered a series of brutal blows to the back of Israel's head. He was too aggressive. The younger wrestler intercepted a powerful swipe from his opponent's right arm and took hold of a solid two-on-one. The Olympian quickly circled to face his challenger and, as he did so, Israel jammed the muscular right arm back into his throat and shot a blast double with amazing speed. Israel's powerful legs drove the Olympian up into the air and then straight onto his back for a three-point takedown. It galvanized the crowd and the spectators watched in fascination as the Olympian scrambled off his back and went into defensive position. Immediately Israel went in for a leg-lace but his opponent kicked out like a mule and he was unable to make the turn.

With twenty-five seconds left in the match, Israel was leading 8-5. Francisco and the five very supportive members of Israel's cheering section were bubbling with fervor. It was not enough to stop his champion opponent. With seventeen seconds remaining, the Olympian secured a vicious front headlock. Right hand cupping Israel's chin, his left arm took hold of an under-arm hook and the Olympian threw him back over his own head and down onto his shoulder blades. It was an incredible throw and it tied the match up 8-8 and sent it into overtime.

Both wrestlers started overtime a bit more cautiously; it was sudden victory and the first athlete to score would win the match. The Olympian was the first to make a move. He came in high, hunting for an upper body-lock, and then shot in low on a double-leg. Israel kept good standing position, however, and his forehead blocked the brunt of the shot and his forearms smashed into his opponent's trapezoidal muscles. His right hand clubbed the back of the Olympian's head and he brutally attempted to bounce the Olympian's face off the mat, just like Father G had instructed him for over a decade.

Against any lesser opponent the technique would have succeeded, but the Olympian's neck was too strong. His toes quickly circled to the left, preventing Israel from scoring a takedown. Israel immediately shot in on a sweep-single to his right, but once again, his opponent countered successfully and avoided being scored on.

The crowd continue to watch in awe as the referee let the match go on and on, with neither wrestler gaining an advantage. Though he had wrestled much longer sessions in the practice room with the priest, this was by far the longest official match in Israel's career. The time clock had just past the sixteen-minute mark when Israel's confidence began to wane for the first time. His opponent was tough, almost as tough as Father G, and his own muscles were beginning to fatigue. He refocused, pushed the pain out of his mind, and feverishly attacked his opponent. He unleashed shot after shot but the Olympian stood strong and skillfully countered each attempt.

Panic registered within Israel's brain and, for just a split second, he let his eyes check on the time clock. It proved to be costly. His opponent came in with a hammering high-crotch, perfectly hit the corner and just like that, scored the winning takedown. Israel stayed on the mat for a few seconds as the Olympian's arms rose into the air and the animated crowd erupted. The mental anguish of the loss quickly flooded out Israel's physical pain. He shook the Olympian's hand and staggered off the mat into his corner. Francisco wrapped his arms around the young wrestler.

"It was the best match I have ever seen, Israel. You went toe-to-toe with an Olympic wrestler for sixteen minutes and fifty-four seconds, and you were so close to pulling out the victory."

The words did not sink in. Israel had let himself be mentally defeated and it cost him the championship.

I am freaking better than this.

He knew Father G would have found some way to win. Israel's mood was sour well on into the early hours of the morning as he lay awake in the van, reflecting upon the loss and his moment of weakness again and again.

Chapter 36

Xiuhcoatl—Jungles of Oaxaca, Mexico

It was dark inside the depths of the ancient temple. The girl screamed as Tlaloc's fingernails dug into her skin. The old cripple was careful, though, to not draw blood. He had gone to extensive lengths to verify the sixteen-year-old female was a virgin and did not want to violate the sacred ordinance. A nearby flame disrupted the darkness; a feral growl pierced through the air as torches held by several brightly colored eagle warriors ignited.

"Ready," said Secretary Acosta in Nahuatl. The defense secretary was dressed in a simple white loincloth and an elaborate headpiece of bright green Quetzal feathers interwoven with gold. Standing next to him was Tehuantl. The enormous man wore a black loincloth and his bulging muscles were covered in oil, gleaming against the fire. Both his hands gripped a massive *macuahuitl* studded with razor sharp scarlet obsidian. Tlaloc proclaimed the weapon the finest *macuahuitl* ever constructed.

Another growl, much closer this time, echoed throughout the temple's chambers. The girl shrieked in terror as a raging jaguar, half-starved to death, savagely pounced on her and sunk its sharp fangs into her skull. With a wicked sneer of excitement, Tlaloc watched in fascination as the beast tore the body of the virgin to shreds.

"Now!" hissed Tlaloc, also speaking in Nahuatl. He was unable to remove his eyes from the jaguar. Tehuantl walked forward and the beast, sensing a challenge, roared violently. The giant man continued onward and the jaguar leaped into the air to meet him. With one brutish swing of the *macuahuitl*, Tehuantl decapitated the beast, silencing it forever. Tlaloc quickly hobbled towards the jaguar's carcass and motioned for Secretary Acosta to do likewise.

"We must ... hurry," said the old man. He inhaled sharply. "Time is ... of the ... essence."

Ramón nodded and hollowed out the dead jaguar's skull with an obsidian blade while Tlaloc painted Tehuantl's skin in its blood. With speed and precision, the eagle warriors skinned the animal's body with obsidian knives like that used by the defense secretary. A few minutes later, Ramón filled the jaguar's skull with the dead virgin's blood. He handed the skull to Tehuantl.

"Drink ... it," Tlaloc commanded. "All ... of ... it."

While the big man forced the skull's contents down his throat, Tlaloc knelt to face the skeletal representations of Mictlantecuhtli and Santa Muerte. When Tehuantl consumed the last drop of blood, the eagle warriors wrapped the jaguar skin around him. The ancient cripple chanted the sacred words to complete the dark ritual. With a mad look in his eyes, Tlaloc stared into the face of Tehuantl.

"You ... are ... now ... all-powerful." His deep pulmonary breathing was intense. "You ... cannot ... be ... defeated."

Secretary Acosta looked at the blood-soaked jaguar warrior and smiled tightly at Tlaloc. Both men understood the importance of the upcoming event.

The jihadists would not respect weakness and it was critical that Tehuantl win the upcoming match. Sheik Mahdavi Haqqani arrived at

Xiuhcoatl on his personal jet two days ago. Mokhtar had been here for more than a week. Ramón had personally escorted Mokhtar to Teotihuacán, Chichén Itzá, and various sites in Mexico City and Guanajuato. And, true to his word, the secretary of defense let Mokhtar fly in his Mikoyan MiG-35D jet fighter. Yesterday he let the jihadist take the shot.

It was risky, Ramón admitted to himself, *but well worth it.*

They had been traveling in an isolated region in the state of Chiapas when Mokhtar spotted the antiquated Cathedral on top of a lush hillside in a rural mountainous village.

"You have way too many Christian churches in your country, Ramón," chided Mokhtar. "Such a shame that your people have allowed the Catholic infidels to enslave both themselves and this beautiful land. Had it been Sultan Saladin, praised be Allah, arriving here instead of Columbus, things might have turned out differently."

The words had infuriated Secretary Acosta, though he laughed calmly and coolly. "You are right of course, Mokhtar. But it is never too late to change." The defense secretary unexpectedly veered to the east.

Showing off the powerful RD-33OVT thrust-vector engines, Ramón stalled the MiG-35 in mid-flight and the jet fighter nosed 90 degrees like a cobra ready to strike and then slid backwards. It was an incredible maneuver and it left Mokhtar gasping for air. Secretary Acosta smiled, turned the MiG-35 around, and brought the aircraft to a speed of over 1,000 mph in a long ranging loop.

Hand covered in fireproof Nomex, Ramón manipulated the ergonomically designed handgrip on the left side of his seat and pressed the top button with his thumb. Instantly, a high-resolution image of the Cathedral appeared behind crosshairs in the central monitor of the Head-Up Display. The MiG-35 had been equipped with a state-of-the-art T220 targeting pod containing a forward-looking infrared sensor, a laser designator/rangefinder, and a boresight correlator for the automatic lock-on of Kh-29L air-to-surface missiles. A red dot started to blink in the center of the crosshairs.

"Now all you have to do is push the button."

Despite the edge to his voice, it took a few moments for Mokhtar to register that Ramón was serious. He was dead serious. *Certainly there would be grave repercussions for such an act? Does the man really exert enough power here that he could make this all go away?*

A surge of newfound respect resonated within his mind and Mokhtar smiled. He pushed the button, just like Ramón had instructed him. Secretary Acosta veered to the north in a 2.5g turn and, out of the corner of his eye, Mokhtar watched the Cathedral burst into bright orange flames.

Ramón smiled at the recollection of yesterday's exploits, though he would be busy with damage control in the midst of this crucial time period. But he had covered up worse transgressions—much worse. And all that mattered right now was Tehuantl and the outcome of this death match. The Arabs would not respect weakness. But more importantly, neither would their own men; they would lose faith in the Aztec gods and their ability to conquer the enemy would diminish. If Tehuantl were to fail, their entire future would be in jeopardy. He had not seen the jihadist swordsman. He didn't know anything about him. But he was sure the sheik would have brought Saudi Arabia's best.

A significant section of the ancient arena was filled with the most loyal followers of Mokhtar and Sheik Haqqani. They were dressed in crimson turbans and cream-white *bishts* embroidered with black flags of jihad upon their left breasts. The jihadists were trained killers, all of them, and most had participated in many of Mokhtar's terrorist ventures around the world. They were ecstatic about their new mission, one which Sheik Haqqani had called the single greatest jihadi mission in the history of Islam. But now was time for a bit of recreation and they would religiously cheer on their champion swordsman, a brutish beast of a man named Mahmoud.

Mahmoud smiled at the crowd as he thrashed the sharpened scimitar through the air with a force that made it whistle. Like his terrorist comrades, he wore a crimson turban. Cream-white trousers. His massive naked torso was covered in thick black hair, matted to his skin in foul-smelling sweat. He had been trained in all manner of warfare since childhood but had shown an aptitude for swordsmanship. Rumors of his skills had eventually reached the ears of Sheik Haqqani. Both Mokhtar and the sheik had wagered large sums of money on him in many duels and Mahmoud had never been defeated. Three years ago, Mokhtar recruited the beastly man into his special forces unit; strong, brutal, and deadly, Mahmoud had proved himself a considerable asset on numerous occasions.

Despite his outward appearance and own unique brand of viciousness, Mahmoud had been unnerved at this strange, ancient city in the jungle. There was an aura of evil braided into the dazzling colors and magical architecture of the restored ruins, the likes of which the big man, a self-proclaimed murderer, found troubling.

"It is essential that we work with these infidels," Mokhtar had told him. "It is the will of Allah, praised be his name, and he knows that the end justifies the means. And your role will be pivotal in shaping our relationship with them. You must obtain victory."

Mahmoud gritted his teeth in determination and rage. He would not be the one to disappoint the most important figure in Islam since the prophet Muhammed.

Ten eagle warriors, adorned in vibrantly colored *ichcahuipillis* of red, green, and yellow, marched onto the hallowed grounds of the battle site brandishing primitive weapons. An ominous drum beat echoed throughout the stone arena. Blood-thirsty applause erupted as the eagle warriors dispersed to reveal a man as tall as Mahmoud himself. He wore a simple black loincloth and the skin of his large upper body muscles reflected an unnatural shade of scarlet against the sunlight. The man wore a blood-streaked jaguar face on his head and Mahmoud could see the sharp fangs of its teeth. The jaguar warrior wielded a large sword-like weapon that Mahmoud knew to be one of the infamous *macuahuitls* that Mokhtar had described to him. The man swung the weapon with a power and skill that rivaled Mahmoud's.

This is my foe, Mahmoud realized. *This is Tehuantl.*

Mokhtar had told him nothing of his opponent save that he would be fighting with a *macuahuitl* and his name was Tehuantl. The sinister drum rhythm picked up its intensity and Tehuantl marched forwards with menacing confidence. Mahmoud swung his blade though the open air one more time and then strode forward to meet his enemy.

Sheik Haqqani and Mokhtar were both sitting with Secretary Acosta in the small section of the stone arena that, long ago, was reserved for Aztec royalty. The defense secretary appeared calm and collected as he casually spoke of the ancient Aztec rituals and ceremonies once making his people omnipotent.

"Your warrior looks strong," said Ramón, offhandedly and in Arabic. "Regardless of the outcome, the match should prove very entertaining."

"Indeed," replied Sheik Haqqani, his eyes fixated on the two gladiators approaching each other.

Secretary Acosta had impressed the sheik once again, as had Tlaloc. The power and control they exerted was obvious and both of their intellects continued to amaze him. Tlaloc appeared to know almost everything about both Mexico and Saudi Arabia. And Secretary Acosta was not far behind. The two Mexicans were ruthless and seemed hell-bent on accomplishing their mission.

And they despise both Christianity and the Americans as much as I do, reflected the old sheik. *Eccentric, to be sure, but which powerful leader is not? It is Allah's will that we work together to destroy the Americans.*

The inspiring thought made his heart flutter and he looked at Mokhtar's special warriors donning the precious black flag of jihad. They had already begun their training and Sheik Haqqani had been amazed at Ramón's planning, knowledge, and attention to detail. Both Tlaloc and Secretary Acosta had been actively involved in choosing the targeted U.S. cities and Sheik Haqqani had not objected; their research had been thorough and their reasoning precise. Neither Mokhtar nor his most trusted counselors could find any flaws in their methodology.

And the bombs are ready to go, thought the sheik, eyes sparkling.

Secretary Acosta had convinced him well enough how easy they could get through the border—Mokhtar had already been into the United States multiple times. It seemed Secretary Acosta could do anything here he desired.

You have done well, thought the sheik, envisioning the beloved prophet Muhammed welcome him into paradise. *It was through your efforts that the infidels were finally conquered. For your devout service and achievements, you shall obtain eternal honor. Allah is well pleased.*

The *macuahuitl* and scimitar clashed for the first time, and the deafening clang woke Sheik Haqqani from his daydreams of glory. Mahmoud, as instructed by Mokhtar, launched a series of thunderous blows to shatter the *macuahuitl.* Eventually, however, he realized that his instructor was incorrect—the ancient weapon was not brittle. It was, Mahmoud discerned, perhaps more solid than his own scimitar.

The jihadist swordsman's eyes narrowed. He circled to his left and glared at his adversary, trying to gain a mental edge. The maneuver was counterproductive and unsettling. Tehuantl's eyes were glazed and his hardened face was streaked with fresh blood streaming down from the jaguar skin. Tehuantl unleashed a primal snarl and lashed out with his weapon. Then, with a rapid barrage of sharp thrusts, he sent Mahmoud staggering backwards on the defensive.

He's good, thought Mokhtar, watching Tehuantl fight.

The master terrorist had been more impressed with the Mexicans than his grandfather, and he had more grandiose aspirations. And the nearness of it all was surreal. *Surely it was a blessing from Allah, praised be his name, that I was to meet with Secretary Acosta.* Watching the two warriors fight to the death expanded his deep-seated wrath and hatred. He envisioned the devastation he would bring to the Americans.

They will suffer for their arrogance, he silently fumed. *They will be destroyed per their lack of faith in Allah, praised be his name, and the true religion. We will establish a global caliphate and the world will know that I am the true successor to the prophet Muhammed, peace be upon him.*

Mokhtar watched Mahmoud struggle with his adversary and he looked back at the red pyramid. Then he looked at his young bride Hanifah who, though feeling very uncomfortable, smiled back at him. Hanifah had arrived here two days ago with Mokhtar's grandfather. She had no clue that if Mahmoud were to lose the match she would be sacrificed to these heathen Aztec gods. And Mokhtar and the sheik would not obtain the massive amount of heroin that Secretary Acosta had staked on the death match.

But a small sacrifice to make, in the scheme of things, thought Mokhtar. *We have money.* He had enjoyed Hanifah but he was due for a few new wives. *Perhaps I might even take a few of the Mexican girls and convert them to Islam.*

While here at Xiuhcoatl, Mokhtar had witnessed the sacrifice of beautiful girls. "Why do you do this?" he had asked Ramón. "You could just get rid of the ugly ones."

The look Ramón had given him was of scorching contempt. "It would be disrespectful to the gods."

Mokhtar reflected on Ramón's words as Mahmoud lost his balance during a particularly feverish onslaught by Tehuantl. The jihadist swordsman stumbled in the soil and, with alarming speed and force, the jaguar warrior spun around and delivered a back-handed strike that sliced through Mahmoud's right arm. The jihadist screamed as his blood-soaked scimitar fell to the ground and, with one final stroke, Tehuantl sliced Mahmoud's body in two. The arena ruptured with triumphant fury. Sheik Haqqani cringed and Mokhtar swore violently. Both men, however, were nevertheless impressed with the skills and ferocity of Secretary Acosta's warrior.

"Congratulations, Ramón," said Mokhtar, extending his own arm to shake the defense secretary's hand. "It was an exciting match."

Ramón nodded in the affirmative. Hanifah shrieked as two gruesome-looking eagle warriors seized her and carried her away to the red temple. Sheik Haqqani watched on in disgust as Tehuantl cut open Mahmoud's chest with the *macuahuitl*, pulled out his heart, and proceeded to devour it.

Chapter 37

Ciudad Juárez, Chihuahua, Mexico

José Luis Elizondo loaded his AK-47. His upper lip curled and the edges of his open nostrils quivered. The other gangbangers had already prepared their weapons and they were now staring at the morbid artwork spread across the upper back of their leader. José Luis had gotten his latest tattoo just yesterday in a downtown Juárez parlor frequented by big name narcos and he had paid a small fortune for it.

"It's badass, *ese,*" commented Diego, a nineteen-year-old thuggish murderer whose own face and upper body were now so littered with tattoos it was impossible to distinguish the original color of his skin.

The gang leader remained silent and prepared to put on the bulletproof vest one of his cousins had lent him. His latest body art depicted a disturbing, detailed image of a young man being violently slain. Those closest to José Luis could make out the depicted victim was the gang leader's sworn mortal enemy and object of his darkest obsessions; the person who had dominated his thoughts both night and day since his humiliating defeat in the alley of that high school.

And today, thought José Luis, *that puto bastard will die.*

There were five gangsters altogether in the assassination squad, certified killers each one of them and some of the most vicious thugs Barrio Azteca had to offer. Their job seemed easy enough but José Luis was taking no chances. He had been meticulous in his planning. He had carefully studied hourly traffic patterns and had made each of the gangsters study maps of the surrounding areas of the newly constructed Saint Navarro Youth Recreation Center. The gang leader sneered as he silently thought of the complex, though even he had been impressed by its size, facilities, and the number of boys and girls flocking to it. The sheer existence of such a place irked him. When he found out that his eleven-year-old cousin was among those attending, he beat the boy into unconsciousness.

José Luis quickly dismissed such musings. His fight was not with the recreation center or with those impoverished Mexican youth attending it. He focused his attention on Israel and stoked the burning rage that had consumed his soul.

"*Vámonos.* It's time."

Padre Quezada arrived at the parking lot of Ysleta Mission Church at 6:29 a.m. in a white 1990 Chevy van. Isabel, Israel, and Mayrín were already there, waiting for him, in Mayrín's red jeep wrangler. Israel was sitting in the driver's seat. The round priest shook his head but could not help from smiling. *Híjole, I cannot remember the last time he has driven the "Love Bug" that Father G and I both chose so carefully for him!*

"*Buenos días,*" said Padre Quezada cheerfully, as the teenagers entered the van. "I have breakfast burritos and orange juice in the back seat. Help yourselves."

Israel hastily accepted the priest's invitation and finished one burrito before the van exited the parking lot. Just fifteen minutes before, he had completed a grueling two-hour workout and he was famished. It was a solo workout, but the rumor was that Father G would be back in town any day now and Israel was anxious to get back his training companion. The loss in the championships had spurred him to up the intensity of his workouts and he was eager to redeem himself.

Mayrín, however, was too excited to eat anything as this was her first visit to Juárez. Israel had told her about all the projects going on in the Mexican border city and she wanted to be involved. She had always wanted to make a difference—to help those who were less fortunate. And now Mexico was pulling at her like a magnet. She knew today they would be working at the newly constructed Saint Navarro Youth Recreational Center. Israel had told her that many of the children and young teenagers were interested in volleyball and she would be a perfect fit as an instructor and role model.

The van crossed over the Zaragoza Bridge, and Mayrín soon noticed the striking socio-economic differences between the two countries firsthand. Women dressed in dirty rags, carrying babies with glazed eyes, lined the sides of the streets and intersections, begging for money. There was many a young person, seemingly on every corner, wearing the all-too-familiar face of a meth addict—trembling, open sores, hair loss, and loss of skin elasticity. Others were exhibiting signs of heroin addiction—constricted pupils, running noses, flushed skin, and track marks on their limbs. Cocaine addicts were everywhere.

Older individuals with glaring mental deficiencies could be seen on the streets as well, wearing expressions of visible insanity that cruelly cried out to a world which had forsaken them. Mayrín, despite being educated by Israel and the others about the poverty and problems in Juárez, was shocked to witness the heartbreaking scenery in person. She almost cried out in anger at the inhumanity of it all, but held her tongue.

"The city has always had its problems," whispered Israel, "but the narco wars and explosion of drug addicts have totally added a new dimension to it." Mayrín remained silent. A few seconds later, Padre Quezada pulled over on the trash-strewn side of the road and got out of the van.

"What's he doing?" Mayrín asked.

"Saving the helpless," answered Isabel, making a clicking sound with her tongue, "one at a time. He does this every time we come here. He will load them up into the van and then drop them off at a Saint Navarro rescue home before we go to the rec center. He has a whole bunch of health workers who take a look at them and help them."

Through the window of the van, Isabel saw a good-looking young man with a soccer ball and winked at him. "Sometimes," Isabel continued, "he will come by with buses and fill them up with every person who wants to be helped. I think he would like to save every one of them but it's just too hard. For each one he rescues from the streets it seems as if two more come to fill the vacancy. It's almost like, I don't know, almost like Juárez has become a human dumping ground for all the Mexican homeless and the drug addicts and the mentally ill. Maybe for even Central America."

A few minutes later the rotund priest came back with two young women and their babies. A young teenage boy, suffering from the aftermath of a slight heroin overdose, followed them. As Padre Quezada got back on the road and drove to the nearest Saint Navarro rescue home, Mayrín started a conversation with one of the young women named Cina. They discovered Cina was originally from the Southern Mexican state of Guerrero and all her family had been killed in the narco wars. Cina had been lured to the North by the promises of work and she had been employed at one of the nearby *maquiladoras* before they fired her for getting pregnant. She'd been on the streets ever since, begging for food and money so her baby could survive.

Eventually the new passengers were dropped off and taken into the custody of caretakers at the Saint Navarro home. Padre Quezada drove twenty more minutes before reaching their destination.

"Who is Saint Navarro?" Mayrín asked, as the van pulled into the parking lot of the recreational center.

Padre Quezada smiled. "He is one of Mexico's greatest heroes. But his tale is indeed a long one, and I'm afraid we must save it for another day. Come—we have work to do."

There were already hundreds of children and young teenagers in the main gymnasium when Isabel and Mayrín walked through its glass doors. The youth were being led in calisthenics by Sister López. Upon seeing Isabel and Israel, however, the calisthenics session quickly died down and flocks of laughing youngsters scrambled to greet the two American siblings.

"Who's this?" asked a skinny boy named Benito with a mischievous grin, staring at Mayrín. Many others were also interested in his question.

"Hello? Israel's girlfriend," Isabel answered with a wry smile. "She's gonna teach you to play volleyball."

"Wow, she's pretty," said Benito unashamedly. "I want to learn how to play volleyball."

"Me too," chirped in one of his friends. "I want to play volleyball."

Others voiced their enthusiasm for this course of action and soon everyone was in agreement. Most of the boys and even some of the girls seemed mesmerized by Mayrín.

"I've never met a person with green eyes before," said an eleven-year-old girl named Daniela. "They look just like the eyes of a kitty-cat."

"Alright, alright," said Isabel laughing. Unconsciously her fingers touched her turquoise tortoise and she made a clicking sound with her tongue. "Everyone will get a chance to meet Mayrín, but please let her breathe for a minute. She hasn't even had a chance to see what's here yet."

Isabel had told Mayrín about the gymnasiums, swimming pool, racquetball courts, arcade rooms, and medical center and she was anxious to show her everything firsthand. But Israel laughed and spuriously opened a bag of volleyballs, tossing them to the crowd of wannabe volleyball players.

"Let's see what you can do, babe!"

"Well, I guess you are up," Isabel said to Mayrín. "I'll give you a tour of the place later."

Mayrín smirked at her boyfriend. Then she took a whistle out of her pocket and blew it like a military sergeant. "Line up—everyone—lines of ten!" Israel stood stunned. In moments the children were lined up and a few minutes later all the youth were warmed up and learning how to serve a volleyball. By mid-morning everyone was playing their first game as Padre Quezada came by to check on the progress.

"Bien hecho, Mayrín," he said, observing the smiling faces of the children. "They like you."

"Um, I'm just glad you let me tag along Padre. Would you like to try a serve?"

Out of nowhere a runaway volleyball bounced off the husky priest's head, followed by children's laughter. *"¡Ay, caramba!"* exclaimed Padre Quezada, grinning. "I think I'd better let you do the hard stuff."

The priest left the gym and just a few minutes later the children were anxiously engaged in their first volleyball game. It was right before Benito's first serve that Mayrín's alert ears heard the first screams of panic. Her head whipped around towards the origin of alarm. She saw five tattooed gangbangers, armed with assault rifles, marching towards the left corner of the gym—where Israel was horsing around with a group of young boys. Mayrín trembled upon recognizing the gang leader and instantly processed what was happening.

She dashed towards her boyfriend with a sprinter's speed. Reaching full stride, she realized Israel was so engrossed in his horseplay he was oblivious to the gangsters closing in on him. Disregarding any thoughts of her own safety, Mayrín hurled herself at Israel's lower back and tackled him to the gym floor. While in midair the first round of gunfire rocked the facility like a cannon and Mayrín felt a searing, stabbing pain in her upper right arm.

"Get down you fool!" she whispered to her boyfriend, wincing in agony. She felt her head go light.

Now fully cognizant of the situation, Israel clamped his arm around Mayrín's waist and rolled wildly across the floor. Several rounds from the AK-47s tore up the hardwood around them. The children screamed. Some hit the floor and others ran for the exits. Some of the younger ones stood frozen in fear. Isabel, though terrified, quickly collected her wits and guided everyone she could out of the building. But the gangers were only interested in two individuals. More rapid gunfire quickly turned the gymnasium into a war zone. Then, out of the corner of his eye, with dream-like lucidity, Israel saw Alma shoot at the thugs with a machine gun.

"Come and get me *cabrones!"* She went cyclic with the M249.

Two gunmen dropped dead to the floor. Israel perceived a brief respite as the others turned their attention to Alma. Israel yanked Mayrín over his shoulders and ran for the cover of the bleachers. He did not see Alma go down, nor did he see José Luis Elizondo sprint to the other side of the gymnasium to intercept him.

As Alma's body hit the floor, the M249 gently rolled out of her fingers. The two remaining gangsters were so intent on finishing off this strange woman who had killed their comrades they failed to notice their new, more fearsome adversary. He seemingly appeared out of nowhere. Before the thugs could whip around their AK-47s, two .45 caliber bullets ruptured their hearts.

Israel's mind raced as he wove in and out of the iron support framework supporting the bleachers. Mayrín's blood was flowing onto the back side of his neck and he desperately prayed for her life. Soon, he saw the opening that would get them out of the gym. He leaped over the last iron bar and his heart dropped to his gut. One of the armed gangsters, less than ten yards away, stepped forward to greet him with an assault rifle. The thug smiled wickedly to reveal gold-plated teeth, shimmering against facial tattoos. His eyes were cold and empty. His gruesome face exuded bloodlust.

"I told you I'd come back, you *puto* son of a bitch. Now your payment will be your life." He spoke slow and hard and his voice had an ominous edge to it. "I will take the girl and finish what I started."

His fingers adjusted to pull the trigger and the explosive sound of gunfire again echoed throughout the gymnasium. Israel took two steps backwards and prepared for his own death. And then silence. Unexpectedly, Israel felt no pain. He stumbled onward, realizing he could still walk and Mayrín was still on his shoulders. He looked up to see José Luis Elizondo crumpled over on the gym floor.

"Let me see her, Israel." Father G stepped forward and took Mayrín from the arms of a numb Israel. Her face was white. Blood was flowing from her upper right arm. The priest quickly examined her and then took off his own shirt, ripped it in half, and tied it around her arm to slow the bleeding.

"Will she be okat?"

"Yes," answered Father G, observing the injury. "The bullet missed bone. Take her to the medical unit as fast as you can."

Amidst a slew of complex emotions, Israel took off at full speed with Mayrín in his arms. Just as the boy left, the priest heard a stirring from the fallen gangster. He drew his pistols again and walked over to the thug. The gangbanger was wearing a sophisticated bullet-proof vest and it was soon evident to Father G he was not fatally wounded.

The gangster opened his eyes and looked into the hardened, scarred face of the priest. Father G glared at him, recognizing the familiar look of fear. *What are you doing here and why were you coming after Israel?* He would have to find out later. The priest hit the thug in the jaw so hard it knocked him out cold and removed three of his teeth. He quickly loaded the gangster across his shoulders and ran back to where Alma had fallen.

Father G soon discovered that Padre Quezada, Isabel, and some of the stronger teenagers were carrying Alma on a stretcher to the infirmary. It was Sister Arámbula who had insisted the medical unit be constructed into the Saint Navarro Youth Recreational Center. Since its completion, the infirmary had been open to the public—used twenty-four hours a day by a team of three doctors and eleven nurses. The doctor and four nurses currently on duty were in a state of panic, as were the hundreds of youth who had flocked to the visitor waiting area. Sister López desperately tried to calm everyone down as Alma was rushed into the emergency room and placed on a table near Mayrín. Father G dropped José Luis on the floor next to them, and, to the dismay of the nurses, his body hit the floor with a brutal thud.

"He's still alive," said Father G, in response to the stunned and inquisitive looks. "It appears the others are dead but we need to make sure, as well as account for all the children. You'll need to come with me, Sister Arámbula." He wanted to stay with Alma but knew his priority was the youth.

Understanding immediately, Sister Arámbula rushed out the door with him. For those children never having seen Father G, the sight of his face would scare them more than the gangsters. Sister López, whose medical skills now equaled most doctors, immediately went to help with the surgical work on Alma.

"Han llamado a la policía," warned Sister Arámbula. Cringing, Father G nodded in understanding. His presence would raise serious questions by the police officers. Back in the gymnasium, the priest retrieved the bloody M249 and verified there were no remaining dangers. Under the guiding voice of Sister Arámbula, the duo then rounded up the youth from all corners of the recreational center. Ninety minutes later, when the police arrived, Father G made his escape.

"I'll be back later," he whispered to the nun.

Father G returned to the infirmary at 3:05 p.m. Both nuns rushed to embrace him and Padre Quezada made the sign of the cross.

"God be with you, G. Alma's going to be okay," said Sister López tearfully.

"She was shot nine times but thankfully she was wearing the vest," added Padre Quezada. "None of her vital organs were damaged, although she received a fairly severe wound to her left leg and her right ear was destroyed. *Gracias a Dios* she sustained no brain injuries."

Thank God. Father G made the sign of the cross.

Alma designed the cutting edge bulletproof vest at one of the many research laboratories they had established throughout Mexico. They had paid a small fortune for the needed materials.

"None of the children were harmed," continued Sister López.

"Mayrín will be fine also," added Sister Arámbula, her eyes glancing to one of the medical beds. "She save Israel's life."

Father G looked at Mayrín. The injured girl was awake now; color had returned to her skin. Israel was holding her hand and stroking her forehead. The priest deduced she must be the girlfriend he had heard so many rumors about. He walked closer to the medical bed and then halted unexpectedly. The girl was beautiful, to be sure, but there was something else about her, something vaguely familiar. And then he saw the pendant dangling near her bandaged arm. Without a word he grabbed the pendant and broke it from the golden chain.

"Where did you get this?" he demanded.

Mayrín, Israel, Isabel, Padre Quezada, and the nuns stared at him in shock.

"The pendant, where did you get it?" Father G repeated.

Mayrín looked bewildered. *Why is he questioning me like this?* She'd never spoken of it before, not to anyone, but today's events had loosened her innermost reservations.

"My mother gave it to me when I was a small child," she said softly, starting to cry. "Before she died."

Stunned, the priest opened the pendant. For several surreal moments he stared at the tiny picture inside. He then gently gave the pendant back to Mayrín and silently left the medical unit. Sister Arámbula walked over to the bed and gingerly took the pendant from a very bewildered Mayrín. She opened it up to see a small photo of a child, a beautiful young woman, and a handsome young man. *"¡Dios Mío!"* She dropped the pendant onto the floor and quickly made the sign of the cross.

"What is it?" asked Israel. "What the freak is going on?"

"Your girlfriend," said Sister López very slowly, picking up the pendant, "is Father G's daughter."

Chapter 38

Ciudad Juárez, Chihuahua, Mexico

"¿Qué pasa, güey?" asked Officer García, mockingly. His bushy mustache joggled up and down and his jowls rolled in laughter. Handcuffed in the back seat of the Juárez Municipal Police car, José Luis Elizondo ignored the question. His ribs throbbed and his jaw ached. Streams of salty blood were still flowing down his chin from several gaping holes in his mouth. *It'd gone bad,* he thought. *Real bad.* Despite himself, he thought again of the one-eyed man and shivered. He could not erase the terrifying image.

"You were on assignment from the La Línea, right?" probed Officer García. "Interesting they had you *pinches changos* go into a youth recreation center. Who were you going after anyway?"

José Luis did not answer. Until recently, the Juárez Municipal Police Department was synonymous with La Línea. But times were different now; things had changed dramatically. El Chapo and La Gente Nueva were on the verge of winning the bloody battle for Juárez and they now controlled most all police personnel. And José Luis knew that Officer García and his partner, Officer Valenzuela, were associated with La Gente Nueva.

Officer García did not ask any more questions and Officer Valenzuela drove on in silence for fifteen more minutes before pulling into a station on the south side of the city. Both officers dragged the gang leader out of the back seat of the vehicle. Officer García whacked him across the back of his head with his pistol.

"You were smart not to talk, *puto chango* asshole," he said grinning. "But you will. We have developed a unique and successful methodology of making people talk. It has helped us eliminate our competition."

It turned out the proprietary interrogation techniques were not needed. José Luis spilled his guts after two broken thumbs and an electric shock to his genitalia. He told the officers everything about the events leading up to the attack—including his humiliating defeat at the high school. He described the assassination attempt in detail and gave a vivid description of the face that now ravaged his thoughts. Thumbs throbbing, he failed to notice Captain Dante Gutiérrez's eyes widen as he related his terrifying encounter with the one-eyed man. It was a serious mistake.

"Tell me again what happened with this *puto* one-eyed man and leave out nothing," growled Captain Gutiérrez. "All the *pinches* details and the exact truth."

José Luis repeated the story and gave the same vivid description of the mysterious man—the hard, scarred face and the inhuman intensity emanating from his steel-blue eye.

"He came out of nowhere," said José Luis. "He's a *gringo chingado* and has some relationship with Israel. I'm sure of it."

Captain Gutiérrez stared at the gangster with narrow eyes and motioned for his colleagues to take hold of José Luis's arm once again. They forcefully did so and spread it out across the wooden table. The gang leader screamed as Captain Gutiérrez slammed the iron hammer against his right index finger.

"Tell me everything again—from the beginning."

Captain Gutiérrez interrogated his prisoner for thirty more minutes before he was satisfied José Luis Elizondo was telling the truth.

Internally, the police captain was quivering with excitement.

This may be the puto luckiest day of my life.

"Take him to the pink house," he barked at Officer García. "Fetch a doctor immediately and see that he is properly treated. Give him morphine, meth, heroin, cocaine—anything he wants. I will meet you there as soon as I can."

A few hours later, José Luis was flying on a magic carpet. The pain was gone. He would survive and fulfill his darkest ambitions. The police officers had treated him like El Chapo Guzmán since Captain Gutiérrez had left—they brought him high-quality drugs and two prostitutes.

There would be no more pain, they had told him. It was necessary to discover the truth and test his bravery—all prisoners were treated in a similar fashion. But he was special, they had said. He would now be working for El Chapo. El Chapo needed men like him—men who were willing to take initiative and avenge their enemies. And together, they would destroy both Israel and the mysterious one-eyed man. Soon, they had told him, he would meet his new boss.

Captain Gutiérrez entered the pink house at 9:05 p.m. and eyeballed the gang leader once again. José Luis grinned. The captain was accompanied by two men. One was a tall, well-built man wearing decorated military attire. The other was an old cripple—a hunchback of some sort with glaring deformities. Captain Gutiérrez extended both men every courtesy and José Luis noticed the small flicker of fear in the captain's eyes—a look the gangster was intimately familiar with. But it was the face of the ancient hunchback that captivated the gang leader's attention—it bore an expression of cold, morbid darkness; his eyes burned with murder. José Luis stared at the face in fascination.

"José Luis Elizondo!" exclaimed the military man in a charming voice, interrupting the trance-like stare. "Welcome! Captain Gutiérrez has told us of your exploits and skills. You will be a tremendous asset to our organization."

The military man shook the gang leader's hand with a smile stretched across his handsome face. "My name is Ramón Acosta and I am a personal friend of El Chapo." Ramón looked deep into the gangster's cold eyes and spoke slowly and deliberately. "I believe we share a common problem and can help each other out."

The defense secretary lit a cigarette and placed it in the fingers of the gang leader not in splints. "I want you to tell me exactly what you told Captain Gutiérrez about the attack today and the events leading up to it. Leave nothing out."

Though Secretary Acosta was indeed persuasive and magnetizing, José Luis normally would have perceived the evil lurking behind the friendly face. It was an amplification of the evil he himself possessed; dark ambitions which drove him to seek and destroy without conscience. But his senses were dulled by the intoxicating chemicals in his brain. And his desire to believe these men. The gang leader took a deep drag of burning tobacco and told the charismatic military figure everything, in excruciating detail. Once again, he failed to notice the excitement rippling through Ramón's facial features as he carefully described his encounter with the one-eyed man.

Secretary Acosta skillfully and methodically interrogated the gangster for over an hour and extracted every piece of pertinent information. When he was done, he looked over at Tlaloc, who slightly nodded his confirmation. Before José Luis knew what was happening, Secretary Acosta reached out with his right hand and grabbed the skinny gang leader by the throat. Even Captain Gutiérrez was stunned at the secretary's sudden and unexpected bestial transformation. The gangbanger was dead within twenty seconds.

"I totally can't get over it," Israel said, squeezing Mayrín's hand just a little bit tighter.

After Father G left the emergency room, Mayrín opened her soul for the first time in her life. Sobbing, she had told the story of how both she and her mother had been captured many years ago. Mayrín could still recall the details vividly. When the opportunity arose, her mother had sacrificed her own life so that Mayrín could escape. Not even knowing which country she was in, Mayrín was taken to a beloved nun who recognized her imminent danger and hastily arranged for her departure to Spain. She had lived as the adopted daughter of the nun's sister and her husband ever since.

"I just wanna see my father," said Mayrín. The nuns had explained to her yesterday how Father G needed time to compose himself.

"He has suffered much," Sister Arámbula had told her. "And this change his life very fast. He is in emotion shock. He loves you so much and wants to say much to you. But right now, he not know how to say it."

"Hello? Just a few more hours," Isabel replied. She was in the back seat of the jeep, leaning up against her friend Sergio as much as she could. She was as caught up in the drama as anyone. Sister López had informed both Isabel and Israel that Father G would be returning to El Paso this evening, and that they needed to bring Mayrín to the Ysleta Mission Church at 8:00 p.m.

"And then you have to tell me and Sergio *lo que pasa!"* exclaimed Lucía. She was sitting on the other side of her boyfriend in the back seat. We could make a *telenovela!"*

Israel was not listening to the conversation. He was in a state of emotional turmoil and anxious to see Father G as well. The priest had raised him like his own son. Father G had been his singular role model for more than a decade and Israel only hoped he would meet the priest's expectations as the boyfriend of his daughter. Though in a bizarre sort of way, it was kind of like he was dating his sister. But he was deeply in love and the thought was not that troubling. *Dating Isabel would be strange,* he thought. *Isabel is my sister. In the end, it will all get ironed out.*

Mayrín kissed Israel on the cheek as the jeep traveled east down U.S. Highway 62 on a dark and cloudy Sunday afternoon. She had been extremely lucky. The gunshot did not cause any serious damage—she hadn't even told her aunt and uncle about the injury. She was still in pain but it had subsided over the last twenty-four hours, though this was partly due to her jubilation of being reunited with her father.

Despite her wounded arm and the incredible events of yesterday, Mayrín had wanted to go to Hueco Tanks, a Texas State Park about thirty-five miles northeast of El Paso. Israel had been skeptical, but Mayrín had convinced him it would be good to get away for a while—the solitude of the nature park would help clear their minds and revitalize them. Isabel decided to tag along as well and they had invited Sergio and Lucía to join them. Mayrín had come to love the park, often referred to as a sacred desert sanctuary, for its beautiful scenery and the ancient imagery left behind by Native Americans. They had trekked to the hills for thousands of years to collect rainwater accumulating within the many natural rock basins. Israel and Isabel had always liked the park as well. Father G had taken them there since they were children. Both enjoyed hiking the many trails and Israel was especially fond of rock climbing. Isabel loved to watch the birds and other wildlife.

When Israel turned north on Ranch Road 2775 he saw the black SUVs approaching in the rear-view mirror. They were driving fast, dangerously fast, and he slowed down the jeep to let them pass. And then Isabel screamed. Assault rifles appeared from the dark-tinted windows and a barrage of gunfire destroyed the tranquility of the surrounding desert. Dust, sand, and creosote bush kicked up into the air just a few feet from the jeep. Israel floored the gas pedal, bringing the jeep to its top speed of 110 mph while bullets continued to pepper the asphalt and desert terrain all around them.

This can't be happening, thought Mayrín. *Not now. We are in the United States, not Mexico!*

"Oh my God!" screamed Lucía.

Three SUVs were chasing them down and gaining ground quickly. Mayrín braced herself against the front seat and looked at Israel; his hands were gripping the steering wheel so hard that veins were popping out of his forearms. A psychotic intensity blazed in his eyes—dramatically different than moments ago.

What the freaking hell? "Hang on!"

A few seconds later he slammed on the brakes and rubber burned asphalt as the jeep jumped from the highway and landed onto a desert trail. And then he floored the gas pedal once again. Two of the SUVs followed them, *sicarios* unleashing another series of rapid gunfire that came dangerously close to the speeding jeep. All passengers now screaming, Israel raced the jeep through the desert scrublands, weaving in and out of Texas mulberry and Mexican buckeye trees.

At the breakneck pace, one of the SUVs veered off to the east. The other continued to gain ground and the sound of gunfire was nonstop. Israel swerved hard to the right and took the jeep into a clearing sparsely populated by isolated boulders and four-wing saltbush. Once again, Israel brought the jeep to full speed and headed directly into the open desert.

For close to ten seconds Israel floored the gas pedal. The leading SUV held tight on their tail. Isabel and Lucía could make out the tattooed facial features and cold, dark eyes of the gunmen—they were grinning wickedly and their bestial stares sent chills through both girls. Then, unexpectedly, Israel slammed on the brakes and hammered down on the steering wheel. The jeep swerved so hard to its left that it skidded out of control for a considerable distance before rolling over on its side.

He was the only one among them aware of the oncoming cliff, barely visible to the naked eye. As the spines of a prickly pear cactus ripped into the flesh of his left forearm, Israel heard the gunmen's screams as they plummeted to their deaths on the jagged rocks below. He wasted no time in maneuvering out of the jeep and, with brute strength fueled by adrenaline, lifted it back on four wheels.

"You all okay?" he asked, sliding back into the driver's seat. Both Mayrín and Isabel were speechless but faintly nodded in the affirmative. Sergio and Lucía were too shocked to do anything but they seemed alright. Turning the ignition key, Israel breathed a sigh of relief as the engine roared to life. Jamming his right foot down on the gas pedal, he immediately drove north, up to the edge of the hidden cliff, and snaked around its border.

"Dude, what the hell just happened?" Sergio finally asked. No one responded.

Isabel was crying. Her whole body was shaking. "It's just like the orphanage!" For the first time in years she brought up the taboo subject.

Israel did not answer. He was thinking the same thing.

After traveling a few hundred yards, Israel rambled onto an old desert trail he had encountered years ago. He had a photographic memory. Father G had told him this at a young age. It was a gift, especially when it came to the outdoors. He could recall the exact details of every creek, hillside, and grove of trees he ever laid eyes on. And he desperately needed that gift now. Rocketing down the dusty trail, he prayed for the safety of his passengers.

Another SUV appeared, approaching from the west, moving quickly, and a barrage of gunfire pounded against the giant rocks surrounding the jeep. Israel swerved the jeep maniacally to the east and the door grinded against volcanic stone to generate fiery trails of sparks and diabolical screeching that ricocheted off the red and white boulders with fierce intensity. For the time being, he had gotten them out of view of the gunmen, and out of the direct line of fire.

"Dude, what is happening?" yelled Sergio.

Israel ignored him. Lucía, Isabel, and Mayrín remained silent; their skin had gone ashen and their bodies were numb. Lucía had buried her head in Sergio's chest. Isabel's eyes were closed and her arms were folded, fervently praying to her Creator for deliverance. Mayrín's eyes, however, were feverishly searching for the pursuing vehicle that would surely appear again any second. Heightened adrenaline sharpened Israel's every sense; the skin on his face was stretched tight. His only advantage over his pursuers was his intimate knowledge of the terrain.

Another fusillade of gunfire crashed against a red overhang as the SUV finally materialized and a shower of rock fragments rained down on the jeep. One fragment, the size of a marble, hit Isabel on her right shoulder. She opened her eyes from prayer. She looked forward and sound finally came to her lips.

"What are you doing?" she screamed.

"Dude!" shouted Sergio.

But flashbacks of the massacre at the orphanage had consumed Israel. He wanted to kill all these bastards. "Brace yourselves!" Israel shouted through clenched teeth. The high-powered SUV was on their tail and closing in fast. Gunfire continued to fly around the jeep and shattered brittle boulders pocketed with fissures. Just a few feet from the rocky top, Israel cranked the steering wheel to his right—while continuing to accelerate. The jeep shot off the hilltop at an awkward angle and landed on the slope of the opposite side of the hill with a jarring force that almost rolled it off an overhanging ledge. Struggling fiercely for control, Israel somehow managed to bring the vehicle to safety and then quickly cut back to his left without looking back.

The enemy SUV was unable to replicate the skillful maneuver. Mayrín, still fixated on their pursuers, screamed violently as she witnessed the pointed end of a large, irregular-shaped rock smash into the front-windshield of the out of control SUV and demolish the bodies of the driver and front passenger. Bright red blood spurted out of the windows to paint a ghastly pattern on the rock.

"Almost freaking there!" exclaimed Israel, adroitly navigating downwards through the boulders dotting the steep hillside.

They made it to the base of the hill and followed a dusty trail through the flatlands. The trail eventually led to a narrow passageway within the confines of two dirty-white granite walls. They travelled for some three or four miles through the rocky corridor while everyone silently tried to regain their mental composure. Nervously holding her turquoise tortoise, it was Isabel who finally spoke.

"I don't understand it. Why are they trying to kill us?"

Israel did not answer. He was thinking the same thing. The men in the SUVs were not teenage Barrio Azteca gangbangers—they were highly trained cartel hitmen.

And I killed them, he realized. The thought chilled him. His rage faded. *I am directly responsible for the killing of another human being.* But then he thought of his sister and friends. *I must protect them at all costs. If it means killing, I will do so. Their deaths are justified.*

The priests and nuns had always taught him the importance of self-defense. He was aware of the tremendous evil in the world. Still, he disliked being a killer. He tried to shake it off and his mind raced to make sense of what was happening. *The U.S. is supposed to be off limits. Was José Luis Elizondo really that high up in the narco world? What the freaking hell is going on?*

He forced himself to think clearly. Getting everyone to safety was his only concern and he knew exactly where they were and the best route to get back to El Paso. His hawk-like eyes had just seen the landmark he was looking for and they were heading directly towards it—a giant multi-colored boulder with an ancient painting of a faded yellow sun at its base. He knew that a few hundred yards to the right of the boulder was a small dirt road leading back to Highway 62. Israel continued to push the jeep to its limits and rounded the boulder sharply.

And then they heard gunfire.

Israel continued to floor the gas pedal but felt himself lose control of the vehicle. Rounds from FX-05 Xiuhcoatl assault rifles punctured all four tires of the jeep. He heard the roar of the last remaining SUV and watched helplessly as the vehicle pulled out and veered directly at him. Airbags shot out, smothering the faces and upper bodies of Israel and Mayrín, and the jeep came to an abrupt stop.

Israel desperately tried to shift into reverse. He could not—the jeep's engine had been permanently damaged. Before he could get out of the vehicle, the butt of a FX-05 Xiuhcoatl launched through the driver's side window and hit him directly on the temple of his forehead. It knocked him out instantly.

Sergio and the girls realized what was happening and screamed. Heavily tattooed hitmen, armed with assault rifles, swarmed around the jeep and two of the men pulled Mayrín out of the passenger seat. She responded by spitting in the face of one of the assailants and punching the other one with a surprisingly solid right hook. Another thug hit her in the chin with his gun and she lost consciousness. The *sicarios* pulled Sergio and Lucía out of the jeep and Isabel watched in slow motion as one of the assassins pulled out a pistol and shot the couple in the back of the head.

"Get them all in the back," growled one of the shorter hitmen. The SUV had been outfitted with thick steel armor and was undamaged. "You!" the man barked, pointing his right index finger at Isabel. She almost fainted from fear. "Tell the pale rider he has five days to turn himself in or these other two die! You understand, *puta?*"

Isabel stared at the man with a blank expression.

"The one-eyed *gringo,*" the thug snarled, growing impatient. "You know him?"

It's Father G, Isabel realized, shivering in terror. *They are after Father G.* Without realizing it, Isabel nodded.

"Then go tell him, *pinche puta!*" the man snarled. "Now! The highway is five miles south so I suggest you get moving!"

CHAPTER 39

MEXICO CITY, MEXICO

"ANOTHER DRINK, GENERAL?" ASKED THE cocktail waitress with a smile. She had been instructed, in no uncertain terms, to extend the man every courtesy.

"*¿Por qué no?*" replied General Martínez. He laughed heartily. "And one for my date also, *por favor.*"

Things were going well for the general and he was in a good mood. Three weeks ago Secretary Acosta had given him high command of the 44th military zone in Miahuatlán, Oaxaca, and he was already reaping the benefits. Clinging to his left arm, the high-priced prostitute giggled and reached for another margarita. Grinning charismatically, the general studied the peculiar architecture of the mansion and listened to the catchy tune of "Cuerno de Chivo" sung by Los Huracanes del Norte.

Known for his insatiable appetite for women, General Martínez had a pencil-thin mustache, beady eyes, and a pot belly difficult to stuff in his uniform. He also possessed the highest rank of any military officer at the party and was the most feared. Less than two months ago, he personally tortured and murdered the former general of the 44th military zone and then hand-delivered his entire family to Secretary Acosta.

General Martínez took another sip of vodka and his eyes widened in astonishment. Standing in front of him, wearing a provocative red taffeta dress and expensive black stiletto heels, was the most beautiful woman he had ever seen. Fiery diamond earrings hung from her earlobes and sparkled radiantly next to her full, moist lips and gleaming white teeth. More diamonds, all of exquisite color and clarity, some in excess of ten carats, decorated her finely formed neck and shoulders. Her long, dark hair flowed down the back of her neck to her buttocks and accentuated her trim figure. The stiletto heels highlighted the shape and firmness of her legs. The woman galvanized him.

"Good evening, General," the woman said in a coquettish tone. She was smiling seductively and the twinkle in her eyes drew a nasty look from the high-priced escort wrapped around General Martínez's left arm.

"And good evening to you, *señorita,*" said the general in his most charming voice, ignoring the sting from his escort's fingernails. He could not take his eyes off the woman in the red dress and, studying her carefully up and down, quickly reached the conclusion she possessed everything he longed for and then some. A fine connoisseur of all feminine jewelry, the general estimated her necklace alone to be worth a small fortune. The woman's beauty and style made his high-priced prostitute look like a common street whore.

Unashamedly, the woman in red reached out to caress several of the highly-polished medals on the left breast of the general's military jacket. She ran her fingers through the silvery strands of his epaulette and across his flabby left pectoral muscle.

"I would be very interested in learning how you came to acquire these tokens of bravery," she said in a husky voice, once again ignoring the icy stare of his escort. Her honey-brown eyes danced wickedly and ever so slightly, she ran the tip of her tongue across her upper lip.

It was too much for General Martínez. Burning with desire, he rounded on the prostitute, stuffed a wad of bills into her hands, and gave her a menacing look that said her services were no longer needed. He devoted his full attention to the woman in the red dress.

"Of course, *señorita,* of course; it would be my utmost pleasure. Can I get you a drink?"

"Sí, General," replied the woman in red, gently running her fingers across his right hand. "I would like that very, very much."

Two hours later General Martínez and the woman in red entered room 223 of the Fiesta Grand Chapultepec Hotel. The general was mad with passion and it took all the woman's resourcefulness to keep him under control. "General," she giggled, her hands caressing his shoulders as he sat on the luxurious king-size bed and unbuttoned his shirt. "There is something I've wanted to do all evening. But you have to close your eyes!"

General Martínez laughed boyishly. *"Bueno, señorita, bueno.* You win. You can do anything you like, but you must hurry."

"Oh I will, General. I most certainly will."

The general closed his eyes with an expression of overwhelming lust. And with surprising strength and quickness, Sister López knocked him out with an iron pipe wrench she had previously planted in the room. The nun made the sign of the cross and then hastily keyed her cell phone. "It's done." She kicked the unconscious General Martínez hard in the groin.

A few minutes later, a breathless Armendáriz arrived in the hotel room carrying a leather duffel bag. He looked down at the general's limp body and then at the nun. She had retrieved the wallet from General Martínez's pants and was studying the technically advanced integrated circuit chip on his military identification card. "Nice work Sister."

Sister López grunted an inaudible reply. Both Armendáriz and

Alma had convinced her that she was the only woman they knew who could get General Martínez alone in a bedroom. Neither Padre Quezada nor Father G knew about what they had planned, and Sister López had no intention of telling them.

"I'll take it from here, Sister López," Armendáriz said softly. "You've done fabulous."

Sister López saw the determined look etched on Armendáriz's tattooed face and handed him the general's identification card. She stood up on her tiptoes and gently kissed him on the cheek.

"God be with you, Matías," she said reverently. "I'll be praying for you."

The nun then used the bathroom to change into the jeans, t-shirt, and tennis shoes that Armendáriz had brought along in the duffel bag, collected the general's car keys, and left the hotel.

Once the nun was gone, Armendáriz undressed General Martínez, pulled out a 9mm pistol, complete with silencer, and put a bullet through the back of his head. Using a surgical Gigli saw, he removed the right index finger from the dead man's hand. And, a few minutes later, removed his left eyeball.

The iron door creaked open. Mayrín looked up from the corner of her cell and saw four rough-looking men in military fatigues. She tried to suppress her tears. Wolfish grins broke out onto the soldiers' tattooed faces upon seeing her for the first time. Despite herself, Mayrín sobbed harder and screamed.

From the opposing cell, Israel cursed fiendishly. Saliva spewed from his mouth. He ripped the porcelain toilet from its base and slammed it against iron bars and concrete. The men in Mayrín's cell ignored him. Two of the men grabbed Mayrín's arms and tried to grab more. She bloodied one man's nose with a strong kick from her right leg before she was completely subdued.

Amidst Israel's violent cursing, another man entered Mayrín's cell, a strange-looking hunchback. He was old, very old. His body was crippled and his face was deformed. But it was something in his eyes that terrified Mayrín into silence. All color drained from her face as she stared into the blazing black eyes and felt the stinging chill of something much worse than death. It was as if this man had the power to devour her soul.

"Hold ... her ... tight," the hunchback commanded. Israel exploded in furor and the other men grinned. Mayrín's body went rigid and she screamed.

"Interesting," the ancient cripple said after a few seconds. He took a deep, ragged breath. "It is ... a good ... omen, ... howbeit, ... unexpected." The hunchback turned around to give Israel a look of utter disdain. Israel cursed the ancient man and, after a few seconds, Tlaloc faced the soldiers.

"She is ... a ... virgin," the hunchback hissed, to the bitter disappointment of her captors. "She is ... not ... to be ... touched. ... Go and ... get her ... prepared."

Two hours after they had taken Mayrín, Israel was led from his cell and brought into a room at gunpoint. His hands were tied behind his back and a leather cord was wrapped tightly around his neck. His left eye was purple and swollen and his face was cut and bloodied. Several of his ribs had been bruised and the whole of his upper torso was aching. Four men in military uniforms shoved him into the center of the room and loosened the slack on the neck cord. Israel coughed violently. He tried to clear his injured throat and then gulped for air. Trying to regain his composure, he looked around for a few seconds to get his bearings.

The room was decorated with images of Santa Muerte and grotesque-looking statues. Standing in from of him, wearing a decorated military uniform, was a large, lean, athletic man with hard, confident eyes, and a powerful square jaw. He had a thick, neatly trimmed mustache underneath a sharp, pointed nose and high cheekbones. And he was eerily familiar.

Israel took a deep breath and turned his eyes into daggers. "Where is Mayrín?" he growled. "Where is Isabel?" He already knew Sergio and Lucía were dead. He had seen their bodies.

The man's lips twisted. "Your sister is safe, Israel. Mayrín, however, is another matter. She is being dealt with accordingly. An unfortunate circumstance, I'm afraid. Her fate is now beyond my control." The man offered Israel a glass of water. Israel refused it.

"Do you know who I am?" the man asked.

Israel did not answer, glaring at the man in hatred. Unbridled rage was building up inside of him to a level he had never known.

"My name is Defense Secretary Ramón Acosta," the man said. "I am the most powerful man in Mexico and soon will become the most powerful man in the world."

"You're a narco bastard!"

Secretary Acosta ignored the comment. His demeanor did not change. "During my tenure as the Mexican Secretary of Defense, I have implemented certain policies and procedures that have proven valuable. One such example has been the development and utilization of a Nationalized DNA Database. We have DNA profiles of every man in the Mexican Armed Forces and quite a few of the general population as well."

The secretary's eyes narrowed. "We also have DNA profiles of everyone suspected of getting in my way. Do you know the value, Israel, of using DNA as a biometric tool as opposed to using fingerprints or retinal scans?"

"I really don't give a rat's ass!" Israel shouted. "I want to see Mayrín and I want to see her now!" Israel's face was hard and cold, but the first tremor of trepidation quivered within his soul.

"It enables one to discover familial relationships, Israel," Secretary Acosta said harshly. "It allows me the opportunity to properly retaliate against a man's parents, siblings, children, and wife."

Israel's eyes bore into his face with a look of immense, burgeoning hatred.

"We typed your DNA, Israel," Secretary Acosta continued, "and ran it through our database. This morning an unexpected discovery was brought to my attention. It appears that we are related. Closely related." Secretary Acosta studied Israel's face intently. Mixed emotions were growing within the secretary as he analyzed the boy's features. "Are you familiar with a Catholic priest named Father Navarro? Were you a resident of the Hope of Mexico orphanage?"

The question came as a complete shock. *How does he know about Father Navarro and the orphanage?* Long suppressed memories, terrible recollections of watching Father Navarro writhe in pain, burst into his forethoughts. Secretary Acosta adroitly observed his reaction.

"I suspected you might. He was clever to rename you, Jacob. Did Father Navarro tell you he was your grandfather?"

The question numbed Israel's mind. "That's not true."

Secretary Acosta's eyes narrowed. "I'm afraid it is true, Jacob. And, in a roundabout sort of way, I am related to Father Navarro also. Because I am your father."

Israel let the revelation sink in and felt a chilling sensation sweep through his body. Again, he remembered Father Navarro's body contorting violently against the inverted cross. "Bullshit," said Israel, as harshly as he could. "That's impossible."

The secretary laughed strangely. "Why would I lie, Jacob? I, too, did not believe it at first, until I saw you up close for the first time. You have the eyes of your mother. And," he continued, staring into Israel's eyes, "of your grandfather." For a split second the secretary studied Israel's body. "Though you have my physique."

The secretary's features hardened and his eyes blazed with frenzy. "Now listen to me very carefully, Jacob. Inside your veins flows the royal blood of Aztec nobility. We are transforming Mexico and we are on the verge of reclaiming its former power and glory. The vulgar injustices Christianity has wreaked upon this land shall be avenged. I am offering you a prestigious position in our organization and a chance to become part of history. It is your destiny."

A complex jumble of emotions boiled within Israel's mind and soul, unleashing a primitive wrath he could not contain. He slammed the back of his head against one of the guard's faces behind him and heard the crunch of bone grinding into flesh. Hands still bound, he came after Secretary Acosta in a rampage. The secretary responded with a left hook that knocked Israel unconscious.

"I'll give you some time to think about it."

At 2:04 a.m., Armendáriz arrived at the security entrance of a military grade barbwire fence on the southwestern outskirts of Mexico City. The dark sky was thickly blanketed with clouds and thunder cracked from somewhere behind them. White lightning flashed, revealing a series of concrete buildings rising a few hundred yards away. Dressed in a t-shirt and blue jeans, Armendáriz rode a black motorcycle. A backpack clung to his shoulders. Rain drizzling across his face, he turned off the engine, dismounted the motorcycle, and keyed his cell phone.

"I'm here."

Seconds later, a large metal dock door on one of the concrete buildings creaked open. A wavy block of light disrupted the morning darkness once again. Amidst another round of thunder, the engine of a camouflage Panhard VCR Armored Personnel Carrier rumbled to life, exited its concrete home, and drove to the main entrance of the security fence.

Colonel David Contreras Zepeda popped the driver's hatch of the vehicle, eyed Armendáriz and then the black motorcycle. An olive-green beret covered the colonel's thick mane of gray hair and a full beard and mustache helped mask his unusually large nose. "You alone?" Colonel Contreras asked, in a deep, booming voice.

"Yes," replied Armendáriz.

"The money?"

"Part of it's here. You'll get the rest when I get what I need."

"I want all of it now, *cabrón.*"

The headlights of the military vehicle brightened, beams shot into the tattooed face of Armendáriz. Unflinching, Armendáriz stared at the colonel with narrowing eyes.

"Then the deal is off," he said, masking anxiety. He turned around and reached for the motorcycle.

"*¡Espérese un momento!*" bellowed Colonel Contreras, a little too eagerly. "Lemme see what you got!"

Forcing himself to breathe slowly, Armendáriz turned around and unstrapped the backpack. He unzipped it and lifted out a steel-plated case. He opened the case into the headlights; the contents glittered. A bald man wearing wire-rimmed spectacles got out of the Panhard VCR. He was small in stature, clean-shaven, and dressed in a dark, double-breasted suit. The gated door of the security fence swung open and Armendáriz walked up to the well-dressed man and let him examine the merchandise. The man's eyebrows hiked up and he nodded in the affirmative to Colonel Contreras.

"Give him the case and get inside the vehicle," ordered the colonel. Armendáriz obeyed and followed the bald man into the personnel carrier.

"The value?" the colonel asked Armendáriz, driving back to the concrete building.

"250 million U.S. dollars."

Colonel Contreras looked into the rear-view mirror. The bald man in the suit was studying the gems with an elaborate eyepiece. He nodded to confirm the veracity of Armendáriz's response.

"The rest?" the colonel asked.

"Once I get what I need, a truck will arrive carrying two billion in cash and gold."

Colonel Contreras remained silent. He had good sources claiming Armendáriz always delivered, though this was by far the biggest transaction anyone was aware of. If things went smoothly, the colonel would become one of the richest men in Mexico overnight. The colonel drove the Panhard VCR into the docking area of the building and the thick metal door slowly sealed the entrance behind them.

A slew of armed guards patrolled the facility and it was more technically sophisticated than Armendáriz expected. Most of the technology, however, had been shut down. There was a state-of-the-art full-body scanner at the first security checkpoint, but it was not operational. All video cameras were off-line.

Colonel Contreras led Armendáriz past the guards and into the heart of the complex. They passed through two more non-operational security checkpoints before descending an elevator to a level a surprising number of feet below ground. Armendáriz followed the colonel down a concrete corridor and into a server room. A single monitor was powered on, sitting atop a plain desk.

"You have thirty minutes."

Armendáriz knew exactly what he was doing and went to work

fast. He inserted General Martínez's ID into the card reader next to the monitor. He then pulled out the severed finger and eyeball of General Martínez from the backpack and peeled off the saran wrap from the digit and organ. Holding his breath, Armendáriz pressed the tip of the severed finger onto the fingerprint sensor and, simultaneously, positioned the eyeball opposite the retinal scanner. Two seconds of agony passed before Armendáriz confirmed he was logged on.

Exhaling, his fingers rapidly pounded on the keyboard and he hashed out a series of LINUX commands. Praying, Armendáriz keyed the final character of the network password he had bought a few hours ago for ten million U.S. dollars. A new screen popped up on the monitor. His eyebrows arched and his pupils dilated. For several seconds Armendáriz remained shell shocked as he gazed upon the computer monitor. He quickly made the sign of the cross.

"Son of a bitch."

He shook his head, slapped himself, and downloaded everything that would fit onto his specialized flash drive. He was done in twenty minutes.

Colonel Contreras was anxiously waiting at the door of the server room when Armendáriz walked towards him. "You were fast," he said, proceeding out to the corridor. "So we good? I got about forty-five minutes before I gotta power up the machines."

"We're good," Armendáriz mumbled. He followed the colonel back to the elevator, still stunned by the information on the monitor. He forced himself to clear his mind and relax. "The truck should be here now."

The colonel grunted an acknowledgement upon entering the elevator. Both men remained silent as they walked back the same route they had come. Inside the docking area, Colonel Contreras pressed a button on the control panel near the first security entrance. The large metallic dock door slowly rattled open and Colonel Contreras motioned for

Armendáriz to climb back into the Panhard VCR. Armendáriz did so and was greeted by a dozen soldiers waiting inside, armed with FX-05 Xiuhcoatl assault rifles. Faces hard and featureless. Armendáriz said nothing. Colonel Contreras turned the ignition key and drove back to the entrance gate of the perimeter security fence. Parked thirty yards from the motorcycle was a dirty-white 18-wheel freight truck that seemed to have been deserted.

"Where's the driver?" asked Colonel Contreras, getting out of the personnel carrier.

"Gone," answered Armendáriz. "The truck now belongs to you, as well as everything in it."

"Open it," commanded the colonel. "If you have delivered everything you promised, then our business is done."

Armendáriz walked over to the 18-wheeler, followed by four armed soldiers, and opened the back door of the freight trailer. The soldiers' eyes bulged upon seeing the large stacks of cash and 100 oz. bars of gold. They quickly climbed inside to examine the merchandise. Armendáriz, heart beating erratically, followed them. Hastily, he went for his helmet and other possessions lying in the northwest corner.

Armendáriz slammed on the helmet and turned around to jump out of the trailer. His lungs stiffened. Pointed directly at his chest were six FX-05 Xiuhcoatl assault rifles. Colonel Contreras took a step forward with a grin upon his face—the first time this evening Armendáriz had seen him smile. *"Bien hecho*, Armendáriz, well done *cabrón.* Your word is indeed as good as gold. But I'm afraid I can't let you leave."

Armendáriz made his decision instantly. Bullets sprayed onto his specialized armor as he jumped down and sprinted onto the open ground, pressing down on the remote detonator previously hidden in his helmet. The freight truck exploded with the sound of hell and the soldiers screamed in agony as billowy flames ate into their flesh.

Armendáriz smashed into dirty asphalt, severely injured. Several bullets had penetrated flesh and he was badly burned. Wincing, he made the sign of the cross and prayed. He then slowly stood up and hobbled to the motorcycle. With tremendous effort, he secured his backpack, straddled the machine, and rode off.

Father G slowly opened his eyes and gazed at the opaline-white tomb directly in front of him. Against the light of the flaming torches, his eyes fixated on the strange color of the Cross of Lorraine decorating the white marble. There were other tombs in the cavern as well, some very ancient, all housing the sacred remains of Red Crusaders. Father G was only interested in one of them. Underneath the ruby within the cross, the letters "SAINT NAVARRO" were engraved into the embedded gold. Unconsciously, the priest's fingers tightened around his own Cross of Lorraine.

Scorching memories of his own torture flooded into his mind with a morbid clarity he thought he had long forgotten. Learning of the abduction of his daughter and Israel had devastated him. Recognizing his mental descent into the dark abyss, the priest forced himself to breath steadily and attempted to refocus on the waning light.

What would the old man have done?

With intense effort, Father G concentrated on the pleasant image of Father Navarro's smile and got down on his own knees. He prayed like he had never done so before.

Twenty minutes later he was interrupted by a strange rustling sound. He abruptly stood up, drew both pistols, and turned around. Limping towards him was a bloodied and battered Armendáriz. His jacket was torn to shreds. Amidst the body art etched into his brown skin, Father G could visualize the golden tattoo of the Cross of Lorraine covering his left breast. The priest ran to him. Armendáriz, with his last bit of strength, shoved a backpack into Father G's arms before collapsing onto the mosaic floor. Armendáriz looked up with a strange smile as he uttered his final words: "Thank you for saving me, G."

Chapter 40

Xiuhcoatl—Jungles of Oaxaca, Mexico

Israel woke to a hammering headache and the strange, ominous rhythm of pounding drums. His wrists were throbbing. He looked down to discover he was handcuffed and chained to a stone wall in some type of dark chamber. He was naked except for a loincloth. A flaming torch perched near the opposite wall allowed him to observe that his skin had been painted blue. He lifted his jaw and discovered a life-size painting of an Aztec warrior near the torch. His eyes homed in on the man in the painting: The warrior emanated strength, confidence, and power. But it was the Aztec's face that shocked him—the sharp pointed nose and high cheekbones. *Like mine,* Israel realized, *I look like this man.* It mesmerized him.

"It's about time." The voice was familiar, and it cut deep into Israel's soul, bringing him back to reality. He turned his head to see the face of Secretary Acosta.

Is it true? Is this man really my father?

Secretary Acosta probed the eyes of his son.

"I'm giving you another chance to consider my offer, Jacob. Come with me now and you will be spared. Come with me and I will make you powerful. Come with me and I will set Mayrín free and I will make her your queen. Together, you shall rule Mexico. We will restore glory to this land and obtain vengeance on all who have robbed us."

Israel looked at the torch. Sparkles of hope blossomed within him. *I can be with Mayrín—right freaking now. All I gotta do is give him my word. She would live. I would live. We could be married. And the good we could do for Mexico. This man is powerful, of that there is no doubt. He loves Mexico...*

Dazed, Israel looked back at the Aztec warrior in the painting. His eyes fixated on the man's face and a foreign, almost psychic, emotion took over his mind, as if he were going back to another place and another time. In some type of trance, he visualized himself in the painting, as if he was somehow connected to this Aztec warrior—the same noble blood flowed in both of their veins. Suddenly and shockingly, Israel's eyes darted to Secretary Acosta. It was then that Israel knew the secretary was his father: Acosta also shared the same facial features as the man in the painting. And the almond-shaped eyes were identical.

He studied his father, differently this time—with an expression of empathy. His eyes flickered to the painting. Both men's faces were stunningly similar, as were their body types. *He is powerful and athletic, just like me.* He had always wondered about both his parents. Of his origins. Of his roots. *Do I have any siblings? Biological siblings? Who was my mother? My grandparents?* He remembered what his father had told him about Father Navarro. Instantly, almost spiritually, he knew it to be true. *He is my grandfather.* Flashbacks of the old priest on the cross surfaced to his forethoughts. They ignited the first sparks of anger. He thought again of Mayrín. *I can save her. I can be with her. I can love her.*

But at what cost? The question crashed into his brain. He pictured the dead bodies of Sergio and Lucía in his mind. *It would be a complete betrayal of their lives. It would go against everything that I have been taught and everything that I stand for and everything that I am.* He thought of Father G. *What would the priest do?* He knew the answer immediately. He remembered the agony of seeing Mayrín touched by the strange hunchback. He remembered the children, his friends, massacred at the orphanage. He remembered again his grandfather on the cross.

"Why did you do it?" Israel asked unexpectedly. "Why did you torture Father Navarro and why did you force me to watch?"

Secretary Acosta's demeanor hardened.

"To show you the weakness of Christianity—to help prepare you to meet the true gods—the gods of Mexico and of power."

"And the children you killed at the orphanage," said Israel. His eyes drifted and his anger rose. "And Sergio, my best friend, and Lucía!" Adrenaline pulsed through Israel's veins. *Father or not, this man was evil.* He exploded. "You bastard! I will not accept your offer. You psychopathic fucking murderer!"

The defense secretary flinched. He carefully studied Israel's face. Once again, Ramón Acosta envisioned Father Navarro. The resemblance to the old priest was disturbing—the eyes, the jaw, the forehead. He thought of Mónica and visualized the face of Rene. *My true son.* Rage flashed within Ramón. *He is too weak. He is incapable of inheriting my legacy.* Acosta now understood what he had to do. He made the decision instantly.

"Mayrín will die. We have also discovered she is the daughter of the man we are looking for. He will die also."

The words knifed through Israel's gut. He lashed out at his father in frenzied rage.

"He will come for you, you lunatic son of a bitch! He will come for you and he will kill you!"

Secretary Acosta's eyes went cold. He let the hatred and fury flow within him as he stared at the face of his bastard son.

"I sincerely hope he tries," said the secretary, walking away. "When you die, Mayrín will suffer a horrific death, just like your mother."

Israel roared and ferociously yanked at the chains holding him captive. Thrashing against his imprisonment, he felt the metal cut into his wrists. Blood streamed down his legs as he continued to batter himself—without concern for his body or his life. Screaming, he fought an unwinnable war until fainting from exhaustion.

"You're up next."

Israel's eyes opened and he discovered he was still a prisoner in the dark chamber. Acosta was gone. Israel's head jerked towards the origin of the gruff voice. A few yards in front of him stood two large muscular men. Both men were dressed in some type of body armor decorated with vibrant red, blue, and green feathers. Helmets fashioned like fierce eagle faces with opened beaks covered both of their heads. They carried swords, of some sort, along with battle shields adorned with brilliant purple and yellow depictions of death. The macabre artwork on the shields circumscribed a silvery skull that glimmered threateningly in the firelight.

"Where am I?" Israel asked, his mind flooding with darkness. "What the freak is happening and where is Mayrín?"

Both men smirked and walked forward. One of them bound Israel's neck with a cord while the other unlocked the chain holding him to the wall.

"Secretary Acosta has chosen to give you an honored death," said one of the men, forcing Israel to his feet. "They are hoping you put on a good show."

The news was not good and Israel, half-choking and gasping for air, forced down waves of panic as he was brutally marched out of the prison chamber and into an ancient limestone corridor. The corridor was lit by sporadic flaming torches and, despite his pain and dark swirling emotions, he could clearly see the walls were covered in ancient paintings of Aztec warriors wearing gruesome masks of jaguar and eagle heads. The Aztec warriors in the artwork were dressed like his captors and they also carried colorful shields and swords dripping in blood.

Picking up its intensity, the eerie drum beat reverberated throughout the corridor like thunder, adding yet another hellish dimension to this living nightmare. Depictions of severed heads, torsos, and limbs were ubiquitous in the paintings and the skin of the sanguine body parts was colored in blue. Israel now understood that he was to become some sort of sacrifice. Morbid statues and murals of gory violence clouded his vision and it soon became difficult to distinguish reality from the gruesome art. He only knew he was marching to his death.

Is Mayrín already dead and did she suffer?

The thought tore at his soul and he stumbled to the stony ground before being jerked back up to his feet. He pictured his father's face and he started to tremble.

Not caring now whether he choked to death, he collapsed to the ground again. One of the eagle warriors yelled something and several more men appeared to help carry him onward. Israel was lifted into the air, his neck cord loosened a bit; some of his mental faculties returned.

So this is it, Israel reflected, closing his eyes, *this is how I am going to die.*

He'd never really thought about how he'd depart this world, though the deaths of his friends and family had defined his life. He envisioned the massacre at the orphanage and wondered if he would see his childhood friends again—and Sergio and Lucía. He'd always been taught that life on earth was a short journey in the eternal scheme of things and that death was not something to be feared. A scripture, one of his favorites, came to his mind with sudden force—*Yea, though I walk through the valley of the shadow of death, I will fear no evil: for thou are with me; thy rod and thy staff comfort me.*

He thought of the meaning of the verse and abruptly made the realization that, though short, his life had been good: he had striven to be a decent person; he had striven to follow God; he could die in peace. His thoughts went to Father G, the man who had raised him like a son and taught him how to be a man.

What would the priest do in my situation?

It was not a difficult question to answer. Though he never talked about it, Israel knew that Father G had been brutally tortured and somehow escaped. He suspected the priest had been a victim of the narco violence plaguing the nation. He also now knew Father G was fighting back.

I will honor him, Israel decided. *I will die like a man.*

A newfound strength swelled within his soul, wiping away the pain and bringing with it a sense of peace.

I will go down fighting no matter what is waiting for me.

He closed his eyes tighter and commenced to pray, just as he had been taught since childhood.

Inside one of the spacious rooms in the stone arena, Sheik Mahdavi Haqqani fervently shook his head in rhythm with the ominous drum beat. Black flags of jihad, embroidered with the single Arabic word "Punishment," displayed alongside ancient murals of Aztec death rituals. Rabid, bloodshot eyes, bulging out of their sockets, gave the sheik's gaunt face a seemingly supernatural appearance and the multitude of jihadi warriors clamored at his every word. The jihadists were every bit as zealous as their beloved sheik. Mokhtar Haqqani suspected more than half of them were certifiably insane.

Not that it matters, he reflected. *In many cases it has proven advan-*

tageous, and now each of the soldiers can and will complete the sacred tasks assigned to them.

The jihadists had been trained extensively in the operation of the "Suitcase Bombs" and the detonation protocol was not difficult. The weapons, all one hundred of them, would be transported across the northern border tomorrow. Secretary Acosta's men would be guiding each of the suicide bombers to his city of destination in the United States.

The sheik had used a considerable part of his wealth to purchase the bombs from the Russian mafia; the rest of his money he had given to Secretary Ramón Acosta. Each of the portable nuclear bombs had an explosive charge of one kiloton, equivalent to 1,000 tons of TNT. Once detonated, each bomb would destroy everything within a half-mile radius of the epicenter. Winds would carry the nuclear fallout and the radioactive iodine would float for miles. Ten of the bombs would be strategically placed in Washington D.C. and another ten would go to New York. The eighty other bombs would be detonated across critically important cities and sites. The United States would collapse in chaos.

Proudly looking across the fanatical faces of his men, Mokhtar Haqqani could scarcely believe the moment was here at last. He gripped the hilt of Zulfiqar tighter and peered down at the double-bladed sword. It was becoming increasingly difficult to contain his emotion during his grandfather's speech.

"Your glory will be infinite and your names shall forever be etched into eternity," Sheik Mahdavi Haqqani bellowed, "the mighty Prophet Muhammed, peace be upon him, will greet you like a brother and personally escort each one of you to your seventy-two dark-eyed virgins. Their beauty shall be beyond compare and you shall reign in paradise in palaces of pearls."

And the Great Satan will finally be brought its knees.

Mokhtar had conjured up images of the devastation and death toll for months. It would launch the apocalyptic war and the entire world would see that he was the great Mahdi—the chosen one. He was absolutely certain of it. His grandfather would depart from this earth soon; the only thing that kept the ancient sheik going was his obsessive yearning to see the start of the great apocalypse and the emergence of his heir as Mahdi.

"On this very sacred and solemn occasion," the old sheik continued, in a voice disguising his age, "Allah has seen fit to unite us with our Mexican brethren to fulfill his will. It is his desire that we pay respect to the rituals and ordinances performed by our allies. One day, after we have defeated the most abominable of our enemies together, our allies shall be brought to know the goodness and peace of Islam. Go now, my beloved children, those who shall shortly receive glory and honor without bounds, go and enjoy these festivities that your minds may be prepared for the holy mission that Allah requires of you."

A tumultuous applause reverberated throughout the stone architecture.

"Allahu Akbar! Allahu Akbar! Allahu Akbar!"

"Kill the infidel! Kill the infidel! Kill the infidel!"

"Death to America! Death to America! Death to America!"

The violent chants eerily merged with the wicked pounding of the drums. The men wrapped themselves in the black flags of jihad and continued their chanting as they departed from the room to the open air of the spectator seating in the arena. Before joining the impassioned suicide bombers, Mokhtar raised Zulfiqar to his shoulder and swung it hard.

The sword sung a haunting tune as its blades sliced through the air. Mokhtar then walked to his grandfather and, with tears in his eyes, embraced him.

Israel felt a rush of cool air and a drizzle of rain brush against his skin. Opening his eyes, he became acutely aware, once again, of the terrifying drum beat. He barely had time to brace himself as he was thrown to the ground. One of the strange eagle warriors cut off his neck cord while another unlocked his handcuffs.

Israel scrambled to his feet and, while watching four eagle warriors run away, discovered a weapon on the soil in front of him. Against the backdrop of the drums he could make out the frenzied noise of the crowd. He quickly looked around and observed he stood in a coliseum, brilliantly colored and decorated with the same types of morbid statues and murals he had seen in the corridor.

Lightning flashed across the sky, illuminating a giant red pyramid. A scream of horror pierced through both the drum beat and crowd noise. Israel looked up and felt his muscles weaken. The sight paralyzed him—he almost fell to the ground. Atop the pyramid, dressed in a thin white dress and chained to a statue of a grotesque beast, was Mayrín. Next to her, clothed in jaguar skin, was the hunchback whom Israel had seen in his jail cell. He was carrying an obsidian knife and, even from the long distance, Israel could make out the twisted smile across his deformed face.

The panic he had just defeated started to resurface before the calming words thundered into his soul: *Focus on what you can control.*

Israel took a deep breath, loosened his muscles, and bent down to collect the weapon. It was a sword of some type, like the one he had seen in the hands of the eagle warriors, constructed out of hard wood and prismatic blades of obsidian. He picked up the weapon with two hands and, to the delight of the crowd, swung it hard into the open air. The fiendish beat of the drums ceased abruptly, and another scream of terror echoed throughout the coliseum. It numbed Israel's brain.

Inadvertently, Israel's eyes went to Mayrín before noticing a yellow blur coming directly towards him. A devilish howl jolted him back to reality.

A large jaguar, half-starved to death and moving with incredible speed, pounced into the air with a gaping mouth and made for the kill. Time froze as Israel gazed onto the knife-like fangs and claws of the beast and then, with incredible reflexes and strength, he swung his weapon like a battle axe. Making a gruesome sound, the obsidian blades severed into flesh and bone and ripped open the chest cavity of the jaguar.

Crimson blood splattered onto his blue skin and, now oblivious to both Mayrín's screams and the uproar of the crowd, Israel yanked his weapon out of the dead animal. The pent-up rage and hatred for these psychotic narcos materialized onto his outward appearance. Veins bulged from his hardening muscles. He snarled and prepared to do battle with anything that came his way.

As his senses sharpened, he noticed the slew of dismembered body parts scattered throughout the arena. Amidst the bloody flesh and fragmented bone, he could see blue skin and he unconsciously inspected the coloring of his own body. A fresh, exuberant applause erupted from the crowd causing Israel to hone in on his new enemy.

Calmly walking towards him was a large man wearing the helmet of a jaguar head. Neon green Quetzal feathers protruded from the back of the helmet, fluttering against the cool breeze. The man wore a black loincloth streaked with red. Some type of armor, resembling the spotted coat of a jaguar, covered his torso and legs. The strange jaguar warrior carried a brilliantly colored shield on his left arm. His right hand grasped one of the sword-like weapons.

The jaguar warrior's muscles stood out rigid underneath his armor and Israel guessed the man outweighed him by a good fifty pounds. Israel gripped his own weapon tighter while feverishly analyzing his own predicament.

He's gotta be more skilled with the primitive weapon than I am. Father G had trained him extensively in hand-to-hand combat with a variety of weapons, including swords, but this was quite different.

He's also bigger and stronger. I'll have to offset the disadvantage with speed and quickness. The real difference will be in my own conditioning and mental toughness.

Israel's lips twisted. His open nostrils flared. His facial muscles contorted violently. His eyes narrowed and blazed with hellfire. He walked forward to fight.

"The boy doesn't seem scared," Mokhtar said casually. Ramón grunted a reply. He had not told the jihadist guest he was the father of the blue-skinned fighter and he did not intend to do so. The secretary was interested to see how long his son would last against Tehuantl. *But I will not be displeased when he dies.* The boy reminded him vividly of his grandfather; ugly flashbacks of the priest rushed through his mind. Yet, the boy's courage impressed him. *Noble Aztec blood does indeed flow through his veins. But it is tainted. He must die.* Ramón hadn't told Tlaloc about the unexpected news. He would not do so until the boy's body lay scattered around the arena with the rest of the corpses. And the girl's heart was torn from her chest.

It's almost, he pondered, *as if the old man has been resurrected from the grave.* Tlaloc had given him the whereabouts of Father Navarro's daughter all those years ago. The cripple had been eager for him to rape the girl.

The old priest somehow keeps fighting back, Ramón thought.

Father Navarro was dead, of that he was certain. They had tortured him well enough a decade ago at Tamoanchan. But the priest had escaped before he could see his dying face and that fact alone almost irked him more than the destruction of his military compound. *The pale rider,* Ramón thought grimly. *It is that man who rescued Father Navarro. It is that man who demolished Tamoanchan. It is that man who attempted to thwart our efforts in Juárez and the whole damn country. And we still don't have him! Three days since we sent him the message and he has not turned himself in!*

"What's wrong, Ramón?" asked Mokhtar with a strange grin. Secretary Acosta was trembling; his jaw muscles were wrenched in an inhuman sneer. "Relax, my friend!" Mokhtar continued. "You are not the one fighting."

Chapter 41

Xiuhcoatl—Jungles of Oaxaca, Mexico

Thunder cracked to mask the first sound of clashing obsidian. Israel half expected his weapon to shatter as it collided against its opponent, but the *macuahuitl* remained whole. Yet the force of the encounter sent shock waves down both of Israel's forearms. His left hand inadvertently loosened its hold on the handle and he barely recovered in time to combat the counterattack of the jaguar warrior. Israel gripped his weapon tighter with both hands and circled to his left, eyes boring into his enemy's face.

Tehuantl held his *macuahuitl* with one large hand. A mocking smile played across his lips. The expression enraged Israel and he sprung forward aggressively. Both his elbows popped up and his weapon savagely cut through the drizzling rain. Tehuantl expertly sidestepped the blow and thrust his own *macuahuitl* upward while rolling his right wrist counter-clockwise. One of the obsidian blades lunged forward and Israel felt its sting as it shaved off a piece of his left ear. Bright red blood splattered onto the blue paint of Israel's torso, and the crowd roared their approval.

Ignoring the injury, eyes steady, Israel took two steps backward in retreat. Tehuantl's taunting smile broadened and he pressed his advantage by launching a direct frontal assault. His *macuahuitl* sliced through the air with humming force and several rapid thrusts caused Israel to back up awkwardly and lose his footing. Just as Tehuantl swung a powerful backhand, Israel shuffled hard to his right to regain position. He narrowly missed the oncoming obsidian blades.

Relax, Israel told himself, fighting back panic. *Fear will destroy you much faster than your enemy.* It was one of the first lessons Father G had taught him. But the jaguar warrior was quicker than he anticipated. And more skilled.

He's toying with me. Beads of blood dripped on his shoulder from his injured ear. *Waiting for the right moment to kill.*

He wiped away the disturbing thoughts and discovered he was facing south. Despite himself, his eyes went to the top of the red pyramid. He could see Mayrín staring at him, terrified.

It was a torturous sight and he rounded on his enemy with renewed determination and fury. His mind raced, processing the first few moments of battle.

His balance is slightly off, Israel suddenly realized, *and he carries his weapon too low.*

Instinctively, Israel rotated the grip on his own macuahuitl. The weapon was sturdier than he expected and it glided through the air smoothly, as if its designer was aware of general aerodynamic principles.

Vivid streaks of lighting lit up the coliseum once again; thunder pounded the Mexican jungle, bringing with it a blanket of rain. Israel slowly backed up on the dirt floor and circled to his left, eyes zeroed in on his adversary. His left foot stepped into something soft and slimy and he looked down for a split second to grimly discover he was treading through rotting human guts escaped from a blue-skinned torso. His feet changed directions and, now moving directly backwards, he carefully stepped over the bloody corpse in retreat.

Tehuantl, sensing weakness, rushed forwards. It was then that Israel attacked. Raising the *macuahuitl*, Israel stormed at his enemy, swinging his weapon at the white fangs of the jaguar mask.

The attack was unexpected. As Tehuantl's right foot slipped in bloody intestines, Israel's *macuahuitl* flew towards his face. The jaguar warrior recovered his footing just in time to brace for the attack. He lifted his shield to cover his head but at the last moment the *macuahuitl* stopped in midair. Israel changed levels, crouched low, and thrust his weapon towards the open skin below his enemy's right knee. It found its mark and the obsidian blades cut through flesh. Tehuantl countered instantly, and it was only because of his practiced reflexes that Israel avoided the oncoming blades—perilously close to his own ribcage.

Tehuantl's mocking demeanor transformed to rage. He snarled and launched into an onslaught like a demon from hell. His weapon crashed downwards and it took all of Israel's strength and skill to defend himself. Sparks blasted into the jungle air as the obsidian blades collided again and just before separation Tehuantl sliced his weapon downward. Obsidian tore into Israel's upper shoulder, flaying off strips of blue skin. Blood jetted onto Israel's hands and he desperately tried to maneuver his weapon into defensive position.

Roaring with fury, Tehuantl viciously swung his *macuahuitl* from side to side, forcing Israel to go on all-out retreat. Bloodlust stained onto their faces, the spectators cheered wildly in anticipation of an upcoming kill. Thunder cracked again and the rain intensified. Israel's right foot slipped onto muddy soil and Tehuantl seized the opportunity and delivered the most powerful blow of the fight: his *macuahuitl* crushed into Israel's, jamming obsidian blades into hardened oak, locking up the two weapons.

With almost inhuman strength, Tehuantl hammered Israel into the ground and then pulled back—hard, expertly, and ruthlessly. Israel's *macuahuitl* sailed towards the center of the arena and Tehuantl quickly raised his own weapon, preparing a death stroke. The deadly blades missed Israel by mere inches as he rolled hard and fast to his left. He sprung to his feet like a jungle cat and, going purely on instinct, ran for the wall separating the fighting pit from the stone seating tiers.

Tehuantl followed him in a bloody rage, slashing his *macuahuitl* down from his shoulder just as Israel reached the barrier. Without breaking stride, Israel leaped skyward and clambered up the wall. The force of Tehuantl's blow shattered a rough piece of ancient limestone and the fragments sprayed onto Israel's legs like daggers as the *macuahuitl* barely missed his body. Still moving at full speed, Israel recoiled from the wall and launched himself at the statue of the Third Lord of the Night. His feet crashed against the outstretched stone arm of the Aztec deity and it broke off at the shoulder as Israel vaulted back onto the jungle floor of the arena. The stone limb, flaming torch in hand, fell to the earth near Israel's landing. In one fluid motion he took hold of the arm and hurled it towards the pursuing jaguar warrior.

Tehuantl roared as shards of fire burned his face. The brief interruption in his pursuit allowed Israel the time necessary to reach his own *macuahuitl* and wrap his two hands around the handle. Muscles fiercely contracting, he lifted the weapon off the ground and pounded it through the pouring rain like a sledgehammer. It met his enemy's obsidian blades head-on and the tremendous force of the blow lowered Tehuantl's *macuahuitl*. Body crouched, Israel switched to a single, righthanded grip on his weapon. His left fingers clenched together and he swung his arm upward in a wicked arcing motion. The punch found its target; Israel's left fist felt cartilage crush against bone and blood.

A purple-hued streak of lighting burst across the indigo sky. Chilling thunder exploded in the background. Before this fight, no one in the arena had seen Tehuantl injured before. Nor had they seen one of his battles go on for this long. Ignoring the inquisitive stares of the sheik, Mokhtar, and other terrorists, Secretary Acosta sat utterly fixated on the battle. From atop the great red pyramid, Tlaloc also stared at the fight in shocked silence.

Standing beside him, chained to the statue of Mictlantecuhtli, Mayrín was quiet also. Despite the knowledge of her imminent death, she felt a calming pride in how Israel had fought and it gave her courage.

Against the subdued noise of the crowd, Tehuantl growled and ripped his weapon upwards with such raw power that Israel almost lost hold of his own *macuahuitl.* The jaguar warrior went berserk. He attacked in frenzy, holding nothing back. Israel found himself once again trying to shield his body against the vicious onslaught and he was forced to maneuver into defensive position.

But his confidence was growing now; he could observe his enemy was breathing heavily and despite the savagery and skill of the attack, the strikes were becoming less powerful. Israel was not fatigued—his workouts had intensified since his defeat at the U.S. Nationals and he was among the best-conditioned athletes in the world.

As the match goes on, you will become stronger.

The words which the priest taught him at a young age echoed throughout his mind.

The rain poured harder as the bottoms of Israel's feet dug into the mud. He went on the offensive. He feigned a low thrust towards Tehuantl's injured leg and then swung the *macuahuitl* towards the large man's ribcage. The jaguar warrior was slightly taken back by the power of the blow and was forced break off his own attack to counter. For the briefest of microseconds, time passed in slow motion as Tehuantl looked into the boy's eyes: There was no fear. Among the multitudes of opponents he had faced, this boy was the only one who had not been scared. The knowledge settled uneasy within him as he recognized the new power and strength behind the boy's attack.

All the spectators watched in stunned silence and bizarre fascination at the turn of events—all except one. The sheik stared due north. His leathery skin was ashen and sweating. His ancient body was trembling. He could not blink. Recognizing the sight was indeed real, his heartbeat slowed to a dangerous level. He watched the silhouette materialize with growing terror. But he was not certain until lighting streaked across the dark sky once again and the unmistakable image of the pale horse imprinted into his brain.

The realization eviscerated his body, mind, and soul. The beast which had haunted him so thoroughly, the beast which had become master of his sleep, the beast which had driven him to the edge of insanity, had finally come to seek revenge. Before the sky darkened, his heart beat for the last time. The sheik crumpled to the stone floor of the arena seating, unnoticed by all around him.

Against the monstrous thunder, Israel picked up his pace. He swung the *macuahuitl* again and again—furious strokes that increased their intensity and power as Tehuantl became more and more fatigued. A strange torrent of lightning illuminated the sky. And all eyes were fixated on Israel's weapon as it blasted through the rain and sliced through the right wrist of the jaguar warrior. Tehuantl's bloody, severed hand fell to the stone floor, along with his *macuahuitl.*

Israel pivoted backwards on his left foot and launched a vicious backstroke that hit just below the fangs of the jaguar mask. The razor-sharp obsidian blades crashed into Tehuantl's jugular vein and the raw power behind the blow propelled the weapon onward through flesh and bone. A burst of hot blood sprayed onto Israel's face and chest as the head of the jaguar warrior went sailing through the air.

And it was at that moment that all hell broke loose.

Gunshots from a M230 30mm automatic cannon exploded into the royalty section of the arena. The sheik's dead body was crushed by a huge chunk of limestone. Mokhtar was sent sprawling to the bottom and his turban set ablaze. Screaming, he clawed at the headpiece until a flying corpse smashed into the back of his head. Secretary Acosta had been the only one with the instincts to run. He almost reached the mid-level exit before a chunk of molten magnesium from a cannon shot collided against the left side of his face. He blacked out instantly.

More gunfire blasted into a band of eagle warriors on the south side of the ancient arena, dropping warriors across the base of the red pyramid. Simultaneously, a barrage of AGM-114 hellfire missiles pulverized any section of the coliseum close to a black flag of jihad.

Israel did not look at the pale flying war machine that had just entered the arena. Ignoring the gunfire and demolition, he raced towards the south side of the fighting pit at full speed and scaled the twelve-foot stone wall.

Lowering levels, he launched himself through the air and crash-landed onto the limestone courtyard. A panicked eagle warrior fleeing the chaos saw Israel and lunged at him. Israel's left fist shot out like a bullet and smashed into teeth and bone. The eagle warrior's body went limp and crumpled to the cement floor. With a wicked combination of desperation and rage burning within him, Israel rushed towards the pyramid, bulldozing over several other eagle warriors fleeing for their lives from the deadly fire of the M230 cannon. Other warriors, however, including some just escaping the destruction of the arena, saw Israel sprinting and realized his intentions. They went after him.

The deathly-white gunship slowly crossed the arena, bombarding both enemy and military sites with Hellfire missiles and CBU-103 cluster bombs containing 200 softball-sized pieces of encased explosives. Rounds from the M230 cannon mowed down every narco and terrorist in sight.

The aircraft was Alma's masterpiece. She had been obsessed with its development for over six years, ever since Padre Quezada purchased it from Lockheed Martin with the help of two corrupt congressmen and a U.S. Senator. It was a variant of the UH-60M Black Hawk helicopter specifically designed for rescue missions.

Alma had outfitted the aircraft with wings and an impressive array of artillery to transform it into a war machine. Miles of silver wiring linked up the avionics, engines, visual aids, and weapons systems—all controlled by a vast network of on-board computers. The 30mm M230 cannon could fire twelve high-explosive dual-purpose rounds a second with pinpoint accuracy. More than 300 Flechette and HEISAP rockets were loaded into four CRV7 rocket pods hanging from both wings of the aircraft. The projectile bodies contained explosive zirconium incendiaries capable of torching their targets. Mounted on rails underneath the helicopter's wings were twenty-two Hellfire air-to-ground missiles, laser-guided from the cockpit for pinpoint accuracy. Each hellfire missile was capped with a 20-lb explosive and dual-shaped charge warhead capable of taking out all known armor.

Behind the M230 cannon, Father G continued his rampage. Most of his focus, however, was at the top of the red pyramid. The priest suddenly unstrapped his harness, vacated the co-pilot seat, and lunged through the gateway leading to the cabin.

"Lower!" he shouted to Alma. "Get me down there!"

As the chopper descended, Father G strapped a M4 carbine across his shoulder and gripped the three-inch thick nylon rope coiled near the starboard sliding door. Padre Quezada squirmed into the cockpit with surprising agility and took over the cannon. And, as rounds from the cannon began firing once again, Father G opened the starboard sliding door, launched into the air, and roped towards the base of the temple.

He landed hard against the red limestone, on one of the terrace steps about forty feet from the temple. He opened fire, killing all enemies within shooting range. Above him, Padre Quezada blasted away at the enemy with the M230 cannon and a fresh wave of hellfire missiles and aerial rockets demolished the surrounding military infrastructure. Father G tightened his grip on the M4 and his facial muscles had almost relaxed when he saw shimmering blackness slice through the pouring rain. The priest turned hard to his right, whipping his rifle into firing position. He was a split second too late. Razor sharp obsidian ripped into the hardened metal of the M4 and rendered it useless. The priest immediately discarded the broken rifle and both hands dropped to his hips. Before the eagle warrior could swing the *macuahuitl* again, three rounds from a Colt .45 dropped him. Father G fired eight more shots into a group of eagle warriors and had scaled five pyramid steps when he felt something strong clamp down on his ankles. It happened with such force that Father G lost his grip on the pistols. As his upper body fell to the floor of the pyramid step he simultaneously contracted his body and kicked out with everything he had.

Face slamming into limestone, Father G reached back to his left calf. With a vicious stroke, the priest plunged his trusted bowie knife towards his feet and into the heart of a crazed jihadist. As Father G loosened the knife from the corpse's ribcage, he saw two eagle warriors charging up the pyramid, *macuahuitls* in fighting position. Leaving the knife, the priest's right fist sprung out like a rattlesnake and shattered the leading man's jaw, knocking him out. Lowering his body, narrowly avoiding the oncoming *macuahuitl* of the second eagle warrior, Father G came up swinging and felt his left fist smash deep into the eye socket of his enemy. In less than three seconds, he collected his pistols, replaced magazines, and blew every surviving eagle warrior to hell.

The priest then frantically scaled the top pyramid steps. And felt his body go numb.

Directly in front of him was his daughter. Since seeing her in Juárez, Mayrín had consumed his thoughts. And there she was again, now screaming in fear and displaying such a look of unbridled terror that he felt like his mind would shatter. A hideous-looking creature, an ancient crippled hunchback, was holding his daughter captive with an obsidian knife at her throat. In one single instant, all the pain and anguish he had suffered over the years came back with vengeance. His body reacted to his mind's paralysis. He couldn't move.

Tlaloc grinned as he saw his chance. They had typed this girl's DNA and linked it to the unknown profiles of their mortal enemy. He knew this girl was the pale rider's daughter. And he had anticipated his reaction. In one fluid movement, born out of sheer hatred for the man attempting to destroy his destiny, Tlaloc threw the obsidian knife at his nemesis. The knife sailed through the air with surprising velocity. It found its target.

Stunned, Father G dropped his pistols and stumbled backwards. His eye flickered downwards to see the primitive black weapon sunk deep into his ribcage, through a deep tear in his bullet-proof vest. Shocked, he looked at the beautiful face of his daughter one more time and then staggered backwards and collapsed off the temple edge.

Tlaloc sneered and went after him, determined to destroy the pale rider once and for all. Oblivious to his surroundings, he surged forward but was stopped in his tracks. Bewildered, his hands shot up towards his throat to alleviate the pain. The rusty metal ripped further into his skin, bloodying his torso.

In desperation, determined to destroy this psychopath, Mayrín pulled ferociously at the chain. She had managed to get the metal links tight around Tlaloc's neck and she pulled for her very life, and for the life of her father. The metal cut deep into the flesh of her forearms and the pain shot new waves of energy into her body. Within seconds, Tlaloc's lifeless body went limp.

Mayrín closed her eyes briefly, rolled out her right arm to loosen the tension of the chain, and then shrieked. A crazed jihadist, macuahuitl in hand, was running directly at her. She closed her eyes again, harder this time. She then heard a scream of death—but it was not her own. She opened her eyes to see Israel, both hands gripping a *macuahuitl*; the weapon was lodged deep within the jihadist's chest.

"Israel!" Mayrín screamed, in a fresh wave of sobbing. Her tear-soaked face was ashen, but she was otherwise unharmed. Israel looked at her momentarily and then quickly searched the area for enemies. Other than the butchered remains of the terrorist and the body of Tlaloc, they appeared to be alone. He could hear the low-pitched growl of the helicopter and, now that he understood the aircraft was on a rescue mission, the noise was like music. Israel frantically tried to free Mayrín's limbs from the iron chains and was unsuccessful. The growl of the helicopter intensified and Israel glanced up to see the aircraft was directly above them—Sister López was lowering a rescue ladder from the cabin.

Israel's eyes then focused in on Tlaloc's corpse and he saw a key attached to a belt. He quickly removed the key and freed Mayrín; she immediately ran to the temple's edge. Israel followed her. Father G was kneeling in a pool of blood on a terrace step just a few feet below.

Israel watched in dread as the priest slowly rose. Blood gushed from a gruesome-looking wound in his chest; fragments of black obsidian lay scattered at his feet. Mayrín rushed to her father's side, followed by Israel, and both of them helped Father G back up to the base of the temple. Israel felt like his lungs had been knifed. He loaded, gently as he could, the bloody body of the priest across his shoulders.

"Go!" he yelled to a weeping Mayrín. "I'll follow you!"

Mayrín slowly climbed up the first few steps of the rescue ladder and Israel, with Father G slung across his upper body, followed her. And then Israel froze. The deadly sound of gunfire pounded into his ears. He looked to his immediate left to see another jihadist, both arms attached to a *macuahuitl*, fall to the ground. Israel whipped his head upwards to see smoke pluming from a 12-gauge shotgun held by Sister Arámbula. Israel exhaled, ascended the rescue ladder, and with the help of Mayrín and Padre Quezada, maneuvered the wounded priest into the helicopter.

Father G was gently laid on the floor of the cabin, still bleeding heavily. Sister López quickly started to bandage his wound and, during the process, he looked directly at Padre Quezada and spoke unexpectedly and surprisingly calm.

"Did you get everyone?"

"Yes," replied the husky priest. His eyes moistened. "I believe so."

"Good," said Father G, his eye closing, a gentle smile drumming across his lips. "Good. I..."

A deafening explosion interrupted his last words. It rocked everyone on board.

Titanium clashed against steel and the helicopter screeched like a wounded falcon. Alma jammed the rudder pedals and slammed forward the cyclic stick against the back noise of electronic audible warning signals and flashing lights. Wisps of gun gray smoke seeped into the cockpit from air-conditioning ducts. Alma managed to steady the aircraft somewhat but it was going down, fatally wounded by an unseen RPG.

The tail rotor failed and the chopper fell harder. To compensate, Alma slammed the cyclic stick to the left and the aircraft spun violently out of control. Father G was thrown completely out of the helicopter and his body landed on the floor of the coliseum. The helicopter crash landed on the ancient limestone and smoldering rubble once composing the western seating area of the arena.

Pain blazed up Father G's upper body. His eye stared for a moment at a recently restored statue of Tezcatlipoca, one of the nine Aztec Lords of the Night. And then he saw the two men. One crazed man, wearing a green turban and a white *bisht* streaked with blood, was running directly at him. Embroidered onto the *bisht's* left breast was the black flag of jihad. The man's face was burned, mutilated, and displayed a wild look of insanity. His right hand held an ancient-looking sword with two blades.

Father G willed himself to remain conscious. His jaw clenched and he grinded his back teeth together, letting the battle fuel of adrenaline seep into the depths of his body and mind. Forcing his numb right arm down, his fingers fumbled at his hip. With alarm, he realized his pistols were gone. He had no weapons.

His eyeball rolled in its socket. The swordsman was almost upon him. Frantic, he reached down onto the soil with his left hand, desperately trying to push himself backwards. In the process he felt something slice into the flesh of his palm. It was a weapon and, like the priest, it had been ejected from the helicopter during the chaotic descent.

Blood flowing freely from his half-bandaged wound, Father G got to his feet. Mokhtar raised Zulfiqar above his head and screamed barbarically.

"You have destroyed everything, infidel!" His voice had the tone of a twisted psychopath. "It was me! I was supposed to be the Mahdi!"

With rage fueled hate, Mokhtar swung Zulfiqar towards the priest. It sang as it twisted through the air, and then, colliding against the Sword of Aragon, the sword of Islam shattered. With one powerful blow, Father G sliced through Mokhtar's midsection and cut his body in two. He turned to the other man.

The man's appearance defined hell. Half of his face had melted off; the other half was charred black. His eyebrows and eyelids were gone. Fire had burned off his hair and scorched his scalp down to bone. His clothes, smoking and flickering with neon embers, had seared into flesh. Yet the man from hell could see clearly and his muscles and reflexes were as functional as ever. He had a RPG launcher loaded onto his right shoulder and was aiming it at the grounded helicopter, completely obsessed with its destruction. His right index finger was preparing to pull the trigger when the flashing ice-blue metal rifled through the air and cut off half his right hand.

It all happened within microseconds. Butchered fingers reached for the fallen RPG launcher. Father G's single eye homed in on the man and identified him immediately. Rage consumed the priest's soul. His jaw clenched savagely and frothy bubbles of pink saliva spewed from his teeth. Blood flowed from his chest to the ground, from his scalp into his eye. He was fading fast. His wound was fatal. He had known it since the black obsidian first penetrated his flesh. But his life was not yet over. Pupil dilating wildly, his single, steel-blue eye bore into his mortal enemy, emanating a determination that could conquer hell. For the last time, the priest realized his singular purpose in life had once again changed: He had come full circle; to save his friends and family he must defeat Ramón Acosta. He forced his rapidly deteriorating body to move full speed and launched himself at his nemesis.

The priest's forehead slammed into the secretary. Both men hit the floor of the arena, but Acosta came up on top and he came up fighting. His punches were fast and powerful and one of them pounded into Father G's ribcage. The priest roared, twisted his body at a strange angle, and, with incredible skill and speed, secured a leg lock around Ramón's neck. It was then, as blood burst through the charred scarring on his disfigured face, that the defense secretary recognized the priest. He couldn't believe it. It was that American bastard: DEA Agent Dan Kasper. And he was very much alive. And he was the pale rider.

Acosta's eyes locked onto the steel-blue eye of the pale rider with demonic hatred and then flickered upwards. Staring directly at him was the morbid face of Mictlantecuhtli. The secretary cleared his mind and summoned the power of the Aztec god with all his spiritual and mental energy. And then, slowly, somehow, he slid his left hand towards his own hip. He drew a Glock pistol and fired it.

The bullet blew off Father G's left thumb and forced him off the leg lock. The priest's arms shot out and his fingers clawed into the skin of Ramón's right arm. Snapping his head forward, the priest's teeth tore into the flesh of Ramón's wrist. As the pistol ejected from his bloody hand, Acosta's left fist smashed into Father G's wounded ribcage, the force of which sent the priest to the ground.

The secretary made no effort to retrieve the gun. He went for the closer weapon, the one laying at his feet in the grip of Tehuantl's severed hand. The fingers of his left hand wrapped around the handle of the macuahuitl, the bloody stumps on his right hand joined them. Father G dove hard and fast, feeling the stinging blow graze his skull. Ramón relaunched the weapon and, as the priest came to his knees, the Sword of Aragon clashed into ancient oak and obsidian.

Father G rose, blood dripping everywhere. He saw the secretary's eyes dart to the RPG launcher and then to the helicopter. Tightening his grip on the Sword of Aragon, he stepped forward to fight.

Acosta's fury was diabolical. The *macuahuitl* spun as it slashed through the air, singing a tune from the depths of hell. And, once again, it was met by the ice-blue blade. Sparks burst through the air like frayed wires of lighting. Father G pounded the sword again and again, wicked strokes that cleanly shaved obsidian blades. Yet Acosta countered brilliantly. The *macuahuitl* sliced through the air like a mutant, diabolical hummingbird. The priest's blood was flowing strong, his head was light; he could feel himself slipping away. Willing his muscles to obey, he summoned all his energy into one final stroke.

The ice-blue metal of the Sword of Aragon flashed and the blade screamed as it pierced through the air, sinking deep into the *macuahuitl* and almost, though not quite, cleaved it in two. Secretary Acosta ripped his weapon upward at the perfect moment. The top half of the *macuahuitl* sailed through the air, and with it, the Sword of Aragon. Father G fell to the ground. He had nothing left. His mortal enemy stepped forward, broken weapon in bloody, mutilated fingers. Lighting flashed and the edges of the deadly obsidian blades reflected an eerie glow. What remained of Secretary Ramón Acosta's hellish face displayed the unmistakable look of triumph.

I have failed, thought the priest in disbelief. *I have come this far to fail. I have let down my friends, my daughter, Father Navarro, and God.*

The priest's eye continued to stare in abhorrence at both Ramón Acosta and the deadly obsidian blades rising upwards. And then, as he started to give in to the waves of failure, he saw the metallic shimmer of ice blue. The blade of the Sword of Aragon had just pierced through Ramón Acosta's heart. Father G watched in astonishment as the defense secretary's lifeless body crumpled to the jungle soil. Directly in front of him, two hands grasping the hilt of the shining sword, was Israel.

For a few seconds, the priest stared at the boy, and then, strangely, his eye rotated up to focus in on the hideous statue of Mictlantecuhtli. It reminded him of the giant saguaro cactus he had become so familiar with the days after his torture—the cactus that he stared at, years ago, for endless hours while asking God to die. Strangely, it now reminded him of how much he loved this country.

His eye flickered from the statue of Mictlantecuhtli to gaze upon Mayrín. She was kneeling and holding his hand. Israel was right beside her. Standing behind them were Padre Quezada, Sister Arámbula, Sister López, and Alma.

They are all alive, he realized. *They are all safe.*

Weeping, Sister López slowly moved forward, fell to her knees, and pecked Father G's scarred cheek. And, for the first time, she kissed his lips. As the nun stood up, her eyes locked onto his face, he returned a look of mutual understanding. Then, with intense effort, he moved his left hand up to gently caress Mayrín's face. He loved her beyond belief and the knowledge she was alive and well filled him with joy. She looked just like her mother, the woman whom he had so desperately yearned to be with for all these years. Now, finally, he could join her.

His eye then rotated to look at Israel. With his last bits of strength, the priest's right hand clenched the golden Cross of Lorraine and he freed it from his bloody neck. Both of his hands grasped Israel's fingers and Father G slid the golden cross into the boy's palm. Father G spoke his final words slowly, deliberately, and with extreme effort. "In time, Padre Quezada will explain to you the meaning of the cross. The cross, the sword—they are your destiny."

Israel slowly started to pull his hand away. "You don't understand, Father G. You don't understand my true identity." He motioned to Ramón Acosta's corpse. "That freaking monster is my father."

But the priest tightly held onto Israel's hand. "I know," he said softly with a gentle smile. "I have always known. Take care of Mayrín and remember to walk with Christ."

With those words, the dark clouds of humiliation, self-loathing, and depression, which had been mounting inside of Israel like a tidal wave, instantly evaporated. Unconsciously, the fingers of his right hand felt the strange gemstone embedded within the gold cross. And as the priest's spirit left his body, Israel, tears flowing from his eyes, saw an expression he had never seen on his mentor before. It was a look of peace.

THE END

Author's Notes

Part I

Prologue) The introduction to the Mexican Drug Wars as described here is historically accurate, per my own understanding.

Chapter 1.) The man with no name, to become 'G,' later identified as DEA agent Dan Kasper, is a fictional character. Enrique "Kiki" Camarena was a real-life DEA agent and Miguel Ángel Félix Gallardo (incarcerated at Almoya de Juárez prison at the time of this writing) was a real-life drug lord known as "El Padrino"—"The Godfather." The description of Camarena's capture and torture is historically accurate.

Chapter 2.) Ramón Acosta, Héctor Vásquez, General Huerta, and Tlaloc are fictional characters. The Aztec ruins in the jungles of Oaxaca, to be known as Xiuhcoatl, are also fictional, as is the association between drug cartels/corrupt officials and modern Aztec human sacrifice re-enactments. Mictlantecuhtli, Mictecacihuatl, and the Lords of the Night are actual Aztec deities and their descriptions in this novel concord with existing specimens and general knowledge of the culture. "Santa Muerte"—"Holy Death" or "Death Saint" is a personification of death whose image is venerated and worshipped throughout Mexico. The popularity of Santa Muerte among the Mexican Cartels and gang members is ubiquitous and undeniable. Many anthropologists trace the current Santa Muerte phenomenon in Mexico back to the ancient Aztec obsession with death.

Chapter 3.) Father Navarro is a fictional character, as are all characters in this chapter. The Virgin Guadalupe, as described here, conforms to reality and the events surrounding her origin are historically accurate, as understood by the Catholic Church.

Chapter 4.) The Jarabo family is fictional.

Chapter 5.) Both the Vargas and Navarro family are fictional as is the Catholic Monastery. The Sinaloa Cartel is real, as is drug lord Héctor Luis Palma Salazar (incarcerated in a maximum-security prison in the United States at the time of this writing). The description of the Cristero War is historically accurate. The scripture quoted by Adela Jarabo is found in Revelation, Chapter 6 verses 4-8.

Chapter 6.) Sister Arámbula and Sister López are fictional characters. *Johnny Got His Gun* is a novel written by Dalton Trumbo and was made into a motion picture. "One," a highly popular heavy metal song created by Metallica, is based upon the novel.

Chapter 7.) Emiliano Zapata was a real revolutionary and his popularity is widespread across Mexico. All the Mexican presidents mentioned are real, as are all the mentioned drug kingpins and relevant narco figures. The descriptions and developments of the rise of the Mexican drug cartels, apart from the involvement of Huerta and Acosta, are historically accurate, as best understood by myself in the murky world of *el narco.*

Chapter 8.) Miguel Hidalgo was an actual priest and is considered one of the heroes and founding fathers in Mexico. The brief description of the history of Mexico and the caste system is historically accurate, as are the events of Miguel Hidalgo's life and death.

Chapter 9.) Pedro Avilés Pérez (a.k.a. "Don Pedro"), whose skull was fictitiously collected by General Huerta, was an actual drug kingpin who died in a shootout with the *federales.* Benjamín Arellano-Félix (now deceased) and Juan García Abrego (incarcerated in a maximum-security prison in the United States at the time of this writing) were real drug lords. Part of General Huerta's character was created after Santiago Meza López (a.k.a. "El Pozolero"—"Soup Maker"). Meza López (now incarcerated in Mexico) was a high-profile drug dealer who confessed to dissolving more than 300 bodies in acid. Major Lugo, Roberto, and Pancho are fictitious characters.

Chapter 10.) The video scene was adapted from a real-life event depicted in *El Narco: Inside Mexico's Criminal Insurgency*, by Ioan Grillo. In the actual incident, the kidnapped child is male. It is uncertain what exactly happened to the child in the video.

Chapter 11.) All characters mentioned here are fictional.

Chapter 12.) The narrative's timeline is designed to coincide with the rise of the cartels and the relative historical events described are accurate, per my own understanding. The military compound Tamoanchan is fictional as is Mayor Carrasco. Joaquín Archivaldo Guzmán Loera (a.k.a. "El Chapo"—"Shorty") is a real person, the most notorious drug lord in Mexican history. At the time of this writing, he had escaped from Mexican prison for the second time and he had been captured again. He was incarcerated in the maximum-security prison Puente Grande, and his capture and stay there, as described in the novel, is, more or less, accurate. Juan José Esparragoza Moreno and Zulema Yulia Hernández (now deceased) are real individuals. The warden and prison guards mentioned here are fictional.

Chapter 13.) Javier Rayón is a fictional character. The ancient history of Mexico described by Father Navarro is accurate, as understood by myself. *Fire & Blood*, by T. R. Fehrenbach, was used heavily as reference material. Nezahualcoyotl was a historical figure and is the author of the poem quoted in the chapter.

Chapter 14.) The Hope of Mexico orphanage is fictional, as is Jacob and all the children characters.

Chapter 15.) Manny Morelos Fernández is a fictional character based upon David Barron Corona (now deceased). Barron was the leading hitman for the AFO and one of the most notorious narco enforcers in Mexican history.

Chapter 16.) The Red Crusaders are a fictional organization based upon several entities associated with the Knights Templar. The recollections of the martyrdoms of the early Christian apostles, as well as the events leading up to the downfall of the Templars, are historically accurate, according to my understanding. The Cross of Lorraine is an authentic symbol.

Chapter 17.) J. Jesús Blancornelas (now deceased) is a historical figure as well as his partner Héctor Félix Miranda (also deceased). The description of the events surrounding the publication of "Zeta," as well as the assassination attempt on Blancornelas, is historically accurate, as understood by myself. Gabriela Guerrero Contreras and her family, excluding Blancornelas, are fictional characters.

Chapter 18.) The description of Badiraguato is accurate. The Aztec specimens described in Tlaloc's museum are based on authentic artifacts. Jesús Malverde is a cultural icon within certain segments of the Mexican population.

Chapter 19.) La Zona Del Silencio—The Zone of Silence—is an actual area in Mexico and the description of events occurring insides its borders is accurate. The description of the events surrounding La Noche Triste, The Sad Night, is also accurate, according to my understanding. No one really knows what exactly happened to the Aztec/Spanish treasure.

Chapter 20.) Matías Armendáriz Carrasco and all characters mentioned in this chapter are fictional.

Chapter 21.) All characters mentioned in this chapter are fictional.

Part II

Prologue) The description of events surrounding the turn of the century in Mexico and Ciudad Juárez is historically accurate, according to my understanding.

Chapter 22.) Yvonne Siqueiros Murguía and her son Esteban are fictional characters though the massacre at Villas de Salvárcar is depicted as historically accurate as possible. It remains one of the more notorious events of the drug war in Juárez. Los Aztecas is an actual Juárez gang with ties to the Juárez Cartel during this period. The Artistas Asesinos is also an authentic Juárez gang with ties to the Sinaloa Cartel.

Chapter 23.) All characters in this chapter are fictional though the Barrio Azteca is an actual El Paso gang that was associated with the Juárez Cartel during this period.

Chapter 24.) Raúl Soto Borja-Díaz is a fictional character, though La Línea was the actual enforcement wing of the Juárez Cartel and was comprised mostly of policemen. Descriptions of the cartels, its members, and the events surrounding the drug war in Juárez, are historically accurate, per my understanding. Mexican President Felipe Calderón did send in the army to Juárez, though General Ortiz is a fictional character. The exact relationship between military personnel and the cartels is somewhat uncertain, though there is widespread speculation that at least some of the armed forces were working for the Sinaloa Cartel in the fight for Juárez. El Chapo did escape from Puente Grande prison in 2001 and was the major proponent for expanding the influence of the Sinaloa Cartel across Mexico.

Chapter 25.) Officer Gustavo Portolatin Alamán y Escalada and his family are fictional characters. The Monument to Fallen Police is authentic, as is the infamous "For those who do not believe" list. The list was successful as a terror mechanism in the eradication of La Línea by the Sinaloa Cartel, as understood by myself. The Mission of Our Lady of Guadalupe of the Meek Paso del Norte is authentic and its history is accurately described. The cavern system underground the Juárez/El Paso metropolis is fiction. Padre Quezada and Alma are fictional characters.

Chapter 26.) The description of the history of the Ysleta Mission Church and Tigua Indians is accurate, according to my understanding. Hundreds of young women were mysteriously murdered in the infamous Juárez femicide and the killings and their aftermath have been a topic of many novels and several motion pictures.

Chapter 27.) Reynaldo Balcázar and his gang members are fictional characters, though the massacre at the Casa El Aliviane drug rehabilitation center did take place and is, more or less, consistent with the description in this chapter. Los Reyes Ciegos is a fictional neighborhood based upon areas in Juárez and other poverty-stricken human residences in the world.

Chapter 28.) The Navarro family as described here is fictional, as well as the sword of Aragon. The seal of the Knights Templar is described accurately, as is, more or less, the founding of the organization. Hugues de Payens and Godrey de Saint-Omer are two of the founders of the Knights Templar and they were stationed in Jerusalem at the Temple Mount in the given period. Whether they discovered an actual treasure has been a topic of debate for centuries.

Chapter 29.) The statue of Jesus Christ at Mount Cristo Rey is authentic, as is the description of the location and its history.

Chapter 30.) José Reyes Ferriz was the mayor of Ciudad Juárez during this time period. Pedro is a fictional son of the mayor. The university, streets, and sites mentioned in this chapter are real.

Chapter 31.) Los Zetas is a real criminal organization founded by former members of the Mexican Special Forces. Though Los Zetas did turn against their former employers—the Gulf Cartel—during this period, the massacre at the party in Matamoros is fictional. Antonio Ezequiel Cárdenas Guillén (a.k.a. "Tony Tormenta"—"Tony the Storm") (now deceased) was a co-leader of the Gulf Cartel. Aside from their relationship with Ramón Acosta, the account of the founding of Los Zetas and their deeds is historically accurate, as understood by myself. El Pastor is a true-life evangelical priest who does live in Juárez and his story is described accurately, according to my understanding. El Pastor was introduced to the world in the non-fiction book *Murder City: Ciudad Juarez and the Global Economy's New Killing Fields* by Charles Bowden.

Chapter 32.) Sheik Mahdavi Haqqani, his grandson Mokhtar, and all the Saudis mentioned in this chapter are fictional characters. The timetable of the mentioned terrorist attacks is accurate, as are the locations and number of reported victims. Zulfiqar was, per legend, an authentic sword and though hazy, its history and mythology is described accurately, according to my understanding. The present location of Zulfiqar is unknown, although one theory says that the Mahdi (Messiah) will return to Earth with the sword.

Chapter 33.) All characters mentioned in this chapter are fictional.

Chapter 34.) Livia, Yadhira, and César are fictional characters. Galdino Mellado Cruz (a.k.a. Z-9—now deceased) and Gonzalo Geresano Escribano (a.k.a. Z-18—currently incarcerated in Mexican prison) deserted from the Mexican Special Forces to help found Los Zetas, as described in this chapter. Raping and pillaging migrant groups, as well as a host of other criminal activities outside of drug-trafficking, has become part of Los Zetas modus operandi. Z-59, Z-84, Z-91, Z-99, Z-110, and Z-119 are fictional characters.

Chapter 35.) The U.S. Freestyle and Greco-Roman National Championships take place each year in Las Vegas, Nevada. The championship wrestling match featured in the chapter was based on the third Greco-Roman match at the 2008 Team-USA Olympic Trials between Dennis Hall and Brandon Paulson in the 55-kg weight class.

Chapter 36.) All characters mentioned in this chapter are fictional. The depicted death ritual, though fictional, is meant to help capture some of the more violent aspects of the Aztec sacrifices.

Chapter 37.) All characters mentioned in this chapter are fictional.

Chapter 38.) The police officers, now controlled by the Sinaloa Cartel in the novel, represent the status of the drug war in Juárez turning in El Chapo's favor. Hueco Tanks is a real location on the outskirts of El Paso. Amazingly, during the peak of the drug violence in Juárez, the bloodshed on the other side of the border was kept at a minimum. Statistically speaking, El Paso, Texas, ranked as one of the safest cities in the United States during this time.

Chapter 39.) All characters mentioned in this chapter are fictional, as is, of course, the holy tomb of the Red Crusaders. The use of DNA as a biometric tool, including the ability to discover familial relationships among individuals, is described accurately.

Chapter 40.) The relationship between jihadist terrorists and corrupt high-ranking Mexican officials is fictional. Descriptions of ancient Aztec murals and statues are based on historical entities.

Chapter 41.) Jaguars and eagles are ubiquitous among ancient Aztec culture and warfare, and the descriptions of various warriors are designed to depict the actual clothing, adornments, and weaponry of the culture.

Acknowledgments

I have attempted to weave in a fictional narrative within a historical setting and, albeit the employment of some minor liberties, have attempted to remain consistent with the timeline and factual events of the so-called Mexican drug wars. I have also attempted to interlace the story with salient episodes and facts of Mexican history which I feel are relevant in understanding the rise of the cartels and the resulting violence in the country. In addition, I have introduced some non-fictional material into the story which is somewhat outside the scope of Mexico, its history, and the drug wars.

That said, I would like to acknowledge the following journalists and authors in whose work I have consulted and referenced: Ricardo C. Ainslie–*The Fight to Save Juárez*; Malcolm Beith–*The Last Narco: Inside the Hunt for El Chapo, the World's Most Wanted Drug Lord*; Chris Blatchford–*The Black Hand: The Bloody Rise and Redemption of "Boxer" Enriquez, A Mexican Mob Killer*; Blog Del Narco–*Dying for the Truth: Undercover Inside the Mexican Drug War*; Charles Bowden–*Murder City: Ciudad Juarez and the Global Economy's New Killing Fields*; Charles Bowden–*El Sicario: Confessions of a Cartel Hitman and Murder City*; Michael Deibert: *In the Shadow of Saint Death: The Gulf Cartel and the Price of America's Drug War in Mexico*; T. R. Fehrenbach–*Fire & Blood: A History of Mexico*; Barbara Frale–*The Templars: The Secret History Revealed*; John Gibler–*To Die in Mexico: Dispatches from Inside the Drug War*; Ioan Grillo–*El Narco: Inside Mexico's Criminal Insurgency*; Jerry Langland–*The Rise of the Mexican Drug Cartels from El Paso to Vancouver*; Robert Ryal Miller–*Mexico A History*; Terrence E. Poppa–*Drug Lord: A True Story: The Life and Death of a Mexican Kingpin*; Ruben Quezada–*For Greater Glory: The True Story of Cristiada, the Cristero War and Mexico's Struggle for Religious Freedom*; Teresa Rodriguez–*The Daughters of Juárez: A True Story of Serial Murder South of the Border*; Michael E. Smith–*The Aztecs.*

I also scoured the World Wide Web for information in this novel and consulted numerous internet articles, websites, and blogs. I would specifically like to acknowledge the authors and researchers of Borderland Beat and Blog del Narco.

About the Author

Joel Galloway was raised in the mountains of Idaho where he developed a passion for hunting, fishing, and athletics. He is a great enthusiast of the sport of wrestling and has competed and coached for many years. For close to a decade he lived on the U.S./Mexico border as a missionary and student, eventually graduating from the University of Texas at El Paso (UTEP). He's followed the so-called Mexican drug wars with fascination and extreme concern, the subject eventually becoming the impetus for this novel. A voracious reader, his writing has been influenced by Wilbur Smith, Bernard Cornwell, Cormac McCarthy, and J.R.R. Tolkien. He and his family currently live in Northern Virginia where he works as a government contractor, assisting in the defense of the United States. This is his first novel.

Please visit: www.crusaderbook.com